Dark Coven

Nick Brown

Published by New Generation Publishing in 2015

Copyright © Nick Brown 2015

First Edition

The author asserts the moral right under the Copyright, Designs and Patents Act 1988 to be identified as the author of this work.

ISBN 978-1-78507-542-1

All Rights reserved. No part of this publication may be reproduced, stored in a retrieval system or transmitted, in any form or by any means without the prior consent of the author, nor be otherwise circulated in any form of binding or cover other than that which it is published and without a similar condition being imposed on the subsequent purchaser.

www.newgeneration-publishing.com

Nick Brown has an archaeological background and is the author of the highly acclaimed 'Luck Bringer', 'Wooden Walls of Thermopylae', 'Skendleby' and 'The Dead Travel Fast'.

Praise for Nick Brown's books

Luck Bringer, nominated for Historical Novel Society book of the year

"This is a fascinating and entertaining book and makes the reader feel as if he were present together with Mandrocles, the Luck Bringer." Antonis Mistriotis, author of '507-450 BC - The 57 Years Which Gave Birth to Democracy'

"Every serious student of this period of history should read this book. In all respects it is exquisitely crafted." Historical Novel Society; editor's choice

"Fleshes out the life of the true historical figure, Miltiades, and brings the ructions of the Arab Spring crashing into life." Cheshire Life

"Fast-paced and based on meticulous research, it tells it like it most probably was, stripped of the hype, but none the less moving for that." Indie Author Land

The Wooden Walls of Thermopylae

"Nick Brown is the Hemingway of the ancient world." Lucy Branch, author of 'A Gift Rarer than Gold'

"Historical fiction at its best; this book indicates a confidence which reflects a lifetime of study." Robins Reviews

"A well written and gripping story." Historical Novel Society

"This book lives and breathes history." Nubian Times

<u>Skendleby</u>

"Something creepy afoot." Big Issue

"Gripping and genuinely creepy." New Edition.

"Echoes of the ghost story master, M.R. James." I Like Horror

"A heartily recommended read for all thriller and horror fans." Horror Cult Films

"I wish the book had been longer." Sexy Archaeology

<u>The Dead Travel Fast</u>

"Sent chills down my spine; a thrilling read from start to finish." Jessica Ward, author of 'The Path of Destruction' series

"Exquisite dialogue creates such an involving story that you'll find it hard to tear yourself away from the pages." Horror Cult Films

"It's crying out to be made into a movie!" Spectral Times

"A fantastic genre-bending experience." Web Weaver

"An imaginative chiller mixing horror and thriller fiction with a twist of Quantum strangeness." Indie Author Land

Also by Nick Brown

The Ancient Gramarye series

    Skendleby

    The Dead Travel Fast

The Luck Bringer series

    Luck Bringer

    The Wooden Walls of Thermopylae

For my family who put up with and support my writing

"Ye shall not make any cuttings in your flesh for the dead."

"Regard not them that have familiar spirits neither seek after wizards"

Leviticus 19 verses 28 and 31

"One way to think about it is that other universes coexist in the same space as ours, like ghosts."

Howard Wiseman in New Scientist

Chapter 1: The Coven

The rain that lay in pools covering the poorly drained flatlands beneath the Edge for most of November was caught out, like everything else, by the sudden sharp cold snap. Livestock penned into the reduced acreage of relatively dry land now faced a lack of water, flood to drought overnight as ice interred the fields.

Kelly Ellsworth pulled back the curtains from her south facing window and found the world changed. The ceaseless rain and dank grey cloud had been replaced by a light too bright to stare into as it flashed off the silver sheets covering the fields. She knew instinctively that today was the auspicious day she'd been waiting for.

She stood for a moment staring down from her second floor room in the seventeenth century converted hall at the sparkling light in the fields. The warmth radiating from glass windows, which stretched from the tip of the A frame roof to her bedroom floor, filled her with a delightful sense of promise.

Her slight figure, covered down to her knees by the plaid work shirt she slept in, might have been mistaken for that of a child. An impression reinforced by the fine blonde hair that she wore long, and which flowed over her shoulders.

After basking in the warmth and the light she turned and padded across the beige carpet that covered the entire second floor of the barn and made her way to the bathroom: one of three shared by the Coven. There were only two rooms occupied on this floor but the third would be filled on Sunday by a friend of Rose's.

The intensity of experience in the house had been heightened when Rose moved in: she was the only one of them to have genuinely witnessed the occult and this made the community more authentic. Rose claimed she didn't like to talk about it to those who'd not seen what she had.

All the same, it gave her an edge in the pecking order and this, along with the way she came across as everybody's favourite older sister, made them seem more like a family.

Well, maybe not everyone's favourite sister. Kelly had noticed that Margaret, who owned the house (a consequence of her messy divorce from "that bastard Ken"), seemed less bubbly since Rose's arrival. Before that Margaret, who ran a holistic healing centre and wrote a psychic imprints column for 'Pagan Universe', had been their spiritual leader.

In fact, Rose had confided in Kelly that, although she wouldn't hear a word said against Margaret, it was obvious that "she had issues with status" and that these were blocking her spiritual development. Rose had then smiled sympathetically and said:

"But that's probably the fault of that man who let her down so badly, and we've all been in that situation, haven't we, love?"

Kelly, not wanting to disagree, had nodded. She'd been in that situation herself but was not convinced by Rose's analysis of why Margaret had become more introspective. But she was too happy in this house to want any friction creeping into their community and pushed the image from her mind; this was her home now. She looked forward to Sunday and the new arrival who would have the room next to hers.

In the bathroom she opened the cupboard under the mirror and took down the pregnancy testing kit. In her mind she was already certain of the result, but she needed to be sure before she told the others; told them they now had what they wanted, that their circle was complete and would remain unbroken. She wanted the moment to be perfect when she told them because it would be the first time in her life that she would be the centre of attention, the first time she would be important because of herself.

She left the testing kit unopened on the surface by the hand basin and walked downstairs: she decided she should meditate and pray to the mother first. The great house was empty and this always felt a little spooky. Despite the soft carpet underfoot there was always a faint after sound of heavy feet on stone floor. But the sun flooding through the floor-to-ceiling window of the Gathering Room drove any anxiety away. This room was the most beautiful place Kelly had ever seen. It was the type of space only a caring community of women could create.

To the side of the great hearth, now occupied by a flame effect gas fire in a massive grate (log burning had been too smoky), Margaret had designed a plinth, eighteen inches high. This was covered in a soft, thick white rug and was where they constructed the circle then sat to communicate with their inner beings and the unseen spirit world. Kelly sat cross-legged, enjoying the soft tickle of the rug on her naked calves and thighs. Leaning back against the lathe and plaster wall beneath the statue of Vesta, goddess of the hearth, she luxuriated in the sensations, watching the motes of dust circling in the shafts of sunlight.

Margaret loved this room. She had stripped it of any last vestiges of male imposed crassness left by Ken and created the Feng Shui vibe of spiritual awareness that nurtured their community. It was a place to be savoured and, as Margaret often said:

"We don't need to wear a hair shirt here, this is a community of women who've earned and appreciate their comforts."

Gazing across the room towards the large oak table still covered with bottles of Prosecco and Pinot Grigio from the previous night, Kelly agreed with her. Well, not fully agreed because she hadn't really earned anything yet, but then again she had a different role and last night had been about celebrating that.

At first she'd been uncomfortable with this role; neither Margaret nor Olga her partner had mentioned it when they first discussed her joining the house. The dancing dust motes trapped in the sunlight were hypnotic and she began to drift into recollection.

It had started in Starbucks, where she'd been crying into a tasteless Latte. She was only in there because she had nowhere else to go. Zak had been two timing her and when she confronted him instead of apologising and telling her he loved her he had…

She had to stop to control herself: this bit still hurt more than it should. Instead of telling her he still loved her, he dumped her. Told her she was too clingy and it was time to move on, and that's what he did. He moved on without paying back the student loan she'd lent to him to part finance the car and sharp clothes he said he needed to break through to the big time. Then with no money and non-attendance at exams, she found herself out of uni and crying in Starbucks. It had changed her life and she knew the mother had caused it, made it happen for her.

Her first awareness of the happening had been a gentle touch on her arm. Looking up she saw a large Nordic looking blonde woman standing over her, a look of concern on her handsome, strong-jawed face.

"Forgive me, but you looked so unhappy, would you mind if I sat down for a moment?"

Thus she met Olga, her first contact with the community. She couldn't remember much of their conversation, only that at the end of it she was left with an address and an invitation to the house for that evening: it was fate.

She took the 157 bus from the city centre to the end of the line. The ride took well over an hour as she moved through inner city regeneration, decaying inner suburbs, affluent outer and satellite suburbs and at last into the country. The bus stopped in a lay-by next to a rural pub; opposite there was a church and nothing else but fields. A couple of miles away a wooded escarpment reared up sharply out of the plain; the bus pulled off quickly as if it wanted to get away. It was growing dark.

Kelly had the instructions Olga had given her but it was assumed she'd be driving. She didn't own a car and hadn't the money for a taxi. By foot and public transport it wasn't so easy. She found the lane leading to the track that led to the house but the five minutes that Olga had told her this would take was more like an hour on foot.

It was hard to tell where she was, high hedges obstructed her vision either side of the lane. Only once did a car pass her and for that she was grateful as she had to scramble into the hedge to get out of its way. The further she walked the darker it grew, and the more uncertain she felt: what was she doing here? The day had already been bad enough. How much more gullible could she get? It was the story of her life over and over again. Some night bird was making a noise in the branches over her head and there was rustling in the hedgerow.

Now she was frightened, she could have been lured here to be murdered or raped and no one would miss her. She felt the tears start again but it was the thought that no one would miss or care if she died that kept her going. There was nothing to go back for anyway, so, pulling up her coat collar, she trudged on, trying to shut out the sounds.

Seconds later she found the track snaking away to the right. It was narrower and darker than the road and uneven underfoot. She wondered how cars would get down it in bad weather, but she followed it. It was dead black now: the moon and stars were swaddled in thick layers of cloud and no light came from streetlights or windows. There were no streetlights or windows out here.

She could hardly see her hand in front of her face. Then she hit a thorn hedge; the track had ended. She groped around before realising that it had veered away to the left and she followed it, keeping her hand on a field fence that marked its right boundary. This time she didn't miss the turn: she just followed the fence line, concentrating on the ground beneath her feet. She was congratulating herself on this when she realised it had become brighter and looked up.

It was there, a few hundred yards ahead of her, three stories, massive, the windows pouring out light; something out of a fairy tale. She stopped worrying about how she'd get back: she wouldn't be going back.

The track had become a drive, emerging from the claustrophobic confines of the hedge and sloping gently down towards the house. Her arrival was no surprise; security lights picked her out as she made her way along the gravelled path. Before she reached it the front door opened. Olga, dressed in a dark green dress, waited for her in the open doorway. To Kelly's relief, she was smiling a welcome.

It was the smell of the house she noticed first, a mix of scents: beeswax, perfumed candles and fresh cut flowers. Olga ushered her into a huge, softly lit room with a massive old fireplace and some type of raised platform next to it. There were seven women in the room; all of them older than her. Standing in the centre was a tall, red haired woman who looked to Kelly to be in her late thirties. She was wearing a long, clinging black dress and was holding a wine glass. Olga steered Kelly over to her.

"Kelly, this is Margaret, she's the head of our rather special little group."

She leant across and kissed Margaret on the lips almost proprietarily as she said this, which struck Kelly as strange.

"Welcome to our community, Kelly, from what Olga has told us you will fit in perfectly."

And, apart from the introductions, that was it. Someone gave her a glass of white wine and not long after, dead tired, she was shown to her room: she was in. But it hadn't been as simple as that - nothing ever was - there had been a price. Something she hadn't expected and could never have imagined.

Looking back they had tried to prepare her for it, but she'd been too naive to pick up any of the hints. So, when Olga and Margaret took her to one side to put the proposition to her she'd been shocked, and then outraged. Her first reaction had been to storm out, but where would she go? The thing that hurt most wasn't the ethics of what they wanted but the fact that during the three months she had lived with them she had filled the role of baby in the house. She had been petted and pampered and confided in because she was no one's rival, even Rose had recognised this when she arrived. Now they wanted a real baby.

She sulked for a bit and then agreed, reasoning it would give her status: she would become the representative of the mother in the community. It had been a logical decision when she reviewed her options; it gave her security because she'd have what they needed. It would also bring her closer to the inner circle: Margaret, Olga and Jenna had connections with other occult groups and knew things the rest didn't.

It was particularly the case for Jenna, who was small, dark haired and sour like a crab apple. She had been ejected from a long-standing, more powerful community for reasons Kelly couldn't discover except that it was the consequence of a bitter feud. There were things that these three knew that weren't shared with the others, but, apart from by Rose, it seemed that this wasn't resented.

In fact, the relationships in the community worked well; there was little friction and the members contributed to the subsistence of the house according to their ability to pay. Not that this was a problem to any of them except Kelly and Rose as they all had successful careers. As Jenna often said, they were "sisters who had broken through the glass ceiling".

Any problems there were came from outside. Kelly heard Margaret talking to Jenna about a hex fetish that had been pinned to the front door one night, a disgusting thing of feathers, blood and bone.

Then there were the bouts of late night phone calls, always the same recorded message, always the same threat or curse. Jenna blamed this on bitterness from an unbalanced member of her previous community. But Kelly observed the upgrading of the house security system and worked out that one of the reasons they had voted to allow Rose to join the community was her knowledge of the horrific aspects of treading the left hand path. Rose was still on sick leave from her job with the county archaeological unit as a consequence of her experiences.

The nature of the engendering of the community's child had been another sticking point in Kelly's willingness to represent the mother. In fact, it had almost split the community. Kelly had assumed that the act would take place at a clinic using the sperm of a donor, a methodology supported by Rose, Ruth and Ailsa who adopted well-rehearsed arguments from the dialectic of sexual politics backed up by personal experience.

However, Margaret, Olga and Jenna insisted on tradition and the old ways. There was to be an act of sexual magic practised on the most auspicious day, involving all of them. Kelly made the mistake of asking if she would have any choice regarding the father but quickly realised this was a faux pas, which was scorned and dismissed by both factions. Tradition prevailed and it became apparent that Jenna had already identified and made overtures to a prospective candidate, a man of impeccable pagan credentials with close links to Wiccan communities and experience in the field supported by impressive recommendations and testimonials.

Arrangements were made for a procedure that would not contaminate the ambient spirit of the house, and which would be strictly ceremonial. Kelly was allowed to see a picture of the donor, who looked presentable but resembled a member of a prog rock band from the 1970s. However, any idea she had of a private half hour in bed with him was soon dispelled. The act would take place clothed in the middle of a circle formed by the community holding hands and chanting sacred incantations. Rose and Ailsa were against this but were outvoted.

Kelly was allowed a few minutes to familiarise herself with the donor, Cadellin. He had long hair and a wispy sandy beard but was otherwise a reassuring presence. His earth name, he told her, was Keith. The act itself, for which she wore a long robe with a slit up the front, was embarrassing, and during the course of it she kept her eyes tightly closed. She realised that the ordeal had ended when Keith tensed and then emitted a stifled grunt, followed by a polite round of applause from her house sisters.

Keith's performance of the sacred fertility rite had the merit however of being thankfully brief. In that respect, if in nothing else, Keith/Cadellin lived up to his testimonials and once he was out and had readjusted his robe he left the house. Unorthodox and embarrassing as the rite had been, it catapulted Kelly into a position of status in the community. She was, if anything, more petted and treated as the baby of the house as they waited to see if the magic worked.

Now, as she sat on the plinth in her sleep shirt enjoying the tickle of the carpet on her bare legs she prayed that the test would show positive. She prayed not only because she didn't want to go through the performance with Keith all over again, but also because the community needed some good news. There had been elements of discord inching into their lives, some of them creepy. Although the others tried to keep Kelly out of this they often failed to notice her and she watched and listened, missing nothing.

Margaret was particularly edgy. Kelly heard her talking to Olga late one night in the kitchen after dinner when the two of them stayed on drinking wine after the others had drifted off. Kelly had been sitting alone in the large, wrought-iron framed conservatory that led off from the kitchen with her Iphone, networking. Now she tuned in to the end of her housemates' conversation.

"No, Olga, I'm sure it's not coming from the Wiccan scene in Macclesfield or Bramhall: we know most of them, they're okay. Maybe more traditional than us and we've had our run ins, but they wouldn't do this. Why would they need to? We may be much richer than them, but we're no threat. Well, not enough for them to do this."

"Even the ones who think they're vampire witches? Anyway, who else could it be? Who else have you cut across badly enough for them to want to do something like that?"

"Nothing: that's just it, we've haven't hurt anybody. We weren't involved in whatever went on at Skendleby and messed Rose up."

"Funny it all seemed to start up after she arrived though, isn't it?"

"Rose has nothing to do with this Olga. Whoever's doing this is sick."

"Well, why we don't try the police."

"And say what? That we've had a curse put on us. Oh yeah, I can see them taking that seriously."

"But we're really isolated out here."

"Leave it now, it's getting late, come to bed."

Kelly heard them get up and leave the kitchen. She sat on alone for a while wondering what it meant. That had been two nights ago and new electronic gates had been ordered like the ones sealing off the mansions of the footballers that littered the surrounding landscape. She decided she couldn't wait any longer and dropped down off the plinth, heading for the bathroom.

The results confirmed her expectations; she was pregnant. Her world had changed and now she would change. There was no one else in the house: the others were out making money or, in Rose's case, negotiating a return to work package. The day was beautiful - she would go out and walk through the fields. She set the alarm system, double locked the front door behind her and then cut round the back of the house and climbed over the stile onto a footpath.

Her head buzzed with ideas and fantasies as she crunched across the frost covered fields. She lost track of both herself and time until she was surprised to find that she'd reached the cricket club; she'd no idea that she'd come so far. The cricket ground, shrouded for the winter, looked vaguely threatening and in normal circumstances she would have turned back but today, in the sun and fired up with dreams of the future, she still wanted to walk.

She knew that if she crossed the ground there was another footpath that swung round in a great circle and passed within a mile or so of the house. She'd been told that from this path it was possible to see Sutton Mound, a sacred burial site where two lines of earth power intersected.

Although the jobsworths at the archaeology unit, who Rose worked with, said it was just a bog standard Bronze Age bowl barrow and there were no such things as lines of earth power, Kelly knew different. Margaret had explained that it had been a centre of pagan spiritual energy for millennia and, for those who knew how to look, energy could still be found. She crossed the pitch, walked past the boarded up pavilion and climbed the stile.

On the other side the land fell away and the low lying waterlogged fields were covered in a series of frozen pools of water, some as big as boating lakes. It seemed warmer this side and a miasma of mist was rising off the ground. Down here the day seemed a lot less cheerful. But it was only after she had crossed three of these fields that Kelly became aware of the noise the fields were making. A sound of shifting and cracking: it seemed to emanate from the ground itself. Kelly thought about turning back but didn't want to retrace her steps to where the noise had started, so instead she increased her pace.

And there was something else; the mist was gathering behind her, closing off her retreat. She carried on through a landscape that suddenly began to feel hostile, listening in alarm to the snapping and cracking sounds all around. The brightness of the day was gone, replaced by a shadowy, obscure world, misty and insubstantial. All ideas of Sutton Mound disappeared and she had to concentrate hard on following the path. She didn't want to get lost so she lumbered on through the shifting gloom with the still silence punctuated by the sharp dislocated cracks.

Time and distance seemed to have lost meaning as she moved, or seemed to move through this strange quantum miniverse. Then her foot landed on something slippery without purchase and went from under her; she hit the ground with a jolt.

Ice: she'd fallen on ice. Now she recognised the source of the disorientating noise. The ice was expanding and beginning to break up. She laughed at the realisation, laughed at herself, at how pathetic she had been to frighten herself like a child. She got up, brushed herself off and moved on.

The ground began to slope upwards. Bit by bit the mist dispersed and within minutes she was able to recognise where she was. The path split and she took the left fork which narrowed to run between low fences. To her right she could see a large old house at the far end of a paddock. To her left were great rolls of waist high bramble, like barbed wire. The fence ended at a stile which she crossed, but the bramble continued on the other side.

She hated bramble like this, had ever since she was little. There had been some on wasteland by the house where she lived with her mother before social services had taken her away. Once some bigger girls had pushed her into it and she had hung there, caught fast by the sharp thorns catching on her dress. It had seemed like she had hung there for hours, cut and torn by the thorns, listening to the rustling sounds from deep inside the thicket.

She forced herself to look straight ahead, away from the tunnel of thorns. That's when she saw the hooded figure walking towards her. There was something about it that made her want to turn and run: an instinct to preserve the new stirrings of life within her. She began to turn round but then common sense kicked in: it would mean going back past the brambles and down into the mist and crackling ice. So she just carried on and quickly realised she'd done the right thing. The figure ahead wasn't that much bigger than she was and the threatening hood was just a hoodie over a running top. She laughed at herself for a second time, everything was alright.

The figure was close now and had pushed the hood back off. Kelly's relief was complete, she knew this person. They approached each other smiling and Kelly put her cheek forwards to accept the kiss of greeting, slightly surprised as this was only a chance acquaintance, someone she'd only met a couple of times at pagan fairs. Still, she went through the respected response and turned the angle of her face to accept the proffered peck on her left cheek.

The brambles came back into focus with the sideways movement of her head and held her attention for a fleeting instance. The mouth darted away from her cheek as she stared at the sharp points of the brambles and moved upwards. There was a searing pain, something tearing in her left ear, then a hard punch in her stomach. She staggered back, her hand moving from ear to belly. She felt something wet, saw blood on her hands. How could that have happened? The pain from the ear was worse. She looked up and saw that there was a bloodied blade that looked like it was made of stone in the hand of this casual acquaintance of hers. She wondered what had happened and if she could wind it all back, like on Sky Plus. She couldn't understand what was happening, her mind wouldn't work: it was like this was being done to someone else.

Then instinct kicked in and she did what she should have done before; she turned to run. But now there seemed to be something wrong with her legs, they began to sag under her. Hands grabbed her by the shoulders and turned her round, the face she looked into was smiling at her and she saw the knife rise again. Her eyes seemed to be losing their focus. She tried to think what to do but couldn't. Then the surface of the earth shifted and she was tipped into the brambles, left hanging there. This wasn't fair. Why did things always happen to her? She began to cry, the pain was excruciating, but fortunately it didn't last; soon, like everything else, it just slipped away.

Chapter 2: Should Have Left Them Buried

"Stop it, stop it, for God's sake, turn the fucker off, turn it off, them's bones, them's human bones."

The digger didn't stop. Just kept on coming with the massive shovel ramped up to take its next bite of earth as it worked remorselessly towards the old chapel. Dave didn't dare get in front of it so he just kept on shouting and waving his arms.

Must have had some effect because with a choke that ended in a whine the engine died and he was confronted with the furious red face of Jed Gifford glaring at him from the cab. Dave wished not for the first time that the economy would pick up so he could move on to a proper job and away from Jed. You only worked for him if you were bent or desperate: he was known for his brutality even in the rough end of Bollington. He knocked his missus about and she was a saint. Dave couldn't understand why she stuck with him.

These were, in fact, the qualities that had got Jed working for Si Carver. No one else round here would work for that bugger and certainly no one would have taken on this job. So Carver had to pay over the odds to get the area between the side of the Hall and the crumbling chapel of the Davenports cleared. Carver wanted to build a heated swimming pool that would start under the hall and then emerge covered in glass, which on sunny days would roll back at the click of a switch and become an outdoor pool.

Carver's wife, Suzzie-Jade, had seen one featured in *Hello* magazine and thought it would add class to the estate. There were problems of course, the chapel was listed and shouldn't be touched: one attempt to demolish it to make room for another hole for his golf course had already been scrapped when local busybodies complained to the local authorities. Carver hoped that the construction of the pool would structurally weaken the chapel sufficiently to give him a valid excuse to pull it down and replace it with a bar and pool changing suite.

Carver hadn't told Jed all this of course, but had said enough for him to understand that if the chapel were, unfortunately to be irretrievably damaged, then there would be a bonus coming his way along with the contract for the new building. Jed knew he could drive a hard bargain: Carver no longer had a tame councillor in his pocket to help with planning, the last one having killed himself. Jed also understood that part of his being paid considerably over the odds for this work was for his discretion.

Jed might be bad and bent, and he was both, but he wasn't stupid and he knew how to keep his mouth shut if it paid enough. He also understood that Carver was not a man to cross. As he often said to his cronies in the pub, "takes one to know one".

What Jed wasn't privy to was Carver's real motive. The chapel scared him, or rather what he thought lurked inside it scared him. He hadn't exactly seen it but he'd seen where it had been: noticed its absence if that made any sense. Most of the time it made no sense to Carver, but all the same he knew it was there and he knew that it knew he knew: and in a way that made it worse, even after he'd had a few whiskeys. During the goings on with the Skendleby mound last Christmas it had got so bad that he'd had to take tablets for his nerves: like losers did.

Dave knew enough to know that finding something dodgy underground near the chapel would not go down well with Jed, and he was right.

"This'd better be good or you can say goodbye to this job."

"Look down there, towards the chapel wall."

"So what, you find bones underground all the time, innit."

"Yeah, but not like this. Look, there must be more than one body."

"So, it'll be a fucking graveyard."

"Don't think so, Jed, the crypt thing is round the other side. And look at them bones, them's been badly knocked about. See that skull, it's like it's been smashed in. This isn't natural."

"So, no harm done then, only us seen it."

"Think about it, Jed, this can't be kept secret. The villagers know what we're doing here, they'll have clocked the JCB. Davenport and the vicar saw us yesterday."

"So?"

"So, they'll 'ave reported us to the council already; we could get a visit any time and if they find out we've tried to cover this up it could be real bad for us and…"

"And what?"

"Well, remember them attacks last year? Police never cleared them up, they're not even sure they found all the victims, and seeing how a lot of it went on round here, we don't want to…"

Dave trailed to a stop, but he'd said enough - Jed got the drift.

"Shit, just what we fuckin need. Carver's out, better go and tell Jordan."

Carver's wife, Suzzie-Jade, was referred to as Jordan on account of her alleged resemblance to the erstwhile lingerie model: not to her face, of course, although she would probably have been flattered.

Inside the Hall, Suzzie-Jade was at that moment relaxing after a session with her personal trainer. She was customising her fingernails to match the new furniture in the much altered banqueting hall. The Hall had already been greatly improved by having most of its clunky and depressing internal features ripped out and replaced with more streamlined modern ones. It was part of her project to try to get *Hello*, or maybe, to be realistic, one of the lesser mags to cover her makeover.

The emphasis in the space was now chrome and white wood, with violet furniture in a neo-sixties G plan design. It was good but still lacked something and Suzzie-Jade was wondering if a Banksy-type street life mural would make it complete. She was disturbed by a banging outside followed by one of the staff, Marika she thought her name was, entering the room.

"Men outside, say there is problem and would you please come to see."

Suzzie-Jade had never actually seen the men up close before and wasn't impressed by Dave, who she thought looked like that meerkat off the adverts, but she followed him, tottering round the site workings in her heels. She was even less impressed with Jed who, despite his attempts at ingratiation, came across as his brutal self. But it was obvious from their furtive manner that something was wrong, something that Si wouldn't like. The bones didn't look particularly interesting to her but now the men and the servants knew about them she knew she'd have to do something. She tried Si's mobile but got no answer so told Marika to call the police.

****

When the call from the council came through to the archaeology unit, Dr Giles Glover wondered what he had done this time. Since his suspension for professional misconduct over the Skendleby excavation he'd never been able to feel easy, aware that his reinstatement had been touch and go and that he had influential enemies both in the university and at the town hall. He'd even been warned by the chief of planning that if he ever got the slightest opportunity he'd have him out of his job.

"Just make one mistake, Glover, and you're finished, and with all the cuts no one will stand up for you next time."

And Giles knew he was right. But the call wasn't about that, it was worse; it was about Skendleby, and if there was anywhere he never wanted to see again it was that place. It didn't make it any better that he'd been half expecting it; Ed Joyce, the parish vicar, had rung him a couple of days earlier to say that things were going on there that shouldn't be. So he took the call with some trepidation.

"Hello, Giles Glover speaking."

"Sam Mendes from the Liaison Unit. We've had a request from the police for someone to go and look at some remains they're examining at Skendleby Hall. Can you get across there now?"

"What? At such short notice? We've loads on here."

"It's not a request in the literal sense, you know how it is."

So, ten minutes later, Giles was steering his car towards a place he'd hoped never to set eyes on again. But he didn't have time to brood on it as driving was more difficult than he'd expected. The cold frost that started the day was now augmented by a sporadic mist rising from the ground and forming dispersed patches that he drove in and out of. He'd just negotiated a particularly dense clump on a sharp bend where the road first met the estate boundary when he was passed at speed by a black Range Rover with opaque windows. As it accelerated onto the straight he was able to read the number plate. It bore the legend 'SI 2', he knew its owner: a man who, like the hall, he never wanted to see again. The black car slowed slightly to negotiate the turn into the estate, but had to stop as the electronic gates had not quite opened. This enabled Giles to follow it unseen down the drive. Parked in front of the Hall's front door were a couple of police squad cars and a scene of crime van.

'S1 2' screeched to a halt by the van, its door flew open and a stocky man with a polished shaved head and wearing a too tight black suit climbed out. He paused long enough to shout at the tanned blond woman who had come out to greet him, then disappeared at running speed round the side of the hall. Giles parked up by the police cars and as the woman began to ask him who he was he pointed to the cars and said:

"I'm with them."

Then he rushed off after Carver, ignoring the cry of:

"How long is this all going to take?"

The sound of shouting directed him to a patch of dug-up-earth by the old Davenport chapel. An area was taped off and a small tent had been erected. Two disgruntled men in work clothes stood by a bulldozer, smoking and watching the altercation between Si Carver and the police. But it was less an altercation than a harangue.

"What are you doing on my property wasting public money? Your Chief Constable's a friend of mine: we do things for charity together see, and he'll be pretty bloody angry when I tell him about this."

Giles recognised the officer in charge, he had good reason to: it was the same man who had interviewed him twice about the series of attacks round Skendleby last Christmas. He obviously resented being shouted at by Carver, but was doing a good job of keeping his cool.

"Mr Carver, we're here because of your wife's phone call. Your men working on this area have uncovered human remains. These have to be investigated."

"Bollocks! They're right outside an old church, what would you expect to find there? You never heard of graveyards?"

The officer, DS Anderson (Giles suddenly remembered his name and rank), started to reply and Giles could tell his patience was beginning to wear thin.

"Mr Carver, all I can say is....."

He broke off, having noticed Giles standing behind Carver; he looked almost pleased to see him.

"Dr Glover, thanks for coming so quickly."

Whatever he might have said next was lost as Si Carver turned round and saw Giles.

"What you doing here? Who let you in? I told you last time, if I ever saw you again you'd regret it, remember, yeah? Last time cost you your job."

Carver's face was swollen red with rage. Giles knew he was an aggressive bully but it flickered through his mind that even for Carver this was an overreaction. It seemed to Giles that this wasn't just anger: the man had become unbalanced. However, he didn't need to respond as Anderson stepped in.

"Dr Glover's here because we asked him to come: he can verify that the remains belong to an historic context and then this ceases to be a crime scene. The sooner he does that the sooner we can get out of your way."

This didn't appease Carver.

"What, let him poke his nose about? You must be joking. You don't know how much trouble he caused last time. There's no way I'm having him on my land."

"Well, in that case, Mr Carver, you would be obstructing the police in carrying out an investigation of..."

Carver cut him off.

"Oh, I get it: this is a fix up, innit. This is part of the fucking conspiracy to stop me bringing this place into the 21st century. Well, let me put you fucking straight..."

But he never got the chance to put him straight as Anderson's mobile rang.

"DS Anderson. Yes Ma'am, we're near there now. Ok, we'll get over straight away. We're more or less finished here."

It was clear from the look on Anderson's face that whatever he was being told was serious and Giles and Carver, in the way people do at such times, just watched and listened. Anderson finished the call and, ignoring Carver, shouted across to his team.

"Pack up, we've got a real one: looks like it's starting again."

He moved off and then hesitated. Turning to Giles, he said loud enough for Carver to hear:

"Check the site over to confirm our diagnosis, please; if you encounter problems we can come back with a warrant."

Then he was gone and within seconds Giles could hear the sound of engines starting up. Carver and Giles looked at each other, frozen in a moment of neutrality. What they'd heard hadn't specified what was starting to happen again, but they were both pretty certain they knew what it was. Behind them, over by the silent bulldozer, they heard Dave mutter to Jed:

"Been better if we'd left them buried."

Chapter 3: Investigating Officer

Vivian Campbell checked her lipstick in the mirror and saw her strong black face staring back at her with a familiar questioning look. In five minutes she would have to face the press: tell them it had all started again. So why was she so bothered about how her hair looked? Maybe it was a mental self-defence mechanism, but all the same it irritated the hell out of her. The options open to her were limited. She'd hoped that the retro Whitney Houston look circa the mid 1980s would have complimented her strong jaw line and high cheekbones, but it hadn't. It looked a mess, stuck out over her ears. Thank God she hadn't had it lightened, that would have drawn everyone's eyes to the mess.

She thought again of the irony of being back in Manchester just as her career in the Met had been taking off. The aftermath of the Stephen Lawrence case had certainly made things easier: although there was an element of whispering that people like her only got on because of their skin colour rather than their ability.

This didn't bother her much; she had no doubts regarding her ability. In fact, she hadn't experienced much racism herself, at least not in the way it was conventionally conceived. It was racial conflict of a different type that had driven her family south from Oldham to London. Negative interaction between the Afro-Caribbean and Pakistani communities which culminated in the torching of the Caribbean club in Glodwick. This had been the last straw for her dad: he was a maths teacher and there was plenty of demand for those in London.

Her family had had aspirations for their kids; two of her brothers were doctors and the third had served in Afghanistan along with Prince Harry. She'd been good at school, loved sixth form college and got a first from the London School of Economics. But her decision to join the police, the Met in particular, had surprised everyone. In fact, some of her more political white friends had been quite hostile. It was her dad who had helped her to make the decision. He'd taken her to the park they used to go to when she was little and they'd sat on a bench. She could still see the sun sinking behind the buildings across the river as she heard him say:

"This is our country, Vivian. We're English, a new type of English and as such we need to take some responsibility for the way the old place is run."

It hadn't quite worked out like that but in general, she guessed, he'd been right in the way that quiet, good men often are. Ironic all the same that the reason she'd been catapulted back to Greater Manchester had been her high profile role in 'the headless body in the river' investigation. A murder case with its convoluted roots deep in African witchcraft. Seems you can never entirely escape the tentacles of history. What she'd had to deal with there still gave her nightmares and in a strange way she felt it had somehow cast a stain on her inner life. Another reason she didn't want to be here dealing with this. But, as always, it was politics that pulled the strings.

Pressure had been put on the Chief Constable by the press and by prominent citizens who felt threatened by the previous year's unsolved killings. As a result a deal had been done. So here she was. She touched up the glossy lipstick and walked out to face ordeal by the press.

DS Anderson was standing by the entrance to the briefing room. He'd been part of the team who'd failed to get any results and she wondered if he, like others, resented her presence. If he did she wasn't going to give him the satisfaction of showing him she was nervous. She stared straight into his face as she walked past and was surprised when he gave her a thumbs up, smiled and said:

"Good luck, Ma'am."

She mumbled a quick "thanks Jimmy" and, feeling slightly better, walked into the briefing.

Once inside, seated with the others behind the long table that seemed to feature in all such briefings, professionalism kicked in. She watched the assembled journalists twitch with impatience as the Chief gave his plodding and pedantic introduction: they knew something had happened and they wanted to pitch into the new girl. He sensed this, came to a stop and then said:

"Now, to brief you on the new development, I'd like to introduce Detective Inspector Campbell who has been seconded from the Metropolitan Police on account of her experience. She will be heading up the case."

A rustle of expectation ran round the room and all the cameras were trained on Viv. She knew she looked good on camera so smiled and held the moment until she knew they were all ready to listen. Then she tried to explain the inexplicable.

Yes, she could confirm there had been another attack and that it had been fatal. She could also confirm that the victim was a young woman of unknown identity, and that they believed the attack was linked to the ones that had occurred at the end of the previous year. Yes, she could confirm that there were particular and disturbing features to this crime. No, she would not reveal what these were.

She was asked if the police had any leads and paused, wondering whether to give the normal guff about a number of promising lines of enquiry, but found herself saying that there weren't. Then came the question that she both expected and dreaded.

"Amanda Gordon, Sky News. Is it the case, DI Campbell, that you have been seconded from the Met because of your experience with witchcraft?"

"I wouldn't have put it like that, Amanda, but it is the case that I have experience with a team who successfully cracked a ritual murder."

"Well, yes, but it was a ritual involving witchcraft, wasn't it? And that's why you are here. So my question is: are we dealing with some type of satanic group?"

"We have no evidence of that and I would advise against attempts to talk up a scare story."

"But people are scared! Sorry, Geoff Oates, the Mail. Following the outbreak of attacks at the end of last year, which the police failed to solve, there were rumours of a mysterious curse and now you've been put in charge. Your most high profile case was concerned with an African witch cult. What are we to read into that?"

"Look, I admit that this is a complex case, Geoff, but all I'm prepared to say is that this was a frenzied attack and the public need to keep calm and be very careful. However, this will not be possible if wild speculative rumours are aired."

She wanted to shut this down now and could tell that the Chief did too: he was sweating, but the question he most wanted to avoid was shouted out.

"What does this say about the effectiveness of the local police if they have to bring you up from London?"

She was ready for this.

"It demonstrates the effectiveness of partnership and co-operation between branches of the modern police service."

A bureaucratic cliché but it worked as a conversation stopper. The Chief rasped into her ear:

"Take one last question. Take his, Jim Gibson's, he's from the local rag but he's steady and relies on our co operation more than the nationals."

Viv looked where the Chief indicated and saw a heavily built middle-aged man in a sports jacket with his hand raised.

"I'll take one more question and I think it would be appropriate to give it to the local paper, Mr Gibson?"

The reporter seemed surprised to be recognised but asked:

"Is it true that the attack took place near to the Skendleby estate?"

Viv was relieved at the banal and non-searching question and answered:

"Yes, I believe that it was fairly near."

"Do you understand the significance of that location in the last spate of attacks?"

There was something here that Viv didn't understand, but the Chief obviously did and didn't like it. He blustered:

"Right, that's it. We've said all we're prepared to say now but we'll keep you informed. Thank you very much, ladies and gentleman."

He stood up and shepherded Viv out of the room, saying as much to himself as to her:

"These bloody things have got worse since they moved all those BBC buggers into Salford."

Viv made no reply and he began to move off then checked and said, almost as a throwaway through gritted teeth:

"You didn't handle that too badly."

She watched him shamble slowly off to deal with the rest of the day's back-to-back crises, feeling grateful that she didn't have his job. The feeling didn't last: Anderson was waiting for her and she could tell by his face the news wasn't good.

"Well done in there, Ma'am, could you to come to the morgue? There are things you need to see."

Unlike in TV series, the forensic pathologist had no quirky or endearing characteristics, just a bedside manner entirely appropriate to her environment.

"Sorry this took so long, it's been a complicated one, but I can give you some preliminary findings. I can't fully vouch for any of them yet, it's too unorthodox. I think there's enough hard evidence though to link this with the attacks last Christmas."

Viv watched Anderson put his hand to his head as he listened. She took in the artificial brightness of the lighting in this grim chamber and knew that what came next would be bad.

"For one thing the knife wasn't metal; it was made of some type of stone."

"Just like last time. It must be linked, we never released any of this stuff to the press."

The interruption came from Anderson. The pathologist ignored him and carried on.

"There were traces of stone - some form of flint, perhaps obsidian from the colouration - left in the body. I've sent it off to the labs for petrological analysis and they'll probably consult the archaeology research unit in Sheffield. They have a high degree of specialisation."

Viv wanted her to shut up about this and get on with the summary: her body language must have been eloquent as she resumed it.

"It was a frenzied attack. Death wasn't instantaneous and yet the victim appears to have put up little resistance: no evidence beneath the fingernails to help with DNA. However, the body was moved after the initial attack, which must have taken place near a patch of brambles judging from the evidence on the clothes.

"The wounds of the initial attack comprise of a tearing of the left ear. It was done by human teeth, but surprisingly there's no trace of forensic evidence for you there. There is a stab wound to the lower stomach, which may have been intentionally targeted as the victim was in the early stages of pregnancy and a series of puncture wounds to the neck and shoulders. That concludes the first phase of the attack."

Viv cut in:

"What do you mean, first phase? Wasn't that enough to kill her?"

"Oh yes, more than enough: one of the neck wounds alone was sufficient for that."

"So, what do you mean by second phase?"

"The second phase was a type of harvesting. Look, you need to see this."

The pathologist pulled back the sheet covering the pathetic remains.

Viv had been through this many times before and after the torso in the river, thought that nothing could shock her. But this, this was different. The torso had lacked features, resembled a butcher's carcass, been anonymous. But this was so…so pathetic, fragile, vulnerable. The face looked so young, so surprised, it wasn't right. She felt a hand on her shoulder; Anderson's, his skin was ashen. He shouldn't have been so familiar to a superior, particularly a woman, but she appreciated it and for a few seconds they were human beings. But they had work to do. Work that could stop this happening again.

"Thank you, I think we've seen enough, perhaps you would summarise your findings on the second phase."

"Certainly, if you think you're ready for it."

Viv could see this wasn't meant kindly, the pathologist was barely suppressing a smirk. She wanted to slap her but instead said:

"Get to it as quickly as possible, please."

"Well, as you've seen in the second phase, the killer cut out selected bones and removed them, again using a stone knife. I think this was done in two stages. A couple of finger joints were removed where the attack took place. Then it looks like the body was moved for the extraction of the more complicated ones, probably to avoid being seen. Whoever did this must be very strong."

"Is that all?"

"It is until I get the test results back. I'll let you know as soon as I can."

Viv nodded then turned to walk out followed by Anderson. She was glad to be out and needed some space to think. But before she could get that Anderson said:

"Christ, I was dealing with the skeletal remains at Skendleby Hall when this job was called in."

"And you think the two are linked?"

"No, I'm not saying that. Well, not now anyway, that'll wait until Glover gets back with his findings."

"Who's Glover?"

"A local archaeologist we use. Interestingly, he was on our 'to interview' list during the last spate of attacks. Only circumstantial though."

"Why would you…?"

She didn't get any further. A young policewoman called down the corridor to her.

"Ma'am, I think we've found out who the victim is."

Chapter 4: A House Divided

In the squad car on the way to the house, Viv tried to prepare herself for what would follow. The memory of the woman identifying the body was still fresh in her mind. The distress had been genuine; well, it was more the shock, but then again there was no other reaction when faced with a sight like that, it had shocked her and she'd had plenty of experience.

But there was something else she'd sensed in Margaret Trescothic. She'd been very reluctant to talk about her community; there were things she wanted kept hidden and there were things that frightened her. Things that almost made Viv as nervous as the mutilated body of Kelly Ellsworth lying on the slab just inches away from her right hand. Not that she thought the woman had any direct responsibility for the murder, but she knew that once they began to ask questions they'd unearth things it might be better to leave buried.

She was brought out of morbid reflection by Anderson, who said:

"You were asking about Skendleby Hall. Well, if you look to the right you'll see it: that's the estate wall we're driving alongside of now."

Viv looked and saw the weathered red brick wall and then the gates with a long curling driveway leading to the Hall. With its angles and massive chimneys lowering under the dismal grey sky it looked Jacobean and sinister. Set alongside the hall was the old church of St George and its great rectory surrounded by the graveyard. As the car slowed to take the corner, she thought she saw a vague black shape shift jerkily from behind one of the trees. It must have been a trick of the light because when she looked again it was gone. It made no sense, but it felt like someone had just walked over her grave, so she was relieved when Anderson said:

"The hall was owned by the Davenport family for centuries, then, about eighteen months ago, out of the blue, they sold it to a financial wheeler dealer, a nasty piece of work. Sorry, shouldn't have said that, he's close to the Chief Constable. Not that I think the Chief likes him much, but you know how these types operate."

She did, like everyone else who had a pension fund or a job. Anderson carried on.

"Behind the Hall there's a patch of empty ground with some type of ancient burial mound that the locals think is haunted. The archaeologists from the Uni excavated it last summer, caused a lot of local reaction. An attack took place there but it turned out to be unconnected as far as we could work out. It's the only bit of the case we managed to crack: it was carried out by an unbalanced young woman."

"I take it that you don't buy any of this haunted stuff, Jimmy?"

It was meant as a sort of soft joke, but to her surprise Anderson gave a serious answer.

"No, no I don't think so, but then I've no reason to, but one of the lads from the local nick got mixed up in it and is still off sick. Nerves they say it is, but that's not what you get if you talk to him. Perhaps you should, his name's Barford."

Wanting to lighten the conversation, Viv asked:

"Why do they call you Jimmy when your name's Peter?"

For an answer, he put back his head and chanted:

"Oh, Jimmy Jimmy, Jimmy Jimmy Jimmy Anderson."

"Oh yeah, I get it, like the cricketer, but you don't look anything like him."

"No, but I open the bowling for the division and for Rostherne, and it's better than most nicknames."

They were on a minor track now, no buildings in sight, then the car turned a corner and there was the house.

Viv's first thought on seeing it was that it must have cost a fortune, even here so far from London property prices. But as she was processing this another perspective on the house hit her out of the blue.

There was something wrong about it. She'd had intuitions on cases before, all good detectives did, but about people, not about places. Since they'd passed Skendleby Hall she'd felt uneasy with the countryside. It felt like a place where bad things happened or rather, that it acted as a magnet attracting them, taking what was twisted in people and amplifying it. Once she admitted the thought she dismissed it, she was a rationalist and, if not a fully paid up card carrying atheist, she was certainly a fellow traveller. It was the only topic over which she and her dad fell out. She may have dismissed the thought but she couldn't shift the feeling. Fortunately, she had no time to reflect further: the car stopped and she saw the front door opening.

****

The session in the house proved frustrating: although on the surface the women cooperated, there was something lurking below that neither Viv nor Anderson could get a handle on. The nature of the community in the house hadn't helped either. What sort of set up was this? It felt somewhere between cult and coven, but with strong overtones of 'ladies who lunch'. "Pinot Grigio Witches" Jimmy had called them back in the car and, although she laughed, Viv saw what he meant.

But there was a definite pecking order in the house, even though only five of the seven women were present. The two missing were the newest and were both archaeologists who Jimmy remembered from the Skendleby investigations. This seemed not only too much of a coincidence but also creepy.

They were shocked by the murder and Margaret, who identified the body, looked like she'd been crying ever since. They were scared too, yet despite this, Viv knew they were withholding. But her impression from the morgue was compounded: there was something else besides this, something they wanted kept hidden. Something that made Viv want to dig away and expose the roots. In particular, she wanted to interview Olga and Margaret again, and this time away from the house. She also wanted to see if the interview room at the station would loosen them up.

Although as the investigating officer she was meant to be impartial, Viv hadn't taken to the two women. For a start they cold-shouldered Anderson, made it plain that they only wanted to talk to her, not only for gender reasons she reckoned. If they were to be interviewed they wanted the senior officer. She could accept that - it happened.

What she particularly didn't like, and which always got to her, was their assumption that because she was a woman, and particularly a black, professional woman, they were all on the same side and that she would be sympathetic. In fact, more than that; like she would be grateful for their empathy. They hadn't alluded to her as a sister but it had come close.

Overt hostility, racism, Viv got it from time to time, particularly in her job, but she recognised it, learnt how to deal with it and with the dickheads who spouted it. But being patronised by 'bien pensants' who didn't know her, had no idea of who she was and how she felt, yet thought they could categorise her on account of her appearance, grated on Viv. There was a lot of it in London and now Viv realised it was here too. She was still brooding over this, over Olga in particular, when they turned into the police compound.

In the incident room some shots from the morgue were pinned up on the board. Lumps of meat divorced from the sweet looking young girl they had once comprised. She didn't want to look, having seen the real thing, and didn't have to as the door opened.

"Ma'am, DS Anderson says that the archaeologist you want to see is here."

He was sitting in one of the small interview rooms with a plastic beaker containing some nasty hot drink. She liked to see them when they weren't aware: gave her a better feel for them than when they were on their guard. This one looked like he should be teaching sociology in one of the new universities, was curly haired and dishevelled. He had the residue of a tan so must have been on holiday recently but the thing that hit her most of all was how troubled he looked: sad rather than guilty she reflected as an afterthought. She walked in.

"Dr Glover? Detective Inspector Campbell, thanks for helping us out."

He did a double take (Viv was used to men reacting to her like this on first sight), then he put down his drink and got up to shake hands.

"No, please sit down, would you like another drink?"

From his quick refusal, Viv got the impression that he was pleased to have got rid of the first one.

"So, I take it you can confirm that the remains you found at Skendleby are historic and unrelated to any current enquiry?"

"Yes, but..."

He hesitated and she had to prompt him.

"Go on, but what?"

"Well, yeah, they're historic, from two different periods actually, and er.... look. I'm sure they've got nothing to do with what you're investigating, but there is something odd about them."

She watched his face as he spoke, he looked troubled and she knew there was something that he couldn't talk about. What was bothering him? She said nothing, left him the space to fill.

"There are the remains of two individuals from different periods, from the contexts I'd say separated by about two hundred years, well there or thereabouts. Timescale maybe between fourteenth and seventeenth centuries."

He paused again and she had to prompt him.

"And that's odd, is it?"

"No, not as such. The odd thing is...the odd thing is, er...that, and I can't be sure of this, but..."

She smiled encouragement.

"Come on, Dr Glover, you're not on oath, you can speculate."

"Well, without ruling out ground disturbance, animal movements, etc., both bodies seem to have had certain bones removed."

A shiver ran up and down Viv's spine, a premonition of what was coming. She asked:

"But couldn't natural causes account for that, like the ones you haven't ruled out?"

"They could, but it's the same bones on each body; the one the workers found and the one we found directly underneath. There are marks of butchery where the bones were severed."

Another pause, Viv sensed he was really troubled by this but prompted him.

"Underneath?"

"Yes, and hardly disturbed, so therefore almost intact."

"Bit of a coincidence?"

Dr Glover ignored the irony.

"If we'd more time I could be surer, but Mr Carver wasn't too happy to cooperate. He blames us for previous stuff."

Viv thought: *Carver, so that's the owner, the one Jimmy didn't like.*

She said:

"Don't worry, if this turns out to be police business he will afford you all the time you need."

Giles continued.

"It's the same bones with both bodies and if it was done by an animal, it was an animal wielding a sharp knife. Not many of those round here. Two burials separated by a couple of hundred years, one on top of the other. It's like whoever did the second knew about the first."

Viv thought to herself: *and now there's a third and he knows more than he's saying.*

She asked coolly:

"Do you always move from excavation to conclusion so rapidly, Dr Glover?"

Her tone had been harsh and ice cold. She regretted it, she didn't want to put him on his guard: it was shock at the coincidence that made her snap.

He replied with a whine:

"Well, you said I should speculate and that's all I did."

He clammed up, she'd been clumsy, he knew more and she wanted that knowledge. She was sure now, he understood the link between this and Kelly's death and that made him the killer, or at least a leading suspect. She softened her voice.

"I'm sorry, it's just that what you said was unexpected but could be particularly useful, and there is more, isn't there?"

He ran his fingers through his tangled hair and for a moment Viv thought he looked like the little boy he must have been. What was eating him? She didn't have to wait long for the answer.

"Look, this will seem mad and its freaking me out, and I've been thinking about it ever since I looked at these bones, but...."

"But?"

"But I've seen it before"

"What, on a different site?"

"No, it wasn't archaeology at all, it was meant to be a holiday."

"You've lost me, Dr Glover."

"In Greece, Samos, this summer. Where I was staying there was an outbreak of killings, the same things were done to the victims, the same bones."

He put his head in his hands, and declared:

"Oh God."

****

Later, after Giles had been given the stuff about his rights and locked up for the night, Viv took a coffee to the incident room. Outside it was dark and dank, inside the windows were misted up. Anderson greeted her.

"Well done, Ma'am, looks like you've wrapped this up. How did you get him to talk?"

"I'm not sure; he just came out with it as if he needed to talk. He was under no pressure. Didn't you say that you'd interviewed him earlier this year? How did he seem to you?"

"Ok really, we had nothing on him, he seemed alright."

Anderson broke off and picked up a plastic cup. Taking a gulp from it, he realised the coffee inside had long been cold and spat it back in disgust before continuing.

"But then they all do until you nail them. Anyway, it must be him, how else would he have known about the modus operandi about all the detail of the bones? And making up all that crap about Greece is what clinches it for me. I suppose they'll want you back in London now."

"I think that's a bit premature: he's not even being charged yet. We've no evidence really so tomorrow we'll follow all this up. It's been a long day so well done everyone."

Viv refused the offer to go for a drink, it wasn't her way of operating, and got up to leave. A few paces down the corridor a young detective, whose name she couldn't remember, called to her.

"Ma'am, the data we put out has got a match. I've got the details here. Not just one murder but a series with the same MO, this summer on Samos, Greece. The senior officer there's called Theodrakis."

Chapter 5: Not What I Wanted to Find

He swerved, just managing to prevent the car from crashing into a hedge and skidding onto the grass verge at the lip of a ditch. The engine stalled. He turned off the ignition and got out, cursing himself for his stupidity. He should have been concentrating on the difficult pastoral visit he was about to make: or at least concentrating on his driving.

But ever since he'd uncovered those papers in the archive it had been difficult to think of anything else. Giles had directed him to them, those papers, the ones Tim Thompson had tried to hide because he was afraid of what was in them. He'd been right to be afraid: now Tim was dead, killed in an apparently random attack in Nice where he'd been researching Skendleby connections. Except Ed didn't believe there was anything random in Thompson's death.

It was one of the only things he didn't believe these days. Since his experiences with Skendleby he'd changed from an agnostic priest in a crisis into a devout priest worried about how much there was to believe. He had no worries about his faith which sustained him: rather he feared all the other things that existed outside of it, and which most people choose not to see. He fished a battered cigarette packet out of the pocket of his parka and lit up, trying to concentrate on what he had to do next. While he was doing this he noticed that just ahead of him the road forked. He must be nearly there.

He'd had to think hard about making this visit: the house had acquired quite a reputation, not a good one. He discounted most of the stories, but there had been problems. What's more, he wasn't sure if he'd be welcome: as an Anglican vicar he was probably regarded as one of the enemy. The house wasn't even in his parish, strictly speaking, being over the other side of Woodford, but then again it wasn't really in any parish and he was the nearest priest to it. But after the killing he felt he had a duty to go and offer what help he could. At least that's what he told himself, but deep inside he knew that wasn't the real reason driving him.

The real reason was a creeping suspicion. It was all starting up again, and what he'd unearthed in the archives made him wonder if this killing was connected. He was going to reassure himself much as to reassure them. He threw down the cigarette and got back in the car.

At first sight, the house failed to live up to its reputation: it looked the type of place only someone with a great deal of money could afford, but wasn't in the least sinister.

He pulled to a halt, noticing the wind had got up in strength, forcing the trees surrounding the house to shake their heads in some wild dance. As he got out of the car a sharp shower of hail was blown horizontally across him stinging his face and his scalp through his thinning hair as he ran for the front door. He waited outside and, continuing to be drenched by the squall, wondered if the bell was working. He was about to ring again when it opened and he found himself looking at a round-faced mousey-haired woman that he recognised but couldn't quite place.

"You'd better come in."

She led him through a large reception hall which he couldn't take in as his glasses misted over with the contrast in temperature: he sensed she was sniggering at him, at which point he remembered her: Rose. She'd been badly injured just before they'd excavated 'Devil's Mound'. But he'd no time to test this hunch out as she walked through a door directly opposite and he followed, trying to wipe his glasses on a less than clean handkerchief.

The room he followed her into was everything he wanted the rectory to be: elegant, modern and with an atmosphere you could sense as you walked in: welcoming and peaceful, perfect for meditation or prayer. It also looked frighteningly expensive.

There were three women in it sitting on a couple of sofas by the great fireplace looking neither peaceful nor welcoming. He recognised one of them, striking rather than pretty, with masses of coarse black hair tied back in a ponytail. Leonie, she'd been on the Skendleby dig too. What exactly was going on here? He was relieved that he didn't recognise the others who Rose introduced as Ailsa and Ruth, neither of whom looked anything like the stereotype of a witch but would have blended in well as teachers or office managers.

"This is the Rev Joyce: he likes to be called Ed."

Ed recognised the mockery in her voice and saw Ruth and Ailsa dutifully smile while Leonie just looked away as if he wasn't there. He wished he wasn't too, but sensed that there was something wrong here, quite apart from the reaction to the murder of Kelly. He began to make his sympathy pitch but a door opened and two women walked in. He watched as the eyes of the women on the sofas locked onto them, with what looked to him like expectation. Except for Rose, her expression was harder to read. She introduced him to Olga and Jenna.

"I was explaining to your friends that I'm here to express sympathy, and to offer any support I can in these most difficult times."

It was Olga who answered. Ed found her strangely attractive: she was strong built with long flaxen hair worn in heavy plaits. She reminded him of a Valkyrie from the Ring cycle.

"Thank you, that is kind, but we have our own spiritual support network here, something more sustaining than your dead man nailed to a tree."

Ed was used to his faith being ridiculed; even so, this seemed a particularly abrupt, not to say archaic, response; more a declaration of hostility than a refusal. Also, it was unexpected: there was a lot of alternative religion round here on the fringe of the Pennines, always had been, and in general Wiccans and other pagan alternatives rubbed along with their Christian counterparts quite well.

"Well, the offer's still there, and please don't underestimate the dead man nailed to a tree, remember he came back to life and that resurrection brings hope to all."

A year ago, Ed wouldn't have said that, he'd have just blushed and walked off, glowing red with embarrassment. But since his experience resealing the tomb at Skendleby he'd been travelling through a different landscape.

"Don't try to patronise us, Reverend Joyce, I choose my words carefully. You're not talking to weak fabulists with heads stuffed full of Margaret Murray nonsense about unbroken millennia of secret rituals, of the Twilight saga or Buffy the Vampire Slayer.

"Ours is the practice of now, the power of stone, of herb, of blood. The community of women evolves and that is what you and your male God fear. I will concede that you may think you act out of kindness, but really you act out of anxiety and the desire to control. And this community is for women who have escaped that control and are evolving a more imaginative and spiritual space."

Ed could see that the others, to various degrees, agreed and he was aware that all the while Olga had been speaking, Jenna had stared fixedly at him, unblinking, hard-eyed. Grief took all types of form and as a vicar he'd seen most of them. But this was something else and it disturbed him, and not on account of himself or his faith. It wasn't the words: the faith and gender dialectics he was familiar with. He would have liked to have talked to Olga one-to-one, but that wasn't possible so he prepared to leave.

"Ed, what are you doing here? How lovely to see you."

The voice came from behind and he turned to see a tall, redheaded woman, and with her, Claire. She came across to him and kissed him on the cheek; it was the first warmth he'd felt since arriving at the house, and he was delighted to see her. As he lowered his face to return the kiss, his chin snagged briefly on the large intricate necklace she was wearing. It was white, like polished bone or ivory, but he couldn't imagine that anyone with her sensitivities or belief system would wear either of those. Perhaps it was synthetic or some type of stone, but he had no time for further reflection.

"Ed, let me introduce Margaret, it's her house and I'm sorry but I've been monopolising her."

Ed said hello to Margaret who shook hands and smiled at him with more warmth than any of the others had. He could see they were staring at Claire as if she were the centre of the community. Well, all except Olga who looked pretty sour, but Ed thought perhaps that was her default setting.

"I just came to offer my condolences and any help that I could give."

He paused.

"But apparently that wasn't needed."

Claire smiled back at him.

"No, it seems I've got that gig, Ed."

"I didn't know that you were connected."

"Well, it's a small world and I think my brand of psychic healing will be sympathetic. Listen, I'll walk you out and we can catch up."

It was only later, when he'd had time to think about it, that he realised she'd seemed completely at home there: in fact, she'd acted as if she was the hostess and that the house and the community were hers. At the car he'd asked her how Giles was. She'd giggled before replying.

"Oh, he's only gone and got himself arrested!"

Ed stood there waiting for the punch line, a look of humorous expectation covering his face

"No, I mean it, they're still holding him."

"But what for? Is he all right, are you?"

"Me, yes, of course I am."

"And Giles?"

"Just typical of Giles, isn't it? He's managed to get himself arrested as a suspect for the murder: this one here, how ridiculous."

She laughed.

"But I expect they'll soon let him go, he'd have no idea how to kill anybody poor darling. I better go back in now, Ed, they'll be waiting. Byeee."

When he got back to the rectory, Mary was out. He remembered she'd gone to the theatre group's technical walk through preceding the dress rehearsal. He wasn't sure if he was pleased or not: he needed time to think and did that best alone, but the rectory was vast and rambling and isolation fed paranoia. He went through to his study and took out the documents he'd copied: the ones Thompson had found and then hidden before his death. The Davenport file from the fifteenth century he'd have dismissed as the product of a ruined mind a year ago, but not now. The other file, if a specialist in the field like Thompson had not verified it, he'd have considered a forgery, and a potentially valuable one. It was a previously unknown and unpublished document, found in the Davenport archive and dating to the early years of the seventeenth century.

To Ed's amazement, the author was the Queen's notorious conjuror and alchemist, Dr John Dee. Ed knew that Dee had been the warden of Manchester College from 1595-1608 and had kept a diary which Ed, in fact, had seen in the Bodleian Library as a student. There had always been conjecture that because of its occult and heretical nature, much of Dee's work had remained hidden. John Aubrey, the seventeenth century antiquarian, had indeed suggested in his 'Brief Lives' that only a third of what Dee wrote ever came to light. Ed wished that this extract had remained similarly occluded.

Before he began to read he tried to make some sense of his visit. He'd found the woman Olga compelling, almost erotically so, and this unusual reaction disturbed him. He wanted to talk to her again but considered that was probably not a good idea. Meeting Claire had thrown him, particularly her light-hearted treatment of Giles's arrest, but at least with her the women in the house were in good hands. But why had the girl from the house been killed and why were the police not releasing any information?

Why had he found the texts on the day the news of the murder broke? They dealt with ritual killing, the taking and secreting of bones for future use as trophies: bones. Like the Neolithic bone he'd been told to bury in the church crypt after the sealing up of Devil's Mound. He remembered the unearthly singing he'd heard as he'd done this.

Please, God, this killing wasn't connected. Please, God, it hadn't started again.

Chapter 6: Greeks Bearing Gifts

The cell door opened; a metallic spike of noise.

"Get up and come with me."

He took his hands from over his eyes and blinked into the light, anything was better than spending another moment in this cell with its hard pallet and cloying smell of antiseptic masking undertones of vomit and urine. He got to his feet and shuffled after the police guard feeling unreal in the overalls they'd made him wear when they took his clothes. He made a mental note to remember that however awkward the police may seem when you meet them, on the street it was infinitely better than when they invite you to stay over at their place.

On TV shows suspects get a cooked breakfast, he'd had nothing since late afternoon yesterday; perhaps they were trying to break him down. Or perhaps what the Daily Mail was always on about was true: the public services were inefficient and shambolic. Maybe McDonald's should run the country's law and order service. At least he'd get a sausage and egg McMuffin.

A door was opened and he was shown into a dimly lit room. He recognised the bitch who'd tricked him then locked him up, the detective from Skendleby, and a man who he guessed must be the duty solicitor. He remembered asking them to contact Claire and wondered if they had. He knew he should feel frightened but this last year he'd been haunted, threatened and terrified to such an extent that they'd already turned the volume up to eleven. He remembered that Theodrakis had used the phrase "walking through hell", and he hadn't quite got it at the time; he got it now.

There was one consolation, however: when you walk through hell things can't get much worse.

"We'd like to ask you some questions, Dr Glover. Have you any objections?"

He giggled, couldn't help himself. It was so ridiculous, as if he were in a position to refuse. It was the pallid male cop asking, not the beautiful black one. He supposed she would watch till he made a mistake and then swoop for the kill. And he would make a mistake; there were so many to choose from, so many things he couldn't afford to tell them. Things he'd seen here and in Greece, things he'd done, things he should have done, things he'd hidden...

He must have lost himself in the train of thought because the woman suddenly leaned forward and said sharply:

"I hope you are going to be co-operative, Dr Glover, because saying nothing and giggling like an idiot isn't improving your already very difficult position."

For a moment he considered replying "no comment" like the criminals on TV do moments before they confess, but he managed to pull himself together.

"No, I'm sorry, I think I'm a little disorientated."

"Would you like a drink?"

"Please, I'd like a coffee."

They brought him a coffee and so it began. It went as he'd expected. He couldn't explain why he'd been able to describe the taking of bones from a body that exactly matched the murder. He couldn't convince them that he had no part in the similar attacks the previous year, and he couldn't make them believe that his presence at the scene of a series of gruesome murders in Greece with the same MO was merely a coincidence. He almost agreed when the female cop synthesised his replies for him.

"So, Dr Glover, you agree that you've been on the scene of savage brutal killings both here and in Greece. You also agree, despite the fact that neither the police in Greece nor here released any evidence concerning the peculiar method of these killings, that you were able to divulge it with great accuracy to me yesterday. What would you consider was the common factor in all theses killings?"

"I can see what you're trying to get me to say but what I told you came from archaeological sites which, apart from the recent discovery at the Hall, date back to the Neolithic, about five thousand years ago."

"Ah yes, I remember. I also remember you saying that all that evidence has, rather inconveniently for you, gone missing. Whereas the evidence of the vicious sickening murder of a young woman, which we have managed not to lose, you were able to describe accurately. Could you explain that for us?"

"No, you don't get what I'm trying to say. I know what it sounds like but…"

He ground to a halt, but they were still waiting.

"But…"

He put his hands over his face.

"Take him back to the cells; give him time to think up some more sensible answers."

Later in the cell, he wondered why he hadn't mentioned Theodrakis. But perhaps Theodrakis didn't really exist, perhaps he was mad, perhaps he had done it just like they said. It seemed it could get worse than walking through hell. He lay down on the bunk and started to cry.

****

Back in the incident room, Viv had just factored a conversation with the investigating officer on the isle of Samos into her already cramped schedule for the remains of the day. The political situation in Greece, she knew, was continuing to deteriorate with daily acts of civil disobedience filling the democratic vacuum. So she didn't expect much from Astinome Syntagmatarchis Theodrakis, but she was grateful that he was going to take the time to ring her.

In the meantime, Jimmy was reading the files sent through from Greece. She planned to spring the fruits of this on the suspect in the hope that this triangulation of guilt would make him crack then confess.

She was reasonably confident; it was a technique that had worked for her previously and she took time to think of her other preoccupation: where to live. She didn't know how long she'd be here and didn't want to stay in her present accommodation. She'd talked to her dad about the advisability of climbing on to the property ladder; she could afford something quite smart here which she couldn't in London. There were available new build apartments all over and she had an appointment to see one in Didsbury.

She'd left the mess of her emotional life in London so was in no hurry to get back. Here she was a strong single woman with a reputation unsullied by the aftermath of her last affair. Well, it had been an affair to him: it had meant more to her. So she would keep open her options to apply for a permanent transfer to Manchester if this went well. If it didn't and she went back she could rent out the apartment: prices would rise again, recessions never lasted forever. She got no further; Jimmy was back in the room.

"I've read the files, boss."

She relished the title: it was the first time anyone here had called her that.

"Go on, what have we got?"

"Plenty from this: it's pretty weird though, and some of it's hard to believe. But I'm sure we've got our man, it's the same thing over there, you know, the cutting out and taking of bones. Seems the whole island was in a state of terror: thought it was the work of the Devil. One of their senior detectives was among the victims, hope that doesn't spread."

"Stick to the facts."

"Ok, well, like us, they never released the details, yet our archaeologist knew them."

"Thanks, that helps: I want you to go back to the women's house and take statements, see if you can establish a motive."

"But why? We've got it wrapped up here. He knows how it was done, which only the murderer could, and he's no alibi."

"Maybe. Ok, probably, but we've not got all of it. No motive, and we're still waiting for forensics on him."

"Wouldn't they rather see you, Ma'am, they blanked me but opened up to you."

"That's exactly why you should go. Sorry."

After he'd gone she read the Greek file: most of it made little sense, particularly the abrupt way the case was closed: a strange mixture of fortuitous suicides and mob rule taking its own savage vengeance before the police could make an arrest. But the killings were certainly similar, if not identical. There was some terrible agent at work here, and one she couldn't equate with the collapsed archaeologist in the cells. The Greeks obviously hadn't suspected him of anything.

And there was something else bothering her: the feeling of menace she'd experienced on the way to interview the women hadn't evaporated, and although the evidence pointed relentlessly at the archaeologist, something inside nagged away at her that maybe it wasn't that simple. Time was moving on; she got up and headed for the interview room.

They'd already brought him in and he sat slumped in the plastic school chair, hands on his lap. She felt a strange rush of sympathy for him. The room stank, an odour she couldn't categorise, but rank all the same.

"I hope you intend to be more cooperative this time, Dr Glover."

"I tried to be last time: I just don't know how to answer the questions."

"Well, you can start off by telling me about your experiences on Samos."

Giles pushed his hands through his hair; he was sweating, on the point of tears.

"It was meant to be a holiday."

Suddenly, Viv's intuition clicked in and her reservations vanished: it was him, he was guilty, she could almost smell it on him.

"But there was more to it, wasn't there?"

He nodded and she thought for a moment that he was about to confess.

"So, go on, tell me what happened."

"There were things going on over there: fires, killings, murders - right across the island and I got mixed up in it."

"How did you get mixed up?"

"I was given these bones to look after."

Viv felt the hairs on the back of her neck stick up, the duty solicitor leant forward to speak but she held up her hand and he kept silent.

"Bones?"

Giles sat thinking how to answer, and in the quiet Viv could hear the monotonous tick of the electric clock on the wall. The stench in the room seemed stronger: they sat waiting for him to continue.

"They were bones that had been found on an archaeological site."

"And why did you have them?"

She could see from his expression he knew where this was taking him. He didn't answer. She saw the sweat beading his face. His stomach rumbled; he belched and put his hand over his mouth. Soon she'd have him.

"They were meant for the police."

"Why was that, Dr Glover, if they were ancient bones? What would the police want with them?"

He didn't answer, just sat with his eyes closed rocking backwards and forwards on the cheap chair. She repeated.

"Why would the police want them if they were ancient bones?"

He appeared to have stopped listening.

"They wouldn't have been interested in ancient bones would they, Dr Glover? But they were interested in your bones, weren't they? So what do we deduce from that? As you've stopped talking I'll fill in some of the blanks for us shall I?"

She gave him a chance to answer but he didn't so she went in for the kill.

"I can fill in the blanks because I've read the Greek police reports on the case and in a few moments I'll be talking to their investigating officer, then I'll know exactly what you were up to on Samos. And I can guess that the bones you had on Greece were the same type that you told us about here. I'm right, aren't I?"

It was a rhetorical question; she had no intention of letting him talk, yet.

"So, let's think about what type of bones the Greek police would have been interested in shall we? We know it wasn't ancient bones. But the bones you had weren't ancient bones were they, Dr Glover? No, the bones you had were modern, very modern, weren't they?"

He didn't answer; she raised her voice and it seemed to fill the small, fetid room.

"They were modern bones, the bones of the victims, weren't they?"

There was a weak semi-audible reply.

"Yes."

"Sorry, Dr Glover, you'll have to speak louder for the tape."

But he never got the chance to: the door opened and a police woman came in.

"Sorry to disturb you, Ma'am, but they said you'd want to know this at once. There's a Syntagmatarchis Theodrakis of the Greek police on the phone wanting to talk to you."

Chapter 7: The Devil's Mark

"After much agitation and discmforte in a storme of hayle, thunder and lyghtening rode beyond Stopford to the halle at Skyndleby; where despite feares for the poore health of my son, plague being rife in Manchester, stayed the night in order to perform certain actions, much against my wille."

Ed leant back in his chair, a sick feeling in the pit of his stomach: he knew enough of the author by now to understand that his usage of the word 'actions' meant conjuring up spirits. So had Tim Thompson, he'd underlined the word. He also knew that Dee, in his published diary, claimed to have burned all papers recording such actions. Well, it seemed he hadn't and that either he or someone else had preserved and hidden them. He sat in an agony of indecision; he was fairly certain what he would find if he continued reading.

He walked to the window. Outside it was murky, the light opaque and uncertain. He thought he saw movement in the trees at the edge of the graveyard. He hoped it was just his eyes playing tricks in the gloom, he didn't want to see the thing lurking there that drove him to the fringe of madness last year. He was a stronger man now, but even so there were things walking the earth that no one could face down, and he should know he'd tried. But he also knew you couldn't dodge what was coming: God wouldn't let you.

He went back to his desk where the manuscript lay in the pool of light from the Angle poise lamp and sat inside the comforting illuminated circle to think. He knew that John Dee, conjuror to Queen Elizabeth, had been given a living in remote Manchester to get him out of London for some undisclosed reason. Ed had seen Dee's desk, with the Devil's mark burned into it, in the old college buildings by Manchester Cathedral. He remembered that some scandal had led to Dee's move to Manchester.

The posting had been tantamount to exile, but had turned out to be worse than that. He'd walked into something that his reputation ensured he'd never be able to wriggle out of. It was just his luck that his time in Manchester coincided with an outbreak of one of the periodic infestations of evil at Skendleby; this one occasioned by the necromantic dabbling of one of the Davenports at the end of the fourteenth century. Ed's friend, the last of the Davenports, called it their legacy. Ed thought that Dee's arrival in Manchester must have seemed a blessing to the Davenports. Not a blessing for Dee, though, as the next highlighted passage clearly demonstrated.

"I discovered they had meddled with bones to avert somme spelle or treacherie; this they in divers ways shewed me. Yet in defence of my soule I sweare that when I was prevailed upon to trie my power the girl was already somme time dead. Being dead when first I arrived."

The mention of a ritual using human bones gave Ed the horrors; it was too close to his own experience. Dee had been through the same nightmare as he had, but it brought no comfort and there was worse to come.

"Heere in Skyndleby there seeme to be shadows that hover and flit rounde aboute the halle and churchyard. The place is bleake and emptie save fore a ridge with rockie edge that reares up out of the dismal plaine. Nearabouts there is a small mounde of dark repute whiche I feare Sir Edmund in his anxietie has tampered with."

Dee's thoughts mirrored Ed's initial impressions of the area. It seemed that Dee had trodden the same path he now trod, the path which had driven Heatly-Smythe to suicide in the eighteenth century. There was one sheet of text left to read, and Ed was pretty certain he knew where it was leading.

"They had assayed some actions of their own: being led to these by a local cunning woman who I believe better shoulde weare the title of sorceress, or as Cicero woulde style it Witch. I thinke that by this acte she meante them evill not good."

A picture of the women's house entered his mind, particularly the image of Olga with her heavy flaxen hair in braids. Then he thought of Claire: what had she been doing there? Why did she seem so at home?

But lucky for the women that she was there rather than the Witch that Dee wrote about, who had preyed on the Davenports. All the same, she'd taken the news of Giles's arrest very calmly: seemed to find it amusing. This had reassured Ed at the time, but Giles had still not been released. The police hadn't named him, just confirmed a man was helping with their enquiries. He'd seen it on television; the elegant black woman heading up the case had refused to answer any other questions. He didn't want to dwell on the implications of this so he turned back to the text.

"It came upon me with awfule force that this my presente situation is what Mr Walker, my Skryer, had seene in the crystal severall years befor but whiche did at the time make none sense. Now him being deade, killed somewhere in the region of the empire known as Hungary, I no longer have the powre; the local skryer, Mr Hikman, whom I begin to mistrust, being a man of no skill. Nowe I muche wish I had heeded Mr Walker's warning."

Ed recognised these references from his own reading of Dr Dee's diaries, and the fact that they seemed to validate the authenticity of the document made things worse. But he only had one brief paragraph to go.

"We travelled to a farm some little distance away towards Handeforthe assayed an action but have little faith that it can take effect, they had meddled too muche already. Before we started I did meete the cunning woman who did looke at me in a strange and chauncey fashion. I liked not this looke. Today I received news from Manchester that my poore boy is deade. I am cursed"

That, to Ed's relief, was the end of the main body of the text. There was just one other sentence that appeared after a gap, at the foot of the page, as if added later in great haste.

"There are shadows, something watches."

****

He sat for a moment in the silence as the psychic anguish of those last words resonated across the centuries. Then he got up and crossed to the window; outside it was now fully dark. High above the trees patches of dirty ragged cloud were being blown across the pitted face of the moon. The wind must have got up while he was immersed in his reading, as if the words themselves had the power to conjure a storm.

He considered taking the papers to Davenport, feeling that the old man's stoic common sense would give him the perspective he needed. But since his stroke, Davenport was fragile: so maybe it would be better done during the hours of daylight. He was considering rereading the text when he heard the chime of the front door bell. Some seconds later, the door of his study opened.

Mary came in and Ed could see from the shadows thrown across the hall behind her that there was someone waiting .

"Ed, you've got a visitor and you need to see her, I think there's something wrong."

Mary seemed unsettled, which was unusual: of all the people he knew, his wife was the least likely to overreact. As he was thinking this Mary showed in the visitor. She was striking in a gaunt way. Tall, she was wearing a deep red, knee length dress that gave her a slightly dated look. Her face, although beautifully shrouded by long black hair, seemed slightly too sharp and there were dark hollows under her eyes. Ed vaguely recognised her from somewhere, but couldn't place it. Mary made no introduction, just said as she left the room:

"Let me know if you decide you want a cup of something."

So it was left to the woman, who Ed judged to be in her early twenties, to introduce herself.

"You are priest, no?"

"Well, yes, I can be described that way but if you are looking for a Roman Catholic…"

She cut him off.

"No, there is no Catholic priest near here, only you. Besides, it is you I need to talk to in this moment."

"Well, what is it that I can do for you? By the way, I'm Reverend Joyce, but please call me…"

Again she cut him off

"Of course, I know who you are, I know much about you, many times I hear Mr Carver talk of you."

"Well, I hardly think you'll have heard much good about me from Mr Carver."

"No, nothing good: is all bad."

She hesitated for a moment then added softly:

"Very bad. He thinks that you are a very bad man. But I need to talk to you."

"So, do I take it that you work for Mr Carver?"

"Yes, sorry, I should have say, my name is Marika, I am his housekeeper. I am Slovenian, come here to work."

Ed finally placed her, she was one of the ever-changing relay of Eastern European girls that Carver employed, on the cheap and, Ed expected, illegally, to run the Hall. None of them lasted very long if the village gossip was to be believed.

"Well, how can I help you, Marika? And perhaps I can offer you a cup of tea and a piece of cake?"

"Thank you, no, there is not time and I will be missed."

He was sorry for this, he could tell that she had been tempted by the offer of cake, she looked too thin, not fashion model thin, poverty thin.

"Perhaps you should take some cake with you. I hear life isn't too easy in the Hall working for Mr Carver."

"It is not so hard, he is not a nice man but I have known worse. He does not beat us or make us give blow jobs like others. In fact, I think he hardly sees that we exist. Perhaps

I will take some cake but first I must tell you about what happens in the hall."

"Things to do with Carver?"

"No, but things that frighten him, things that should not be there, shadows of things you cannot see. Two girls have left because of these things."

"If it's so bad, Marika, why don't you leave?"

"If you had ever been to my village you would not ask such a thing, there is no work, the economy is broken."

She looked uncertain what to say next. Ed thought she was wondering how much she could trust him. Then she went on.

"Where would I go? I am not legal, I have not papers: anyway, my family need the money I send home, and at least here I do not have to be whore."

She looked Ed straight in the eyes as she said this last bit, as if challenging him to judge her. He didn't.

"I would like to help but I don't know what to do. Mr Carver doesn't like me, he's reported me to the police, he'd not listen to anything I said."

"But you are brave man: I watched as you danced and prayed with the spirits by the mound last year. Other priests would not have done that."

He was shocked that he had been seen and didn't know how to reply; he'd hoped the ritual he'd performed was dead and buried. She carried on.

"Carver is frightened, he think by destroying old building and replacing with new he is safe. But he does not understand, he has no belief. Each change wakes the bad thing more. Even the birds: great black crows, like vampires, would not stay by the Hall anymore. Have you not noticed how empty are the trees?"

Ed had noticed: not that he would ever forget the feeling of those birds as they swarmed over him by the mound, pecking and tearing. Even though later he came to understand that in some strange way they had been helping him, he was relieved that they'd left the area. Now it occurred to him that if what she said was true, the disappearance of the birds was something to fear. He was so lost in thought that he didn't reply. Marika carried on to the point she had come to make.

"It is your duty as priest to stop this thing: you have done it before, there is no one else who can."

She must have noticed that he was trying to object, and put up a hand warning him to stop.

"No, you will listen. You must stop Carver from knocking down the chapel and building his development by the mound. I know this you will do because you know what happen if you do not. You have read about murder of poor girl, do you want more added to your list of sins? Now I must go back, you will give me the cake?"

A minute later, Ed waved her off from the front door and watched as her slight figure, clutching the pathetic parcel of cake wrapped in cling film, merged into the dark. Something inside urged him to call out to her to come back: apprehension triggered by a dread of what consequences this meeting might provoke, and by how vulnerable she looked. But just as he opened his mouth to shout, his mobile rang and he fished in his trouser pocket to see who was calling. Then his automatic response overrode his intuition.

"Hello, Reverend Ed Joyce speaking."

"Ed, I know this must come as a surprise but I need to talk to you: it's Olga Hickman."

It was a surprise and an image of the woman tossing her head as she had lectured him filled his mind, to be replaced by the realisation that she had called him Ed, as if they were close.

"I'm a bit busy at the moment..."

She talked over him.

"Ed, this is really important; I know we got off to the wrong start but I need to meet you. Something is dreadfully wrong but I can't discuss it over the phone."

"Well, I..."

"I understand that you might not want us to be seen together, it doesn't need to be local, my business takes me all round the region."

He understood the point and the image of a clandestine meeting gave him a slight frisson of anticipation, but it would not do and he started to object.

A couple of minutes later he was replacing the mobile in his pocket, having agreed a time and place. He was trying to justify this to himself on the grounds that he had gone to the house to offer help, so he could hardly refuse it at the first request. Then the image of Olga was replaced in his mind by a vague recollection that it was the second time that day he had encountered the name Hickman. Then it hit him: Hickman was the name of the skryer Dee had used and mistrusted.

It was only then that he remembered Marika - but by then she was already approaching the back door of Skendleby Manor.

Chapter 8: Less Said Soonest

In the car, Anderson even made an attempt at conversation; what right had he to act friendly as if they were old acquaintances. At least they were in an unmarked car, rather than a squad car, but even so he got them to let him out a couple of blocks from the house. He could imagine all the hands twitching at the lace curtains if they'd dropped him off outside. Maybe he was becoming paranoid, but considering the course his life had taken over the last year perhaps paranoia was the logical response.

He felt confused, dirty and ashamed, but there was something else: he felt unreal, as if his grip on what had happened was too tenuous for him to cling to. No one had been to see him and for all he knew no one had tried to find him. Perhaps he was dead and this was indeed Hell.

But he found he'd retained enough humanity to check that he didn't smell too much before he reached the front door. It was like history repeating itself, and he remembered his first stressed out visit to Claire when he had been equally unsure of his reception. Now he loved her totally: she'd saved him, changed his miserable life. So why hadn't she tried to contact him while he was detained? He told himself that perhaps she had tried, but because of the circumstances of his arrest, the police had kept him screened off from anyone. They had treated him like shit, the remembrance of it made him want to cry.

He'd gone there to help, and they'd tricked him into telling them things he didn't understand. He'd been honest with them and they'd locked him up. They'd had no motive and no evidence, but even when they let him go they offered no apology, not even an attempt at an explanation.

All she had said, that bitch, the one who pretended to be understanding then tricked him and locked him up on his own for almost three days, was that following enquiries in Greece they were releasing him. Enquiries were still ongoing and he was not to leave the area. Even he had worked out that they had no forensic or even circumstantial evidence to link him to the victim. No apology: the last thing she had said before telling Anderson to take him home had been:

"However, you need to be very careful for two reasons, Dr Glover: first because you are still very much part of our enquiries; but most important is the fact that the only people who know the method of the killing are us, the murderer and you, assuming, for the moment, that the last two don't constitute a single category. So, if any of the details leak out we'll know who to come for won't we?"

Of all the things that had been said to him in there this was the most chilling. It chilled him so much that the protest he'd been about to make concerning their lack of evidence turned to ashes in his mouth.

He'd reached the house by now: up until this point he'd not been able to work out if it would be easier if Claire was out or in, but her car was parked up so the choice didn't need to be made. He was leaning against the door fumbling for his keys, but needn't have bothered as the door swung open and he almost fell inside. Claire must have seen him and been waiting. She said:

"You smell awful, get upstairs, I've a bath running."

He went: it avoided having to ask her the things he wanted to, for the moment at least. She did baths well: perfumed oils, scented candles, the whole works, and he needed them to wash away the smell of the police cell and the sweat of his fear. After a few moments the door opened and she entered carrying a steaming bone china mug.

"Here, drink this, don't worry, it won't put you out, quite the opposite if anything. When you come down we'll have a glass of wine and you can talk."

Then, almost without moving, she was gone. He lay back in the bath sipping the infusion, whatever it was, staring out through the partially steamed up window at the bare trees tossing their heads in the wind at the edge of

Lindow Moss. He began to sense the fear draining out of him, and by the time the water had flowed from hot to tepid he felt ok, even vaguely aroused.

When he got downstairs, enveloped in a bathrobe, she was sipping a glass of wine and listening to a jazz trio playing a surprising version of Purcell's Dido's Lament. She got up as he entered and he saw she had changed and was wearing the soft, clingy, long white wool dress she had worn on their first date. He suspected she hadn't anything underneath, which was confirmed when she stepped across to him and into his arms. She locked her mouth onto his and he realised how much he wanted this. He had pulled the hem of the dress up to her buttocks when something clicked in his mind, reminding him there were questions he needed to ask. He pulled his mouth free to speak but she said first:

"Giles, baby, don't let a little misunderstanding over a few silly bones get in the way of what really matters."

As she said this her hand had been inching its way down his chest towards his groin. As it reached its target, any idea of what he wanted to say evaporated.

Later, as he lay in bed listening to her soft breathing and watching the lashing rain being driven in waves across the orange streetlight outside, an unwelcome thought came to him. How did she know about the bones?

****

Viv understood she'd reached a crucial point in her relationship with the Chief Constable. He'd spent the minutes since she entered his office cursing over her handling of the arrest, without giving her chance to answer. She'd bitten her lip up to now, but it was getting to the point where it was too provocative to keep silent.

"We look like bloody idiots, like we've no bloody idea what we're doing. They make a big bloody noise about sending us some bright lass from London to show us how it's done. Might have been better if you'd spent a bit more time on the beat: did me no harm, waited to do my qualifications, turned fifty before I started a management course. MBA it were. Now I've got Carver on my back for releasing that bloody archaeologist and Jim-bloody-Gibson after me for letting you arrest him in the first place. Now you tell me..."

But she'd heard what she needed to cut in.

"Excuse me, Sir, but how could they have known that he was being held? We released no details."

"No, but news travels fast and we have to keep our constituents in the loop."

"That could have compromised the case."

"Don't you talk to me about compromising the bloody case, it weren't me who arrested him before even bothering to check with the Greeks. Didn't it occur to you at the time that he might have been helping them? Like it turns out he was."

She decided to let him talk himself out.

"And now, and now, the bloody Greeks are interested in our killer, seems they think it's connected to theirs, which makes me think they're not so sure they cracked their own case. So what do you think they want to do now? Well, I'll tell you, because it seems that your little chat with bloody Zorba went so well that they want to send someone over here."

Viv didn't think she'd got Theodrakis's first name over the phone, but she was fairly sure it wasn't Zorba. But he was still going.

"That'll look really good that will, first we get sent you and now they're sending a Greek to show us how to do things. A country where the banks have closed cos there are no bloody jobs, no bloody currency, no bloody government, and where the police all wear armour and carry guns, except now there's no bloody money to pay them, so there's no bloody law and order either. They'll be sending us John Terry next to teach us about fair play."

He paused, out of breath, and she wondered if this was the point when she could restore an element of perspective, but he started laughing.

"Or send Sarkosy to join our high jumpers, or Berlusconi to be the next Archbishop, or Louis Suarez to teach us self control."

He got out a handkerchief to wipe his eyes.

"Ok, I've got it off me chest and I heard what you said about talking to Carver and Williams, you were right on that. But I meant what I said about Zorba: he goes with your team. But it's a strange one that, he outranks you and it seems he's well connected politically, so why do they want him sent over here?"

He was serious now. She found it hard to get a fix on him. He was hard to categorise because underneath the 'good old boy Lancashire hillbilly shtick' there was an acute mind, which he obviously sometimes was at pains to conceal.

"Anyway, apart from the cock up over the arrest I suppose you're not doing too bad; Jimmy seems to rate you and, on the whole, he's a good judge of character. So now I've bollocked you we can get on as before."

He picked up the phone.

"Bring us two teas, please. Oh, and some of them assorted chocolate biscuits."

Then he turned back to Viv.

"So, now tell me honestly; what the hell's going on?"

The admonishing was over and normal service resumed. Although not wanting to be, Viv was impressed with the way the Chief Constable was able switch from one style of operating into a more relaxed one. The tea was brought in; she composed herself to make sense of what she was going to tell him, sat back in the chair and crossed her legs.

"The evidence takes us nowhere, I suppose that's why we questioned Glover, and there weren't any other leads. Compared to this, the London case was uncomplicated. There we had a torso in the river: neither prints nor head, but at least a dossier on similar and related cases, information to share, even cultural clues pointing to where communities could help us. Here there's nothing: no context, no motive, no background. It's as if this isn't real, like it's some type of horror film, nothing makes sense."

She paused for a moment then asked:

"Sir, I need to ask you why there was such a delay in linking these attacks, why so little information was shared and then, after all that, why I was drafted in? It looks like the approach to all this has been turned on its head."

The Chief Constable grimaced and ran his large hands across the stubble on his beefy head before answering.

"I'll tell you this only once, after that don't ask me again. We didn't connect the attacks at first because there was no motive, no similarity between the victims and no common MO. It just seemed like an unrelated series of events: the early ones weren't hurt badly, it was only after a couple of months that we got the first fatality. When we looked more carefully, it seemed there might be a pattern that linked the university with the estate at Skendleby. But we were warned off, well not quite warned off, but it was made fairly clear that there were some important planning developments scheduled for round there, and that since nothing we'd come up with to date led anywhere near an arrest, or even a lead, there was no point in causing a problem."

"So, what changed things so much that I was drafted in?"

"That's the strange part: seems that somehow the developers themselves got the shit scared out of them in some way. One of the political backers killed himself, leaving a suicide note that implied there'd be more killings. After that, having been told to lay off the case, we were told to speed things up. Only apparently, and I quote, 'the local wooden tops weren't up to the job', and that's where you come in."

He put his head back in his hands and said in a quieter voice:

"And perhaps they were right, we had no bloody idea. But then again, we'd had our hands tied behind our backs. Anyway, since then there's been another killing so, as the met superwoman, you need to come up with something pretty bloody quick."

"Ok, but you're going have to back me up over some strange decisions."

"Understood, it's that type of case."

"Well, the only thing that seems to tie all this together is that, just like you said, the attacks run from the university to Skendleby, and it all kicked off once the excavation there started."

"Hang on; you've already made us look stupid by bringing that archaeologist in for questioning then holding him."

Viv sighed, exasperated.

"Yes, I know, that was a mistake: but there's still a connection. He led the excavation and was then disciplined for some weird attempt to close it back up. He then goes to Greece where there's an outbreak of similar attacks, and he knows stuff about the bones and rituals in the killings. Stuff that we don't know. We should try a different approach on him."

Now it was the Chief Constable's turn to sigh.

"You've not much chance there, you'll be lucky if he doesn't make an official complaint."

"I hope he's still too scared to try that. I sent Jimmy to take him home, try and appease him a bit, you know, good cop, bad cop. He should be back by now, I'll get him in and see how he got on."

"You'll have to wait for that, I've sent Jimmy to the airport to pick up Zorba."

"Well, in that case, fill me in on the developments planned for the Skendleby estate by the influential Mr Carver, because I want to interview him soon."

"I'd stay clear of him, at least for now, you've stirred up enough trouble as it is. He doesn't welcome any attention and his money's a significant part of economic regeneration round here, so we try to forget about the dirty way he made it."

She could feel the petulant scowl rearranging her facial expression as she folded her arms tightly across her breasts and said:

"I can't accept that, Sir. Skendleby is central to us stopping these killings and if you don't let me investigate the leads I need to then you're stopping me doing my job, and if that's the case I don't see how I can continue here."

"They said you could turn awkward, said that all the smiley charm was just a front and that underneath it all you were a real ball brea…"

He paused and quickly corrected himself.

"I mean an iron fist in a steel glove."

She said nothing, just stared at him, aware of his discomfort. Let him stumble on while she tried to work out how to move things on. He continued to stumble but without any sign of concession.

"Look, leave Carver alone, at least until you've got something concrete. There's no connection to Skendleby in this last killing."

"Except that it took place less than two miles away."

She knew she ought to back off a bit, but also knew her own fixed mind. Her dad said she was like a dog with a bone, would never give way when she knew she was right. Instead she dropped into the intervening awkward silence:

"I'm sorry, Sir, I can't carry out this case with one hand tied behind my back."

Then she added, against her better judgement,

"Even if it is inside a steel glove, or a velvet glove as the saying actually goes."

"I meant exactly what I said and I mean this too, so listen carefully. Stay away from Carver."

Deadlock. How long they would have remained staring at each other in stony silence and who would have given way first they never found out. There was a knock on the door and a uniformed sergeant who Viv didn't recognise came in.

"Sir, ma'am, I thought you'd want to hear this right away; there's been another killing. This time on the Skendleby estate, right by the Hall.

Chapter 9: Dazzle to Drizzle

The dazzle of sunlight reflecting from the shiny white paper blinded him, making it too painful to read. He fished, with eyelids half closed, for the shades trapped in the lining of his jacket pocket. Eventually he worked them free and fixed them over his blinking eyes: Lion Square settled into a tenebrous and more comfortable prospect. Life was returning to normal, or as normal as it was possible to get these days as many ordinary people, guilty of committing atrocities in the aftermath of the murders, tried to forget their actions. To Theodrakis, it had been like the violent orgies of The Bacchae out of the pages of Euripides: the return of ancient horrors.

Greece was holding its breath but the economic crisis was still biting and the few cafes still open were crowded with people huddled under sun shades, stretching out hours over a single coffee and glass of water. It was late in the year yet still the heat was intense; water was limited and fire warnings were in place. This was when the island was meant to get its rain and the newspapers were postulating that ecological catastrophe had arrived and summer would never end.

After a moment, he restored his gaze to the short document and introductory letter. The latter was from a friend of his father's at the ministry in Athens, and in an attempt to soften the blow it addressed him by his first name, Alexis. The document was more formal, in that he was Astinome Syntagmatarchis Theodrakis and he was directed to assist the Greater Manchester Police in their attempts to bring to justice a serial killer.

It stank of an excuse to get him out of Samos, out of Greece: but why would they want that? He had wrapped up the case pretty neatly, and as Greece was tumbling out of the euro zone and into anarchy he guessed that the Grafficocratia in the capital had more important matters to deal with as the lull in the rioting was probably only temporary.

This took him onto another more frightening train of thought, one that six months ago he would never have considered and would have regarded as the product of a broken mind. But his experiences on Samos had changed him irreversibly, so he let his mind wander onto the message of Vassilis.

And not only Vassilis: he forced his memory back, back to the terrifying moment in the bar in the village. The moment when instead of sitting across the table from Captain Michales, he found himself looking directly at the messy, degraded corpse of Samarakis, staring in horror, unable to move as the partly decomposed jaw started to move and the vocal chords began functioning one last time. The apparition told him he was not finished with the horrors on Samos, but that he was doomed to follow them somewhere colder, somewhere from which he may never return. Then it was gone, morphed back into Michales.

Maybe as a one-off he could have dismissed this as a delayed reaction to the shock his system had been dealt by his experiences over the preceding couple of months. But it wasn't a one off: Vassilis had told him something similar and hinted that there were forces beyond his understanding which controlled his destiny and his movements, and that the free will he thought humans possessed was merely an illusion. Even Yaya Eleni warned him that the events on the island would sweep him up and carry him off in pursuit of events, and now, out of the blue, his superiors were ordering him to England.

The thought of Hippolyta's grandmother tore at his heart; leaving Samos meant leaving Hippolyta. Leaving his one love affair and the only successful physical relationship of his life. How could he tell her? How could he leave?

He signalled to the waiter that he wanted to pay and braced himself for the usual argument. Since the end of the killings he'd been credited with almost supernatural powers, and everywhere he went people tried not to charge him. This was very different from when he first arrived: then they'd seen him as an evil influence from Athens, perhaps even in league with the killers. He supposed he'd have to go through pretty much the same process in England. He'd already spoken to the English officer in charge of the case on the phone, she had no idea of the horror she was up against and he envied her this temporary innocence. What advice could he give other than run away? Despite his reputation he knew he'd been little more than an ineffectual bystander to what had happened on Samos. Forces beyond his understanding had ended the spate of unnatural ritual killings, for reasons he couldn't even guess at. He didn't even know if the good guys, if there were any, had won.

Waiting for the bill, he read the orders again.

"Following the approach of the Greater Manchester Police in England through the correct diplomatic channels, we are transferring you for a temporary posting. You are to assist the chief investigating officer there on enquiries into a series of attacks that have similarities with those you so successfully investigated on Samos. This has been sanctioned at the very highest level in the ministry in Athens. Further instructions and travel arrangements are being sent separately."

That was all, a short paragraph that dissolved his happiness and threatened his very existence. The irony was that at first he'd hated Samos, regarding it as a medieval backwater. Now he loved it, and had been angling for his posting to be made permanent. He felt that they owed him enough to make that happen. He had nothing against England, he'd done a year at Cambridge and quite enjoyed it, but that had been through choice.

He gave up waiting for a bill that obviously would never arrive, left some coins on the table and moved off. Before he spoke to Hippolyta about the posting he'd see if he could find Vassilis, see if he would help. Like everyone else on the island he had stayed away from the Vassilis estate since the lynch mob had torched it after the killing of Antonis and the disappearance, presumed dead, of Alekka.

He didn't know what he'd find up there but had an idea that some trace of Vassilis may still be around. The mob hadn't been able to find him and in any case, Theodrakis was pretty certain that whatever Vassilis was, he was way beyond the power of mob vengeance.

He was about to call for a police driver when he thought better of it: no point in stirring things up again. He hated driving but reckoned this time he needed to. He was concentrating on controlling the car so much that he was half way up the isolated track leading to the Vassilis estate before he noticed that everything had changed.

Long before the estate boundary, the track just petered out. He knew it was the right track so despite all the evidence he continued driving in the hope the track would resume. Then the car ploughed into a grove of olives and refused to move on. He was sweating now, beginning to doubt his hold on reality. He got out.

Above him he could see the great slab of out cropping rock from which the Vassilis mansion projected. Even that looked different, but it showed him he was in the right place and, slightly reassured, he began to walk towards it. The reassurance drained away with each step. By the time he reached the point where the fences guarding the compound should have been his mouth was dry with fear and his heart was racing. He fumbled to light a cigarette to steady himself as he tried to understand what he was seeing.

Nothing: seeing nothing; there was nothing and it was obvious from the mature trees and rockslide that there never had been. At least not in this world. No house, no gardens, no chapel, no cricket pitch or helipads: nothing. It wasn't that it had been destroyed. It had never existed. He sat down on a fallen tree trunk. A lizard basking in the sun scuttled off: the climate had obviously disturbed its routine too. He thought of the Lost Domain in Fournier's book: it was the closest he could get to an explanation. Like in the book he and hundreds of others had experienced and existed in something that wasn't real. Without meaning to he started to laugh, a hysterical reaction he couldn't stop until he choked on smoke and gave over to coughing.

Some questions filled his head: where had he really been when he thought he'd been talking to Vassilis in the house? Where had all the people at the dinners and cricket matches held here been? What had the mob that believed it had burnt the place down really done? He had no answers. He began to think back over Vassilis and the conversations they'd had.

Now here, slumped on a real tree in a garden that had never been, he began to reinterpret those conversations. It was clear that what he had taken as metaphor and allusion in Vassilis's conversation had been literal, if a metaphysical proposition can be regarded as such. The talk of entropy and simultaneous parallel multiverse had been meant. He remembered something else Vassilis had said, which he had taken as hyperbole at the time.

"Humans are very easy to reprogram."

It was as if some type of glamour had been cast over them, a type of projection. This took him nowhere and he felt the hysterical laughter building up again. Sometime later, he was not sure how long, a thought, or rather suggestion, came clearly to him.

"Go to the beach taverna in Limnionas."

Clear, but not his thought. In spite of that he had no better idea and badly wanted to get out of this place. Not that the place scared him, there was nothing here to do that: it was empty. Rather it was the thought of what was missing. He was also very sad and could feel tears on his cheeks. He stood up and looked down the slope towards the sea and was shocked to see the ancient site where the bones had been taken. So that, at least, had been real. He didn't want to be here so turned round and stumbled back to the car as quickly as he could.

He must have been in a dream driving to Limnionas because he arrived without knowing how he got there. Near the shoreline, a fisherman sat by his beached boat mending nets. There was no one else around, it was dusk and in the west the sun was turning the sea into a pool of crimson as it sunk. Despite the hot weather, the tourist season was over and the place was dead, suffused with a late autumnal melancholy.

He trudged down the beach towards the taverna but could see no light. When he walked onto the terrace it was empty, the tables and chairs had been moved inside for the winter. The terrace was covered in a patina of windblown sand; all it lacked was tumbleweed blowing across it to present the complete picture of desolation. What had made him come here? He got out his cell phone to ring Hippolyta then decided what he had to tell her was better said face to face. He turned and noticed that there was a scrap of paper weighted down by a lump of rock on the terrace wall. There was a simple, scrawled note written on it and an arrow pointing to the far end of the beach.

"Come to boat house."

He looked in the direction the arrow pointed. At the end of the bay an olive clad promontory stuck out into the sea, with part way along it a small jetty. Somewhere above it, in the grove, he thought he could make out a faint flickering light. In the minutes it took him to cross the bay the light faded further as a sea fret drifted in across the beach.

The jetty was rotted through and collapsing into the water. Above it were the remnants of a boat house long since abandoned to its slow decay. There was no one there and he decided to go. Then, on a sudden impulse, he decided to try and find the source of the light and began to walk up the slope through the olives whose branches seemed to whisper as he brushed against them.

He caught glimpses of the light, like a Will-o'-the-Wisp through the trees as he walked; it seemed to be leading him further into the wood. Then he was in a glade staring at the shell of a long disused wooden summer house, through one of the glassless window frames he saw the light, then it vanished. The place was very silent, very still: numinous. He knew something was about to happen and stood waiting, the hairs on the back of his neck prickling.

He saw her, thought he saw her for a moment, not the full person of course: that wouldn't be possible, just a phantom, an outline of what had contained her. He knew who it was, what it had been.

"Alekka, what's happening? Where are you?"

"Where? Now I'm nowhere, although a trace of what was may still register here. Perhaps rebuilding for next time. Here again if needed, or some other world."

"Why?"

"Why here? Before the end I was happy here for one brief instant."

Then she faded, everything became indistinct. He was trying to think of the question he should ask when he heard her again, this time inside his head.

"Where you are going you may never leave, but there is help if you look for it."

Silence. He thought it was finished and she'd faded back into the ether, but then, almost as an afterthought:

"And Steve, later when the time comes, you will need Steve."

Then he was alone. Alone and it was fully dark.

****

Something strange happened just after takeoff. The aircraft climbed into the clear blue sky over Mycale then out to sea as it gained height before circling to fly back over the island. Then suddenly, as it passed above the rugged spine of Mt Kerkis, it entered thick cloud. Theodrakis craned his head back for one last look, maybe his last glimpse of Samos, but it was like a pair of curtains had been closed, shutting the island out.

He was displaced and bereft, remembering his last night with Hippolyta. They'd clung together in bed, miserable and unable to sleep, dropping off just before dawn to be woken almost immediately by the alarm call. She had pleaded to go with him, cried, said she might never see him again. But how could he take her into what he was about to face?

Even the logistics of the journey were a nightmare. Athens Airport was closed down by political action and tourist flights were no longer running. The only option had been a local flight to Thessaloniki followed by a plane to Vienna, a four-hour wait, and then a flight to Manchester. His worries that the hanging about and airport food would lead to a blocking up of his digestive system were quickly confirmed, and it was a costive and unhappy man who disembarked at Terminal One.

He trudged along the seemingly endless glandular corridors towards immigration reading the proud claims on the walls that Manchester had won the Airport of the Year award and thinking how bad the others must be. After a prolonged queue at customs control, where half the desks were unmanned, he emerged blinking into the arrivals hall.

He looked around at the people waiting to meet and greet until he saw a tall, fair-haired man in a cheap suit holding a sign which he recognised at the fourth attempt as misspelt and ungrammatical Greek. Well, at least they'd made an effort. The man introduced himself as DS Anderson, took one of his cases and they left the building.

Outside it was cold with a drizzle of sleet and freezing rain that began to splatter his pastel linen suit. He shivered. Just before they reached the car, Anderson's mobile rang. He excused himself and turned to answer. About fifteen seconds into the call his manner changed and Theodrakis saw the little colour in his naturally pale face drain away.

"Sorry, Sir, but there has been a change of plan: there has been another attack, close to here and the boss wants us both on site."

Theodrakis felt his blood run cold. It had started already and he had been sucked in. Maybe he would never get out of here. He was so overwhelmed by this that he never heard Anderson's unnecessary next sentence.

"So, the hotel will have to wait."

Chapter 10: In the Pit

The drive to the murder site reawakened in Theodrakis memories of what a strangely inhospitable country England was. Particularly here. Cambridge had been strange but urbane, here it was too cold, too green, too wet. It didn't help that on landing he was immediately rushed off to a murder scene. He didn't like the look or feel of Skendleby Hall from the moment the car turned down the long drive, but there wasn't much time to dwell on it.

The car pulled up next to a collection of police vans and cars. Anderson opened the door and he got out into the cold spitting rain. Behind the Hall a gaggle of cops, some in uniform, some in plastic sterile suits and some in plain clothes, milled around a damp, sombre pit. He knew what would be lying in it, could anticipate what had been done to it. This wasn't new to him: it was what had brought him here.

And yes, there it was, fragile and broken, sprawled in the puddles of cold wet clay at the bottom. He felt a bitter taste in his mouth as bile rose in his throat. A girl, dark haired, maybe pretty once. This made it worse. He thought of Hippolyta and was glad she wasn't here. He could see from the distortion of the arms and legs that there had been cutting, harvesting of small bones. So they'd been right; it was happening, it had moved here. He noticed the police had shifted aside to let him look; they knew who he was. What would they expect?

Anderson was speaking, speaking to him. He tore his eyes away from the pathetic bundle lying on the cold damp ground and saw that a woman was looking at him expectantly. Striking looking and perhaps beautiful in a powerful, angular way. Taller than him, probably heavier too. Anderson had been introducing her but he hadn't been listening. She held out her hand and said:

"Syntagmatarchis Theodrakis, I'm Vivian Campbell, investigating officer."

He took her hand. She looked tired, unwell. He felt a rush of empathy. He'd been where she was: alone, bemused, afraid. He'd only just got away from it and now he was back.

"Pleased to meet you, Inspector, permit me to compliment you on your Greek pronunciation."

"Thanks, glad I was able to get my tongue round your rank, but it's all I know and I got that bit from Google Translate."

He smiled, her handshake was firm, her palms soft, but there was a trace of sickly odour on her breath that she'd tried to disguise by sucking mints. Before she could speak again he gestured towards the body and said:

"Would I be correct to guess that there was no sexual assault but that bones were removed using a crude blade?"

It sounded so dispassionate, almost indifferent in English, made him sound uncaring; in Greek it would have sounded more emotional, came across better. But she seemed almost relieved.

"Yes, just like that. You've seen it before?"

"Sadly, and it doesn't get easier."

"Do you want to go down and take a closer look? We can get you a sterile suit, save your clothes."

"Go down? No, I don't think so. I know what I'd find."

He looked around, then said:

"But you could tell me about that building over at the pit's edge. Is it as old as it appears?"

Viv looked surprised at this. Theodrakis supposed she'd soon learn, probably the hard way, how unnatural this was - just like he had.

"Old? Yes, I think so, it's the chapel of the Davenport family, the oldest thing on site."

He nodded, flicked at the raindrops spattering his suit, then said:

"I suspect there are much older things, timeless things, whose significance we can't even guess the purpose of, deep under it."

Viv didn't reply and Theodrakis could tell that she could make no sense of what he was saying. Also, she was sweating, despite the cold, and he sensed she was unwell: distressed and unwell. He asked:

"I think it would be a good idea to have a look at this chapel and perhaps even underneath it."

"Ok, but why? These attacks are scattered round this area, they're random and we've not attached particular importance to any location. The bodies have just been dumped."

"There's nothing random, it's just that your thinking isn't aligned with the intelligence behind this."

He could tell from her face that he'd gone too fast, she was rattled; he should have waited until he was less travel weary and dislocated. But standing there, seeing the same horrors in a fresh context jarred his judgement. He'd started so he'd finish.

"We should look at the building, the ground. Ancient ground has significant attributes, it can't be ignored. The archaeologist who we spoke about, the one I met on Samos, it might be a good idea to ask him to help investigate…"

He was interrupted by one of the forensic team working below in the pit.

"We've done all we can here for now, Ma'am."

"Ok, send me the preliminary report as soon as you have it."

Theodrakis could tell Viv wanted to be away from here. She turned back to him.

"You'll have to excuse me, Colonel Theodrakis, I have to go somewhere else. DS Anderson will look after you and we'll get together properly tomorrow."

She looked around.

"Where's Jimmy?"

A uniformed WPO replied:

"He's over in the house, helping with the interviews."

"Well fetch him and ask him to take care of Colonel Theodrakis."

She turned and walked off towards a small Nissan, and, after fumbling for her keys, drove off, leaving Theodrakis to his own devices in the cold, ignored by the other officers. He was watching her car's rapid progress down the drive when he overheard one of the male officers behind him.

"Looks like Black Beauty didn't fancy hanging about too much, eh?"

He was just trying to work out what the heavily accented English slang meant when there was an explosion of shouting as he saw DS Anderson confront the man.

"You better keep your mouth shut, Johnston, because if I hear anything like that out of you again you'll not have a job. Racism, sexism and criticising a senior officer in one statement should be enough to satisfy any disciplinary panel."

"Sorry, Sarge, didn't mean nothing, just a joke like."

"Pity to end a career because of a stupid joke, not that your career's likely to amount to much."

Theodrakis could see that the young officer had gone pale and that Anderson's own pale face was red with anger. He realised now the meaning of the man's joke and understood the admonishment, but there was something else in Anderson's reaction, something that went beyond just the professional. Anderson must have realised that Theodrakis was watching intently because he turned to him and said:

"Sorry about that, Sir, we take casual racism, however it's meant, seriously these days, even from a stupid young lad like him."

But Theodrakis carried the impression that they were both aware that the cause of Anderson's anger was down to something else, even if he didn't know what. To move things on he said,

"DS Anderson, on Samos I met an archaeologist who works near here. I'd like to get him to take a look at that chapel."

Anderson's reply told Theodrakis that he was prevaricating.

"Well, the boss would have to authorise that, Sir."

"Even so, it couldn't do any harm contacting him. I know you've already spoken to him; it's why Inspector Campbell telephoned me in Greece."

Whatever Anderson's reply might have been he never found out. There was a shout from the pit.

"Sir, come quick, see this."

He ran to the edge of the pit and looked down: the earth had opened up. Two officers were struggling to haul one of the forensics team out of a hole that had opened up below him. As his head appeared above the surface he shouted to Anderson:

"Sarge, you need to see what's down here, it's a mass grave."

****

She couldn't quite place when it started, but the feeling that someone was watching her was fully realised by the time she parked her car in the cramped bay across the road from the flats. She was uncomfortable and edgy and tried to put it down to it being the wrong time of the month. But it was more than that. She felt threatened, unsafe. She pressed the button to lock the car and the noise of the click as the locks engaged seemed unnaturally loud. Pulling up the collar of her raincoat against the chill she crossed the road and, to take her mind off uncertainty, looked closely at the sprawling block of new flats she was headed for.

They occupied the entire length of the elongated new road that followed the course of the old rail line, now being converted into the Metro South route. Four stories high, faced in faux Victorian brick with a scattering of faux Edwardian decorative stone effect features. The flats subverted the balance of the old village.

Over thirty years, Didsbury had shifted from respectability, to boho chic, to centre for stag and hen parties. Now, as the brochure promised to its target of young professionals, these apartments were:

"A statement that affords you the ambience and comfort you need to be you in a successful modern world."

To Viv, the flats seemed like a cross between a hotel and a banlieu or favela for yuppies.

The sky had grown dark and she hurried into the lobby where the agent, Tim, was waiting. He greeted her with a casual smile and a "hi", seeming to suggest that this was where they both belonged. She turned her phone off and looked round at the lobby: it had a defined sense of dislocation, a transitory feel emphasised by the eye straining artificial lighting and the showroom furniture that no one ever sat on.

It couldn't have been more mundane, yet for a moment she thought she saw a figure in a long black coat looking at them from a corner. But she hadn't time to look because Tim was already well into his prematurely intimate and slick spiel, and by the time they moved towards the lift the figure had gone.

In the apartment, one of hundreds identical in the block, Tim was able to demonstrate how this development, catering to the successful, fast-moving modern professional, came with all the individuality that "you" deserved. The building noise from the Metro work site could have been a disadvantage but, according to Tim, this was the last piece of the jigsaw making it the perfect location for a fast-moving world, and if Viv was quick there was a window of opportunity for a fantastic deal. It was immediately available and seemed to make economic sense, so Viv duly went through the window.

Walking back to the car slightly dazed at her decision, she thought she caught a glimpse of Jimmy's pale face staring out from the window of a bistro. But it couldn't have been because he was meant to be looking after the weird Greek.

She thought about going back to the station but felt too awful. She'd been on the go for the best part of three days with only sporadic episodes of broken sleep. So she went home: let the chief take the heat like he was paid to do. The flat emptiness of the city centre rented apartment made her glad she was buying in Didsbury.

She tried to put the feeling of being watched out of her mind, rationalising that she imagined she'd seen Jimmy because it was when he'd first driven her past the Skendleby estate that she'd thought she'd seen that ragged figure flitting between the trees. She knew from her academic research that feelings of paranoia like this were often a symptom of having to deal with the type of things she had to deal with. But she couldn't shift the unease.

She felt terrible and bloated. She thought she smelt and considered a bath, but instead took some tablets and tea to the bedroom, put on her pyjamas and wrapped herself in the duvet. After reading it twice but still unable to focus on a piece in The Guardian about the Hubble Space Telescope, she curled up into a ball of aching sweating misery and tried to sleep.

But sleep wouldn't come and she found the illustration from the article of the furthest recordable frontiers of the universe stamped across the inside of her eyelids. So huge and real that what happened on this tiny planet, whose own galaxy was only a pinprick in the picture, was of no account, no more than the slightest tremor of an eyelash. The thought of insignificance conjured a worse image of the meagre broken body of the girl sprawled in the pit where it had been dumped.

There was something way beyond the ordinary in these killings, some dimension hovering just beyond her peripheral vision, something essential to understanding the case that she couldn't quite capture. The nearest she could get to it was that somehow time and reason had slipped out of kilter, but that wasn't much help. There was no motivation in these killings, at least not one a modern mind could comprehend. But in each case, a close link with the past and its legacy. Theodrakis had got this at once, but his only contribution had been to suggest they get the archaeologists to investigate the Davenport Chapel. No wonder it had taken him so long to crack the Samos case.

There was something more wrong about these killings than any she'd ever known, and this was beginning to frighten her. It was a horribly predictable modus operandi; a purposeful, almost clinical cutting and mutilation of each victim using a stone blade. Never any trace of sexual assault. That poor girl, alone in a strange country: she'd been left, used up and discarded like an old rag doll while the multiverse wheeled and expanded into the void, immense and uncaring. Viv began to sniffle and cried herself to sleep.

Chapter 11: Unwanted Connections

Gradually, through the fog of sleep, she became aware of shouting and banging at the apartment door. Bleary eyed, still half asleep, she stumbled over to open it, realising when she did so that she'd made a mistake. She found herself face to face with Anderson. One look told her that he was more embarrassed than her, if that were possible. She wouldn't have wanted to come face to face with her subordinate in night attire at the best of times, and certainly not unwashed and wearing men's pyjamas. Fortunately, there was no time for a further chapter in the comedy of manners.

"Ma'am, you've had your phone off so the Chief sent me to get you," he said by means of apology, and before she'd unscrambled her brain quickly enough to reply he'd added, "You're wanted at Skendleby Hall, there has been an incident."

Before she mumbled that he could wait in the kitchen while she dressed he said, with unexpected tact:

"I'll wait in the car if you don't mind, I've got some reports to tidy up."

Ten minutes later she joined him in the car and was surprised but pleased to be handed a black coffee in a Costa carton. She took a sip of the steaming liquid, and as the car pulled away, Anderson said:

"Bit unexpected this, isn't it? We're warned to stay away from Carver and now he wants us over there."

"Any idea why?"

"He's had some type of scare apparently."

"Suppose that's a bit of a break for us. Thanks for the coffee by the way, I needed it. Where's Zorba?"

"Asleep in his hotel bed I hope."

After that Anderson drove in silence and Viv drank the coffee, both were uncomfortable: some unquantifiable intimacy had impinged their routine. The gates of the hall were open and as they wound their way along the drive they could see that Carver already had company: a couple of four wheel drive vehicles were parked up next to three squad cars. A harassed WPO greeted them at the door.

"I'd better warn you, Ma'am, he's not in a good mood."

She was right, he wasn't, and he made this clear almost before they were through the door and into the lobby.

"Took you're time, look I've had to bring in me own security."

He pointed to two heavy, meat-headed men wearing bulging jeans and hoodies. They were standing either side of the entrance to the old Davenport drawing room, now a games room.

"And there are more outside. Now I have to pay for safety with me own money as well as pay the taxes what pay for you."

Viv had dealt with his type before. She knew there was no point contradicting any of this, that it was best just to let him talk himself out. They walked into the games room where Carver threw himself onto a huge white sofa that looked to be covered in some type of antelope hide. She gazed around at the pool table and various game consoles scattered around and noted the absence of any staff. She wondered if they'd all made a run for it, scared they'd meet the same fate as Marika. Perhaps Carver picked up on this because he broke off from his tirade to remark:

"And the maids have done a flit, so I'll have to get in a couple of girls from the club. Cost more they will, English girls more greedy, innit."

When given a chance to speak, Viv asked:

"So what is it that actually happened last night, Mr Carver?"

When it came to specifics he was hesitant and Viv got the impression that beneath the aggression he was frightened.

"That hole you made in the pit: it came out of that, must of come out of that."

"Sorry, you've lost me."

"It was by the house, right by the house. But there's no footage on the CCTV. The cameras cover all the grounds; I had them put in last Christmas when we had the problems. You can't get anywhere near without them cameras picking you up. So it come up out of the hole, must have."

He came to a stop and Viv thought for a moment that he might be on the brink of tears, but he managed to pull himself together and return to his default setting: aggression.

"I was told I'd have protection, told there weren't nothin to worry about, that you lot had it covered. Well you bloody haven't, have you? Well have you? I told you where the trouble was coming from, who the troublemakers were, but you did nothing. Now there's a tunnel they come out of leading from the church, obvious, yeah - but you missed it."

Before Viv could get her head round this thesis and reply, Anderson said:

"I know you're shaken up, Mr Carver, but you can't seriously think that the Reverend Joyce or Sir Nigel came crawling along a tunnel to attack you. Would you be frightened by either of them anyway?"

The words had the intended effect, Carver blinked.

"Well, who is it then? Who killed the girl and who was here last night? What are you going to do about it?"

This was easier to deal with. Carver reminded Viv of a sulky, spoilt child. She said:

"I can assure you, Mr Carver, that we'll take every step to ensure your safety. Until we effect some resolution we'll provide twenty-four hour protection."

"What about the pit, the tunnel? I want that looked at then blocked off."

"Consider it done. Now we need a full statement."

Later, walking back to the car, Viv said to Anderson.

"Well, that's moved things on, we've access to Carver and we can look at what's under that pit: you'd better have the archaeologists standing by for that and arrange for

Joyce and Davenport to be questioned, best do this by the book."

Anderson started to say something about mending bridges with the archaeologists when they saw a figure running towards them.

Dressed in a lime green, skin tight designer tracksuit, blonde plait bobbing out of the back of a baseball cap, heavily made up and jogging like a show pony, the figure slowed as it approached. Viv noticed that the woman was wearing black woollen gloves with some flashy rings over them. She stopped by them and removed her headphone earpieces.

"Don't know why I bother with all this, Si never takes no notice, is all for show with him. He's never up for it, doesn't really like women, hasn't even tried it on with the foreign sluts who work here. He'd notice if I didn't bother though. I could of done better, used to be engaged to a footbawla. Still, not done too bad here, have I?"

When the stream of consciousness slowed Anderson said:

"This is Mrs Carver, Ma'am."

"Call me Suzzie-Jade, it's more social, not that there's much socialising in this dead shithole."

Viv assumed she was referring to the area not the Hall, but it might have been both. She asked:

"Would you mind telling us if you saw the intruder last night?"

"Didn't see nothing, went to bed early, bored out me head, took a couple of pills and went straight asleep. Freaked Si out though, never seen him this scared, not like the man I married really. Ok, see yu laitaa."

Viv started to assure her that they now had full police protection but she didn't seem that interested and jogged off towards the Hall.

****

Inside the hall, in the state- of-the-art gym, Si had taken a drink into his top of the range Californian hot tub and was on the phone to Jed Gifford.

"Listen, Gifford, I don't care what plans you've got, you get your arse over here right now and bring your shovel monkey with you. I'll give you twenty minutes, no longer."

He tossed the phone back into its niche in the tubs' music centre and lay back against the jets as the old skool gangsta rap flowed through the speakers. Gradually, his heart rate slowed and he began to feel better. At least now he had a course of action. He hated waiting, always had. Waiting for his step mum to get home in the early hours of the morning while his baby half sister screamed the house down. Waiting for his dad to get out of prison - not that he saw much of him when he was out.

But he'd seen enough of him to learn that there were only two types of people: winners and losers, mainly losers, and that if you wanted to stay a winner you didn't take no prisoners. So he played hard, broke the rules; well, with his start in life he'd had to. He'd been a tough kid and it helped that he quite liked to hurt people, not that he did any of that himself these days. He was respectable now and delegated. It hadn't been easy and he'd had to get out of London pretty quick, but he'd made it. He was established, owned a stately home, knew the people who counted, had a trophy wife.

The thought of this most recent acquisition soured his mood a bit: maybe she hadn't been such a good bargain. He'd have to rethink that one before long. She cramped his style, but even in a city like Manchester that prided itself on its pluralist approach to sexuality, you still had to put up some sort of front, particularly when you had to mix and do business with some of the people he had to.

Gifford, trailed by the shovel monkey, real loser that one, was shown in by one of the meatheads. Si liked to receive people when he was in the tub like this. Got the idea from a Roman king or something like that he'd seen in a film. It made them uncomfortable having to stand there while he lay back with a drink. Gave them a good look at his shoulders, chest and arms, let them see how pumped he was. He been put through a lot these last few days and now someone was going to pay for it.

"What took you so fucking long, Gifford? I told you twenty minutes."

Always a good start that line, even when they weren't late. He could see Gifford hated it and wanted to react. He loathed being shown up, liked to play the bully himself. He responded peevishly.

"Weren't my fault, couldn't find Dave."

Si chuckled to himself, it worked every time; he'd admitted to being late when he wasn't. He snapped back:

"Wasn't the shovel monkey I told, it was you. What I say you do, geddit? Good, now I'm giving you one chance to put right the damage you did when you found them bones."

Si enjoyed letting them squirm for a moment, then dropped it on them.

"I bin thinking. All this trouble comes from one thing. One thing that's holding up the development and causing all these problems here. So, if we get rid of it then the problems go with it."

He paused for a moment, suddenly realising how right this was and wondering what had led him to think something so far outside his normal philosophy. It wasn't the illegality that bothered him about what he was going to order the men to do. It was the fact that he was in some way buying into an equivalent of the poncy crap they spouted in the church. This was some type of change and he wasn't in control, didn't know where it was leading. For a moment he no longer felt like the Roman king or whatever, he felt hesitant. Then he remembered how all of this was getting to him, didn't want them to see him indecisive. Anyway, wherever the idea had come from it was a good one, and besides, he'd gone too far to turn back.

He needn't have worried about the effect of the pause on Jed and Dave. They understood what a right bastard he was and knew he was dragging things out cos it made it worse for them.

"So now, you're going to take your JCB and demolish that mound the archaeologists messed around. Understand? You're going to flatten it and anything that's in it. I don't want nothing left. No sign of where it was, like it never existed."

Jed couldn't help himself.

"No way. No one in their right mind's gonna touch that bugger. It's cursed, protected like, can't be done."

Si said nothing, just waited for Jed to continue.

"Anyway, it's against the law, innit, criminal offence."

Si couldn't prevent himself laughing at this.

Jed snapped:

"No, won't do it, can't. Get someone else."

Then the bit Si always enjoyed the best. He said very slowly, like he was speaking to a child.

"You'll do exactly what I fucking tell you. Know why? Otherwise I'll withdraw my protection, Jed. Then that loan shark you're so deep into will be able resume making his little visits. Know what I mean? Then there are those things the police were so interested in. Then there's........."

Jed had no choice and raised a hand in a gesture of surrender.

"Ok, we'll do it, long as no one stops us."

Si was disappointed not to be able to table his entire manifesto of threat, but he'd got his way, like he always did when people had no choice.

"Now, who could stop you when I own the land?"

They sloped out of the room, with Si's final blessing following them:

"And make sure you don't fuck it up."

He turned the spa pumps back on and sunk back to enjoy his power. But he couldn't, unease began to build and he could feel his gym built muscles tensing as his heart rate increased.

****

To Dave, the noise of the JCB seemed enough to alert every copper for miles. He was sweating and wanted to run for home, but he was as scared of Jed as Jed was of Carver. So he tried to pretend it wasn't happening, that it was just a bad dream and soon he'd wake up. But by the time the spluttering JCB chugged through the gate into the deserted archaeological site this was no longer possible. The wind had got up to gale force and a mass of grey clouds were chasing each other into increasingly ominous shapes. He looked up and said to himself, as much as to Jed:

"Jesus, look at that, they weren't here before. Where have all them fucking crows come from?"

Chapter 12: Strange Bedfellows

Sitting in the car, engine turned off, wiping at the misted-up windows ineffectually with the back of his hand, Ed wondered again what he was doing here. The 'here' being illegally parked in front of Wrexham station. It had started to rain and the emerging passengers were swaddled in hats, scarves and hoods, or crouched under umbrellas. What if he missed her?

But then, unmistakable, she emerged and came striding across the road towards the car. More statuesque than he remembered, she was wearing a white jacket, stretched taut across the bust, and her strong legs were sheathed in a tight, calf length purple skirt. Not conventionally attractive, she was more like striking, and he was toying with Junoesque as the appropriate epithet when she opened the passenger door and struggled into the passenger seat, having to hitch up the tight skirt to manage. The windows misted up again.

Ed could feel himself blushing and was pleasantly relieved when she said:

"This'd give everyone who knows us something to gossip about, talk about dangerous liaisons."

He recognised the reference to the film, otherwise he'd have felt considerably more nervous, which he became after she followed up with:

"I see you've got into the spirit of things and come in disguise."

He felt at his neck, replying:

"Yes, I felt it advisable to discard the clerical collar."

Then he mentally cursed himself for the pomposity of the reply. Why could he never get it right? But if she minded, she didn't show it.

"If you take the first right there's a quiet pub after about a mile where we can talk undisturbed."

He wasn't really a pub man but it was a good idea and he pulled away from the curb, aware of her proximity and the scent of her perfume.

It wasn't difficult to work out why the pub was quiet. They took their drinks, a gin and tonic for her and lemonade for him, to a sticky table flanked by torn and dirty seats.

"Told you it'd be quiet, never anyone here. Good thing too, don't we make a strange pair?"

She giggled and before he got chance to reply she'd moved on.

"You know, you need to do something with your hair, Ed, that scruffy long look ages you."

She sounded almost flirtatious and he kept his eyes on the smeary lemonade glass. Apart from a radio playing softly somewhere there was no other sign of life in the pub. He muttered:

"What are we doing here, Olga? What do you want?"

"I need you to listen, listen with an open mind. Don't judge me on your experience at the house the other night."

He nodded assent, knowing he was going to hear something he didn't want to. He felt strange and out of time; the radio and the table sticking to his hands could have been in another universe.

"Something's wrong, Ed, out of step with reality. I'm frightened. I'm talking to you because I know more about you than you think. You're the only person who'd understand and..."

She paused and her generous lipsticked mouth fashioned a moue of disgust.

"And you know that woman."

He began to protest, she held up her hand to cut him off.

"Please listen."

"Claire's a friend of mine, you mus..."

She cut him off.

"She's not, not at all what you think, not what anyone could possibly think. Just listen, give me a few minutes, please listen."

He was sweating, something was happening, something wicked was coming, he needed time to think. He got up and went to the bar. Eventually the barman appeared from somewhere deep inside the building and served him. He changed his own drink to whisky and went back to listen.

"It started to go wrong last Christmas after you carried out your exorcism at Skendleby. I don't know what you did but I felt it. Around then, Margaret got the idea of the baby. It was like a Damascene conversion, no discussions, not even with me, and I share her bed. Sorry if you're embarrassed by that, Ed."

Ed shook his head, hoping to appear at one with the sexual zeitgeist, but he thought he might be blushing. Olga smiled, said:

"No need to be embarrassed, we all lead complicated lives and mine's considerably more complicated than most, which I hope you'll discover."

Then she continued:

"I didn't know where the idea came from at the time, but I'm certain it wasn't Margaret's."

"So whose idea was it?"

"Save that for later please, Ed. I don't want to go there yet. She talked me round, she's so lovely and she's been so hurt, so together we convinced the others. But even so, I knew this birth meant something more to Margaret than the rest of us, but didn't suspect what. So when a week or so later I happened on Kelly in a coffee bar it seemed like fate, and I suppose because it was me who found her I began to believe in Margaret's project."

She broke off. Ed thought she was trying to fight off tears, which surprised him. She seemed so powerful, so in control.

"That poor innocent, sweet girl. I wish I'd never drifted into that coffee house, I only did it on impulse."

Ed handed her his handkerchief, she took it with a nod of thanks.

"Then, gradually at first, things began to change in the house, not just the atmospherics. After the impregnation ceremony it escalated: nuisance calls, really nasty ones, acts of petty vandalism, then we started discovering disembowelled animals at the front door, you know: crows, rabbits, weasels. Cut up with precision, not done by other animals. Margaret blamed Ken, her ex-husband, but I've doubts about that, it makes no sense. I think she's hiding something else. Trouble is, as an explanation, it plays to the sexual politics of some of us: Rose and Jenna in particular."

She must have noticed he looked surprised.

"I think you got a false impression of us, Ed. I know we came across as pretty hostile but that was down to the circumstances. We're a group of women who want to live a spiritual life independent of men, not hostile to them. That's why everything is so wrong."

He said nothing. Since Skendleby he'd developed into a good listener.

"Then that hateful killing: poor Kelly, never hurt anyone. Why kill her? I've done nothing but think about it ever since. All I've come up with is that she wasn't the target, it was the life inside her."

Ed couldn't help himself, blurted out:

"No, you can't say that, how would anyone even know she was pregnant?"

"Good question. She'd told Margaret she thought she was and Margaret told me. No one else in the house knew as far as I know, but I suspect one other person did. That same day, Claire turned up offering psychic healing and Margaret accepted. She feigned surprise, but when you're close to someone you know them. I know Margaret was expecting Claire, I could see they were already very close. I've got two questions for you, Ed."

He waited, knowing that his world was beginning to turn, but there was no time to think about what was coming.

"We've got a new member of the community now, someone I think you know: Jan. So the first thing I'm asking is: why are there three women who were damaged on the Skendleby dig living in our community of seven? They couldn't wait to get away from here last year, so what could be strong enough to bring them back?"

He didn't know and for the moment wasn't bothered, he was too intent on what was coming next: the thing he was dreading.

"What is Claire?"

He swallowed his whisky in one gulp.

****

Within a couple of miles of Skendleby, the weather started to change. Ahead of them they could see dark grey cloud masses blown around by an increasingly strong wind. The drive back had been a strange mix of fracture and intimacy. Ed was both disturbed and attracted by Olga and couldn't deny he felt a strong tug of intimacy. He knew she wanted something but also that she seemed to get him, had worked out what he really was beneath the awkward and shallow surface. So he'd been able to be honest with her once they left the pub and were sitting in the car.

"I can't give you answers, not now, I need to think. I can't even tell you what really happened last Christmas, well, not yet, maybe later. But you're right, there is something happening again, something that shouldn't be happening. I can't understand why Rose, Leonie and Jan are living so close to Skendleby. The place almost killed Rose and damaged the others so much it drove them away. They'll be more likely to talk to you than me. As for Claire, I owe her so much, without her I don't think I'd have made it. But…"

He faltered. Olga smiled, encouraging him to continue.

"But, when I saw her at the house, I don't know what it was, but something was different. Different, and it just felt wrong. That's all I can say for now. But, there's a couple of things I think I need to share with you."

The wind was beginning to buffet the car, forcing him to struggle with the steering and pause momentarily.

"I've been examining some previously unknown sources concerning the Skendleby estate. They were run to earth by a researcher working with the archaeologists, just before he was murdered in Nice."

The murder of Tim Thompson in Nice and the deranged letter he'd written only hours before were beginning to seem frighteningly linked with their current problems. Another of the restless dead that hovered above Skendleby. But he pressed on.

"Thompson's research led me to concealed Davenport papers and extracts of the journals of Dr John Dee that he'd obviously been at pains to hide. Conflating the two, it's pretty certain that over the years there have been several attempts to exorcise Skendleby from whatever lurks under that foul piece of ground. But the worse thing is…."

"Go on, Ed."

"Look up there, oh God, they've come back. It's starting again."

Above them, wheeling in the wind torn air, was a dense mass of black carrion: crows, rooks, magpies and ravens.

"They're over the mound, something's happening."

He took a sharp right turn onto a track leading to an open field gate. In the field beyond adjacent to the Skendleby mound, two men were shouting at each other while trying to get a heavy bulldozer to start. Ed excused himself to Olga and began to walk rapidly towards them, stumbling over the uneven turf in the swirling storm blasts. When he was about fifty yards away he heard the engine begin to splutter into life and he realised what was going to happen. Heart pumping, he began to run, shouting:

"Stop, you mustn't do that, this site is protected. I must insist you move away."

The destruction and reopening of this site was his worst nightmare, and it overrode any of the dangers of interrupting the work of two hefty and obviously angry men. He was close now, less than ten yards away, and for the first time they noticed him. The bigger and nastier looking man was climbing back into the cab. Ed grabbed at his left arm to stop him.

"Stop, please stop, you don't know what you're doing."

The man shook him off and he fell into the mud on all fours, losing his glasses. He heard the roar of the engine, felt it begin to move forward. So, scrambling to his feet, he managed to get round the front of it, where he stood gasping out like a distressed asthmatic child.

"Stop, please, please stop."

For an instant as he stood there, the mound behind him, the birds wheeling and cawing above, he thought it wouldn't stop. Thought that he would be ploughed into the mound to lie with the bones and whatever else lurked underneath. The shovel brushed into him but stopped, and he found himself confronted by the driver. A jowly, stubbly, red-face man, apoplectic with rage.

"You fuck off out of here or I'll fucking bury you under it."

"No, please, I'm the vicar, Reverend Joyce, call me..."

"You're a fucking joker is what you are."

He was swung away and out of the bulldozer's path, and he saw the man pull a clenched fist back to smash him in the face. On the periphery he was aware of the other man ineffectually attempting to intercede.

"Jed, don't, it'll make things worse."

Ed was closing his eyes to block out the impact when he saw, coming from behind his right shoulder, another fist covered with rings crunch into his assailant's head. The man seemed to crumple up before collapsing incrementally to the earth.

Chapter 13: From The Other Side

Theodrakis tore himself out of the nightmare and jerked awake, hoarse screams reverberating inside his head. The same dream, the English dream. Now that he was in England it was worse.

Despite the cloying hotel heating system he was cold, yet the crumpled bed sheets were wet and sweat stained. He went into the coffin sized bathroom and splashed water from the tiny washbasin over his face - he needed a shave. He wanted Hippolyta, which speaking to her last night had exacerbated. She'd told him her crone grandmother Yaya Eleni was having visions, and although non-specific they spoke of danger for him. Hippolyta wanted to join him in England, but having recognised what he'd seen yesterday he wanted her as far away as possible.

He wondered what time it was. His body clock wasn't working and he'd been constipated since arriving at Manchester airport. He was considering asking reception for the nearest pharmacy when his phone rang.

"Syntagmatarchis," it sounded like Syntmarchers. "Theodrakis, it's DS Anderson, can you be ready in half an hour, Sir, we're sending a car."

It was a relief to be doing something, but he could have done without the assault on Greek pronunciation and replied:

"Good morning, Anderson, I'll be outside the front door and Colonel Theodrakis is sufficient."

He dressed with care, determined not to be contaminated by the shabby chain store fashion of his new British colleagues. Reluctant to face the hotel breakfast, he patronised an adjacent coffee house for an espresso. It was cold on the street and as he was opposite Selfridges he bought an expensive but heavily lined Herringbone overcoat, which struck him as elegantly English but made him late. Anderson was in the hotel lobby looking none too pleased when he returned, and he greeted him with a dyspeptic:

"You've got your chance to see the archaeologist now, Sir"

But not immediately it seemed. First there was a briefing in the incident room. He hated incident rooms: their grisly photos, x-rays, samples and artefacts. They were bad enough in Athens, but the English seemed to make a religion of them, which he found almost pornographic. Thus immersed in the gruesome evidence he had his first real experience of DI Campbell.

He'd been surprised when he'd first seen her. She wasn't what he'd expected and would have been unusual in the Athens office, never mind Samos. So he empathised and was disposed to like her and ignore that it was her case, even though he outranked her by several grades.

"Good morning, Colonel Theodrakis, I hope you've settled into the hotel while they're looking for somewhere more suitable for you."

She was taller and maybe more broad shouldered than he was, and still looked unwell. This couldn't disguise that in a strong, rugged way she was beautiful, like Michelle Obama crossed with the Williams sisters. He knew she was waiting for him to say, "Please, call me Alexis." Everyone had to be a friend these days.

"Thank you, Inspector, I believe we go to visit Dr Glover today."

She seemed vaguely disappointed with this reply and he noticed a flicker of irritation cross Anderson's face.

"That's this afternoon, we've a session to bring you up to speed first."

The briefing lasted two hours. Theodrakis listened selectively and contributed nothing; he knew he was there to give specialist advice, not do the legwork that would solve the case. He wasn't sure it could be solved anyway; they were dealing with things way beyond their capabilities. From his ordeal on Samos he knew they'd only make progress if their objectives coincided with those of more ancient forces. He sat and looked at the pictures of the poor mutilated girls with horrific injuries with which he was so familiar.

The victims, these and the ones who would follow, were not even significant as people, they just supplied a commodity. With these things, humans as individuals didn't even register. His new colleagues didn't realise this yet and he pitied them.

He pitied himself too, always being moved to alien environments, dependant on the comfort of strangers but comfortable with no one. He could sense their disappointment. To this was added a measure of awkwardness when his only contribution to the briefing was a comment entirely irrelevant to the case.

"These days in Greece, Zorba is not a name parents often give to their children."

****

For Viv, the car ride to the archaeology department at the university was uncomfortable and embarrassing; the Greek said nothing and she was wondering how to handle Dr Giles Glover. She felt awful, not only physically, her perspective was bleak, always bleak. She felt a shroud of uncertainty covering everything. She was lonely, anxious and worried that she was slipping into clinical depression. She sat in the back with Theodrakis, wishing she was in the front with Jimmy. She supposed the Zorba gaff hadn't helped much.

They drove through the neo-Gothic arch into the university quad. The archaeology unit was housed in the basement, and to use the adjective utilitarian in relation to it would have flattered its ambiance. Once they passed through the shabby institutional door labelled GMAU, with its peeling green paint, they found themselves in a cavernous office. The ancient desks and shelves were scattered with books, papers and artefacts and were occupied by one smartly dressed woman and a series of scruffily dressed students and ex-students whose taste in fashion and hairstyling had frozen in time the day they'd graduated.

Sitting in the centre at the largest desk, shaggy haired in some sort of olive green knitwear smock worn over a faded white T shirt and baggy Primark jeans, was Giles. He made no attempt to rise and greet them when Viv, followed by Anderson, entered. It was exactly the difficult start Viv had anticipated. He barely favoured them by bothering to look up.

Then something surprised her, altered her perspective. The look of sullen resentment on his face vanished and was replaced with a look of delight that transformed him, made him attractive, desirable possibly. She felt Theodrakis push past her and Anderson, striding towards the central desk. Giles almost leapt out of his chair, scattering piles of paper. They met halfway, paused for a moment as if to shake hands when, to Viv's amazement, they hugged each other, pulled apart and stood smiling like lovers. Giles spoke first.

"Poss pas, ese kalla?"

"Ne, ne, poli kala, k sis?"

Then they laughed and this time did shake hands. She knew neither well but even so it was like looking at two different people, and suddenly it made things seem easier. Not for Anderson apparently, he was scowling as if Theodrakis had defected. She seized the moment to move things on.

"Thanks for agreeing to see us at such short notice, Dr Glover, I appreciate this must be difficult for you."

For a moment he seemed about to make some complaint but instead said:

"I've got the bones, the ones from the pit, and some others from below in the meeting room, it's more private in there."

The meeting room was even less welcoming than the general office, if such a thing were possible. One table, a scattering of classroom style plastic chairs, no widows and in the centre of the table - seeming to dominate the room -

a green plastic collecting tray, which contained a selection of stained off-white bones.

They arranged themselves round the table beneath a humming strip light, Theodrakis and Giles sitting across from Anderson and Viv.

"I can offer you coffee but wouldn't recommend it."

She declined, then asked:

"What can you tell us about the samples, are they relevant?"

"Depends what you mean by relevant, they all predate your case by hundreds of years."

She knew he was cagey, reluctant to say anything that might incriminate himself, and said:

"We know from Colonel Theodrakis that you helped him materially in Greece, we know you have no connection to the killings, we've apologised unreservedly, but we need your help now. Please help us understand the context of the evidence."

He nodded and laid the bones out in front of him like a card dealer in a casino.

"Well, the most interesting thing about this collection is the assemblage."

He must have noticed their blank looks.

"I mean, it's not the individual bones, it's that they're all together in one context. These bones cover several thousand years. This one here's the most recent, probably late Tudor, and they get progressively earlier until we get to this. This isn't natural."

He gently picked up a fragile and degraded sample about the same dimension as a child's finger.

"This is over five thousand years old, Neolithic, same as on Samos. Here, take it."

He passed it across and placed it gently in the palm of Viv's hand. It was light, as if it had no substance. Then she began to feel it, not physically, more like it was burrowing into her mind, seeding pain and terror. Everything else in the room diminished, the walls seemed to recede, the voices faded. Then the feeling had gone. Giles was standing over her with the bone in his hand.

"Sorry to snatch it from you but it looked like you were going to drop it; it's very fragile and incredibly rare."

She didn't respond, just sat there watching the room return to normality. He was still speaking, but now in a concerned tone.

"Are you ok? Do you want some water? You look like you've seen a ghost."

Jimmy was hovering over her.

"Ma'am, do you need to get some fresh air? We can take a break."

"No, I'll be ok in a minute, I just felt a bit dizzy. Perhaps we should have that coffee you offered."

Giles left the room to get some. She noticed Zorba staring intently at her and made a mental note to stop calling him that, even in her head. His expression was somewhere between concern for her and alarm at something else. Something he knew that she didn't. What was going on here? The coffee came in: it was as bad as Giles had predicted. He resumed his analysis of the bone sample; this time avoiding any class participation. She found it difficult to concentrate; something inside her was already repelled by these bones.

Giles was concluding when Jimmy asked:

"So, all these bones were cut from different bodies?"

"Yes."

"Over thousands of years?"

"Yeah."

"So why do they all end up jumbled together?"

"I'm not stating the obvious, but they're together because they've been deliberately put together."

"Why?"

"That's what I can't tell you, sorry. But you might be interested to know that there's a strong possibility that the cutting-out was performed while the donors were still alive."

"And always the same bones: fingers, toes?"

"Always straight bones, but not always extremities. Some of these bones would have been very difficult to harvest. On Samos there were bones from the shin and forearm as well as ribs."

"The same pattern across thousands of years and the same technique as in our murders. Why?"

Viv saw that Giles looked away briefly before answering.

"Don't know, frightening isn't it?"

After they dropped Theodrakis off at his hotel, Anderson said what they'd both been thinking.

"Our silent Greek friend's more intimate with Glover than we knew."

It puzzled her too, she nodded.

"And I know we've got nothing on him, Ma'am, but Glover knows more than he's saying. What's he got to hide?"

She didn't have the answer but she felt frozen inside: they were being sucked into something they couldn't handle, something unknowable."

****

When Giles got home the house was in darkness. Claire didn't get home for a couple of hours, during which time her phone was switched off. When she got back she seemed excited, he thought he detected the trace of a different perfume on her dress. He poured her a drink and began to tell her about the police visit.

"Theodrakis was with them, felt good to see him again, someone who understands. There was no time to ask him about Steve, thought we'd invite him round for dinner."

"Maybe later on, he's heavy going. Tell me the rest."

When he'd finished she got up and took his hand.

"Come on, let's go to bed, it's an auspicious night."

He didn't know what she meant by that but followed her up the stairs. As they reached the bedroom she said:

"Forget Theodrakis, I think the woman sounds more interesting, let's invite her"

Chapter 14: Olga Alone

It took some time for the frightened, ferrety man and Ed to get the unconscious driver loaded into his van and then driven away. Olga considered suggesting that she and Ed repair to the pub, he looked as if he could use a strong drink, but reckoned that, as this was his parish, he'd be compromised. So instead they agreed he would ring her tomorrow to discuss what to do next. It was probably better to get back home as her right hand was beginning to hurt and she suspected that she might have chipped a bone in her index finger. She'd found it quite satisfying managing to knock the man threatening Ed out with one punch, it was something she hadn't done for some time and she was pleased she'd not lost her touch. It might be a problem explaining it all to Margaret, however.

She needn't have worried about that because she arrived home to something more serious. As she pulled into the drive she saw Claire coming out of the front door looking pleased with herself. She made no effort to acknowledge Olga, just got into her car and drove off. Margaret was in the bedroom smoothing her hair down: she looked flushed and acted embarrassed.

"Hi, Olga, love, you've just missed Claire."

"I know, I saw her drive off."

She kissed Margaret, detecting the vague scent of an alien perfume. For a moment they just stood looking at each other. This was a first: their relationship was loving and supportive, with an ease of communication bordering on telepathy. Olga teetered on the brink of asking something that could smash all that beyond repair, and she knew Margaret was thinking something similar. So they stood in silence, feeling as if the house itself was holding its breath. Olga blinked first.

"I'm going to make some tea, do you want some?"

"Thanks, that would be lovely. I'll help you make it"

They went through to the kitchen where Olga saw two wine glasses in the sink.

Later in the evening the community came together for their regular house meeting. Candles were lit on the plinth and they sat on cushions in a semi circle, sipping from goblets of white wine. They were seven again as Jan had newly arrived and this was her first taste of house ritual. Olga couldn't make her out, she was different from the other two archaeologists: the bitter Rose and cynical Leonie. She was nice, eager to please but edgy, haunted almost, something compounded by premature streaks of grey in her hair.

Olga and Margaret hadn't spoken since the wine glasses in the sink incident. They hadn't agreed not to talk, just stayed in different parts of the house, and now, as Margaret opened the meeting, Olga could feel a tiny tangible fracture growing in the spine of their partnership.

The three archaeologists sat next to each other, which was understandable but not good for the balance of the community. But why were they here? Why should three women who'd been damaged by Skendleby and tried to escape it opt, a few months later, to join a community almost within sight of the place that scared them? Why choose a Wiccan lifestyle? Had the three of them made an individual lifestyle choice, or was something else linking them?

Olga was suddenly overwhelmed by a feeling of loss for Kelly and missed the first part of what Margaret said to open the session. By the time she picked it up she realised they were debating ways to oppose the Skendleby development and Jenna was speaking. Olga had never really taken to Jenna. There was something competitively feral about her, a disposition to be against things, to hate rather than love. She was certainly against the development.

"Now they're talking of a bigger slice of the green belt: two thousand five hundred houses, not just nine hundred, on top of the leisure centre, hotel and shopping mall. Can you imagine how that's going to change the peace of the place, never mind the fact that the roads won't cope?"

Ailsa, who always tried to be fair and balanced, interrupted.

"Yeah, but there's going to be some affordable houses built, you know, starter homes."

"Don't be so naïve, Ailsa, it's about profit."

"But it's still got to get planning consent."

"And you think that's not going to happen? Get real."

"Well, since all that stuff came out after Councillor Richardson's suicide, it's seems to have slowed down."

"And you think that he was the only councillor ready to put his hand out? Between Carver and the council they own all the land. That last propaganda leaflet we got from the council said the project was shovel ready."

Olga saw Rose and Leonie nodding encouragement as Jenna made her points; this wasn't how the community was meant to be. Ailsa made one last try.

"Perhaps what just happened on his estate might make it more difficult for him."

"For Carver? Do me a favour! I wouldn't be surprised if that pig didn't kill the girl himself."

The mention of the killing was too close to home. It brought back Kelly; Margaret held up her hands and said:

"I think we agree that we'll oppose the development, but the killing of that poor girl is connected to what I want to propose next. We can't be sure if there's a connection with what happened to poor, dear Kelly, but something terrible is happening here. First we had the threats; the foul stuff smeared on the front door, the Hex fetishes. When we lost Kelly, we lost the baby that would have been the centre of our community, the sign of our renewal. Now…"

She paused and Olga saw that she was close to tears.

"Now we're rudderless and threatened. Why would people want to threaten us? What have we ever done to deserve this?"

Rose said:

"I thought we'd already established that it was your ex-husband behind all that, dear, you know what men can do."

Olga saw that Jenna was nodding like she was enjoying this. But what Margaret said next chased any other thoughts from her head.

"This afternoon I had a consultation with someone you already know. Someone with more experience of this than any of us, who was closely involved with whatever it was that happened in Skendleby last Christmas."

With a sinking feeling in her stomach, Olga worked out where this was leading. She tried to catch Margaret's eye but Margaret averted her gaze.

"Someone with powers of psychic healing, someone who can put us back on track and help replace what we lost in Kelly. Someone who understands what our community needs and is prepared to help us."

Olga knew what was coming next, couldn't believe it, and just sat speechless as she heard Margaret say, like someone pulling a rabbit out of a hat:

"Claire Vanarvi."

Olga found herself protesting before she'd thought it through, precipitated by hurt and something stronger, which gnawed away inside her.

"Why Margaret? We hardly know her; she never showed any interest in us until what happened to Kelly. It's not the way this community works."

Margaret still wouldn't meet her gaze but said:

"Olga, you know how threatened we are, you must understand we need some help; something's targeting us, you know that as well I do."

Before she could begin to answer, Jenna cut in.

"And who would you suggest, Olga? That pathetic little priest who made a fool of himself here the other day?"

"No, obviously not, I'm just saying that..."

But Jenna hadn't finished yet.

"And, by the way, what happened to your hand, Olga? You've not taken to fighting again, have you?"

While Jenna was getting her jibe in, Olga watched the faces of the archaeologists. They knew Claire, how would they react? Some of the telepathy with Margaret must have survived because she called out.

"Please, please, we mustn't be like this; we have to support each other. I'd like to hear what our newer members think about Claire's offer; they've known her the longest."

Rose shook her head.

"You'll have to rely on Leonie and Jan, I only saw her from a distance. I was in hospital when she got involved with the excavation."

"Yeah, and I only saw her a couple of times. Jan's the only one who really knows her."

All eyes turned to Jan; she looked nervous, like a child cross-legged on her cushion.

"Well, I don't know her that well and most of what I do know comes from Steve."

She blushed and glanced towards Leonie. Olga thought: *there's a history here we don't understand.*

Leonie said:

"Don't worry about that on my account, Jan, as far as I'm concerned you were welcome to him."

Jan took a deep breath.

"She was around the dig after the excavation of the mound. Giles relied on her a lot. In fact, he moved in with her. When I saw her she seemed really nice. I left the dig soon after, went back to live with my dad in Glasgow, I wasn't well and it was getting to me."

She looked round at them and Olga guessed she wasn't sure how much to say; obviously there were things that no one outside that dig was supposed to know. Margaret coaxed her gently.

"Please, Jan, it would be really helpful if you'd tell us as much as you can."

Jan nodded, then continued.

"Ok, Steve got quite badly damaged by what happened to him at Skendleby. He had a sort of breakdown and came up to Glasgow on Christmas Eve. That was such a lovely surprise, well, at first it was."

She pulled a tissue out of her sleeve, dabbed at her eyes and blew her nose, then looked at Margaret and tried to smile.

"Sorry, this is difficult for me. Steve said that if it hadn't been for Claire something terrible would have happened to him and Giles. He said they and some others owed more to Claire than anyone else could ever imagine. He didn't say what, he didn't want to talk about it, so I didn't ask. In fact, I didn't want to know, the little bit I'd seen was enough to stop me sleeping for weeks."

Olga, like the others, was hanging on her every word; there was something awful and authentic in the broken and partial account of the Skendleby excavation. It cast a dark spell over the room. So much so that Olga thought to herself: *if it was so terrifying and did that to you, why are you here? Why did you come back?*

"Steve had been through so much, the physical effect of the attack on him was bad enough, but the mental scarring was worse. I thought he'd be all right after a bit and that we could be happy, but it didn't work out that way."

She paused and snuffled again, dabbing at her nose with the fragmenting tissue. They waited for her to continue and the candles lighting the room flickered. Jan pulled herself together and carried on.

"The horrors came back, he felt watched, haunted really. He used to ring Claire every night for reassurance. Then..."

Her voice faltered and silence covered the room. She looked like she was going to cry but with an effort said:

"Then, just before Easter, he disappeared, went to the Greek isle of Samos. Last I heard of him was in a letter from Giles saying he'd retreated into a monastery out there. While he was on Samos, Tim Thomson, the archivist who worked for us on the Skendleby dig, was murdered in Nice. Sorry, I'm rambling, it's meant to be about Claire."

Margaret walked over to her and topped up her glass. Olga and the rest sat in trance-like silence. After she'd filled the glass, Margaret placed her hand on Jan's diminutive shoulder saying gently:

"Go on, Jan, love, take your time."

Jan gulped down half the glass in a couple of swallows, spluttered then picked up the thread.

"All I'm trying to say is that Claire's good, Steve trusted her, Giles loves her and she did something at Skendleby that seemed to hold back the dark. But despite that it seems she couldn't save Steve or anyone else. So how can she…"

She came to a stop and finished off the wine. Out of the intervening silence Margaret said:

"Thank you, Jan, that was very brave and I think it constitutes one of the strongest character references I've ever heard. So we can take a vote on my proposal, which is that Claire comes to our next meeting with a view to becoming an ex-officio member of our circle. Those in favour."

Olga saw Ailsa and Jenna raise their hands with Margaret. Margaret smiled at Jan who also raised her hand, followed by Rose and Leonie. Olga saw them all looking at her, but she kept her hand down. What had they done?

Margaret looked at Olga for the first time that evening.

"Not you, Olga. This will be the first time we've not agreed."

She paused, waiting for Olga to relent, which she didn't, and Margaret moved hurriedly on to her main point.

"Well, before we eat, I can now tell you something that Claire has already done for us. She's found a potential replacement for poor dear Kelly. Someone who, like Kelly, has known suffering. Someone abused by her father into a breakdown which Claire was responsible for treating to the point where she has been completely rehabilitated. She too will come to our next meeting."

While Margaret said this Olga had been watching Jan. She was becoming agitated and, as Margaret finished, she blurted out:

"Who is she, what's her name?"

Margaret was obviously surprised by the tone of Jan's voice but answered smoothly enough.

"Lisa Richardson."

Olga saw a look of pure terror cross Jan's face.

Chapter 15: "It's in the 'ouse, it's got inside me 'ouse"

First thing in the morning, the Chief sent for her. The message said it was urgent so she'd had to postpone signing the papers for the Didsbury apartment. She didn't actually mind having to see the Chief. In fact, the only positive vibe about any of this was that she knew he backed her - liked her even. She felt the only reassurance she got came from him; she still wasn't sure if the rest of the team accepted her, well Jimmy maybe.

In many ways she was in a double bind because, behind the politically correct front, she was pretty sure they suspected that having her imposed on them, in charge of the operation, was down to her colour. That would always niggle away at her and as her mood was down it fed on negatives, and the next of those on her increasingly long list was bloody Zorba.

Theodrakis said nothing helpful and made no attempt to bond with anyone. He just stood around, expensively dressed, looking elegant and bored. But she knew that under this reflective surface lay a mound of experience that he wanted kept hidden. He was like an iceberg with the most dangerous eight-ninths hidden below the waterline. She also knew that getting him to share that experience could prove worse than letting him keep it. On top of everything else about him it was his comment about Greek names that was most irritating - a clever bugger remark out of context in a murder enquiry briefing. It had put her on the back foot and embarrassed her in front of her team, and she still felt the shame of it.

By this time she'd reached the door to the Chief's office. She ran her fingers through her hair in a vain effort to push it into some facsimile of neatness and knocked. There was a gruff bark from inside which she interpreted as an invitation to enter. He was sitting slumped behind his desk but, upon looking up and seeing her, managed a smile.

"Come and sit down, lass. I'll send for some tea and a chocolate biscuit."

So far so good then. She slid into the chair across the desk from his and waited for what was coming.

"Something's up at Skendleby Hall. I've had a call on my direct line from Carver, but I'll play you a recording of the 999 call he made first, it'll give you a better idea of how he was feeling."

He pressed a tab on his keyboard and, after the voice of the police operative, Viv heard an agitated voice that she recognised as Carver.

"Get someone here now, emergency. It's come for me, come up out of that hole."

There was a scuffling sound and then the voice again, this time panicked, shouting.

"It's come out of the hole, it's in the 'ouse, it's got inside me bleedin 'ouse."

The Chief switched off the recording and looked at Viv. There was no mistaking the fear in Carver's voice. She asked:

"What happened? Is he all right?"

"He's physically fine and we still don't know what happened: when the local boys got out there they couldn't find anyone. Couldn't find any trace of a break in, couldn't find anything. By that time Carver had regained enough composure to be angry. They got to the Hall just after three and they're still there. I've told them to wait until you arrive."

He poured tea and offered her a chocolate biscuit; she knew she was the only one to get this treatment.

"I'll not play you the conversation he had with me; although he was calmer there wasn't much difference. He's scared stupid and it takes a lot to scare a man like that."

He slurped down some tea before adding:

"It makes no sense but he claims that someone dressed in a type of Halloween outfit got into the house, and he's sure it came up out of the hole under where the girl was killed. He thinks there's some type of conspiracy to scare him out and, believe me, he's certainly scared. So check it out thoroughly, will you? Maybe it's time to persuade our archaeological friend to have a good look at what's under the pit."

She started to protest about having to go back to Giles, but he raised his hand in a signal to listen.

"I know, I know, he doesn't exactly love us at present, so just remind him that this is his opportunity to look around that chapel you said he was so keen on."

She finished the tea and headed off to find Jimmy and Zorba. As they made their way to the car she couldn't help noticing again the discrepancy in appearance between them. Jimmy, like her, was wearing a well-worn suit of similar quality to hers, which had been bought in a Debenhams sale and which she noticed in a mirror was baggy and seated. Zorba looked like he'd just walked out of the shop window of Harrods. They drove through a drizzle of sleet to Skendleby without speaking. At the Hall, as Anderson parked the car, Theodrakis asked her:

"If you don't mind, Inspector, I won't come in with you, I want to have a look round the chapel."

She snapped back at him.

"Why? Have you suddenly become an archaeological expert?"

He ignored the sarcasm.

"No, of course not. But you don't need me inside and it suits me to study the chapel."

A heavily built man with a street fighter's scars and a badly reset nose showed Viv and Anderson into a large room with a full size billiard table and a new stone built bar. Sitting on a barstool, unshaven and nursing a drink, was Si Carver. He neither welcomed them nor invited them to sit, just snarled:

"Well, you've taken your time gettin' here."

"We came as quickly as we could, Mr Carver, and I understand you've had a police presence at the hall since the early hours."

"Well, it's not bleedin good enough."

He took a drink and Viv saw his hand was shaking as he lifted the glass to his lips.

"There has already been one murder here, how many more do you want?"

Viv forced her mouth into a sympathetic smile and asked:

"Would you like to tell us what happened last night?"

Over the next hour, Carver tried to explain what had frightened him. It was a rambling, unbelievable account. But as he talked he convinced them that he believed it even if they didn't understand. Anderson made some notes, then asked:

"Who do you think is trying to frighten you? Who was in here last night?"

"There's a conspiracy to get me out, to stop me development. It all started when the archaeologists messed things up last year. Since then I've had nuisance calls, intruders in the grounds. Then there are the crows, them bleedin crows."

This last reflection halted him in mid-delivery. For a moment it seemed that he couldn't continue, but then he added:

"It's driven me staff away and murdered one and now someone's broke in. What more do you want? What does it take to get you people to do anything?"

Viv saw that he was near the edge and that the drink wasn't helping.

"We're giving this top priority, we'll step up the security and investigate what's under the chapel, although we'll need to involve the archaeologists."

"You said that last time. 'Consider it done', you said. Well, it wasn't, was it? Anyway you can involve whoever you like and put in as much security as you want, it won't do no good."

He clearly was highly distressed, so much so that, for a moment, Viv almost felt sorry for him.

"I'm sure we…"

"You haven't seen it, you don't know what it's like, what it does: you haven't had to live with it."

"Tell us what you want us to do."

"I want you to catch it, get rid of it - I want you to do your bleedin jobs."

"Ok, I understand how you must feel, just try again to describe what you saw."

"I dunno, like I said, it was all in black. It was like bigger than it should have been and in more places. It was old, smelt old; it moved funny, you know, floating about. It knew me. I've already told you over and over."

He was right, he had, but it still didn't make any sense. Viv decided to talk to him again the following day when he'd be a bit calmer. But he hadn't finished.

"Like I told you last time, you need to pull in that vicar, it always comes from his churchyard, and the old fool who used to live here. They're behind this and the protests. How many more murders do you want?"

There was nothing more they could achieve here. She tried to reassure him about the level of protection they were leaving and got one of the local lads in to take a full statement. They were shown out and, as they walked to the car, Anderson said:

"I didn't expect that, not from him. It's normally him who does the frightening. Funny thing is that description of the intruder though."

"Oh, that 'Living Dead' stuff. That was just his nerves and the drink."

"Maybe, I'm sure you're right, Ma'am, but it's not the first time I've heard it. I'm pretty certain I took a statement describing pretty much the same thing during the attacks round here last Christmas, and not from Carver."

Viv never got an opportunity to reply because history was about to repeat itself. Jogging towards them from the direction of the estate wall, this time in a pink Lycra ensemble, was Suzzie Jade. Anderson observed:

"Well, doesn't look like she's too bothered by last night."

"Hiyaa, can't keep away from here then, can ya?"

Viv smiled a greeting and asked:

"Is there anything you can tell us about last night, Mrs Carver?"

"I prefer Suzzie-Jade, I think I told you that last time, but no, they already asked me that this morning."

"Is there nothing more you can help us with? Every little helps."

Suzzie-Jade laughed.

"Now you sound like Tesco! No, I didn't even wake up so I can't tell you nothink, sorry. But I hope that you can sort out all this. It's really getting to Si, making him very difficult to live with. If he's in a bad mood there's no fun for anyone, know what I mean?"

She started to move off, saying to Anderson as she passed him:

"Where do you work out then?"

"Me? Oh, at Total Lifestyle."

"Yeah? Nice. I've got a personal traina, that's why I have to do all this. See ya."

As she moved off towards the front entrance of the Hall, Anderson grinned and said:

"Well, at least she's consistent, I'm almost getting to like her."

If he was expecting any type of banter by way of reply he was disappointed. All Viv said came from the perspective of a more anxious stream of consciousness.

"Look how dark it's getting. Where's Theodrakis?"

"I don't know, Ma'am. He said he wanted to look at the chapel, perhaps he's still in there."

They walked round the side of the Hall, past a couple of sheds and towards the chapel. If it seemed gloomy by the car it was stygian round there, amongst the dark green of the dripping rhododendrons. The ancient stone of the chapel was stained and eroded: it transmitted an aura of decay and neglect which wasn't helped by the pit that stopped just a couple of feet short of it and which was slowly becoming waterlogged.

The door of the chapel was slightly ajar. Anderson pulled at the rusted iron of the door ring and it opened with a creek. Inside it was cold and musty. The woodwork, seat and wall coverings were all mildewed. Viv glanced at the motto carved into the coat of arms above the door as she followed him in.

It read, 'Vigilate et custodite'. She'd done a short course in Latin at sixth form college and knew enough to understand that it said something about watching. As her eyes got used to the murky light she saw a figure sitting crouched on the front pew.

Theodrakis stood up slowly and walked towards them, his expression unreadable in the permanent twilight of the decomposing chapel. Viv decided to say nothing, placing the onus on him to talk, and she was surprised when he said immediately:

"We should talk to Giles; I've arranged to meet him at a pub near here. A pub with an odd name which I've…"

She snapped back. Bit his head off as all her frustration poured out.

"You've arranged! Let me remind you who's in charge of this case. Let me remind you who decides who we meet, where and when. Don't you dare…."

This time it was Theodrakis's turn to interrupt, and he did it by holding up his hands in a gesture of surrender and, smiling an apology, said:

"Please, I'm sorry. I know I've not been helpful but if we go to this pub now, I'll tell you what I know before Giles arrives. I don't think it would be advisable for us to talk in here."

This surprised Viv and she thought: *so he can communicate when it suits him.* She wanted to get away from here too, there was something contagiously unhealthy about the atmosphere in the chapel. She regretted the outburst; Jimmy recognised the pub from Zorba's description and so they set off.

Waiting at the table in the corner for Jimmy to fetch the drinks, Viv felt her mood begin to lift. It had been almost dark as they pulled out of the Skendleby Hall drive, the year was getting old.

Theodrakis took a sip of brandy then talked.

"Please, don't be angry at what I'm going to say. I'll tell you what I know but I'm not sure you'll understand it or find it helpful, at least not yet. In that chapel I felt the things I felt in Samos. Please listen and don't interrupt until I've said it all - it will only make sense to you when you experience more of this. Ok, you promise?"

They nodded.

"I don't think the chapel is real in the way that other places, like this pub, are. No, I can see you beginning to question, don't. There was a place on Samos like this and I think they are connected. That's the first thing I know."

He finished his brandy and rubbed his hands together as if for warmth.

"The second thing is this. On Samos we looked for a culprit. We didn't understand that no one did it, or whatever occasioned it we would never find."

Viv couldn't stop herself.

"But you solved it, you made arrests."

"Yes, we made arrests and yes, the killings stopped. That's true, but only up to a point. We caught people who carried out the physical aspects of the contagion, but they weren't the generative force. They had no reason for what they did, no past record and, in one case, I think it's improbable that the perpetrator had the physical capacity for the attack. There was conclusive forensic evidence, a compulsion to confess, but no logic.

You must understand that there are two simultaneous processes at work here, and your murders are a symptom of something much older and far worse. I can't explain it, but the Skendleby excavation, what I encountered on Samos and your case are just a tiny fragment of something unknowable. If you want to stop this you need to look for someone with no motive, no record and no connection or profile."

Anderson spluttered into his drink and Viv began to protest. Then they were interrupted.

"Well, what have we here? Our old Greek friend, Inspector Theodrakis..."

The voice was amused and mocking. Viv turned to see a strikingly beautiful black-haired woman approaching the table with Dr Giles Glover behind her.

"Hi, I'm Claire, I'm with Giles."

Her eyes were sparkling as she spoke. Viv found her hypnotic but noticed Theodrakis edging back into his corner seat as she approached. Later, when she looked back on the time in the pub, she couldn't remember much, certainly not why Claire was there, just that Giles agreed to investigate the chapel and the pit. But as they were leaving Claire took her hand and held it while she said:

"I'm glad we've met at last, honey, we're going to have some special times."

While she said this she looked straight into Viv's eyes, and when Viv recovered her hand she thought she saw for a fraction of a second her eyes turn jet black.

That night Viv's sleep was disturbed by a nightmare in which a young woman was dragged into some type of tomb beneath an earthen mound, and then walled up alive.

Chapter 16: Dark at Lindow

Early morning in the rectory was disturbed by the phone ringing, Ed reached it first.

"St George's Rectory, Ed Joyce speaking."

"Ed, its Olga, I need to see you."

"I thought we agreed it was better not to ring me here."

"Sorry, this is urgent, we have to meet."

"Well, I think I might have some time later, perhaps this evening."

"No, it's got to be before then, meet me in the lane by the Lindow cuttings in an hour."

"What's all this about, Olga?"

"Sorry, Ed, I can't talk here, try to find out what you can about Lisa Richardson. See you later, bye."

The phone went dead, leaving Ed worrying about what he'd tell Mary. But this paled beside the horrific shock at the mention of Lisa. Life was spinning out of balance again: in the last thirty-six hours there'd been a series of comings, goings and late night disturbances just across the graveyard in Skendleby Hall. Even as he'd been on the phone he'd watched the Archaeological Unit's mini bus turn into the Hall's driveway.

Then there was the question of Olga. His meeting with her had been stimulating but worrying. He couldn't work out his motives or his feelings, but alarmingly he'd felt an erotic charge when she'd floored the thug in the bulldozer.

And now he wasn't being straight with Mary. He told himself it was his responsibility to investigate if the current attacks were linked with the Skendleby exorcism, and he wanted to shelter her from any danger. Some of this was true, as was his worry about what he'd discovered in the archived papers of Dr John Dee. But did this apply to the meeting in the pub and the frisson about Lindow? Well no, he knew that was something else.

By the time he pulled up at the end of the lane by the cuttings he was twenty minutes late. Olga's car was there but she wasn't in it. He got out and looked over the waterlogged cuttings and peat heath woodland. It lay desolate, forbidding and sodden under the cold grey sky.

He didn't like Lindow. Prior to his posting to Skendleby it held only two associations for him: as a sinister place in 'The Wierdstone of Brisingamen', a children's book by a local writer, and as the site of the gruesome prehistoric murder exhumed by police and archaeologists.

"Ed."

He turned and saw Olga emerge from the trees lying beyond a swollen drainage ditch. She looked solid and reassuring, but he felt his heart rate increase at the sight of her.

"Thanks for coming at such short notice; I thought this would be a good place to meet as there won't be anyone else about in these woods on a day like this."

He stepped unsteadily over the ditch and joined her at the edge of the wood. She kissed him on both cheeks and he moved his face awkwardly in response, but there wasn't time for embarrassment.

"Ed, you need to be truthful and tell me all you can about Lisa Richardson."

"But why? I don't think anything that poor un…"

"Because fucking Claire is bringing her to our community, is why. Now do you understand?"

"What Lisa? I thought she was still in the…"

He hesitated.

"Still in the what, Ed?"

"Still in the secure psychiatric ward."

"Oh, great. What was she in there for, Ed? There's something going badly wrong, you must be able to feel it."

"Yes, I can feel it, it's just I thought it'd gone away. But now, I don't think it ever really did."

A keening wind was sweeping across the flatness of the cuttings; it was getting colder. Ed took Olga by the arm.

"Come on, it'll be more sheltered among the trees. I'll tell you what I know as we walk but I don't think you'll like it. Lisa was a damaged young woman with a bullying father, or I suppose an abusive father is a more accurate description. Well, that's what she told me."

"And?"

"And she was a press photographer at the opening of the prehistoric tomb at Skendleby."

"And?"

"I don't expect you to believe this."

"A witch listening to a vicar? What's not to believe?"

Ed smiled at the absurdity of the situation, then made up his mind and told her. A rambling, fragmented and horrific narrative. Olga listened without interrupting then conflated the stark essence of it into an accurate précis framed as a question.

"You're telling me that something got out of the tomb when they opened it, took refuge in Lisa and possessed her, and that she attacked one of the archaeologists."

"Yes, amongst others."

"So, how come she's out now?"

"I don't know, I didn't know that she was...I suppose after the procedure with Claire..."

"What? Claire did something to her?"

"Not did something, she helped."

"Helped? How exactly did she help?"

"In a spiritual capacity. Look, I've already said more than I should."

"No, you've not said enough. How did she...?"

Then the truth Ed was attempting to obfuscate hit her.

"She attempted an exorcism, didn't she? She tried to exorcise Lisa."

Suddenly he wanted to tell her, needed to tell her, needed to share this with someone else, someone who hadn't been part of it.

"Well, I wouldn't put it like that...Ok, all right, a type of exorcism, and it worked, it must have, because from what you say Lisa's recovered."

"So, where did it go to, the thing that came out of the tomb and possessed her? Into Claire?"

"No, of course if that had happened we wouldn't have been able to conduct our act of spiritual sealing, nothing could have worked."

"Ed, there's a lot you're still hiding about Skendleby."

"Yes, and for very good reasons, and believe me, you need to be grateful you don't know; once you do know it's too late."

He pulled away, putting his head in his hands. He knew now it was back, the nightmare wasn't over, he could feel his heart hammering and his mind start to unravel like last time. He needed one of his tablets but he hadn't taken them for months so didn't have any on him. He was jogging around from one foot to the other when he crashed into a beech sapling, which deposited icy rain drops from its leaves over him, almost bringing him round.

It was Olga who did bring him back to his senses; he felt her strong cool hands on his cheeks.

"Ed, come on, it's all right, calm down, breathe steadily - you're Ok. You've told me enough, I won't push you for more."

"No, it's not all right and it never will be. I think your community in its present state is the last place Lisa should be. She was highly disturbed, her father killed himself; she threatened me, almost killed Steve, and two police officers. She did something to the throat of one of them; he had to be invalided out of the force. I think Claire's got this wrong."

"Or maybe, for her purposes, she's got it right."

"No, you're wrong, whatever she's doing I know she'll be doing it to help, to bring good and to heal."

They'd been walking in a circle and were almost back at their cars. He needed to unburden himself of other things before going home. Last year he would have turned to Davenport, but since his stroke the old man was too frail. Outside the shelter of the trees, sleet was being swept horizontally across the bleak peat cuttings towards them – Ed could feel it stinging his cheeks.

Why had he come here? The place felt like it invited evil, welcomed it. He looked across the acres of dark mud, scrub and peat, thinking of the Iron Age murder which was contemporary with the original village excavated at Skendleby. He remembered Giles saying Lindow was where the villagers at Skendleby might have run to after they'd found the tomb. It was such a vast area of peat, he figured there must be other bodies hidden under there.

"Ed, I said do you want to go for a coffee?"

"Sorry, I was thinking about something else. No, I don't want a coffee but there's something else I want to tell you."

They pulled back into the relative shelter of the trees. The light had an underwater murkiness; this wasn't a good place to be. But he couldn't wait, his nerves were stretching, and although he felt cowardly, he wanted to share the burden of anxiety with her. If she was expecting more about Claire she'd be disappointed.

"I came across some papers that had been found under unusual circumstances by an archivist working for Giles. He'd concealed them but left clues."

"Why couldn't he just pass them on to you?"

"Because he's dead. He was the victim of a motiveless knife attack on holiday in Nice."

Ed surprised himself by the matter-of-fact way he dropped such a horror into the conversation, and he saw by Olga's expression that it had disconcerted her. They were standing by a curve in the brook flowing through the woods, just far enough in to be sheltered from the worst of the wind and sleet. He began to articulate his fears about what he'd read and how it was keeping him awake at night.

"The papers, the earliest of which are fourteenth century, link the Davenport family with a local tradition of the supernatural, and not in a good way. But the most concrete evidence comes from Dr John Dee, conjurer to Elizabeth I."

"Yes, I know about him."

"Well, towards the end of his life he was serving in Manchester as rector of Manchester College, which is now a music....."

"I know, get to the point, Ed."

"He got involved in Skendleby; they called him in when something went badly wrong. Reading between the lines it seems that the Davenports were facing something like we are today, and they tried to end it. Not only that but this wasn't the first time they'd tried, and it didn't work. But the worst thing is that it seems from what Dee imputes that this involved removing certain bones from a living victim. The diary indicates this occurred at a farmhouse some distance away, towards Handforth."

He paused, remembering she wouldn't be aware of the significance of the bones, but it was too late, he'd said it.

"Dee links the Davenport chapel with the farm, and whatever it was that happened in the ritual, he also infers they feared some type of entity watching over the mound that was excavated last year."

"Ed, there's a lot you're not telling me."

"I know, but what I am telling you is that history is repeating itself here. Over and over, and it never ends happily. I've got so much evidence, it all triangulates."

He felt overwhelmed; she sensed this and placed a hand gently on his shoulder.

"Sorry, this type of thing is difficult to relate, particularly when you've been involved. It can make you paranoid, so much so that when I read in Dee's journal about a skryer he was using and who he didn't trust I…"

"What Ed? What's so bad about that?"

"A skryer is a type of......"

"I know full well what a skryer is."

"This one was called Hikman, add a c and that's your name, Olga. Your name and an action at a farm near Handforth. You live in a late medieval farm near there, Olga, think about it."

She didn't respond, just looked steadily at him.

"Whatever he saw here messed him up; I think he became deranged because the extract finishes with a terrified reference to something dreadful, which watches from the shadows. Almost the same phrase was used by one of my eighteenth century predecessors in this parish, a man so scared that he preferred to jeopardise his immortal soul by suicide rather than face what he feared."

Olga said nothing so Ed stumbled on.

"Things didn't end much better for Dee. When he got back to Manchester he found that his family had contracted the plague. Soon after he returned to London and disappeared from history."

"And you think that it's all happening again? That whatever you thought you'd achieved at Skendleby has come undone? If you want my help, Ed, you need to trust me, tell me all of it."

"That's a two way street, there's things you haven't told me, like what your coven is really about."

He wanted to kick himself; he'd meant to say community, where had coven come from? Mortified, he kept his eyes down staring at the brook. Particularly at a small layer of dead white fungus that seemed to be growing out of the bank just above the waterline. He hated fungus, always had. It frightened him as a child. He aimed a kick at it. It didn't detach and flow downstream as he'd expected it to, it just flopped into the water and remained inert. Olga was saying something now but he wasn't listening, couldn't listen. The fungus had grown fingers, five of them, and it was attached to something bigger.

"Ed! Are you listening?"

But he still wasn't. He was shifting some sodden conifer branches that were obscuring the main part of the fungus. For a moment he stared back at the wide open eyes that were staring at him from under the water, then he jumped back with a scream.

"Ed, what's wrong?"

"In there, under, look it's there, a body - oh God."

He felt her push past him and heard her scream, then she was shouting at him.

"I know who it is, I know who it is."

Chapter 17: What Was Under The Chapel?

Looking out from the minibus, Giles caught a quick glimpse of Ed in the rectory window. He looked worried, and Giles wished he was with him: he didn't feel good about this. What Theodrakis had told him about the chapel had brought all the horrors crawling back. Following the police car down the drive, Giles had the opportunity to study Skendleby Hall.

Time hadn't treated it well. The ancient seat of the Davenports stood bleak and weather stained against the winter sky. The post Davenport modernisation programme implemented by its new owner looked unreal, like a film set, a perspective reinforced by the plethora of CCTV cameras liberally scattered round the grounds. The combination of archaic decay and modernist vandalism gave the place an aura of desolation and despair, and in that spirit, saving the best for last, came the abandoned and waterlogged pit where the sad and semi-disarticulated remains of Marika had been dumped.

"Sorry about the conditions, but the DI needs this done quickly; our crime scene guys are already in the pit, they'll show you what we need you to look at."

Anderson was by the minibus door waiting for them to get out, huddling behind the turned up collar of his raincoat.

"Mr Carver's been very specific about where you can go and you're limited to the pit and the chapel. Anything else and you have to ask me."

Giles brushed past, tossing back over his shoulder:

"Anything else and I'll ask Theodrakis. He can talk to you."

Theodrakis looked cold and unwell as they shook hands and Giles said, loud enough to be certain Anderson heard him:

"Vu levi sto ekklesia exi?"

It was poor Greek and probably inaccurate, but good enough to irritate the detective. Theodrakis must also have had a score to settle, he replied:

"Nai, nai, parme."

Giles ushered the other three from the minibus towards the pit and followed Theodrakis into the Davenport chapel. Passing under the lintel, Theodrakis indicated the Latin motto and asked,

"So, who's watching now? Whatever it is, I hope we don't see it."

They sat in the front pew for a time, letting their eyes get used to the light. The windows were so cobwebbed and dirty as to be virtually opaque.

"This place looks like it hasn't been used for centuries."

Theodrakis replied with a sardonic smile:

"Well, would you want to spend time in here?"

"No, not here."

"Tell me what you know about it anyway."

"From what we know it's built over an earlier chapel and there are suggestions that this spot might have been regarded as a site of significance even before that, before the Davenports. This current chapel dates back to Richard II at the end of the fourteenth century and was apparently started by a Hugo Davenport who then, for reasons we don't understand, disappears from the record leaving it to be finished by his younger brother, Edward."

Theodrakis interrupted him.

"I think I can tell you about Hugo: Steve showed me that strange letter from one of your colleagues, the one killed in Nice, about the documents he'd recovered showing that Hugo went travelling in Europe after some indiscretion and ended up on Samos."

He looked as if he was about to say more but checked himself, so Giles continued.

"The records must have got a bit mixed up because if all the things attributed to Edward are authentic then he lived to an unnaturally old age. He's also the one who had that motto carved on the chapel. It's the first mention of it, even stranger, the last authenticated documentation of Edward places him at the battle of Blore Heath during the Wars of the Roses, which must be a false attribution otherwise he'd..."

Giles paused and Theodrakis prompted him.

"Otherwise he'd what?"

"Otherwise it would make him older than a hundred."

"We saw stranger things on Samos, did we not? Remember Father John?"

"I'd rather not. Anyway, I suppose we'd better have a look at the crypt. I assume you've got the key?"

Theodrakis produced it and they made their way down an uneven flight of stairs to a solid door with iron studding. The lock was rusted and it took Giles several minutes to get the key to work, then the door swung open surprisingly smoothly and they walked through. Down there they needed torches; Giles was surprised at the size of the space they found themselves in. It was far bigger than was needed to accommodate the few tombs it contained.

"Hardly overused is it? But it's certainly older than the chapel; this must be the crypt of the earlier one. Medieval mortuary structures was my special paper at Uni, you never know when something's going to come in handy."

Giles began to examine the stone catafalques.

"Yeah, look, these are all older than the chapel: it looks like all these must have been laid down when the older chapel was in use, it's as if they stopped using the crypt when they built the current chapel. What's the point of that? Where did they bury the later dead? Where are Edmund and his successors?"

He got no answer, and when he looked round he couldn't see Theodrakis, but he could still hear him.

"Come here, to the right of the door we came through, there are more steps going further down."

Giles was excited now, there wasn't a precedent for this: a deeper layer must be either older or have been submerged to keep something hidden. He could see the light from Theodrakis's torch descending in a kind of spiral; he followed it.

Down there was a deeper shade of dark, and the air lost its fusty, churchy smell, becoming earthy with feral hints of rotting vegetation and animal. His torch traced the steps down: they were uneven, roughly fashioned, and just before he reached the bottom they petered out into a short earthen ramp. He was in a passage narrow and claustrophobic; there was no sign of any torchlight ahead: the passage must twist and turn.

He didn't like it; ever since he'd been inside the Skendleby mound he'd come to hate confined spaces. His heart was pounding. Where the hell had Theodrakis gone? There was a scratching sound, something scuttled across his feet and he jumped back in shock and revulsion, trying to regain equanimity by reminding himself that, according to urban legend, whereever you were, it was never more than ten feet from a rat.

After a few yards the wall on the right-hand side disappeared, leaving his hand scrabbling at dark space. A few feet ahead of him stood Theodrakis; they were in a large chamber where the torch beams couldn't reach the far wall.

Then he heard the sounds: Theodrakis must have heard them too as his torch beam froze in one position pointed at the ground. Giles couldn't suppress a shiver of repulsion at the things that the beam lit up: this couldn't be right, it was surreal, like stumbling into another reality. But there was no time to investigate; the sounds were getting closer. He brought up the beam of his own torch to see what was coming and it showed him only Theodrakis. The Greek indicated he should extinguish the torch and keep silent.

With both torches off, the darkness was total and choking. Giles was inhaling fear with each breath. But what were they afraid of? What did they hear coming? Standing blind with eyes useless, the ears began to compensate, detecting a rhythm to the approaching sounds: a type of dislocated shuffling underpinned by a susurration of murmurings.

So what else was moving about down there, hidden in the dark amongst the things that Giles had seen in the torch light? Then there was the crack of something breaking.

Several things happened at once: the beam of a torch cut through the darkness, and Giles dropped his; there were screams and flashes of light.

****

Viv stood at the window of her new home staring at the metro link snaking away into the cold distance. She felt vaguely guilty; she should have taken the archaeologists to Skendleby instead of sending Jimmy. But at least she'd managed to sign the papers and she was standing in an apartment that was hers: her own space. Something she could never have afforded in a half decent part of London. It felt safe and maybe here she could escape from the night terrors and dreams. Even better, the agent had thrown in several items of the showroom furniture so there wasn't much for her to buy. For a moment she fantasised about hosting some type of housewarming party, but who could she invite and, more to the point, who would want to come?

But the image of the party lingered in her head and prominent amongst the guests, in fact, the only recognisable guest, was Claire, with her silky dark hair and mesmeric eyes. Why? She'd only seen the woman once and now she'd invaded her daydreams as well as the night. There was something compelling about the woman. Viv's first thought had been seductive but, prudently, her emotional intelligence kicked in and quickly censored that. Something compelling that wormed its way into the consciousness and began to pupate. Once inside the mind it wouldn't shift and Viv found herself thinking about that brief meeting, those few words.

There had been something presumptuous and deeply inappropriate in what Claire had said to her. Honey, she'd called her honey; no one had ever called her that. Her reaction should have been either to laugh or become indignant. But she'd done neither. She'd been fascinated and the conversation had dogged her thoughts ever since. Especially the mention of special times they were going to have: that had been overtly seductive but with an undertone, somewhere deep down, of something disturbingly threatening. When Claire had been speaking everything else in the pub seemed to fade away.

Across the narrow strip of grass on the landing of the next block by the lifts, Viv caught an image out of the corner of her eye: someone in black watching her. When she turned to look fully at it all she saw was a group of crows circling in the intervening airspace. She needed to get a grip on herself, the isolation was beginning to get to her. She felt like a fish out of water here. No friends, no support system, a terrifying series of crimes which she had no idea how to solve, and a hostile organisation to work out of. She wished her dad was here, if he were she could allow herself to cry. Maybe she should have told someone in the Met how the torso in the river case had got to her, how the supernatural overtones had darkened her perception. She mentally corrected herself, rationalising supernatural to superstitious, but it didn't make her feel any better. Then, and it was almost a relief for once, her phone bleeped.

"Ma'am, I thought you'd want to know this: a body's been found near Wilmslow, the locals are attending, and they think it's related to the others."

"Ok, send a car and tell Jimmy to meet me there and to bring Colonel Theodrakis with him. Let the Chief know and make sure nothing gets out to the press."

The apartment would have to wait, she headed for the stairs keying Jimmy's number into her cell phone, then the dark figure in the next block reappeared at the window.

****

Anderson was even more relieved than Viv when the call came. He'd had enough of Skendleby and wanted to get away, having learned nothing from the few remaining staff he'd interviewed. He'd wanted to talk to Suzzie-Jade but she was shopping at the Trafford Centre and wouldn't be back till early evening. However, there was something more that made him want to be away from Skendleby, something that he didn't like to admit to himself, something long hidden deep underground where Theodrakis was now.

Anderson was lighting up round the back of the Hall when the noise started. It seemed Carver had been right about something: there was a tunnel. The crime scene people and archaeologists had almost fallen into it when the ground they were working on slipped from under them. They found themselves in a section of partially collapsed passageway. It was damp, dark and earthy with a low roof and seemed to run under the pit in the direction of the chapel. Where it started was less clear as there had been considerable land slippage between the pit and the Hall, and any passage that might have existed in that direction appeared completely blocked. Disregarding strict health and safety regulations, two female archaeologists and one of the CSI guys had crawled along it, negotiating tree roots, animal droppings, feathers and other distasteful debris choking the tunnel floor.

After a few yards, the claustrophobic dank atmosphere became increasingly threatening and they decided to turn back. Then suddenly, the lamp beam tracing the walls faded into the distance and the roof above vanished. They could stand up. Looking around they saw a large subterranean chamber and by the light of their lamps they stared in disbelief at a particularly disturbed mausoleum. From out of the dark, beyond the range of their beams, there was movement, then a pin prick of light. In the darkness they screamed:

"Jesus Christ, Giles, what are you doing here?"

The reply came from somewhere behind Giles, calm sounding, in slightly accented English.

"We got here from under the chapel so, on the assumption that you're not the recently risen dead, I suppose you must have followed a passage from beneath the pit."

Meanwhile, Giles was looking at the visible bits of the chamber. It was bigger than he'd imagined but what he saw didn't allow him to draw any logical conclusions: it was like being in a vandalised archaeological museum of the dead. He could see that his colleagues thought the same, and they didn't like what they saw. Theodrakis asked:

"Have you got a lighting system we can set up?"

"We've got a couple of arc lights in the bus."

"Ok, let's get out of here, catch our breaths and calm down. Then we'll come back for a proper look. I suggest we exit via the chapel. I imagine it's safer than your point of entrance."

A male voice, sounding shaken but relieved, answered:

"You're dead right about that: we fell through the fucking floor."

Sometime later, as Giles was inspecting the catacomb by the beam of the arc light, he wondered whether it hadn't looked better by the dim diffuse light of the torches. It made no sense, well not in an archaeological context, but there was a horrible consistency with the analysis of the bones from the pit.

It was an assemblage not from one period. Even the most cursory scrutiny revealed that the structures, artefacts and fetish objects spanned the millennia. Giles was no expert but even he could speculate that there was stuff here that predated the English Neolithic. There was no precedent and no logical reason for it, outside Skendleby that was. Even the things he'd found in the pit on Samos couldn't compare with this in terms of time span. He wished Steve were here to help him make sense of it and reassure him that he wasn't going mad because any study of this grisly nightmare would feed madness. It was like some macabre Dadaist joke.

So, like Viv and Anderson, but for different reasons, he was relieved to be interrupted when a surprised looking PC came down the passage from the chapel with a message for Theodrakis.

"Colonel Theodrakis, the DI wants you, they've found another body."

Chapter 18: Eliminated From Suspicion

The woman was either in shock or an actor who wouldn't disgrace the Royal Shakespeare Company. Viv thought she was probably genuine, despite the massively improbable level of coincidence. Either way, it wouldn't be productive to interview her yet. The vicar wasn't much better, but for a different reason. Viv sensed he was more worried about the knowledge of his whereabouts becoming known than finding the body. So not much had been got out of either of them yet except that they both had a connection with the victim.

The information from the corpse was starker. It had been cut like the others but there were preliminary suggestions that this might not have been the cause of death. The evidence of bleeding, or, more to the point, lack of bleeding, suggested that the cutting had occurred after death. The brief glimpse of sightless eyes set in the bone white face staring up out of the water suggested intense fear; maybe that had caused death, it wouldn't be the first time. Viv felt a prickle at the back of her neck and turned away shivering.

Cold water was dripping from the trees where Theodrakis and Anderson were trying to light up. Anderson said:

"It's going to take them some time to get all the crime scene stuff before they shift the body, Ma'am, so we'll have to wait a while for any real evidence from here."

"But there's a connection with this one, we have a context, it's become more of a normal case, we can look at motivation."

Theodrakis threw the wet tip of his cigarette onto the sodden earth and shook his head, before saying quietly:

"I think perhaps you're going too quickly. We can't even be sure this falls within the same range of killings. The MO isn't quite the same - this could be something different."

Viv snapped back.

"Well, it can't be a copy-cat killing; we never released details of the method."

"No, I'm not suggesting that, although your faith in our ability to keep the cutting a secret is touching. I'm not saying this isn't connected, just that it's different, maybe deliberately so. Don't you consider it a little peculiar that it was discovered by two people connected with it in life? A bit too much of a coincidence, don't you think?"

"You can't be suggesting that having them find it was part of the plan?"

"Maybe not, but I'm not ruling it out, nor am I ruling out the possibility that this one is different and maybe springs from a different source. Better to liken it to the way an outbreak of plague or a virus spreads. All we can definitely conclude from this is that the estranged husband of Margaret Trescothic can now be eliminated from our enquiries."

"That was the only lead we had, flimsy as it was."

They stood in silence for a moment before Anderson said, and she wondered if it was just to cheer her up:

"Yes, but it strengthens the connection with the women's commune. Remember, the vicar said that it was at Olga Hickman's request that they met here. She had a motive; she'd already complained about the victim, reckoned he'd been stalking the house."

"Come on, Jimmy, you can't think she's behind all this?"

"Well, she's got a criminal record for violence."

"Yes, but a long time ago and in a completely different context."

"All the same, she and the others benefit from his death. It all revolves around that house."

"I disagree, there's no connection with the attack at Skendleby Hall or last year's incidents."

Having set them going on this, Theodrakis proffered his final observation.

"Or it's all part of something bigger and far more complicated. Could be that he was involved in the earlier attacks but outlived his usefulness."

"This is getting us nowhere except wet, we'd better interview the women and wait for what forensics come up with. Let's get away from here."

As they began to move off through the dripping undergrowth, Theodrakis murmured:

"I wouldn't expect much clarity from whatever they find."

Behind them in the growing dark, dim lights flickered through the flimsy walls of the scene of crime tent, and the brook flowed cold over the latest Skendleby victim. Under the tent the sad mutilated remains of Ken Trescothic lay at the end of their journey: pale, soaked and bloodless. The mouth was contorted in a rictus grin of terror and the eyes were open, frozen in their last expression of surprise. The body was partially dressed and the rest of the clothing was scattered around, all of it ragged and filthy as if it had been worn for days by a man on the run. It was lying only yards away from the desolate spot where the Iron Age Lindow man had been unearthed. This was another who had brushed up against Skendleby's curse and died amazed, afraid and unknowing.

****

Viv saw his face change before she'd finished the sentence, morphing into an expression that indicated a far more personal fear than just receiving the breaking news of another killing. On the Chief's advice, she'd gone to speak to Jim Gibson before briefing the press in general. He'd said that Jim could be trusted to act responsibly and not to spread panic, if you were straight with him. But from the look of him it seemed that the panic had already spread: what was he so afraid of? What did he know that the police didn't? She'd have to think about this and of ways to probe him later. Meanwhile, he asked:

"You're sure it's the same as the others?"

"Well, fairly similar, we'll need all the forensics, but they'll be here soon. This takes priority."

They were sitting in Jim's office in the building the Journal shared with the local radio station and the offices of a charity. In the old days, before it became a giveaway and still made money, the paper had occupied the whole building. Through the window behind him, Viv could see the roof and tower of the neogothic town hall, where workers with a cherry picker and scaffolding were positioning a huge inflated Santa. Christmas had crept up on her by surprise.

"That's three then in quick succession and all of them linked to the area round Skendleby?"

She wondered why he'd focussed on Skendleby, only one was from there; the others had been closer to Handforth and Wilmslow. She replied:

"Well, they're all geographically close together but for us that's not the most important factor. When the name of the latest victim is released it won't take your colleagues from the nationals long to work out that there's a fairly close connection between two of the victims."

"How close?"

She wondered how far she could trust him, then took the plunge.

"This last one was on our list of considerations for committing the first of the three."

"And you're sure the Skendleby Hall one's not related?"

"We can't be completely sure about that."

"Ok, then just between us, I promise none of this will get into the paper, what have you got to work on? Because if this follows the same pattern as the attacks last Christmas, the next victims will be in the city. The attacks then stretched from the university to Skendleby."

He checked himself then added:

"Only one of those was fatal though, so these are worse. Your predecessor never really got a handle on the outbreak last Christmas. I know that despite police reassurances everything was cleared up, you've kept the case open. Now it's happening again and you've still no leads."

Viv began to protest but he raised his hands, palms open to prevent her.

"Listen, Inspector Campbell, a lot of strange things happened here last year: I caught a glimpse of them from the periphery and I was scared enough, believe me. I'll play along with whatever line the police come up with, but if this isn't stopped panic will spread and then you'll have all the world's media here."

She thought he'd finished but then, as she watched the lines of worry creasing his forehead, he added:

"Last time I got a gut feeling that there was a link between the developments that Carver is planning and what the archaeologists unearthed at Skendleby, something way more than just the planning issues. It's not the type of thing you expect from a cynical journalist, is it? But whatever it was spread like a virus from Skendleby - and you better be prepared for that this time round."

Outside, Viv noticed that it was beginning to frost up as the light faded: winter had arrived.

****

She had time to worry about his warning again as they skirted the fringe of the Skendleby Estate in the car to the house. Also, for reasons she couldn't fathom, Theodrakis had insisted on interviewing Olga Hickman with her. After work she was going to spend her first night in the new flat and there was a lot to sort out, so she hoped that the interviews would be straightforward. She'd agreed to do the questioning at the house to make things easier on the women, but now she wasn't so sure.

The door was opened by a tearful Margaret Trescothic, and the tears weren't faked: from the puffy redness of her face it was obvious that she'd been crying for hours. They were shown into the Gathering Room that Viv remembered from the previous time. Inside the room, sitting on a sofa by the window, was Olga but she'd not much time to register anything else as the occupant of a sofa on the other side of the room swept across the room and kissed her on both cheeks before she was able to prevent it.

"Seems like you're following me around, honey; should I be flattered or worried by that?"

Claire was wearing a floor length clingy black dress appropriate for visiting a coven; she radiated pleasure and confidence, looking Viv straight in the eyes and giggling. Round her neck Viv noticed a thick necklace with links of what looked like stumps of ivory from different ages. Claire must have noticed her staring.

"Don't you just love it? There's not anything like it; an heirloom or a series of heirlooms. Now it's been bequeathed to me. Seductive isn't it?"

She didn't wait for an answer, just expelled a peal of laughter before saying:

"I'd better go, things to do, people to see, you know how it is?"

She kissed Margaret and waved across the room to Olga who deliberately ignored her, causing another giggle. As she passed Viv on her way out she said beneath her breath:

"We must stop passing like ships in the night, don't you think?"

Then she was gone, leaving Viv feeling strangely aroused and the room seeming empty. Claire had made no attempt to acknowledge Theodrakis, who Viv noticed had crossed the room to sit next to Olga, while Margaret stared tearfully at the space where Claire had been.

There was no purpose in interviewing Margaret; they couldn't get anything out of her beyond a series of variations on:

"I can't believe he's gone like that, it was never meant to end this way."

And:

"If it wasn't for Claire I don't think I could hold myself together."

Neither of these constituted effective use of police time, so, after explaining the process that would have to be completed before she could identify the body and arranging to speak when she was feeling more stable, they settled on interviewing Olga.

She was surprisingly straight forward and cooperative, particularly with Theodrakis when he asked why she and Reverend Joyce had come to find the body.

"I'd asked Ed to meet there because it was away from prying eyes: rather ironic in view of the way things turned out."

Viv had conducted enough interviews to recognise when an interviewee was prepared to talk, and to whom. She motioned to Theodrakis to continue.

"Why? Why did you feel the need to meet with Joyce? Is there something bet…"

She forestalled him.

"No, there's nothing between us: well, not in any way that you'd recognise, although beneath the smarmy surface he's an attractive and sensitive man and that's some compliment coming from someone who doesn't like men much."

"So, why meet there?"

"Because, like me, he feels there's something more to this than just a series of motiveless killings. He was involved with what happened at Skendleby, you should talk to him."

"We will, but please continue."

"There's something about Skendleby that makes bad things happen, makes them recur over and over again. Ed stumbled across evidence of incidents throughout the years in his research. Let me ask you a question: what do you know about Lisa Richardson?"

Theodrakis looked blank and Viv answered for him.

"She was responsible for some of the non-fatal attacks last year and was sectioned into a psychiatric unit. For a time there was a suggestion that her activities were linked to the other attacks, but there wasn't evidence for that. Then we received the full confession for the attacks from the homeless man who later killed himself in custody."

She saw Theodrakis roll his eyes at the mention of the confession and was temporarily thrown off her stride. After a pause, Viv continued.

"After that we were able to treat her as a patient not a criminal. She'd been the victim of abuse which tipped her over the edge, but she's made a complete recovery."

Olga looked sceptical, replying:

"I hope you're right because on the recommendation of the Vanarvi women, who I notice you seem to be on such good terms with, she's about to join our community."

Theodrakis asked:

"And you don't think that's a good idea?"

"No, I think it's a very bad idea, particularly now. But I think you should look into Lisa's relationship with Claire Vanarvi."

She paused before asking:

"Or, has she cast some type of spell on you like she has over everyone else?"

Although the reply was aimed at her, Viv saw that Olga's eyes were trained on Theodrakis as she spoke; she was thinking of a response when to her surprise Theodrakis said:

"Thank you, Ms Hickman, that's all for now but we will need to see you again for a formal statement. Oh, and by the way, what happened to your hand?"

Viv saw her eyes narrow like a cat's as she stared at Theodrakis before answering:

"I hit a man. It was an act in defence of someone else. I can supply witnesses and can assure you there won't be any complaints about it."

"Not an act of defence like the one that put you in prison ten years ago I hope?"

"No, not like that."

Watching the conversation, Viv had the feeling that beneath the surface of words there was something else that she couldn't understand happening between the woman and Theodrakis. Then Olga spoke again:

"So, now that I think we can agree that I've been eliminated from your list of suspects, let me give you some advice."

She looked first at Viv.

"You need to be very careful; you can't just walk away from this: you're being sucked deeper and deeper into something you don't understand. While you…"

She shifted her gaze to Theodrakis.

"…You are in greater danger because you do understand. Or at least understand enough to make you a nuisance, but not enough to protect yourself. I can see from your eyes that you recognise what I'm saying. I don't think any of us is safe."

Chapter 19: Agents of Gramarye

The dead man's face kept appearing every time he closed his eyes; the awful gaze staring out of the pallid flesh. So Ed couldn't sleep and in the early hours he gave up trying. Since then he'd sat in the kitchen drinking tea and waiting for the dawn. At first light he pulled on his jacket and crossed the graveyard to the church. Outside it was cold with a crisp, white hoar frost. Inside the church it seemed even colder, and certainly much darker. He ignored the light switch and groped his way down to the front pew where he went down on his knees to pray. But he couldn't, it didn't always work, but at least the effort crystallised his thinking.

He was sure now. It was stirring, but had it anything to do with him this time? Maybe it was someone else's problem. He hadn't felt haunted and, apart from Carver, hadn't felt threatened. And with what was going on at the Hall, Carver must have other priorities. He hadn't been bothered by the shadowy, disarticulated presence that haunted the churchyard and estate wall the previous winter. It seemed to have been replaced by the jogging Mrs Carver who, if not much more friendly, couldn't be considered threatening.

So, his service for quieting the restless dead seemed to have worked. The mound was dormant and the crows had gone. Then he remembered he'd seen them when Olga had felled that reptile Gifford with one blow.

He sat back and stared up into the distance at the much-repaired medieval roof, indistinct in the half light. But logical thinking worked no better than the attempt at prayer had. He was agitated and restless, knew he wouldn't be able to settle to anything until he'd spoken to Olga. But it was still too early to do that: too early and maybe wrong. He should have confided in Mary. What was he getting himself into? He felt guilty and fretful about this, but it was too late now.

He decided to walk for a while then take Mary her breakfast in bed and see if he could find a way to clear all this up. He left the church and took the path that followed the estate wall, cutting across the cricket ground and circumnavigating the mound. The sun was rising through the bare winter branches to the east, the air was cold and pure and no one else was about. By the time he'd finished half the circuit he was feeling better and paused to lean against a fence to look back across the Skendleby mound at the church, his church.

The high spire covered in frost rose above the dark of the tree line, sparkling in the rays of the rising sun - even the mound seemed benign. He was aware of someone approaching him at speed and turned round to see a figure in a skintight, bright orange running suit. He recognised Carver's wife and mumbled good morning without expecting any response. So he was surprised and almost childishly gratified to receive a cheery "Hiyaa" in return as she flashed past. Perhaps the Carvers were no longer determined to persecute him.

It was quiet, no birds, and he was relieved they'd gone. It still made him shudder when he remembered how they'd swarmed over him, pecking and clawing, smothering him as their foul breath filled his nostrils. He understood now that in some way they'd been helping him, giving him strength. But he also knew that this was against their will, as he'd felt their hate and rage. He took a few deep breaths and was about to continue his circuit when his phone signalled he had a new text - "Ed, can you talk?"

It was from Olga and his heart rate rose as he pressed the button and heard her phone ringing. She answered at once.

"That was quick, Ed."

"I couldn't sleep, I'm out walking. How are you?"

"How do you think? It feels like everything's falling to pieces here. You certainly wouldn't sleep in this house. It seems like every big black bird in the universe has moved into our trees. The bloody things never shut up and they've got to your archaeologist friends, seem to be freaking them right out. But listen, I need to talk to you."

"Ok, go ahead."

"No, not on the phone, Ed, we have to meet."

"That might prove problematical, Olga."

"Fuck off, Ed, you know what's going on. We have to meet, something's really wrong, you know what I mean! Really wrong."

He knew it was, knew there was no going back, only forwards.

"Yes, of course, where would you like to meet?"

"Where the documents are. I need to talk to you and see them."

She sounded rattled, worse than him in fact.

"But they're archived in the Rylands."

"Can you access them?"

"Yes, I've a reader's card."

"Ok, I'll meet you there in about an hour."

He rapidly thought through his day's commitments.

"The best I can do is about two o'clock. I'll meet you in the cafe on the ground floor."

She hadn't seemed happy at having to wait. He felt a twinge of guilt; when he'd last seen her at the murder site in Lindow she'd been close to hysteria. This was followed by three rapidly succeeding thoughts, each worse than its predecessor. The day was colder and a drift of cloud spreading from the west was occluding the sun.

His cognition of the weather was replaced by a shard of mortification. He wouldn't be able to unburden himself to Mary now, he was going to meet Olga which meant he'd taken another step down the road of deception. His mind then leapt crazily back to Lindow. Why had she taken him there? There, to the exact spot where the body had been hidden. Who'd wanted the man dead? Who'd benefited from that death? The women in that house, the women who'd thought the victim, Margaret's embittered ex, was behind the nasty attempts to frighten them out. He tried to block out the next thought but couldn't.

Which of the women benefitted the most? He knew the answer to that. The woman who had succeeded Ken in Margaret's bed: Olga!

He began to walk quickly back to the church, trying to find something positive in all this. It wasn't easy but just as he was walking through the lych gate of his church like a miracle he was hit by a wave of hope, maybe his unformed prayer had been answered.

Claire! Claire was with the women, he could go to Claire. She would make everything right.

****

Olga was already in the cafe when he arrived, halfway through a second coffee and a large slab of Victoria sponge cake, and hard to miss. He wondered again what was he doing here but she'd seen him and was waving in his direction. He wandered between the other tables towards her, recognising in her eyes the expression of need, tinged with vague hope, that he'd seen in the faces of so many parishioners over the years. Need and hope which, in almost all cases, he'd failed to provide.

"Sorry to have dragged you all the way out here, Ed, but things are getting pretty desperate and I needed someone I could trust."

The thought that things must be going badly with Margaret struck him.

"Can I get you a coffee?"

He didn't want one but her trip to the counter would give him some time to think how he was going to play this.

"Here you are, medium Americano, no milk."

He hadn't thought of anything but it wouldn't have helped if he had because she got straight to the point and the comfortable, everyday atmosphere of the café, with its postcards, mugs and the type of stuff pedalled in any upmarket museum, shed their glamour of normality.

"Something's manipulating us; I don't think our community is what we thought it was. I think we might have been lured there to fulfil the purpose of something else."

Listening to this a year ago, Ed would have recommended a visit to the doctor and anti-depressants, but he was a different man now. All the same this seemed a bit radical. He asked:

"Olga, are you sure you're not a bit overwrought? Finding Ken in that way must have been a terrible…"

He got no further.

"Why do you think that three women terrified of Skendleby would all decide, more or less at the same time, to go and live back there? What type of logic is that? No, it's rhetorical, don't answer."

He took a sip of coffee and burnt his tongue. Through the glass walls of the cafe it looked as if it were trying to snow.

"They were contacted, invited. Rose was given details of our community when she was receiving counselling. This personal recommendation was slanted towards her needs. You know, a community of talented women who had been damaged and deprived of their just desserts by men. She was told that there was a vacancy and she should contact Margaret. She was right about that, we were looking for new residents. But how did the counsellor even know about us. When we asked Rose who had given her the recommendation she couldn't remember and, when she asked, none of the hospital staff knew anything about it. Strange, eh?"

"Strange but credible, it's quite possible tha........"

Olga snapped back:

"No, it's not! Just listen, Ed. The next was Leonie. Remember, she was the one who felt she was being stalked last winter; she was scared out of her head. For a time it seemed she'd gone missing. They don't even have her address at the unit. Then one day she gets a brochure advertising our community. She's still got it. But there never was a brochure for the house. Why would we need one? We haven't the heart to tell her. At first she's suspicious, but then she finds a recommendation from an anonymous friend left on her desk. It says the house is safe and spiritual and gives Margaret's telephone number. Once she speaks to Margaret of course, she's sold on the place."

"The brochure's odd, but the note will have been from Rose, surely?"

"That's what we thought, but it wasn't. Rose never wrote it and once you know Rose and what a selfish manipulative cow she is you understand that she'd never want to share the peace of our little family with anyone else. And then there's Jan, the one you know best, such a sweet girl."

Ed thought that if he'd described Jan that way it would have seemed sexist, but as a description from Olga it was just right.

"The way Jan was sourced was the cruellest of the three. She was badly broken up by a love affair with another archaeologist, a real bastard: Steve."

Ed flinched at this description but kept silent.

"This creep had run off to Greece to escape his responsibilities and somehow seems to have disappeared off the face of the earth. Then, out of the blue, a letter arrives with a Greek postmark but no address. It says she's in danger but there's a safe haven where she'll be looked after. Suggests that she contacts Leonie. Leonie recommends it so she contacts us.

"Jenna, Ailsa and I all said no, the house is turning into club for distressed female archaeologists, and of course Rose is dead against it for other reasons. But it's just after Kelly's death and Margaret is too kind hearted, so we take her in. To be fair, she's a good addition, exactly the type of creative, caring woman we need. Now, Ed, tell me, do you consider all that put together as credible?"

He'd no satisfactory answer to that and what Olga said next floored him.

"And now they've settled in, our mutual friend Claire gathers them together, away from the rest of us, and suggests that, as they're archaeologists, they might be interested in exploring the house's past, starting with what may be under the cellar floors. Says it would be a healing project for our community and could turn up something auspicious. What do you make of that?"

He didn't know what to make of it and Olga gave up waiting for an answer and changed tack.

"Why do you think all those birds have moved to the house?"

He thought he knew the answer to that one but decided it was too undiplomatic to articulate that he believed they were condemned to follow the source of the contamination. By the time he'd thought of an answer she'd moved on again.

"Ok, can't put this off any longer, I need to see these last Dee papers you've found."

"Do you think that's wise, you seemed distressed enough as it is?"

She gave him a long look, it seemed affectionate, and answered:

"I can't really explain why but I need to see them because....."

She faltered, he gave her time.

"Because I think that my name being the same as the skryer Dee didn't trust, and who was operating in the vicinity of our community, is more than a coincidence, and I think - no that's not right - more like I feel I'll recognise something in them."

"Recognise what?"

"I don't know, Ed, but I'll know it when I find it."

He took her into the library and installed her in one of the book lined alcoves on the mezzanine at an aged table of dark wood, then went to collect the papers from the archive desk. Once he'd delivered them he wondered if he should stay but she thanked him and waved him away. Outside the light was fading and fog threatened; it was cold and he set off at a brisk pace for the car park. Somewhere above him in the roof line he thought he heard a bird calling and he suddenly thought: what if the birds left the mound, not because it's safe, but because we got it wrong and failed? It's moved on, it's still out there and it's growing stronger.

****

She knew it when she saw it alright; it took away her breath. She felt blind panic building somewhere inside, wished she'd asked Ed to stay. She hadn't felt this bad since her first night in prison. Automatically she switched onto the self control exercises she'd learnt back then. They took some time to work but when they had she'd decided what to do. She'd keep this to herself until she knew how to use it. With an effort of willpower she reopened the book and forced herself to copy out the passage that had shaken her up so badly. By the time she finished she felt drained and unclean, could feel sweat trickling down her back and under her armpits.

She couldn't stay here. The library felt empty, the silence threatening. She thought she could detect a flickering and dimming of the lights. She couldn't bring herself to touch the manuscript and return it, so instead gathered her things and got out of there as quick as she could leaving it on the desk. It was only when she'd got outside that she realised what a mistake that had been. After thinking on this for a while she threw down her cigarette butt and forced herself to go back in. She was sure that the place was darker now but she could see the light from her workspace dimly flickering and headed for it.

The table was bare and the surface was dusty, that was odd. She looked under it, nothing there. Maybe this wasn't her desk. She checked the others, nothing. They must have found it and put it back. She went back downstairs and almost bumped into what she took to be a librarian: an oldish, thin man in black wearing some kind of hat with its brim pulled down, shadowing his face.

"Excuse me, have you taken some papers from a second floor table?"

"No."

"Well maybe one of your colleagues?"

"No, there's been no one in here."

He paused and she felt that he was amused at something. She could only discern the bottom half of his face, in this light it looked grey.

"No, there hasn't been anyone here at all, save you and me. I was coming to tell you we're closed and you have to go."

There was something so unpalatable about the man that she forgot about the papers; just wanted to get out to the street and breathe untainted air. For a second time she found herself lighting up outside the plate glass doors of the cafe foyer that clashed so badly with the neogothic of the library itself. Then a thought wriggled into her consciousness. Chethams College, where Dee had been master, was only a short walk away from here. On an impulse she set off through the murky light towards it.

The area to the far side of the cathedral wasn't a place she visited often. Largely because Victoria station, which lay behind it, had been her original gateway into Manchester and she didn't care to be reminded of those times. Once she'd passed through the late medieval buildings which the planners had relocated to make room for the Arndale Centre at the end of the 1960s, she recognised another reason for not wanting to be here.

This was a strange few acres of ground. Something about it seemed out of joint, something which the spreading fog did little to alleviate. It was a peculiar mix in what, with the exception of the Roman fort, was the oldest part of the city. In this medieval core, ancient buildings, new buildings and patches of waste ground awaiting development, co-existed cheek by jowl.

The waste ground, particularly that abutting the station, was feral and unwelcoming, lying like the ghost of Manchester past. Hovering in the midst of this lay the old

Manchester College, presided over by Dr John Dee, reputedly Queen Elisabeth the first's necromancer. It came to Olga that the custodian in the library she'd questioned resembled the portrait of Dee on the cover of a book she owned.

She turned her attention to Chethams now, a respected but troubled school of music, and stood facing it aware of the desolation of the wasteland and the lack of lighting in the civic buildings. The new football museum was just a stone's throw away, but in this light it may as well have well been in another universe.

It was beginning to freeze as she cautiously picked her way through the murk towards the Chethams buildings, then she stood for a moment staring at the blacked out windows. It was unnaturally quiet here, no sound, not even from the station. Dee had hated it here; hated it for several reasons: its distance from London and the court, and its lack of society. It had marked the end of his ambitions. But most of all, according to what she'd just read, he hated it because it precipitated him into what was happening at Skendleby.

There was a scuttling sound behind like rats in a cellar. Olga turned her head and saw something indistinct growing out of the fog. As it drew nearer she knew it mustn't catch her. It had lured her here and now it would harvest her. She turned and ran. At this stage, logic was still guiding her actions so she headed for Urbis and the football museum, there'd be other people there. But it realised this and moved to cut her off. It moved in a strange irregular way, but quickly, much more quickly than she could, even though it barely seemed to be trying. She changed direction; maybe she could reach Market Street. But she couldn't so she swerved to the left and felt something skitter across her shoulder. It had never been in her nature to scream for help but she did now, only to hear the noise evaporate weakly into the fog.

It was toying with her, driving her where it wanted her. She was running faster, her breath drawn in agonising gasps; she couldn't last long. Every way she ran it was there before her - until she found herself in the filthy alley, Blackpool Fold.

How'd she got here? But she was spent, couldn't go another step. She leaned against the wall and tried to suck in gulps of air. Behind her something reached out almost tenderly for her neck. The touch was imperceptible at first but then she felt it, softly leprous, a mix of hair and skin and rotten fruit. The jolt of repulsion sent a last course of energy through her, enough to send her crashing into something solid and throw her senseless to the ground.

Chapter 20: Makes no Sense

It wasn't as quiet as she'd expected. She'd wondered how it would feel to be the only resident in a large empty block. It wasn't anything like she'd imagined. There was an unsettling amount of background noise rather than the silence she'd anticipated. Not road noise, nor from the metro line. The noise was internal, came from the apartments themselves: the empty apartments. It was ceaseless, a mixture of creaks and scratches underpinned by a strange, unsettling and continuous chattering. There was probably an explanation in the laws of physics but she couldn't think of it. So going to bed early had proved a pyrrhic exercise, a deeply frustrating one as now, in the small hours, having first been unnerved by it then frustrated, she was fully awake.

Awake, isolated and lonely. It had been her birthday and the first she'd spent away from her family. They'd rung and texted but it wasn't the same. She hadn't even any friends up here and no one had seemed to know about it at work. However, at one point, when she was walking back from the upmarket deli with the ingredients for her evening meal, she thought she'd seen Jimmy across the road. For an instant she'd wondered if he knew about it and was bringing her a card or something. But when she looked again he wasn't there and it would have been inappropriate and embarrassing anyway.

The noises ceased as if someone had suddenly flicked a switch. The silence that followed was worse as she lay in the dark waiting for them to recommence. Her mind was racing. Knowing that sleep was now beyond her she got up and shuffled in her PJs and fluffy slippers to the unfamiliar kitchen to make a pot of tea.

Sitting sipping at the mug, she thought of her friends and family in London. She was missing them. She thought about her failed relationship and the lack of intimacy in her life. It wasn't the sex, although she did miss that, more the companionship and contact, having someone to talk to. Social messaging: Facebook, Skype, just didn't do it.

Maybe she wasn't cut out for this job. Maybe she should have told her bosses in the Met how much the last case had got to her and that up here alone she was leaching confidence. Then the noises started again. After the silence it was almost a relief. She went back to bed, pulled the duvet over her head and eventually drifted uneasily into a restless doze.

The noise followed her into whatever level of sleep she attained. One sound in particular was cutting through the others, and she tried to claw her way back to the surface to deal with it. Gradually, as she pulled up through the levels of sleep, she recognised the tones of her mobile. Saw the time; shit, she'd overslept. But when she managed to answer the phone what she was told pushed everything else to the back of her mind.

Twenty minutes later she rushed into the incident room hoping no one would notice that she was wearing the same clothes as yesterday. She hadn't had time to look out anything else, or shower for that matter, hence the lavish application of body spray. She was relieved to see that Anderson didn't look any better. The performance indicators of a heavy night were all over him. He handed her a coffee and they sat down to hear what twists and turns the case was about to make as a consequence of the evidence gleaned from the body of Ken Trescothic.

The unappealing pathologist took a long time to begin, and Viv thought she was milking the moment to maximise her importance. She looked round the table at her team, trying to see from their faces if they respected her. It wasn't a conclusive survey either way, and most of them looked tired and anxious with no trace of the gallows humour usually employed to lighten the evidence of such grotesque and savage atrocities.

She understood why the humour had vanished: this was the second time round for most of them. The first time they'd thought they'd cracked it, now they knew they hadn't. All they had left were the known, and increasingly, unknown knowns of this case and they, like Viv, were expecting further confusion from what they were about to learn. She suspected they'd blame her for this as after all, she was the wonder kid brought up from the capital to show the local wooden tops how it should be done. They needed leadership but she felt too dislocated to lead.

With a clearing of the throat that brought everyone to attention, the forensic feedback kicked off.

"Just for starters, and I'm not sure how helpful this is going be, one of the outcomes from the autopsy and lab tests strongly suggests that Ken Trescothic was the killer of the girl murdered at Skendleby Hall: the DNA found on her is a direct match with his."

She paused for effect and in the silence the implications of this hit Viv like a blow to the solar plexus. She heard herself blurt out:

"But…"

The pathologist favoured her with a wintery smile before saying smugly:

"Yes, inconvenient, isn't it?"

It was more than inconvenient. Viv looked round at the faces of her team, registering their disbelief and disappointment. She filled the silence by stating the obvious.

"And Ken Trescothic has a rock solid alibi confirmed by prima facie evidence for the murder of Kelly Ellsworth. So we have at least two killers, and possibly three."

To stop the murmurs and swearing round the table she ploughed on.

"I know, I know, it's disappointing."

Anderson broke in.

"It's more than disappointing, we've nothing now. No leads, nothing. Just more information that makes no bloody sense."

Grasping at straws, Viv asked:

"What about the DNA found on Trescothic?"

The pathologist smiled, she was enjoying her moment, and replied:

"There wasn't any found; in that respect the killing is analogous with the murder of the first victim, Kelly Ellsworth."

"So, are you suggesting that the killer of Kelly and Trescothic could have been the same person?"

"No, all I'm saying is there's no DNA evidence on either of those bodies, whereas Trescothic's was all over the Hungarian girl. There may be leads in the similarities of the method of killing in the three cases, but even there we found ambiguities. Perhaps it would be best if I gave you the full picture."

She did and it made things even less clear, as Viv found when she tried to explain the findings to the Chief later. She could tell by his face that he already knew the news was bad, and there were no tea and biscuits this time.

"This one makes everything harder. From the condition of him, the contents of his stomach and the state of his clothing, it would appear he'd been on the run and living rough for a period of days. There are no sightings of him or records of contact for three days prior to his death."

"And what are we supposed to deduce from that?"

"I don't know, Sir, but it's almost certain that he died of shock or fright, his body was moved to the scene after his death and the cutting was done somewhere else."

"Was he cut before he died?"

"No, that's another way this one's different."

"Does that mean something went wrong, or that whoever's doing this is changing the ritual?"

"We don't know: maybe they don't need the bones so much, maybe they've got all they need, or maybe he just died of fright before they got started."

"You keep saying they. Do you think we're looking for more than one person? No one could be mad enough to collaborate with this."

"I know, but for some of the things done to the two women, who were alive when they were cut, the killer would have to have superhuman strength."

"What about a cult? There has always been a smattering of Satanists and the like in the vicinity of the Edge."

"But have they ever got up to anything like this? I thought with them it was all role play left over from the hippy craze for Aleister Crowley."

"So, what have you got from this?"

"Nothing, just confusion. The cutting is different in each case and forensics can't rule out that it could mean three different killers."

"All possessed of superhuman strength? Bloody marvellous."

"I think so, Sir. Look, maybe you need someone else to take this case. I'm not sure I'm really up to it. Don't you need someone with greater experience?"

"That's meant to be you, that is, that's why you're here. We don't have a special magic branch as far as I'm aware and excepting the unlikely event of Harry Potter having recently joined the force we're not likely to get one. Anyway, Viv, you know how difficult it'd be to remove you considering the high visibility of your profile. Besides, I've confidence in you."

They sat glumly in silence for a while. Outside, through the frosted glass, it was growing dark. Then the Chief made an effort to move things on.

"And you've got bloody Zorba, he's dealt with a case like this, he must be able to help, you know, take some of the pressure off."

She didn't want to go there. Her last experience of Theodrakis had been enough and she couldn't get his contribution to the forensic session out of her head. He'd sat at the back at the far end of the table, wearing a retro style raincoat unbuttoned over an elegant suite. He reminded her of a character out of a Renoir film from the 1940s, which had been briefly fashionable when she'd been a student. He'd said nothing until the end when she was closing the session down. Then, out of the blue:

"There is one sense, of course, in which this analysis can help us make progress."

Every face, even the pathologist's, turned to stare at him and Viv bit back on the sarcastic comment she had been about to hurl in his direction.

"Perhaps it would be useful to look beyond the evidence which is, of course, contradictory, and concentrate on the intelligence. As Matisse said in a different context, 'when dealing with a convergence of forces a large part is down to the mysterious workings of instinct.'"

Now she couldn't hold the sarcasm back.

"So what does the workings of your mysterious instinct infer from this, Colonel? That we visit the local art gallery?"

"No, although that would probably prove as useful as some of our current activities. I suggest we look at this from a different perspective, that we try to imagine three physical agents of the killing, but only one mind and one purpose playing a very long game."

Viv had closed the meeting down at that point and gone to render her report to the Chief, but the words stuck in her mind. There was something way beyond the a priori about this case, a type of metaphysical mist clouding their vision.

When she got back to the incident room most of the team were still there. Anderson approached, took her to one side and whispered:

"I think it would be a good idea to take them out for a drink, Ma'am."

"That's not my style, Jimmy, you know that."

"Even so, it would be a good idea, morale's not good and you could treat it as a bonding exercise."

"Well, why don't you take them?"

"Because it's not me who needs to bond with them."

She could see from his eyes how serious he was; he was going out of his way to be helpful and besides, what else did she have to do. She called out:

"Ok, it's been a hard day; let me buy you all a drink."

They walked, minus Theodrakis, in a crocodile through the dark of the rush hour to a pub behind the town hall, their way illuminated by the Christmas lights; an incongruous backdrop to their morbid quest. The pub was typical of the faux-traditional modern anachronistic movement that had dominated inner city style over the past couple of decades and was accepted as the norm by punters who probably never knew the far less comfortable original.

It was crowded with a mixture of city types relaxing after a day in the office, and some hard looking specimens whose activities probably never troubled the tax system. Some of the latter obviously recognised them as cops and eased away from the centre of the room to hover at the periphery, making space for Viv and Anderson to make their way to the massive slab of mahogany that comprised the imitation nineteenth century bar. The price of the round of drinks surprised her and, after a few minutes standing in a circle at the bar, they drifted into groups at the few tables where there were seats available. Soon, except for Jimmy, she was alone at the bar, lost in a swirl of captains of commerce and criminals.

"Well, so much for your theory of team building, Sergeant."

It sounded much harsher than she'd intended and she was relieved when he appeared to ignore, it saying only:

"Look, there's a couple of stools over there come vacant."

She followed him across to a small alcove with a high table flanked by two tall bar stools. They sat opposite each other, leaning forwards, elbows resting on the wood and chrome surface. It occurred to her that they probably looked like a couple, and it made her desperately sad. This is probably why she said out of nowhere:

"It was my birthday yesterday."

"Happy Birthday for yesterday then, Ma'am, did you do anything nice?"

"Nothing."

She felt she was on the point of tears sitting in this horrible pub buying drinks for people who couldn't wait to get away from her, in a job she couldn't handle, in a place she didn't have a single friend.

"Do you want to talk about it?"

His question surprised her. Obviously the mask she wore professionally wasn't as effective as she thought. She blurted out:

"What?"

"Whatever it is that's making you so unhappy. The case, Zorba, the team, Manchester. I don't know where to stop."

"No, I don't. In fact, I don't want to talk at all, so why don't you tell me about yourself?"

He talked; she picked up bits and let the rest flow over her. After his progression from a second class degree at a second rate university, the rest got lost in the fog. But she started to feel better and two drinks later found that she'd begun to drip feed bits about herself in reply.

Three large white wines were beyond her drinking capacity, she usually stopped after the one she had to be sociable. The crowd in the pub had thinned out and her team had long since departed, thanking her as they drifted out into the night companionably in dribs and drabs. She was feeling light headed and beginning to wonder how she'd get back to her lonely, but strangely noisy, apartment. Jimmy sorted that out: they'd share a taxi which would drop her off on the way.

On the way back she tried to focus on his face as he recounted some anecdote about her predecessor; it was quite a nice face really. Then they were outside the sterile apartment block where she would re-enter solitary confinement. He was reaching across her to open the cab door when she heard herself say:

"Do you want to come in?"

Chapter 21: From What Universe Does This Stuff Come ?

"You obviously acquired a taste for Greek food over the summer?"

Jim was sitting with Giles by the restaurant's floor-to-ceiling plate glass window, looking out into the early evening Manchester murk at the rear of the town hall.

"Yeah, suppose I did, and this one's easily the best. Good peasant cooking. Oh, and this is on me, Jim. Can't remember when I last paid."

Jim couldn't remember when he'd last paid, either or even if he'd ever paid, and he intended to make the most of it. He'd set this very late lunch or early dinner and expected to pay, which was fair enough as he intended to pump as much information out of Giles as he could, so for the moment he was prepared to let Giles rattle on about his new enthusiasm.

"It's a family run place and an offshoot from the original, smaller one in Stockport. Let me order for us both. Listen, what's really good is revithia for a starter then the rosto with salad. They serve the salad on the plate with it. No upmarket place would do that, but it tastes good so we'll go along with it. Oh, and they do a brilliant red from Nemea at a great price, so we'll have that with it, Ok?"

Seemed fine to Jim who just nodded. By the time the rosto arrived they'd exhausted the small talk. Outside it was as good as dark now and Jim knew he couldn't delay asking the question he'd been avoiding since they'd arrived, but Giles got there first.

"You're going to ruin all this and use the S word aren't you?"

"Skendleby? Yes, how did you know?"

"It's all over your face. You know, the way people who've been contaminated look when the place is mentioned. Why? You got away relatively unscathed last time, why not stay away?"

"Can't, I'd like to but I can't, I have to report what happens, I can't delegate this to anyone else."

Jim paused and took a slug of the heavy dark wine as if to strengthen himself.

"I'm working with the police, whatever they say, they've no idea what's going on. It's all happening again, isn't it?"

"I don't think it ever stopped. I can't escape, but you have: don't go back."

"Tell me what's happening, Giles. What did you find under the chapel?"

"Jim, last time you said…"

"I know what I said last time but things change. Please, Giles, tell me what new horrors you've raked up."

The waiter brought across another bottle. Jim hadn't noticed Giles order it but he wasn't going to refuse.

"Why always me? Why does everyone think this is somehow my fault?"

"Because things happen to you, Giles."

Giles leant over his plate and began to shovel down forkfuls of the tender, slow-cooked lamb. Jim watched and waited until Giles surfaced for air, then asked again:

"Giles, what did you find under there?"

Giles refilled both glasses from the new bottle.

"I've tried to warn you off this, Jim, so don't come crying back to me when it all turns bad for you like last time."

Jim realised he'd hit a raw nerve but sat sipping his wine hoping Giles would open up. He didn't have long to wait. Giles finished his wine, poured another glass, then said wearily:

"I'm out of my depth, Jim. I don't understand what's happening with the archaeology or with my life. You know the police locked me up for a time, said I was a suspect. All I was trying to do was help but that bitch running the case tricked me into saying things then deliberately misinterpreted them. If it hadn't been for Claire I think I'd have gone under these last weeks. Now even she's showing signs of strain."

Jim didn't want the personal stuff, he wanted the story. He asked:

"If you're out of your depth with the evidence why not contact Steve, he could h…"

Giles cut him off.

"No one's going to be getting in touch with Steve, certainly not me and I'm one of the only two people who know where he is."

He added almost beneath his breath,

"The only two people who can properly be considered as alive, that is."

They sat in silence; there was no one else eating. Their table, with its candles, was like the last inhabited island in the dark sea of the taverna. Outside, in the night, streets were being slowly smothered by creeping tendrils of fog.

"I don't know where to start, Jim, before I even touch on what's under the chapel let me tell you about the timescale. There's a stratigraphy down there, Jim! Do you know what that means?"

"Of course, it means you've got layers of things building up on top of each other. That's common enough, isn't it?"

"On occupation sites, yeah, but this is a chamber under a chapel, a type of big, underground hole. No one ever lived there; the place is only about death and what comes after."

"Ok, I see."

"No, you don't see, Jim. You've no fucking idea. I don't see and I've been down there in the middle of all this weird shit for days. So just stay quiet and listen."

Jim kept quiet and watched Giles take a slurp of wine, too much to swallow it seemed as some dribbled out of his mouth and down his chin onto his shirt. He dabbed at it absentmindedly with his food-stained paper napkin before finishing the glass and starting again.

"There's stuff in there which, if it's not a hoax, dates the early phases of that assemblage way back before the Great Interglacial to a time after which Britain was deserted for a hundred thousand years."

"But that's impossible, surely?"

"There's a piece of bone in there which the bone expert at the uni thinks might be from the shin of a Homo heidelbergensis - that would make it about five hundred thousand years old. So yes, it's impossible. It's impossible because what we recognise as Skendleby wasn't even there back then. Since then ice sheets a mile thick rolled over whatever was there then and tore and ground it up into what it is now. See the difficulty, Jim?"

Jim nodded. It was obviously all that was required of him because Giles swept on.

"Then there's the incredible amount of material down there: it's like the ground zero of every cult and fetish on the archaeological record. It's packed with stuff from all over, since the time when Europe was first inhabited, plus some from before that. Very interesting and not in a good way.

"It'll take months to sort it all out, but here's a taste of what we have found. There are stone heads with the eyes scored out and real skulls overlaid with painted plaster faces that have been deliberately smashed. There's even a tree buried upside down like it's meant to be growing down into the earth. There are complete burials, evidence of sacrifices and human bones butchered for eating. That enough for you?"

"There's more?"

"Oh yeah, there's more, plenty more. Listen, you'll appreciate this bit: remember the crows?"

"Crows?"

"Yeah, the ones all over Skendleby before we opened it."

Jim remembered them all right, sometimes he dreamt about them. Giles must have seen the look on his face because he favoured him with a sour smile, belched softly, then said:

"Well, the place is full of their bones; they're in every level like they're some sort of old favourite. There's even a small figurine of a woman's head with a crow coming out of it. Then there's bulls' heads in piles, weird antler tools. We don't even know what some of this stuff is, never mind its provenance or what it means."

"So it must be a hoax."

"If it is, it's one that's been kept up through the millennia because some of these things are in a dateable context. I think we can safely assume that it's beyond the expertise of Carver and it seems that since the end of the sixteenth century, the Davenports have kept it shut down and buried."

Giles let out a loud exhalation of breath, drained his glass, then said:

"Jim, we've been sorting through a stratigraphy of the impossible. There are artefacts we can date, and each level was hidden and kept separate from the others. So we've got some type of sequence. It'll take years to sort it all out. I mean, what kept bringing people here and making them do all this 'Blair Witch' stuff?"

"So, what's your best guess?"

Jim had to wait for an answer: the waiter materialised with two glasses of a clear spirit and exchanged a few words with Giles, which Jim supposed must in be Greek.

"It's raki, good stuff too, on the house."

Giles threw his back in one gulp and stared out at the night. Jim had to coax him.

"Go on, what do you think?"

"Think? Don't really know, it's hard to rationalise some of it. The nearest I can get is that it might have been intended as a protection or antidote to whatever lurks in Skendleby. And whatever it is, it predates the mound we excavated last year. Some of this stuff predates that by hundreds of thousands of years. But we can be pretty certain that whatever creatures laid all that stuff down over the years were pretty desperate."

"So what does this give the police?"

"Nothing, there's nothing. I doubt that there's anything later than the seventeenth century. So they won't be pleased. I won't know for sure until all the bones have been sorted through and obviously their people get first dibs on that. I'm quite sure though that they'll find some pretty close parallels with the cutting of the murder victims."

"What cutting? How do you know that?"

"A bit from Skendleby last year and the rest from what I saw on Samos."

Jim couldn't think of anything else to ask: he'd drunk too much and Giles was drunk. So they sat opposite each other, avoiding eye contact, lost in alcohol-fuelled reverie. After a time, which Jim couldn't gauge, Giles suddenly said:

"As archaeology, nothing about this makes any sort of sense. So it must be the place, somewhere that drags people to it over the millennia to perform these bloody rituals and practise magic. I don't understand any of it, it's not archaeology. I mean, what bloody universe does all this stuff come from? It's like it's both real and impossible at the same time."

Jim thought Giles was talked out, but then, as if dragging something up from the depths of his memory, he mumbled to himself.

"You know, while I was on Samos, Theodrakis interviewed this guy, Vassilis or something, and this guy really freaked him, told him that we miss most of the things that are right in front of us and that most of the stuff we do see is illusion. You know, like multiple universes and all that quantum crap."

He'd started to ramble. Jim was surprised. He'd seen Giles put away far more booze and manage to remain lucid. He was also beginning to think that with Giles in this state he would end up having to foot the bill. He gestured to the waiter that they wanted to pay and turned back to Giles to get him moving.

"Come on, Giles, we need to..."

There was a tremendous crash, something smashed into the window. The glass held and the considerable thing that hit it bounced off. Someone was screaming: Jim scrambled to his feet and headed for the door. Outside, a large, fair-haired woman was lying sprawled on the pavement, her skirt round her hips and her coat open. There was blood on her face and it was seeping from her nose. Her head hung off the pavement over the road at a worryingly oblique angle.

A small knot of spectators had gathered, none of whom looked as if they were in a hurry to do anything helpful. Jim went down on one knee to examine the woman's head and check for a pulse. He was aware of Giles and the waiter behind him. To his surprise, as he touched her, the woman opened her eyes and gasped:

"Where is it? Has it gone?"

Her eyes were wild and it was clear to Jim that she was in a state of shock and terrified.

"No, don't worry, you're going to be all right, help is on its way, just keep still."

"Where is it? Has it gone?"

"No, listen, you've had a nasty shock, you must have walked into the window in the fog."

But he could hardly believe that just walking into a window could cause that much damage. Also, it was clear that she'd been running. A woman standing watching with a clutch of shopping bags said:

"She just came running out of that passage like a wild thing, then turned and hit the glass."

He heard someone else say:

"I called an ambulance, innit."

Jim wondered if they should leave her until medical help arrived, or get her up off the cold hard ground. The waiter was trying to lift her.

"Come on, you, help, we carry her inside, is warm in there, out here she freeze."

Jim was glad someone else had taken responsibility and it wasn't down to him anymore. With Giles's help they carried her into the restaurant and onto the sofa by the bar. As they lowered her onto the cheap fake leather surface she took Jim's hand.

"Has it gone?"

She was obviously concussed so there was no point in reasoning.

"Yes, it's gone. You need to stay still and rest. You must be very careful, don't move until we're sure there's nothing broken."

She didn't seem too reassured and made a move as if to get up. Then there were other people behind Jim. He turned and saw that it was a couple of paramedics. While one of them crouched down by the woman, the other one lectured Jim about having moved the patient and health and safety in general. Over at the bar he could see Giles and the waiter drinking raki.

After what seemed an age they got her on to a stretcher, even though by now she was asserting she could walk and wanted to go home. This was refused and, as she was being taken outside, where light snow was starting to fall, Jim, relieved he had no further serious role to play, asked her if there was anyone he could contact.

"Yes, warn him. It'll come after him now, you need to warn him."

"Warn who?"

"Warn Ed. Warn Ed Joyce."

Chapter 22: Master of the House

The phone was still ringing: why hadn't one of them Polish sluts answered it? Then he remembered they'd gone back home and their British replacements, Tegan and Jay-Jai wouldn't be here till midday: they were sleeping off their early hours' efforts entertaining the punters at one of his 'Elite Nite Club' venues. He'd have to fix that and get some more live-in staff.

The phone still rang, couldn't be interesting, all important calls came to one of his mobiles. The ringing stopped at last; then bloody well started again. The two bouncers who, since the upsets, tended to stay with him weren't sufficiently skilled to answer it properly so had been told not to, and that lazy cow he'd married must be out - no change there then.

Not that he was bothered about that particularly, he preferred it when she was somewhere else, even if she was wasting more of his money. Still, he supposed she had to look the part. He walked a few feet across the room and picked up the handset.

"Yeah, Si Carver, what do you want?"

There was an old, poncy voice he thought he recognised but couldn't place on the other end, but he wasn't left wondering long.

"Carver? It's Davenport, I've details with which I need to acquaint you."

"Too fucking late to try and apologise now, my lawyers have already been instructed."

"Don't be ridiculous, man, I'm not apologising to you for anything, but I am trying to do you a good turn, which, believe me, it would be a grave error to refuse."

Si Carver realised if he didn't reply Davenport would ring off. He couldn't make up his mind whether to answer and show weakness or not listen to what might be useful. But it was possible Davenport might be able to help alleviate what this house was doing to him.

"Alright, but you betta make it quick, I'm a busy man."

For a moment there was a silence at the other end as if Davenport found this transaction as distasteful as Si did, then:

"I won't pretend that I have any time for you or what you stand for, Carver, but I feel that in some ways I haven't behaved the way I should have."

"I already told you, it's too late to apologise."

"We don't apologise to your type, Carver. Now are you going to listen or not?"

Davenport must have assumed that silence indicated assent and he commenced spelling out his warning.

"We left you with a legacy. A legacy we should, or rather I, should have informed you of. I think some of the events you now experience are a direct consequence of that legacy."

"Yeah, and how you going to help with that, then? With the police and the murder and what they found under the chapel?"

Si could tell that the mention of what was under the chapel was unexpected and had thrown Davenport for the moment.

"Didn't know about that then? Not so bleedin clever now, are you, eh?"

"No, I wasn't aware of that but it just serves to make what I tell you of greater import. Listen carefully, there are things in that house, things on that land, that you need to leave alone. Things that have been there for longer than people have, things that don't like being disturbed."

"So, why didn't you do something about it then?"

"We did. We tried for centuries without success. There is only one thing that you can do to quieten them and even that only works some of the time. But these things occur in periodic episodes, you have to get through the episode then it quietens down."

Carver was torn between a horrified need to know more and anger. For the moment, fear held the upper hand.

"Go on then, tell me what I should do."

"Nothing, do nothing, it's the only option you have."

"Nothing, just let it happen? So what about me improvements then?"

"Particularly the improvements. You're stirring things up that you don't understand, things that can…"

But Si had got what Davenport's game was now, and he was going to pay for it.

"Same old game then, this is just to stop me and the development, innit? I got you're measure now, all this bollocks is about that. Well, let me fucking tell you…"

But he got no chance, Davenport rung off and left him hanging. He was sweating, what was wrong with him? This wasn't how he was, he was a winner. He crossed over to the bar and poured himself a drink. He reckoned Davenport had been right about one thing though, and that was the land, well one particular piece of land anyhow: the Skendleby mound.

He needed to deal with that, not the way Davenport meant neither, he needed it levelled. Then it occurred to him that maybe the tunnel to the chapel came from under the mound, not the church. He knew this made no sense but it lodged in his brain. If he levelled the mound, knocked down the chapel then sealed the pit up under concrete, maybe things would get better.

He phoned Jed Gifford's mobile number and after a couple of bleeps the builder answered. He sounded different somehow but emotional intelligence wasn't one of Si's strong points so he ignored it.

"Gifford, I'm giving you one last chance, yeah? You get yourself into that fucking bulldozer and you level that mound. Don't take no one with you this time neither."

Gifford started to whine about something but Si wasn't having any of it.

"No fuck ups this time, last warning, right?"

This time Si rang off. Game over. He flopped onto the sofa and turned up the sound to Sky Sports' boxing coverage. It was the adverts and Ray Winstone was advertising a betting company. He liked Ray, a proper geezer, someone he'd like to have a drink with. He needed another drink, it would help to stop him shaking. Threatening Gifford hadn't helped and he usually enjoyed that.

His mouth tasted foul and he had this constant pain in his gut. It had been there for weeks and stopped him working out. He was putting on weight, getting flabby. He was proud of his body, he built it up with weights: massive biceps, pecs and shoulders, and almost a six pack. He liked looking at himself in the mirror at the gym. Shaven-headed and bulky, a real hard man, that's what he was, a winner.

He liked the other punters in the gym to watch him pump iron, and if he thought that they weren't watching he'd make that loud grunt that pro lifters make to demonstrate the weight of what they are lifting. He liked parking his motor on the double yellows right outside the terrace of restaurants like Pissarro's and Edge Road, where the footballers went. See the ordinary punters staring at him cos he could do what he liked and they had to follow the loser's rules. That showed class that did: he was well respected.

He couldn't concentrate on the boxing; he'd seen the fight before and his mind drifted onto the planning permission for the development. The funding package was there and he'd had his lawyers look into the loopholes that would let him vary the use once the project started. Maybe, when it was all sorted and he'd got the money he needed to cover his problems, he'd move. Maybe somewhere hot by the sea, he deserved it - leave all this behind - Florida or Dubai, somewhere like that, on one of them golfing villages.

Trouble was, there were still glitches with the permission. He'd had to waste money on the wrong people and the ones he threatened didn't have power to make decisions. He blamed Richardson for most of the problems. This brought his reverie up short. He shouldn't have thought of Richardson. He knew where that could lead.

Back when Richardson topped himself, Si thought maybe it was for the best, but not now and for two reasons: Richardson knew how the council worked, all the levers that needed to be pushed and the losers prepared to push them for a fee. The second reason was worse: when he was alive he was useful and could be controlled. Now he was dead he was beyond control, even thinking this freaked Si. He tried to turn his attention back to the boxing.

The channel had reverted to adverts. Ray was back. Si decided to hold off from fast-forwarding until Ray had said his catchword, "Bet naaah", which Si particularly liked. He looked at the screen in anticipation as the camera closed in on Ray's head.

But it wasn't Ray; Ray had gone, it was Richardson. Not the Richardson that Si remembered; the Richardson that was dead. The Richardson that had been dead for some time. Mottled flesh slipping off cheek bones, something that didn't look like an eye in the left socket, the right looking like an overused teabag. Richardson turned his head towards him and a slit in the gelatinous mess that used to be the mouth opened to say something. The bone structure moved but the liquefying flesh didn't as the remaining organic material in the mouth cavity struggled to form words.

Si waited in horror, not knowing what Richardson was going to say but pretty sure that it wouldn't be "Bet naaah". He was right, somewhere out of the pulpy ruin a voice resembling a punctured whistle began to speak.

"It endures, it doesn't fade so listen...."

He wasn't going to listen, not to this. He hit the off button and got out of the room. He needed help but where could a vindictive bully like him look for reassurance?

Upstairs in the master suite he swallowed a couple of tablets and lay on the bed trying to see if deep breathing would calm him down: someone was going to suffer for this. He fantasised over who he'd punish the most and gradually regained a measure of equilibrium.

Sometime later he heard footsteps on the stairs, then the bedroom door opened and Suzzie-Jade bounced into the room flushed and wearing what appeared to be a lycra body stocking.

"Having a little rest are we, babes? Oh, bless."

If there was one thing Si didn't want now it was Suzzie-Jade with her bitchy little digs. She'd been a mistake, she was meant to be for show, not for having to put up with. She stripped the sportswear off in one fluent and, he thought, practised movement, dropped it onto the carpet and headed naked for the walk-in shower, shaking her arse at him as she went.

She was fucking taunting him: now he knew who he wanted to hurt, and rage overcame his past experience of what she could be like. She must have been aware of him getting up and looked over her shoulder at him, affected a pout and breathily mouthed:

"Like what you see, babes?"

Then she giggled and added:

"Oh no, I forgot you can't manage it normal, can you?"

That was it: he was off the bed and on her, grabbing her from behind, forcing her into the shower. She gave a gasp as he grabbed her, pinching at her flesh, but instead of resisting she began to grind her buttocks into his groin. It must have been the rush from the anger because he felt himself becoming aroused. As he was moving her towards the edge of the bath, she said coldly:

"That's it, Si, pretend I'm one of your rent boys, that'll help you keep it up."

Any desire evaporated, was transformed to pure hate; now he just wanted to hurt and drew back his fist for the first blow. But she was both lither and quicker than he was. As he raised his arm for the blow his balance shifted and she wriggled out of the grip of his other hand, turned quickly and shoved him into the bath. While he pushed himself back up she scampered out of the en-suite, scooped up her running suit from the floor and legged it downstairs.

He wasn't going to risk humiliating himself further by chasing her so had to resort to smashing his fist into the door a couple of times. It wasn't the first time this had happened and she'd be back, but he began to seriously think about dealing with her proper at some future date.

****

After the third ring of the doorbell, Ed pulled the door open wondering what emergency he was about to confront; but no crisis could have left him as surprised. So much so, that for a moment he wondered if it was a case of the wrong address. He was dismissing the possibility of someone walking through a graveyard to a rectory as a particularly likely mistake, when he realised he was being addressed.

"Hiyaaa, I wondered if we could have a little chat?"

"Yes, of course, Mrs Carver, please come in."

"I prefer Suzzie-Jade, although I suppose I might have to change that soon."

Now he was completely lost and had no idea what she was talking about. He also wondered about the way she was dressed. Her outfit seemed to bridge the spectrum from tracksuit to lingerie. He pushed any thoughts this engendered to the back of his mind.

"Well, Suzzie-Jade then. I must admit to being a bit surprised at finding you here, I thought that…"

"Yeah, well Si don't like churches."

Then she seemed to change.

"I've been in your church a couple of times when it's quiet. It knows me now, an interesting church: the oldest bits must be early fourteenth century."

Surprised as he was at this, he managed to answer.

"Yes, in fact the most ancient bit of stonework is part of its Saxon predecessor. May I offer you a cup of tea?"

"Be nice, but I haven't got time. Look, I want to ask you what you really know about the Hall. I've not noticed anything apart from our friends the birds but now they've gone. But it's messing Si up and, despite what the police say about us being secure, it's hard to feel it since the murder."

"Yes, that poor girl, I suppose you must feel…"

"Not really, I hardly knew her, but something's changing."

Ed noticed that there appeared to be the start of some bruising round Suzzie-Jade's throat.

"Has Mr Carver been…?"

She followed his stare and replied:

"No, he's not really up to knocking me about, it'd take a better man than him."

Ed had no idea how to respond to her. It felt like he was confronting two entities in one and he couldn't be quite sure which was which. It was most disconcerting. However, he didn't need to worry about how to answer: she was talking.

"Don't take me for stupid, I'm like this because it's what Si wanted, you know, a WAG, but it's all for show, like his big cars. All we've got is a type of arrangement but that's not really working so I'll have to reinvent myself and move upmarket. Any rich vicars going?"

She must have seen the expression on his face and changed her tone. She reached out a hand and patted his with it. The feel of her touch was pleasantly reassuring if oddly cold.

"Only joking, Ed, don't look so worried, I'm no threat to you."

His instinct told him he should be feeling very threatened indeed, but his thinking was confused. She continued.

"But there's a serious reason why I'm here. I've dug around a bit and found out some of the things that you were involved in last Christmas. I think you should look at what's under that chapel. I saw the effect it had on the police and the archaeologists who went down there. Something's wrong and I think you should investigate."

Even as he began to answer, Ed realised that she'd dropped the estuary accent and her grammar had improved.

"I hardly think Mr Carver would agree to that, last time we spoke he…"

"No need to bother about that, I'll let you know when it's a good time. Anyway, I don't think you're half as soft as you make out. You're a much better man than Si is."

Ed hadn't time to agree to either her request or her highly unexpected assessment of him, she was already heading for the front door. She opened it herself and for a moment stood staring straight into his eyes, as if judging him. He found he was spellbound, staring back at a pair of eyes that seemed to change continuously.

"Expect to be seeing more of me, at least in the near future. I think you're beginning to understand, aren't you, Ed?"

Staring at her, this seemed less remarkable than it should have been. She smiled.

"I'll be in touch to let you know when."

She paused for a moment before reverting to character.

"Maybe have that tea next time, vicar, nice to talk, innit. See u laitaa."

The spell was broken.

Chapter 23: The Gathering

Theodrakis requested to be part of the interviews to be held at the women's house in order to confirm the previous statements concerning the death of Ken Trescothic and to open the investigation into the attack of Olga. He could tell this took Viv by surprise but he couldn't read whether she was pleased or not. Anderson had certainly looked relieved at being stood down, which struck Theodrakis as peculiar. He still hadn't figured how the relationships in the investigating team worked, but he recognised the tensions and could tell Viv was uneasy. That she was unhappy with him was apparent and the almost silent drive from police HQ to the house wasn't needed to confirm this.

After a perfunctory conversation about the interviews they were going to conduct and their suspicions concerning Olga, conversation trailed off and they sat together in the back seat gazing out at the low cloud massing in the silver grey sky. Theodrakis had forgotten how oppressive the skies of England could be and North Cheshire was greyer than his memories of Cambridge.

Most of the tension in their relationship was down to him, even though unintentional. In fact, he needed to talk to her, wanted to warn her about what he was fairly sure was facing her. But he couldn't. Part of this stemmed from his awkward reticence, but the major impediment was that until she understood more of the nature of the killings, anything he tried to explain would sound mad. Sometimes he thought he was mad, that he'd imagined what he'd encountered on Samos.

He knew in a sense this was true, and the nearest he could get to an understanding was that the things they faced operated on a quantum scale in an alternative reality where things were different, that they were only able to make progress through being granted a limited window of artificial perception. They could see the bodies but not appreciate the levers and mechanics that ruled the game.

The car slowed down and looking up he saw the electrified iron gates slowly swing open, exposing the driveway to the house. How isolated it was; something exaggerated by the low cloud that limited visibility.

In summer it may look beautiful but he could understand why any threat the women faced must feel magnified out here in winter, with no other houses visible. He guessed that DI Campbell must be feeling the same as she shivered and said:

"Come on, let's get this over with."

He followed her across the frost covering the stone chipping drive towards the front door, which he saw swing open. He followed Viv in: the interior couldn't have felt more different, light warm and comfortable. All the women, except for one, were in what the woman who opened the door, Jenna, described as the Gathering Room. He had no idea what a Gathering Room was but it sounded, to his Greek consciousness, like something out of the pages of Aeschylus. He didn't warm to Jenna either, but there was no time to reflect on that because he found himself gathered into the presence of what Anderson had referred to as the coven.

The first part of the process went quickly; all the women had an alibi for the time of the supposed attack on Olga: they'd all been together in the house. Similarly, their alibis for the attack on Ken were confirmed and verified by an independent witness, Claire Vanarvi, who'd been with them. Theodrakis didn't have time to wonder why she was mixed up in this because Jenna kicked off.

"I don't see why you're here harassing us; we're supposed to be the victims."

Viv tried to explain.

"We understand that, but the circumstances have become more complicated and, as you know, the original suspect has been killed."

It had no effect.

"But that doesn't mean that he wasn't behind all this, does it? And why are you questioning us about Olga, she's a sister? You don't know what you're doing, do you? Easier for you to harass us than catch the men who attacked Olga, threatened us and killed those poor women.

"Please, stop this."

The voice came from behind them; they turned to see Olga, her face bruised and stitched, enter the room.

"It's my fault you're here, we'll go through to the conservatory, it'll be quieter in there."

They followed her, aware of the eyes of the other women following them. For Theodrakis it was unsatisfactory. He'd wanted to talk to the three archaeologists about why they were here and how they felt now they were. He could tell just by looking at one of them, Jan, that she was willing to talk, more than willing - she looked lost and desperate.

The conservatory looked out over neat lawns spreading towards the vague grey bulk of the Pennines. Olga attempted a smile, then said:

"I suppose you know about my time in prison?"

They nodded.

"Do we need to go over it?"

Viv answered her.

"Not unless you think it's relevant. Is it?"

Theodrakis was impressed. Viv was good, he could afford to sit back and listen. Olga cleared her throat before replying:

"No, it's not relevant. Keep it in the past where it belongs. I learnt from it, never been with a man since."

Olga looked at Theodrakis as she said this. He smiled back and said:

"No, me neither."

To his surprise she laughed and said:

"Good, I like you for that."

He saw that it also made Viv smile and reflected that this was probably the only thing he'd said since arriving in this damp pudding of an island that had gone down well. It came to him that the attack on Olga was something different: not part of the pattern and therefore significant.

In his experience these things didn't make mistakes: if it suited them that you die then you died. She wasn't dead, assuming this assault was connected, so it was either a warning or something that they were meant to see. Viv asked:

"So, if it isn't too painful to go over it all again, would you think back to what happened to you, Ms Hickman?"

"Something chased me, chased me through the back alleys of Manchester, like it was herding me, you know, shepherding me in a particular direction."

"What makes you think that?"

"Looking back, I realise that it could have caught me any time it wanted to. It touched me a couple of times, a filthy touch. I'm still trying to wash it off."

"You keep saying it, not he."

"And so would you if it had chased you. I think it followed me from Rylands to Chethams College, and then decided it needed to frighten me. It certainly did that."

She fell silent and Viv prompted.

"And that's all?"

"Yes, that's all"

She seemed to hesitate, then added:

"Except, well except I think it wanted me to knock myself out on the glass of that particular restaurant."

"Why would it want you to do that?"

"Because it achieves two things in one action, frightens me and links me up with two other victims of Skendleby who happen to be sitting in that window and are therefore the first to help me."

Theodrakis could see that Viv had lost patience.

"With respect, Ms Hickman, this is a police investigation, not an episode of Dr Who. It would help if you'd stick to the facts."

"These are the facts; do you think I'm enjoying this?"

Theodrakis cut in.

"Why do think this thing was following you?"

"Because of what I found in Rylands library."

"And that was?"

"I was looking at some documents that Ed, that is, Reverend Joyce, had shown me."

"Oh yes, the companion of your last two unfortunate misadventures."

Viv snapped the caustic remark before Theodrakis could stop her. He signalled they should let Olga continue whilst wondering why it was that powerful women so often treated others with less empathy than they did their weaker sisters or men. After the ensuing silence Olga asked:

"You want me to continue?"

Viv nodded.

"The documents were some pages from the Manchester diaries of John Dee, which for some reason had been extracted and hidden. Dr Dee was…"

"I know who he was, I saw the opera at the Palace. Why were they of interest to you?"

"Because I'm in them."

This should have been a conversation killer, but something tingled in Theodrakis; something raw and partially surpressed in his psyche intuitively recognised the authenticity. He didn't want Viv, who looked as if she was about to laugh, to blow this: he took over the questioning.

"I believe you."

Olga exhaled heavily; she was a tough woman on the verge of tears. She mumbled something back that might have been thanks.

"Take your time and tell us about it."

"Ed found the documents for me, they're just scraps of jottings Dee made, no big deal really, most of his time in Manchester seems pretty dull."

She paused and Theodrakis prompted gently.

"There's an exception though, isn't there?"

"Yes, sadly there is. Dee was asked out to Skendleby Hall; from there he was taken to a farm some distance away to perform what he calls 'certain acts'. It's clear that what he found terrified him and his attempt to perform these actions failed, or even made thing worse."

"And that's all?"

"No. When Dee was at the height of his power he used a type of sensitive, they called them skryers back then, but he'd parted company with his skryer who died somewhere in Hungary, so he had to use a local man who claimed he had the gift. This man's name was Hikman."

"Same as yours."

"Same as mine and what's worse is that Dee didn't trust him and he was proved right. When Dee arrived at Skendleby he found Hikman and a hooded man in the crypt under the chapel with the body of a dead girl. The lord of the manor wasn't there, seems he'd gone away to avoid whatever Dee might do. Dee is at pains to say that the girl was already dead and had been cut before he got there."

"Well he would, wouldn't he?"

Theodrakis put his finger to his lips, indicating Viv should stay quiet.

"Dee's part in this was to accompany them and take the bones that had been cut to the farmhouse, which Hikman's scrying had disclosed, and bury them with 'a significant undertaking'. The situation of the farm and the earth beneath was supposed to have special properties. Or maybe the Davenports just wanted the evidence shifted elsewhere."

Theodrakis asked:

"What about the rest of the body?"

"I wouldn't be surprised if Ed's archaeologist friend doesn't find it under the Davenport chapel."

"And the farmhouse?"

"I'm very much afraid that you're sitting in it. The farmhouse is certainly old enough, this used to be a house and barn. Margaret's husband had it converted."

Viv started to ask:

"So that would mean tha..."

Olga finished the sentence for her.

"That these unspeakable things are buried in the cellars somewhere beneath our feet."

She paused, looking close to tears. Theodrakis asked gently:

"Is there more, Olga?"

"Only if you know how to look for it. After the piece about Hikman and the dead girl there's some rambling about fear and dark shadows, then the diary peters out. There are a couple of blank sheets then the same account ordered differently."

"Why? That doesn't make sense."

"No, that's what I thought at first. Then I looked again, sometimes being a mathematician comes in handy. I put the two versions together and in the differences there lurks a simple numerical code. Probably quite tricky back then but a teenage computer hacker wouldn't be taxed by it today."

"And?"

"And there are a couple of simple differences: the girl was alive when Hikman cut her and the dark shadows have a specific, as well as metaphorical, application. They refer to the hooded figure, hooded not to conceal his identity but to hide his appearance from anyone unlucky enough to be forced into contact with him, if it was a he, which I'm not sure."

An image of the time-eaten figure of Father John on Samos awakened in Theodrakis's memory. Olga hadn't finished.

"There's one other detail. This thing of shadows had a name, Edward Davenport, and that would make him…"

Theodrakis finished the sentence for her.

"About two hundred and fifty years old."

Theodrakis expected this to provoke some protest from Viv, or at least a derisive laugh, but he was wrong, she didn't even react. Instead she asked:

"What do you think is happening then?"

Olga must have noticed a more open attitude because she blurted out:

"Something outside my experience, certainly beyond yours, but I think your colleague, sorry, I don't know your name, may understand more than either of us."

"Call me Alexis."

He noted the look of surprise on Viv's face as he said this: surprise and a touch of hurt maybe. But this wasn't the place to unpack all that, Olga was speaking again.

"But have you any answers for this? Why are Jan, Leonie and Rose here? Three women threatened by the Skendleby outbreak? Why do I find myself living in the same house in which my ancestor performed a piece of magic that involved the brutal murder of a girl? Why was Kelly killed here and the Eastern European girl at Skendleby Hall? Why was I attacked? What happened here last year? They're all related. Put the answers to these together and I think the picture of what's going to happen will become clearer."

Viv placed a hand on her arm, asking softly:

"But what do you think all this means?"

"Something terrible is coming: I think that we've been collected. The elements for some terrible ancient reckoning are being put in place. Soon the gathering will be complete; until then we wait for the agent who will set things in motion. I don't think we'll have to wait long."

****

Shortly afterwards, as Theodrakis and Viv were walking to the car, another vehicle pulled up in the drive. The door opened and Claire Vanarvi got out. Viv noticed that she was wearing the necklace of ivory, it looked bigger somehow. To her surprise Claire made no acknowledgement. Her attention was focused on the passenger door of her car, which was slowly opening. A pale, nervous looking young woman emerged and Claire took her by the arm, shepherding her towards the open front door of the women's house.

Chapter 24: Carcass Breath

"Listen, Ed, it's under the chapel, that's where it happened, that's where we have to look."

It was the third time she'd said this since he answered the phone and he was still trying to get his head round what had happened to her in Manchester. The news of the attack was shocking but in a way he wasn't surprised, he'd noticed the dark energy gathering again.

"Ed, are you listening? We need to get down there, you can fix it, the archaeologist is your friend. Don't you understand that there's a pattern to this? He was the one who looked after me outside the restaurant. Or do you think that's just another coincidence?"

"No, but we have to be sure, wait till I've spoken to Claire."

"She's the last person you should go near."

They agreed to differ and she rang off. He was feeling squeezed and needed someone to lean on. The news that Lisa Richardson was now in the women's house didn't feel right either. He had to talk to Claire.

Before Olga rang him he'd made another connection with the past: Marcus Fox had called him from a phone box somewhere on the Welsh borders following a sleepless night of dark visions and foreboding. Apparently his cottage had no mains services and Marcus didn't have a mobile so he had walked the miles through intermittent snow to the nearest village. In his state of health he must have been desperate to make the attempt. It had been down to the ex-priest's certainty that they'd come up with the plan to neutralise the entity from the Skendleby mound the previous Christmas.

Marcus wasn't so certain now, he'd sounded desperate: desperate and frightened. So much so that it had been difficult to follow his ramblings at first, but once he caught the drift, Ed felt a chill pass through him.

"I don't think it worked, Ed, I've been seeing things that couldn't be real if it had worked."

Ed asked what things, but in his heart he knew and what Marcus said next confirmed it.

"The exorcism, Claire's exorcism of that unfortunate girl. I shouldn't have asked Claire to do it, she hadn't the strength. The creature must have detected her weakness, must have wriggled into the fault lines of her earlier mental illness."

"How can you be sure, Marcus? Everything went the way you said it would and Claire was fine afterwards."

For a moment Marcus seemed reassured, asking:

"Are you sure she's fine? You haven't noticed any change in her?"

"Well, a little perhaps, but that's only to be expected."

"I knew it! Had it worked I wouldn't be haunted by these things. The creature left the Richardson girl but didn't return to the tomb. So where did it go? Oh, sweet Jesus."

There was a pause, Ed found himself shouting down the phone:

"Marcus, Marcus, are you alright?"

Then, from the phone somewhere in the dark among the snowy borders:

"We have to rethink this, Ed, you must be very, very careful, I'm out of time, try to...."

The line went dead. Ed tried to ring back but there was no answer, just endless ringing. He called Gwen in Shrewsbury but only got the answerphone so left a message for her to check that Marcus was all right. Then he fetched the whisky bottle from the dining room and poured himself a stiff drink. He was finishing the second of these when Mary popped her head round the door, telling him to come to bed.

He thought he'd never sleep with the burden of responsibility and the fear of what was coming chasing crazy rhythms through his overheated mind. Gradually he focused on what Olga had said about Hikman and the shadows under the chapel. His last fully conscious thought was that maybe what had happened down there had put a spoiler on their ritual last year.

****

"Sorry to wake you so early on a Saturday, Ed, dear, but I've got Mrs Carver on the phone, she says she needs to talk to you."

Mary passed him the handset and swept the curtains back, allowing a smear of sludgy grey light to creep into the room. He sat up and pressed the handset to his ear.

"Hello, Mrs Carver, is anything the matter?"

"I told you, call me Suzzie-Jade, for the present at least."

There was a giggle and he wondered if he was being mocked but the thought evaporated with what she said next.

"Today's your chance. Si's gone into town and taken them shaven-headed fuckwits with him. I'm going to Barton Oaks so the place is empty. Come in through the gate in the estate wall. I've left it open, the chapel's unlocked."

Ed started to protest but it was too late.

"Good luck, vicar, see yaaa."

Now he knew events were conspiring and an unavoidable decision was microseconds away. His gut instinct was pulling him towards something his rational mind rejected. But he wasn't a rational man any more: he'd seen too much for that to still be an option. However, a glimmer of rationality must have still been fighting its corner because he decided to seek advice before taking any action. He rang Claire, first at home where there was no answer, then on her mobile where he got the answering machine. At the bleep he found himself saying:

"Hi, Claire, it's Ed...er...I just wanted to check something with you."

He stammered to a halt and then added, before he had chance to think about it:

"Oh, and I spoke to Marcus. He thinks your exorcism failed and the thing didn't return to the tomb.... so where did it go? Ring me when you get this please."

He got out of bed and shivering, dressed slowly, hoping she'd ring back but the phone remained silent and inert. It was cold, frost on the windows; the rectory was too big and expensive to heat. Downstairs, Mary wanted to know:

"What did that woman want you for? It's the first time I've spoken to her since they moved in."

But Ed wasn't listening, his mind was elsewhere and after a quick slurp of coffee he got up to go.

"Sorry, Mary, I've a couple of visits to make."

He could see that she was disappointed.

"Oh, Ed, we were going into town to shop for Christmas, you said today was free."

He hated to disappoint her, after all, without her he'd have cracked up long ago, but he had no choice.

"Sorry, but it shouldn't take me long. I'll be back in a couple of hours, we can go then."

She didn't appear very reassured and he shamefacedly shambled out, pausing only to grab a coat and a torch from the cavernous cloakroom under the stairs before leaving the house. He made his way through the graveyard to the Skendleby estate wall, which he followed kicking through piles of frozen, dead leaves until he reached the gate. It was rusted and as he tried to force it open, he remembered the last time he'd been through this gate. It had been with Davenport on the night Liza Richardson ran berserk. Eventually the gate swung back with a screeching sound Ed thought must have been loud enough to wake the dead.

On the other side he peered anxiously around, fearful that maybe this was a set up and he'd be arrested for trespass. But Suzzie-Jade had been true to her word, the place seemed deserted, deserted, cold and desolate. He made for the chapel, keeping under the cover of the trees for as long as possible before crossing the patch of open ground towards the door.

The crumbling sandstone of the chapel stained a darkish green over the centuries radiated decay. He didn't want to be there long so forced himself inside. The door opened surprisingly smoothly and he was confronted with the tombs of the Davenports.

It was still a house of God so his initial instinct was to kneel in front of the altar and pray, but once he was standing before it a feeling of despair swept through him. This wasn't a place where prayer had ever worked. Whatever had been worshipped here, it wasn't his God.

Other than that, by torchlight, the place wasn't intimidating, just bleak, cold and empty. He made his way to the steps leading to the lower level. Down there though there was a different feeling - earthy and morbid. He made his way through the mausoleum architecture, its shape distorted by the flickering torch beam, trying not to look towards the dancing shadows and concentrating on keeping his eyes fixed straight ahead.

This had been a mistake; he shouldn't have come on his own. Then he saw the other steps - rougher, cruder - crumbling their way down to the dark and his fate was sealed. As he began to pick his way gingerly down the worn stone his first reaction was mild surprise: it didn't feel as bad down there as it had in the crypt under the chapel. So when his feet detected the change in gradient at the point where stone step gave way to earthen ramp, he had just enough confidence to carry on.

The passage at the foot of the ramp was cramped and narrow, with a low roof forcing him to stoop. It was a claustrophobe's nightmare, exacerbated by the tree roots pushing their way down into the passage and catching at him like febrile skeletal fingers. It smelt alive down here too, that couldn't be right. His confidence had betrayed him like it had Hector when it made him think that he could face Achilles. He was about to turn and get out as fast as he could when the passage wall to his right disappeared and he was there, in the chamber. The place where Hikman, Dee and, he presumed, others over the millennia had gathered to practise their desperate necromancy.

He moved his torch from side to side, watching the weird shapes the beam flickered through as it traversed the darkness. What in God's name was this? It looked to Ed as if the chamber had collected the essence of every childhood nightmare and made them real. Most of this, maybe all, was pre-Christian, like the complete panoply of the early churches' shibboleths gathered together in one foul cache. It was the morbid compulsion of this that drove him to take his final step away from commonsense and ignore the warning of the fading torch beam.

He made his way between two blinded stone heads set on rough pillars, taking care to avoid a patch of dark organic earth that appeared to defy logic by containing the remnants of a tree growing down into the earth, and picked his way towards an image that the torch beam seemed to have stuck on. It was a slab of rock, resembling a tall altar, which had been painted – it was like the Palaeolithic cave images he'd seen as a boy in Spain.

But this one was far more sinister, depicting the image of a figure with a bleeding gash where the heart should be. But it wasn't the heart he was looking at: it was a head. A woman's head, he thought. A head that had burst open from the inside and was releasing a huge black bird.

Everything about this particular image appalled him, and it engaged his concentration to such an extent that at first he was unaware of the crunching noise his feet had begun to make as he approached this terror of life in death.

Then the torch beam failed and he was plunged into darkness, his squeal of terror amplified to an unnatural volume, which reverberated right round the chamber. Something was round his feet, impeding movement. Then, thank God, the beam was back, weak and indeterminate but he could see enough to get out of there anyway. But first he needed to see what it was catching at his feet.

He directed the puny beam down and saw they were caught up in the leprous white tendrils of some inverted creeper or sucker living its unnatural existence in the dark. Trying not to think about how it had come to wrap itself round his ankles, he pulled his feet free. The tendrils sloughed off with a sickly sucking noise and seemed to retreat beyond the narrow pool of torchlight. He stood shaking in the cold and dark, fighting panic and gasping down lungfulls of the freezing stale air.

The silent dark pressed down on him and he had to force himself to move. It was only then he became aware of the other sound, the crunching sound he hadn't previously paid heed to.

Forcing his gaze back downwards, he discovered the cause: his path to the image had taken him across a litter of skeletons. They were the remains of birds and there must have been hundreds of them. He didn't want to have to walk back through them, to have to touch them in any way, so, unwisely, he hesitated, looking for another way back.

It was while he was scanning the bizarre cavern for an alternative exit that he sensed movement at the chamber periphery. Movement and an intensification of the timbre of blackness; if such a thing could be possible down there.

And a different sound, faint but growing. The nearest he could come to placing it was as a type of rustling. Something rotten was rustling nearby, he could hear and smell it. Now he was terrified, his breath coming in strangled gasps. This was terribly wrong, no human was meant to be in this place. He looked round for the best way to leg it out, but it wasn't a way out that his eyes locked on. The deeper blackness at the very limits of the torch beam appeared to be spreading, growing and moving. It was certainly growing louder.

He couldn't bear to look and then luckily didn't have to as the torch beam died. Died finally, its photons dispersed to another frequency. Jesus, this was worse, now he daren't move, but in the impenetrable blackness he could sense this black mass drawing closer.

The sounds were certainly nearer now. He thought he could feel leprous tendrils re-encircle his ankles and begin to inch up over his socks and under the edges of his trouser legs. He felt the useless torch fall out of his limp hand onto the mass of skeletal bird debris on the floor. He was beginning his first scream of terror when an image of his cell phone came to him. It had a torch app, he'd used it, and he could get it to work down there.

The anxiety of fumbling in his pockets for the phone seemed an eternity, but then his fingers located it. He turned the phone on, its batteries were low but if he got the app it'd last long enough to get him out of there. And it did work, thank God it did work. He directed the beam in the direction he thought was the way out.

There was no way out: he was closed in Hell.

A Hell specifically created for him. Now he understood the sound, it was the soft rustling of ink black feathers. They were all around, crowded densely together, on top of each other: a mass of crows, stacked as tall as he was. He swung the light round three hundred and sixty degrees. They filled the chamber, packed from floor to ceiling, inching towards him - every dead black eye trained on him. All the crows in the world, the universe, and whatever exists beyond.

Not living crows, all the crows there'd ever been. He knew this because there were young healthy crows, freshly dead crows, partly decomposed crows and skeletal vestiges of crows. He spun in a circle, there was no way out now, there had only ever been a way in.

The front row of carrion was almost touching him; he stood in a circle of space with a diameter of little more than a metre. It was a rapidly shrinking circle. The noise was so loud now he almost didn't notice it and besides, he had something else to take his attention.

The smell: the foul taint of their carcass breath. Rotten, meaty and bloody, filling the fetid air of the chamber. He could tell more and more carrion were packing into the chamber, squeezing in at the back and pushing the others further forward. They'd had to let him go last time. Now he was theirs down there in the dark. What had he ever done to deserve this?

Then there was a change: the noise of rustling ceased. Scarce centimetres from him they paused and he could see every living and dead corvid eye fixed on him. There was no sympathy in their gaze, all he could discern was a type of feeding lust. But there was still sound, quieter but no less chilling. The sound of the crows breathing, rumbling back towards the far off walls of the chamber.

The stench of this was suffocating; the oxygen was used up now the chamber was just crows and carcass breath. He didn't want the light any more. He didn't need to see this. He'd done his best, that was all God could have asked of him. He'd failed but at least he'd tried.

He turned off the phone, put it back in his pocket then fell to his knees. In the blackness he felt the bird's begin to rustle the last inches down on to him. He began to pray.

Chapter 25: While Cold Blood is Raining

Giles knew he had to do it; he'd learnt it wasn't possible to avoid fate. He'd been one of the last people Mary had contacted and the fact that he'd been contacted at all was a pretty good indication of the levels of desperation she'd reached. Ed was missing. The last person he'd spoken to had been Mrs Carver at the hall but she wasn't there and Mr Carver wouldn't come to the phone (according to the barely articulate creature who'd answered it).

Ed had gone out for a couple of hours in the morning and now it was only a couple of hours before midnight. No one in the parish had seen him and after his history of mental health problems had been explained forcibly to them, the police were now taking it seriously. Still no leads, so at the scraping-the-barrel stage, Mary had tried Giles on his mobile number.

She'd tried Claire first, who told her not to worry and, certainly, Claire herself hadn't sounded in the least worried. In fact, she'd even made an inappropriate joke that maybe Ed had a lover. This had taken Mary by surprise, she'd always thought of Claire as a caring person. The fact that Giles seemed to take it very seriously was even more surprising: she'd had him down as irresponsible and feckless.

Giles was in the pub when he got the call and he knew at once this wasn't down to Ed's depressive mentality. He thought about contacting the woman who'd smashed herself up on the restaurant window, remembering her warning for Ed.

A split second later he thought of the chapel. The decaying deserted chapel standing sentinel over its underground chamber of horrors. He still hadn't made any sense of what he'd found under there. The nearest he got was an archaeological equivalent to the theory of quantum tunnelling; worm holes through the multiverse. He didn't want to go anywhere near the place, but if Ed was down there he couldn't leave him. His first solution was to tell the police, but his instinct kicked in, this wasn't something they'd understand, certainly not that bitch who'd locked him up. Any connection with Skendleby would just give her more ammunition.

So he had to go himself. He thought about ordering a quick rum chaser to steady his nerves but didn't and left his half finished pint in its half empty pot and went out.

There was light snow covering his windshield and the skies held the promise of heavy falls to come, a whiteout was predicted. It would be freezing under the chapel. The main roads were clear but the minor ones near Skendleby hadn't been gritted and he had to concentrate hard on stopping the car from sliding around. This was good because it prevented any attempt at a critique of his intentions. The only way to reach the chapel without being picked up by Carver's CCTV was by parking on the Skendleby mound site and climbing the estate wall at the back of the Hall. He got his torch from the back of the car and made his way to the wall, being careful not to look at the mound. If anything was going on there he didn't want to see it, he was scared enough as it was.

Each step seemed to make a sound loud enough to wake the dead as he crunched over the earth, which rang iron-hard beneath the frost. He slipped twice trying to climb the wall but on the third attempt managed to push himself over and landed in a heap the other side where, through good fortune, the stunted undergrowth under the trees broke his fall. He was sweating and breathing heavily. It was even darker in among the trees than he'd imagined, and he wondered if he was up to this. Maybe he should climb back over the wall and ring the police from his car. He could have kicked himself: he didn't need to incriminate himself, he could ring Theodrakis.

Then something weird happened. He got a clear image of Theodrakis by the chapel. Not by the chapel when they'd both been there during the investigation, but by the chapel now, in the dark. He turned on the torch, directed it down at the earth and began to pick his way through the wood.

It was clear, crisp and dark and, apart from the occasional crack from a twig underfoot and the sound of his breathing, it was silent. He felt like he'd walked out of the wardrobe into Narnia. The woods had a weird dark magic about them, this must be happening to someone else, it was almost enjoyable.

The snow had started to come down heavily by the time he reached the chapel door; there was no sign of Theodrakis. Giles wasn't too bothered because in a way Theodrakis had played his part by making sure he got there. The feeling of hyper reality sustaining him was heightened by the strange sensation of a rushing noise, which sounded like a great flock of birds suddenly disturbed from roosting, climbing into the sky. He looked up, he was out of the trees and there were no birds.

Inside the chapel he made the sign of the cross. Where had that come from? He wasn't a Catholic, wasn't anything except confused. Footballers did it on TV when they ran on to the pitch but he didn't: even Ed didn't go in for all that stuff. But in a way it gave him an unexpected measure of reassurance so he repeated the gesture when he found himself confronting the altar. He'd hoped Ed would be in the chapel but wasn't surprised when he wasn't because inside him he knew that if Ed was here it would be underground, walking through the underworld.

He forced himself down the steps to the under-chapel. Still no sign, but there was sound, a type of dislocated echo coming from somewhere below. He headed for the steps down and, by the time he'd reached the earth ramp, the torch beam had reduced to only about a couple of meters in length. He didn't feel cold anymore, in fact, it was warm. He remembered Theodrakis telling him something about reality warping on Samos. Well, now it was warping in Skendleby.

At the foot of the ramp he groped his way along the passage towards the chamber. It was definitely getting warmer and there was a thick, cloying odour pervading the passage: rank, sickly and sour. He didn't want to go any further or see what he was pretty sure would confront him in there. He came to a halt, choking on the foul air slithering down his windpipe. He was very alone and thought of Steve, wishing he were there with him. He was too weak to do this alone. Why him, why always him?

The sound had gone now and he'd reached the chamber. As he passed the first of the fetish objects buried there, the unreality of the place almost overwhelmed him: it was a false assemblage. What had put it together? There was no way that these things could ever have co-existed. His feet were moving through soft things that littered the floor. He directed the light down and saw that he was moving across a mass of feathers. Some were shiny black and new, others were mouldering, and some appeared to have been preserved in some perverse embalming process. Then he heard the sound. Low but distinct, a susurration of muted cawing. The torch beam reached the periphery of the source of the chanting and he saw what was in the centre of the beam.

There, a few yards in front of him, the light flickered on a moving black mass. A rippling and slithering contagion of undulating feathery bodies swarming around a static object. A mass so large the beam could only illuminate a fraction of it. Almost by instinct he directed the beam towards the centre of the mass towards what they were worshipping, and it partially revealed the thing at the centre.

He found himself peering at what looked like a crudely sculpted humanoid figure mummified in a cocoon of organic material. In the constantly shifting perspective of occluded vision it was impossible to be certain but his instinct knew what his eyes couldn't grasp. This was the end of the trail; he'd found what had once been Ed.

****

Jed Gifford saw the old man stumble out of the phone booth. He looked frail enough to drop down into the snow beneath his feet. Jed didn't feel cold at all, which was weird because he wasn't wearing a coat. He knew what he was here to do but didn't know why. He couldn't figure how he'd got here, where ever here was. One minute he'd been bullying Dave into buying him another drink in the Bull's Head and thinking about the street walker in Maccy he had his eye on for the way home. Now he was in the middle of fucking nowhere in a bloody snow storm.

So why did he know what he was going to do when he didn't know why or what would happen to him when he'd done it? But there wasn't time to worry about that now because the old man was moving off. He looked like he could hardly walk but he set off up a lane that looked like it didn't lead anywhere. Must be off his head; still, it made it easier with no one else about and it would give him plenty of time to go through his pockets afterwards.

It was dark out here and once the old man had left the light of the call box and the single street light that illuminated the minor junction where it was located, he should have disappeared into the night. But funnily he hadn't, Jed could still see him. Even stranger, the man was walking up towards him, which meant that Jed must have overtaken him and he didn't remember having done that. He didn't even remember leaving his position opposite the call box. Then again, he didn't remember how he got to the phone box either.

He could see the old boy clearly now, he looked like some type of vicar or something. He was unsteady on his feet and Jed knew it had taken quite a lot of drink to give the old boy the courage to set out for the phone.

In fact, Jed knew all he needed to about his victim. Strange that, when he didn't even know where he was. The wind was getting up now, blowing the snow about: it was beginning to drift and there weren't any lights for miles. Best get it done now, shouldn't take long, the old ones were always the easiest to roll. He stepped out of the hedgerow, where apparently he'd been waiting, and confronted the old man.

He was standing right in front of him now, and he'd been right about him being a vicar. He had one of them white collars on back to front. An old, stained one. His face was pinched white in the cold except for his nose and the patches of cheek alongside. They were red and covered in purple veins: the sign of a drinker. He looked as if he were near the end, so what was he doing out here on a night like this?

The old man didn't seem to see him at first, even though he was right in front of him; it was like he was invisible or something. No one blanked Jed Gifford and got away with it, except Si Carver, of course, but he was different. Jed wasn't going to take no disrespect from some old git.

He grabbed him by the throat, wanted to teach him a lesson, scare him into respect before he killed him. It couldn't hurt to have a little fun first, could it? The throat was frail and scrawny yet softish: Jed could have circled it with one hand. The man scrabbled at his throat with both hands. Then, at last, he saw Jed.

His eyes locked onto Jed's, they looked surprised, but, to Jed's surprise, not scared. This took away some of the pleasure, he should be frightened, Jed was a frightening man, at least when his victims were smaller and weaker - which they always were. He'd give him a bloody scare all right.

"See me now, doncha?"

"Yes, I see you."

"You'll know me next time, innit?"

Jed could have kicked himself; there wouldn't be a next time. He wanted him to know what was going to happen, make him snivel. But before he could correct himself the man said something that surprised Jed.

"I knew you as soon as I saw you."

"What do yer mean? You never seen me before."

"No, but I've been waiting for you."

This was really pissing Jed off now; this wasn't how it was supposed to go. He snarled:

"Go on then, you clever little bugger, who am I?"

"My death, I've been waiting for you a long time and now you're finally here, you're welcome."

"What you mean you bin waiting a long time? I just got here."

"You've been shadowing me since I lost my way, you're my punishment and I'm glad it's over, glad I didn't have to take my own life and risk my immortal soul."

"What you mean? What you on about? Listen, do you know who I really am, eh? What I really am?"

"In your corporeal form not really, you appear in many guises, but you're the black dog that's been stalking me."

"Don't you bleeding call me a dog."

"I intended no offence, it was merely a metaphor."

"Call me a fucking metarfour and I'll...."

But he already had and, without noticing, the man's throat was mangled and Jed could see the life draining out of him. This wasn't what he wanted, it was too quick and now he'd missed the best bit. But the conversation had wrong footed him and there was something he needed to know.

"Wait, what's that all about? Who are you? Who bleedin are you?"

It was too late, the man's last breath was being exhaled. As it went there was a hoarse whisper that sounded something like "Marrcuuss Fox".

Jed dragged the body, light as a child's, to a snowdrift building up by the hedgerow. Then he went through the pockets. No point in letting stuff go to waste. There wasn't much, two tenners and a fiver in the wallet and a cross round the neck that he hoped was gold. The small black book of prayers, much annotated, he tossed over the hedge. While he was doing this he heard a growing noise above him. Looking up he saw movement in the bare branches of the trees. Dark shapes agitated and growing in number. Birds, bloody great black birds, like those above the mound the day that fat lezzer had decked him. They shouldn't be about now. What was going on? The thought chilled him. Where was he? How had he got here? Where was he going?

"Jed! Jed here are your drinks, pint and rum, like you said. I've no money left so I'm going. Jed, are you all right?"

His head was swimming. He forced his eyes open and saw that he was leaning on the bar in The Bull's, staring at Dave. What the fuck was happening?

Chapter 26: Seen From An Armchair

The ring of a phone. Getting up from the armchair was bad enough, but after a few shuffling steps across the carpet the chest pain that all day had been hovering just beyond the horizon kicked in. Davenport came to a halt and seconds later the phone ceased ringing. It had been ringing over the last twenty minutes. The first two times he'd ignored it, but there'd been no message on the answer phone and after a short period of time it had begun to ring again. He stood suspended halfway between the silent phone and the refuge of the armchair, trying not to move.

The pain felt like it was splitting his chest and he tried to breathe steady and deep to make it relent sufficiently enough to enable him to totter to the bureau where he kept his tablets. He knew one of these attacks would finish him off, which he thought might not be too bad a thing. He also knew, or rather felt in some way, that this call was sweeping something terrible towards him, something he couldn't avoid.

He'd been dreaming about it, about Skendleby: the mound, the Hall and the chapel. Not normal dreams. In fact, he wasn't even sure he was asleep when they swarmed into his unconscious. All he concluded from these dark occluded visions was that his old inheritance was ready to gather him in. In a way it was a relief. Since he'd moved out of the Hall he'd felt himself begin to dwindle. He shouldn't have run from his responsibility, he'd learnt in the army that you could never dodge the bullet.

More to the point, his moral compass told him that he was responsible, in part at least, for the disastrous excavation and botched resealing of the mound. He'd suspected for some time that their attempt at magic had proved incomplete and the reappearance of the unearthly flocks of black corvids these last days confirmed this. Also, despite the central heating being permanently on and the fires lit, the house was cold. Far colder and also darker than it should reasonably be expected to be.

The pain diminished sufficiently for him to make it to the bureau, extract the tablets and wash them down with whisky and soda. This last detail was forbidden by the doctor, not that Davenport had ever intended to comply with that particular stricture. In fact, the only variation to his pattern of intake since the attack had been to recommence smoking.

He was ready to sit down again but the pain was worse when seated so fortunately, or perhaps unfortunately, he found himself standing by the phone when it again began ringing.

"Davenport here."

There was a delay before there was any reply, as if whoever was on the other end hadn't expected an answer. The voice when it came was muffled and imprecise and Davenport didn't recognise the caller.

"Sorry, I think you've got the wrong number."

Before he managed to replace the handset a more intelligible but panicked reply from his unknown caller jogged his memory.

"Sir Nigel, it's Gwen. Have you heard from Marcus? Is he with you? Please tell me he's there safe with you."

He knew who he was dealing with now, but the voice on the line sounded very different from the calm, imposing but strange woman who he'd collaborated with in their failed act of necromancy the previous Christmas.

"No, he's not here. Why should he be?"

There was a gasp of dismay then a stuttering reply.

"I thought, I'd hoped he might be; he liked you. I've tried Claire, I've tried…"

Davenport thought she might be weeping and his natural kindness and good manners kicked in. He began the process of attempting to reassure her.

"No point in distressing yourself, Gwen, why not explain some of this to me and we'll see what we can do about it."

It hadn't proved as easy as that. She'd taken so long to calm down that during the process his tablets had begun to work their chemical magic. The pain had receded and he'd gratefully slid his weary body back into the armchair before he'd picked up the gist of her anxiety.

"So, since that rather strange and disturbing message you've heard nothing from him, Gwen?"

"No, that's what's worrying me."

"But you've said yourself that he's prone to vanish from the radar for extended periods of time."

"Yes, but..."

"And there's no phone or electric in his cottage in the borders?"

"No, but..."

"And remember, it's snowing pretty hard up there at present. The same snow that, if the weather people have got it right for a change, is going to cause us problems in the next few hours. So he's likely to be snowed in and out of contact, nothing worse than that."

"No, but you don't know him as well as I do, he's troubled. He said he could feel something from Skendleby reaching out for him. He'd realised our ceremony hadn't worked. He said it was far worse and very different from what we thought and that we'd played into its hand and made things worse."

She came to a stop and he heard her snuffling to herself. None of this Davenport understood, and there wasn't time to work it out as she continued.

"He told me he'd been following up some research leads but nothing he said made any sense, that's why I'm worried. I think his old illness has returned. I'm worried he might harm himself."

"Now you've no evidence for that, Gwen."

Davenport sounded calm and logical but he didn't feel it. He felt whatever it was that Marcus had uncovered was consistent with his own fears, and he needed to know what it was.

"So, tell me, what was it that you think put Marcus in this state?"

"I've already told you, it made no sense. He was rambling on about us being tricked, some nonsense about portals and time warping. He kept quoting from Milton's *Paradise Lost*: some nonsense about a demon called Mulciber being thrown out from heaven to land on an island in the Aegean. He seemed to think that we had been tricked into doing something that served the purposes of some power not even from our time or universe."

This certainly made no sense to Davenport and he began to suspect that maybe Gwen was right and Marcus was a risk to himself. Gwen must have picked up on his change of mood.

"That's why we have to find him, he's so disturbed, to such an extent that he even told me to be wary of Claire."

Davenport didn't know why but for a second something deep in his subconscious resonated with the warning. He brushed it away and said:

"Right then, we need to take some measures to ensure he's alright. What steps have you taken?"

"I rang Claire, she wasn't in but I left a long message on her answer phone alerting her to Marcus's condition."

"Including his reservations about her?"

"Of course, if anyone can make him better it's Claire, she has particular gifts and power. You should remember that."

He did remember but again, for reasons he couldn't quite put his finger on, he felt like someone was walking over his grave. Gwen hadn't finished.

"Claire lives close to you, could you contact her and see if she can help? I'm going to ring the emergency services, see what they can do. The snow here is getting awfully deep."

Then the line went silent, she must have rung off. Davenport had forgotten his physical problems but was more troubled in his mind than hitherto. He mixed himself another whisky and soda and slumped with it into his chair by the fire. Debo popped her head round the door and said:

"I'm taking the dogs out before the weather breaks, the wind's getting up and the clouds look thick with snow. Don't you dare have any more of that whisky, you know very well that Dr Padkin told you to lay off it."

Moments later he heard the kitchen door close. He sat sipping the forbidden drink wondering if he'd ever be fit enough to take the dogs out like he used to. Then he remembered that he'd promised to contact Claire. As soon as the thought entered his mind the phone rang. He managed to reach it before it rang off, something he attributed to the efficacious powers of the whisky.

"Davenport."

Again there was a female voice on the other end, but this time one he did recognise.

"Sir Nigel, have you seen Ed? He went out this morning for a couple of hours and nobody has heard from him since."

Mary, Ed's wife, was not sounding her usual level-headed self.

It seemed to Davenport that history was repeating itself. As with Marcus Fox, he was unable to help, but this time he was far more worried. Particularly for Ed, he felt responsible for him, had come to like him as a man. There was something connected and deeply wrong about these disappearances. Why should the two clergymen involved in the Skendleby sealing and exorcism disappear on the same day?

He was still fretting when his wife and the dogs returned shrouded in snow. Looking through the open door he saw that the predicted storm, which had brought traffic to a stop in the South West and Midlands, had arrived in the North. It was early and in full spate.

There was no answer from Claire's cottage, neither from her nor Giles, not even an answering machine, which was unusual. Too unsettled for sleep by bedtime, Davenport remained downstairs in his armchair by the fire.

He would hold his ground and wait, like he had that night in Aden when he'd saved his men and won the Military Cross. What he was waiting for he didn't know but he knew something was coming. But before it could arrive the combination of booze and medication carried him off into an uneasy doze.

In his dream he was back by the estate wall on the day they'd resealed the mound. By the wall, alone and cold, confronting his legacy, the thing his family had feared over the centuries, the awful 'Hades bobbin' image from a Yeats poem. Strange then that when it arrived, its awful dislocated body swathed in corpse wrappings, it seemed familiar rather than frightening as he stared up at its unnatural height.

It was familiar to such an extent that he was on the point of understanding what it was when it stretched out a hideous bone white finger and touched him above the heart. After that any cognition dissolved into darkness. Gradually, a noise of knocking percolated through to his senses. For a moment he considered it must be Debo returning with the dogs. Then he remembered that they'd long since come back and gone off to sleep. The hammering continued and he forced himself out of the chair and towards the front door.

The blast of cold air that greeted him as he opened it froze him to the core. A violently gusting wind blew the heavy falling snow in all directions, including straight into his face. Temporarily blinded, he failed to see who was hammering so loudly at his door at this ungodly hour, but he felt hands grip his shoulders.

He wiped snow from his eyes and found himself staring into the face of a wild eyed Giles.

"Help me get him in, help me get him in, he's freezing."

Davenport didn't understand. All he could see was Giles and he was indistinct in the storm, the howling noise of which Davenport now noticed for the first time.

"Move then, I'll get him in on my own."

Giles turned and crouched down, and in the pool of light flowing from the house Davenport saw the thing. He couldn't believe his eyes at first, but it was there. Behind Giles, foul and besmeared, crouched a hideous feather-covered thing conjured by some ancient shaman. Davenport, normally the most courageous of men, opened his mouth to scream.

Chapter 27: Women's Work

Claire was in sparkling form from the moment of her arrival. She'd swept into the house radiant, leading a pale, short-haired young woman as if she were a present brought as an alternative to wine or flowers. She spread infectious good humour and greeted all of the women with a hug and kiss as if they were long lost friends. All except Olga, that is.

This was the most unusual house meeting Olga could remember, and that was saying something. Margaret had set it up to ratify the proposition that Lisa Richardson should take Kelly's role, with all that implied. Olga and Margaret had argued about it the night before: about Claire, about the community, and about their relationship. It was the first time they'd been like this: spiteful and bitchy - so untypical of both of them.

Olga had moved back into her own room. It felt cold and empty as she lay there weeping with rage and frustration. Neither of them slept and they hadn't spoken since. Margaret couldn't understand why Olga wouldn't back her, and Olga thought that Margaret had been seduced by Claire - in everything the word implied.

When Olga managed to calm down though she realised it wasn't only a seduction there was also an element of psychic coercion, something she had bitter memories of experiencing before. The Vanarvi woman unsettled her. No, it was more than that, she was frightened by her. To Margaret, she appeared quite different and Olga suspected that she had cast a type of glamour over her, like she did over everyone else who was even slightly susceptible.

Now here she was, Claire, holding forth to the community, trilling with laughter and being regarded with something akin to worship. She had introduced Lisa and outlined why she was such a suitable replacement for "our poor dear Kelly". She didn't look suitable to Olga, she looked sedated, but none of the others appeared to notice this detail. Now Claire moved on to something else, something she presented as an amusing anecdote.

"I can't believe how men can be such fools, can you, girls? I don't suppose you've heard this but that ridiculous little vicar, Ed, has gone and got himself lost, I wouldn't be surprised if..."

Then it all suddenly changed. Olga had been watching the look of delighted anticipation on Jenna's face when the timbre of Claire's voice changed. She turned and trained her gaze exclusively on Olga who felt herself frozen, rigid like a stage-frightened actress caught in the spotlight. Claire's next words were directed in a chilling tone only at her.

"But I don't suppose you find this funny, do you, Boxer? I think you rather fancy him, don't you?"

Olga gasped, why did she call her Boxer? How could she know that's what the other inmates called her? Why was no one protesting at this? Why was Margaret still laughing? Then she understood. Here in the house, their community, real witchcraft was being practised for the first time, and she was the only one to see it. The others, clearly, heard and saw something quite different. Something loveable and funny.

"Yes, that's right, Boxer, only you can hear - I'm saying this only to you. In this ridiculous community you are going to be privileged to host the birth of the donor of the last bone we need. The special bone. I know I shouldn't be teasing you like this but it's been so long since I inhabited such an enjoyable body that I can't resist a little amusement."

Olga heard, as if in the distance, a ripple of laughter as the other women listened to the end of Claire's story about Ed. Rose and Jenna were the most amused but Jan barely managed a smile. Olga felt she'd been transported to a different dimension.

"Just watch them lapping it up, Boxer, they love me, don't they? I could get them to do anything. Margaret, for instance, she can't wait to get me into bed; but, of course, you already suspect that, don't you? And believe me, she'll get a shock when I let her, they don't seem to survive my handling very long. Don't imagine you'll be able to warn anyone because sadly for you, my oversized friend, no one will believe a word you say. They'll just agree with me that you're experiencing one of your little episodes. Depression you called it I believe, although that wasn't the term the judge employed, was it? No, for you I'm afraid things are all going downhill from here."

Claire favoured her with the most malevolent smile as she said this. Then Olga felt the voice inside her head begin to withdraw. A snarl final snarl of:

"And of course, if you were stupid enough to attempt mischief we'd deal with you in the same way as all the others."

Then Olga heard, alongside all the rest, Claire's closing remarks.

"But sisters, that's enough of me, and I'm sure you are as delighted by Lisa's pregnancy as I am. So the rest of this wonderful evening should be about Lisa and her thrice-blessed future in this wonderful community of the spirit."

There was a burst of applause and Margaret and Jenna opened some chilled Prosecco. Claire directed a wicked smile at Olga as she led Lisa towards the glasses, a smile that would have driven her from the room had it not been for the look of abject misery laced with terror that she saw in Lisa's eyes.

****

Anderson was about to leave when the call came through. He'd been watching through his office window the scurry of city workers headed for cars, buses or trams to get home before the expected blizzard marooned them. The wintry scene and Christmas lights should have radiated a festive glow, but instead there was a sense of panic. It looked like an evacuation.

He decided to get off home, he was tired and stressed: and it wasn't only this gruesome, meaningless case. He was unsettled. The DI unsettled him, added to which half the time they didn't even know where she was. He took the heat for her but he was getting fed up of that and her behaviour the night he'd taken her home was well out of order. He sympathised with her and supported her behind her back, but there were limits. He logged off, grabbed his coat and then the phone rang.

"Sarge, I've got West Midlands CID on the phone, they wanted the DI but we can't raise her, they say it's important."

Anderson looked out of the window as if expecting a decision from out there; the snow had started to fall, heavy, fluffy flakes sticking immediately on the freezing roads and pavements.

"Put them through."

The voice at the other end sounded like a mix of Scouse and Brummie. It also sounded resentful of having to share intelligence.

"I'd wanted to speak to the DI but you'll have to do."

Anderson ignored the jibe.

"Thanks all the same, I'll do my best to stand in for her."

"We've found a body that might interest you, and you need all the help you can get from what we hear."

Anderson, having learnt at least this from Theodrakis, remained silent and after a time the voice continued.

"The victim's name is Marcus Fox. Messed up well and proper he was too, made the lad who found him heave up his breakfast."

There was a chuckle, then:

"Lots of mess so there should be plenty of DNA for you as well as prints. Whoever did him made no attempt to cover his tracks."

Anderson asked:

"How does this help us?"

"Because our boss thinks there could be a connection with your case. Some strange old bird turned up here the day before and reported him missing. She was agitated, dressed like a bloke and wearing Doc Martens. She must have been over seventy.

"We're getting more of that round here; Shrewsbury seems to be a magnet for pagans, wierdos and all the rest these days. Anyway, the thing that should interest you is that the list she gave us of people who might know where he was included a Dr Giles Glover. That rang some bells and it turned out that he was the archaeologist your lot pulled in and kept for a few days for questioning over the current murders. Strange that, don't you think?"

Anderson agreed and asked:

"Thanks, that's very helpful. What can you tell me about the late Marcus Fox?"

"Not a great deal. He lived like a recluse, kept himself to himself. He had good reason to and all, he used to be some type of vicar specialising in the occult. You know, like out of the exorcist, that type of thing. He got himself in the papers years ago trying to drive a demon or something out of a young girl. Mistake that was because the church suspected him of kiddie fiddling and he had to disappear quickish."

The lack of logic over the victim's decision to get involved in Skendleby must have struck both men at the same time because there was a pause, then Anderson asked:

"So, what's your take on the murder?"

"Doesn't seem to be any reason. He was found in the middle of nowhere near a phone box he'd just been using. It was a hell of a long walk from where he lived, particularly in this weather. So it must have been something serious he had to phone someone about. Snow had covered the body; we only found it by chance when a snow plough trying to keep the road open shifted something that obviously wasn't snow. There was blood all over the place."

"Anything else?"

"Plenty. Must have been set up in advance and carefully planned. Because who would be hanging round in the middle of nowhere on a freezing snowy night on the off-chance of finding and killing a recluse? So he must have been lured out, yeah?"

"Yeah, go on."

"And it was a grudge crime, whoever killed him was enjoying himself, enjoyed messing him up. So it makes sense that it's related to the kiddie fiddling he was involved with way back, yeah?"

Anderson wasn't so sure about this but kept his reservations to himself and listened to the rounding off.

"All we found on him apart from his wallet, which had been gone through, was a list of phone numbers, all from your patch. Apart from Glover do these names mean anything to you: Rev Edmund Joyce, Claire Vanarvi and Sir Nigel Davenport?"

"We're familiar with all of them."

"From last year's attacks, yeah?"

"That's right, but we don't regard them as suspects, in fact, Glover's helping with our enquiries."

"Well, as you've not made any progress, couldn't hurt to look at them again. Soon as the evidence is back from the labs we'll get it straight to you."

He rung off and for a moment Anderson slumped back in his chair watching the snow silently blanket the streets. It was falling heavily and obliterating any glimpse of the Christmas lights. He was about to try Viv's number when his cell phone chimed, the call was from her.

"Jimmy, I need you to mind things for a bit longer."

"Ma'am there has been developments, you need to come in."

She either didn't register this or didn't care to answer, all she replied was:

"Can't tell you about it but I'm following something up, someone wants to talk."

He was about to protest but the line went dead as she terminated the call.

Chapter 28: Shaman

If it had been possible to shock Giles any further then the sight of Davenport clutching at his chest and collapsing against the door frame would have triggered it, but he'd already seen too much that night for his senses to cope with. So, in an almost logical state of psychotic detachment, he prioritised between the collapsing elderly man and the crouching creature behind him in the way a triage nurse would.

He supported Davenport and half carried him across the lounge to the armchair by the fire, lowering him into it.

"What can I get you, there must be some tablets or something?"

"Bugger tablets, whisky."

Giles poured a generous measure into the tumbler from the decanter and then, for good measure, took a swig of the fiery liquor himself. Half of it spilled over his chin and down his neck while the other half he swallowed the wrong way and coughed back up. So, by the time, coughing and spluttering, he'd placed the tumbler in Davenport's hand it was hard to tell which of them was the more likely to expire. But Davenport was a man who'd dealt with more than most and he'd been toughened as a consequence. He was able to speak first.

"What in God's name is that foul thing you brought with you?"

Giles turned and scurried back to the doorway. Davenport took a couple of deep breaths and finished the whisky, thinking he'd need all the sangfroid he could muster in the next few moments. He was right.

Giles was framed in the doorway against the background of swirling snowflakes. He was struggling with some kind of garishly made-up mannequin that constituted a dead weight in his arms. The odd couple swayed and lurched across to the empty armchair facing Davenport's by the fire. With a grunt of effort, Giles deposited his partner into the chair and stood back revealing his burden.

The figure was covered in something like mouldering papier-mâché, was filthy and stained. In the palette of colours, black and smudged brown predominated interspersed by patches of filthy off-white like something painted by Braque during a nightmare. Beneath this hideous carapace there were discernible signs of gentle movement around the chest. So this pupating thing from a Halloween display was alive.

The grotesque presence in his living room made Davenport forget the pain in his chest; he wanted to ask Giles for some type of explanation but couldn't shift any of his concentration from this most unwelcome guest. So he just sat and stared at the abomination occupying the facing winged armchair.

After some moments of study it became apparent to Davenport that this thing was covered in an outer layer of decomposing organic matter, fashioned predominately, it seemed, out of black feathers in a variety of states of preservation. This mouldering outer surface was held in place with a type of sticky substance resembling a nasty mix of bird excrement and mucus. There were other things as well, things that Davenport feared to classify.

The bird thing began to chunter, then to rub with its feathered hands at the blank spaces beneath its forehead, the places in a human face where eyes would sit in their sockets. After a few seconds of this Davenport saw that hidden centimetres beneath excreta bonded feathers there were in fact eyes, eyes that still worked because after a struggle to unglue the lids they came apart. The creature gave a little noise sounding like relief and Davenport found himself staring into a pair of eyes that he recognised.

****

When Giles's faltering torch beam had first illuminated the slithery black mass of feathers his heart had almost stopped. It hadn't occurred to him that there was any way out. He'd assumed he would suffer the same fate as Ed. So it was surprise rather than any other emotion that gripped him when the birds began to edge back away from the priest. For no logical reason he assumed that they were making way for him, the way the crowd at an accident would make way for the paramedics. But they weren't.

They drifted back towards the furthest reaches of the cavern, passing through and over the millennia of accumulated fetish shrines. As they passed him they seemed to move through him. Although he could see them, they didn't seem real. Crowded together, perched in ranks superimposed on each other, the masses of crows, long dead, half dead and seemingly alive dispersed towards the darkness at the cavern's fringe. The susurration ceased and silence regained its hold on the dread dark space.

The scientific rationalist in Giles told him that neither the birds, the fetish shrines nor perhaps even the cavern itself, existed. But the torch was real enough and its beam, grown much stronger now the birds had gone, shone brightly at the mummified statue crouched on its knees. He hesitated before approaching it. A fluttering sound like ghostly wings being flexed told him the birds had gone. The cavern felt different, less threatening anyway, so with nerves slightly restored he began to inch his way forwards.

He didn't know what he'd find but as he gingerly stretched out his hand to test whether the figure was real it moved and he jumped back in shock. Now it looked alive he was more afraid to touch it. As he hovered in a lather of indecision there was a flapping of feathers, which sounded percussive in the cold, silent air. He shifted the torch beam towards the sound.

There, perched on the grimmest of the fetish shrines - the stone woman with a bird bursting out of her head - sat a crow. Huge, covered in night dark feathers tinged with grey, this old corvid monster sat staring at him. Its black eyes seemed to pierce his. Giles wondered if it would attack him. Instead it opened its beak.

"Taaakke him."

It grated the actual words. Giles heard them, astonished. The crow stared at him to emphasise its point and then flapped up off the shrine and vanished. Giles did as he was told and turned towards the priest. To his discomfort, the blind head turned towards him and from somewhere beneath the mass of bird shit and feathers a mouth spoke to him.

"I am both foul and brittle, much unfit to deal with holy writ."

Giles grabbed hold of him, his hands slipping on the slimy covering, and pulled him to his feet. He didn't know where the strength came from but his nerve had snapped. Ghost birds and a haunted chamber were bad enough, but quoting poetry was too much.

****

"I've no idea how I got him up out of there, the stuff covering him must have doubled his weight. The way up is narrow and twisting across steep, uncertain steps."

He stuttered to a halting stop. Davenport prompted him.

"Stress in action can provide extra strength, I remember a chap in Aden…"

"No, nothing like that, it wasn't anything like that."

"Then what?"

"My legs were weak, think I was in shock, and I could barely walk myself."

He paused again, then said falteringly:

"It felt like, like…"

He looked at Davenport as if expecting mockery. The older man said nothing, just waited to hear the rest. Behind them the flames hissed in the fire and the wall clock ticked.

"It felt like it wasn't only me, felt like I had help."

Davenport reached across and patted him on the knee.

"Perhaps you had. Go on."

"That's it really, it was only when I was back on the surface in the snow storm that I began to think again."

Davenport didn't reply, merely refilled his tumbler with whisky. Then between them, with Davenport directing and Giles supplying the effort, they peeled the foul outer layer and the equally disgusting clothes from Ed and manoeuvered him into a warm bath. Giles had talked throughout the operation.

"Couldn't think what to do with him at first, knew I couldn't take him home in this state. I knew that if we went to the Hall Carver would call the cops. So I brought him here, nowhere else really. He didn't say one thing the whole way. One quote from fucking Herbert and that was it. What are we going to do with him?"

They dried him off, put him into a pair of Davenport's PJs and a sweater, then into the spare bedroom with a hot water bottle.

"Perhaps I should get Claire over here."

Giles tried to raise her on his cell phone but got no answer.

"That's strange, I've not been able to reach her all day."

"Never mind that, now he looks half human we need to tell his wife. I thinks he's just about cleaned up sufficiently for her to see without the shock killing her. I can't imagine how you're going to explain this to her, Giles."

But the night had one more shock in store for them. Mary answered the phone at the first ring and said she'd be there in minutes. They returned to the bedroom to wait with Ed until she arrived. Through the open curtains the snow fell in a dense blanketing mass; the wind had dropped. Davenport said:

"Gwen rang tonight, she sounded pretty shaky. If I hadn't seen what happened last year I'd have suspected she'd been drinking."

He looked down at the oft-refilled tumbler in his own hand, emitting a sardonic chuckle before adding:

"She's been prey to a growing suspicion that what we did last year hasn't worked and that Marcus Fox wanted to gather us together again for a purpose not entirely to our benefit. Since then, however, he appears to have disappeared."

He looked at Giles for a reaction. Got none. Giles was lost in some interior daze. The events of the night were proving too much for him. He mumbled, as much to himself as to Davenport:

"A crow spoke to me, a crow; it spoke to me, what's go…"

The front doorbell rang and in the quiet of the night it sounded strangely strident. As if summoned by bells, the figure on the bed opened its eyes and spoke.

"I have been anointed."

Chapter 29: The Beguiling

Maybe Viv should have thought more carefully about how the message had found its way on to her personal cell phone before accepting the invitation. Only a handful of people had that number, people she loved and trusted. She certainly hadn't given it to anyone outside that close circle.

It was only when she was halfway to Skendleby that she began to think at all: before that it was like a type of autopilot had governed her actions. When the intellect kicked back in it commenced with raising the obvious questions. The first was prompted by the traffic reports on the local radio. According to the giggly reporter, the region was afflicted by snowstorms of an apocalyptical severity. These rendered road use at best extremely hazardous and at worst impossible.

So why was she making such good progress? She'd been aware of the snow when she set out and could see it hovering around her but, here she was, driving comfortably at the maximum speed allowed. Now she was almost there, the 'there' being a country bistro across the road from the Hanging Man. As she turned left opposite the pub she saw that its car park was snow shrouded and empty.

The bistro car park wasn't, it had a light sprinkling and a couple of parked cars, and yet she could see snow gusting in the orange glare of the streetlamp. It was as if the weather itself had opened a passage through the snow for her to follow. If she could have isolated and analysed the impulse that catapulted her out into the winter night towards this strange encounter then she might have put it down to instinct and the lack of any other leads. But...

But that wasn't what it was down to. She'd gone because she'd felt compelled. She was a woman of sharp intellect but she'd driven off into a blizzard to meet someone she feared in a remote setting. Even as a plot device in the most tawdry of soaps she'd have hooted in derision. In real life she'd lived it.

She opened the car door and the cold hit her, bringing her to her senses. She could be snowed up here while her officers needed her. A couple of miles down the twisting lanes behind the bistro lay the Skendleby mound. It was the unbidden and unwelcome image of this prehistoric burial mound, lying forbidding and bleak beyond the woods that sent her scurrying across the frozen surface of the car park towards the comforting light that poured out through the bistro windows.

Inside, in the cosy subdued lighting, it was warm and comforting. A Christmas tree twinkling near a log fire at the far end contrasted oddly with the two olive trees growing from huge terracotta pots just inside, flanking the entrance. A smiling woman appeared from behind the bar and took her coat, saying:

"Your friend's over there in the alcove, she's ordered you a drink."

Before she could protest she sensed someone approaching her, and heard a trilling voice.

"Oh, look at you, honey! You must be frozen."

It was like a dream. But there was nothing dreamlike about the two cold hands that were placed in a proprietarily presumptuous manner on her cheeks, or the deep red lips that brushed hers.

"Come over here to our table and have a drink; what a night we're going to have, just us two."

Viv had no choice, one of the cold hands now had hold of hers and was leading her towards the softly lit alcove.

"You'll love it here, honey, the food's really good."

Then, wondering how it had all happened so quickly, Viv was sitting down facing her interlocutor, facing Claire; facing her and knowing why she feared her.

"What's the matter, honey? You've come all the way out here to meet me and now you look like you've seen a ghost and want to run off home."

She paused to pass Viv a glass of white wine before continuing.

"Not that you'll find it as easy getting back as it was coming."

Looking out of the window at the swirling snow, Viv realised what she meant but hadn't time to think on it as Claire said:

"Come on, have a sip of the wine, with that sour look on your face you're beginning to remind me of a sulky girl I met on Samos. She didn't want to play either."

Viv took the glass and gulped at the wine, it was stronger than she'd expected and despite being chilled she could feel it warming her as it travelled down to her stomach.

"There, that's better, isn't it? Take another sip."

She did as she was told, the wine relaxed her, but she wasn't sure if this was a good thing.

"I've already ordered, so we're not going to be bothered by the staff: at last we can get to know each other properly."

Viv sat like a rabbit in the headlights and her mind swerved into questioning why she'd chosen to wear a slinky black dress. Knowing she ought to make some attempt at speech she blurted out:

"Will Dr Glover be joining us?"

Claire squealed with laughter.

"Oh, with lines like that you could make a fortune doing 'stand up'. No, of course he won't be, think about it: he'd cramp our style."

Then a waitress appeared, putting a plate of fish mousse with oysters arranged in a circle around it in front of both of them, before swiftly withdrawing. Claire said:

"Come on, eat up; you know what effect oysters have, don't you?"

Claire refilled the glass that Viv couldn't remember emptying. She picked it up and drank, then started to eat. The food was delicious, although eating the oysters, which she normally hated, left the salty juice running down her chin. It was like a dream where you can't control yourself. But she knew she wasn't dreaming and could see that Claire wasn't eating.

Then she felt the cold hand through her tights on the inside of her thigh. She hadn't noticed when Claire had started to touch her and, for reasons she didn't understand, couldn't move the hand away.

"You see things, don't you, honey? Things that other people don't see, things that you try to pretend aren't there. But they are there. What do you see when you look at me?"

Viv stared back at her, and what she saw made her forget the hand creeping up the inside of her thigh.

"I'm not sure, sometimes a beautiful woman, but sometimes something else, something I don't want to…"

Claire cut her off.

"Now you're talking, that's better; better for you anyway, so now maybe we can have an enjoyable evening without the nasty stuff being necessary."

Viv was wondering what Claire meant by the nasty stuff when she became aware that the sharp fingernails were gently tickling the inside of her thigh, near her groin. She felt herself becoming aroused; how could this be happening? Claire's other hand picked up Viv's wine glass.

"Drink some more of this, you'll need it."

Viv took the glass and emptied it; she was beginning to feel excited in a frighteningly strange way.

"Now you're going to answer a few questions. If you don't I'll take my hand away, and if you give the answers I want then little by little I'll move it further up. You want that, don't you, want it badly? You're excited and terrified, just like I want you to be and believe me, once you're in that state you're lost and the only way you can be found again is through doing what I want."

She was right. Viv's mind recoiled from the sharp-toothed face whose features were constantly sliding into different shapes and whose dead eyes flickered through all the colours of the spectrum like Christmas lights experiencing a power surge. But her groin was trying to push itself towards the gently teasing fingers. The restaurant seemed to have disappeared. She felt as if her mind was opening up to Claire's to receive something, something she recognised as having been lost, something familiar. She heard Claire say:

"So, answer and perhaps I'll let you back into your world and you can run off back to London, that'd be a relief, wouldn't it? Answer well and perhaps if you're lucky I'll give you the other relief you need.

"But before you go getting too excited I want you to tell me something about that funny little Greek detective of yours."

Then, as if from a great height, Viv found herself looking down through a fringe of winter trees at Theodrakis. He was out in the snow, outside an old stone building, she recognised it: the Davenport chapel. What was he doing out there on a night like this? Then she knew, knew what he was after, and the moment she knew she heard Claire's voice, strained and insistent.

"Yes, yes, nearly there, follow him in, tell me what he sees; do this and I'll finish it for you."

But she didn't and Viv didn't follow: a voice cut through to them.

"Hiyaa, fancy meeting you here on a night like this?"

The spell was broken. Viv watched Claire jerk backwards into her seat, spitting like a cat at the newcomer who stood smiling at her. Not quite smiling, her eyes weren't smiling, they were locked onto Claire's. Then she slipped into the seat across from Claire, the melting flakes of snow on her tight fitting jogging suit dripping on to the cushioned seats. Neither of them spoke. Viv watched, the restaurant staff may as well have been in a different dimension. Time was suspended.

Claire moved her hand forward reaching for Viv, but before it made contact Suzzie Jade's hand got between them; she held her palm up against Claire's. There was power passing between these hands, a power transcending anything Viv knew. It was like a display of mime, the hands dancing with each other without touching. Claire's expression of amused control vanished to be replaced by an expression that suggested bafflement, or maybe just surprise. Then it was over and Claire was walking towards the door in the reconstituted reality of the restaurant.

Suzzie-Jade looked shaken. She said:

"Lucky for you I got here when I did, another moment and it would have been too late and you'd have joined all the others who've been used then tossed away."

There was no trace of wag-speak now. Viv hoped she was dreaming, wanted to wake up, but instead asked:

"What's happening? What's happening to me? What are you?"

Suzzie-Jade replied.

"I don't know, I thought I'd grown out of this when I was little. I don't know why I'm here, I just know things, they are beginning to come into my mind bit by bit."

She must have read from Viv's face that this wasn't a satisfactory answer. She stopped and started again.

"It's hard to explain. It's like it's not real, the purpose is, but that's beyond anything you'd understand. You only see what's here, which is a tiny bit of the purpose, just a bit of audit. None of what you see in your consciousness matters at all. The bits you see are no more than steam escaping from a kettle. What's in the kettle is important but the kettle's somewhere you couldn't even imagine. What's happening here to you isn't even real. I can't explain better, it keeps slipping in and out of focus."

Viv couldn't take any more of this, she needed to get out. More than anything else she wanted the normality of police HQ. She rose shakily to her feet and traced Claire's footsteps towards the door. Behind her Suzzie-Jade called:

"You won't get anywhere tonight and anyway, you've been drinking too much."

Viv ignored her and pulled the door open, only to be hit by a blast of snow carried on freezing air. Screwing her eyes together she blinked into the night. The car park was snowbound, the road closed; beyond the church she could just spot the lights of a council snow plough vainly attempting to extricate itself from a drift. Suzzie-Jade had joined her at the door. She said:

"Don't worry, they'll put you up here, it's all arranged. Oh, and one more thing that has just come to me, you need to listen to that little Greek, you can trust him. I think he knows more about this than any of us."

Suzzie-Jade blinked her eyes like someone trying to wake up, then she squeezed past Viv and out into the night, immediately disappearing into the snow as her last words were blown back by the wind towards the restaurant.

"See yu laitaa."

Chapter 30: Within You, Without You

It took Claire some time to recognise it. Recognise her own front door. It took her even longer to figure out what she was doing standing in front of it and where she'd been. In fact, she never made it to the second discovery, her mind being fogged in a mist of amnesia. But she found her key, turned the lock and went in.

It was like seeing the place for the first time. She shrugged off her coat, wondering why it still felt dry despite the snowstorm outside, and draped it over the newel post on the banister. Wandering into the living room, she saw Giles sprawled out on the couch, asleep in front of the wood fire. Poor love, he must have been waiting up for her. She felt a rush of emotion, a surge of love. How long had he been there? She checked her watch; it was after midnight. Where had she been?

Then she noticed on the table by the sofa a wine bottle and two glasses. She picked the bottle up, saw it was Amarone, the wine he'd brought for their first date. It was a romantic gesture he'd obviously intended to reprise tonight, and she saw that he hadn't finished the bottle; he'd left some for her.

Feeling a wave of sympathy for him she picked the bottle up and poured some into the unused glass. Maybe she should wake him, tell him how much she loved him despite the fact that they seemed to be drifting apart. First, she sniffed the wine in the glass, and the rich scent triggered precious memories.

Then everything began to change; it was like someone had shifted the dial on an old-fashioned radio. All clarity disappeared and she began to feel woozy, like she used to during her episodes. She knew what was going to happen next and the thought filled her with terror.

She was losing herself again, becoming something else, becoming part of something greater, something wild, savage, sensual and evil, but worse than that was the strange warping of her eyesight. She could see other things, other places. Just a few at first but then, like someone had flicked a switch, they were myriad.

Her eyes were seeing multiple images, like a fly's. But a fly with infinite optical lenses, with each lens accompanied by its own thought process. This legion of minds occupied myriad spaces in myriad dimensions; her grip on the room slackened.

Each individual thought process was subservient to something more powerful and within milliseconds of realising this, her own mind, will and feelings were reduced to an imperceptible fragment of the collective.

A collective memory of a range of creatures, some of which had been human once, whilst others were biologically different in every way. Then, way down in the deepest depths of consciousness, there were things little more than thinking aspects of strange landscapes, strange rocks on dark pyroclastic worlds long since dead or yet to be born.

Amongst these millions of fragments the real Claire shrunk to an imperceptible ripple of which only flickering images survived. This composite in Claire's form looked down at Giles on the sofa and saw him as weak and contemptible, something that had almost outlived its use and would soon be discarded.

The parasite was controlling her, diminishing her perception as it was all the others it had subsumed across the millennia. So within her form, its latest temporary home, there were myriad visions but one controlling purpose, to which the will of Claire and all the others the parasite had infested were subject.

Now the will was flexing itself, focusing on a single image from Claire's individual memory bank. An old woman with grey hair, wearing a man's dark suit and Doc Marten boots. A ridiculous kind-hearted creature and the beloved saviour of Claire's youth.

As she watched, the old woman, Gwen, picked up her house phone and began to speak. She was worried, worried by the disappearance of Marcus Fox, she was fretting that something evil she had thought was vanquished was in fact stirring. Her actions were driven by a growing terror she had trouble keeping in check.

She was speaking to Davenport, the old man who should have died. She was meddling, trying to arrange a meeting of the same fools who had interfered with the resurrection at Skendleby the previous Christmas.

She wouldn't be allowed to meddle this time. Not now that the coven was gathered, now that the final bone necessary for the rising messiah was almost ready to be cultivated and harvested.

The parasite raised the Amarone bottle to her lips, bit clean through the glass neck and allowed the mix of fragmenting glass and wine to flow down Claire's throat. Having gargled the last mouthful of wine and glass, she spat it out, laced with blood, over the recumbent form of Giles. Then, pausing only to throw back her head and crow with laughter, Claire passed straight through the wall and out into the wild night.

****

Suzzie-Jade couldn't find her keys; in fact, she couldn't remember having left the house. She was cold so hammered at the door which eventually was opened by the Neanderthal form of Si's latest minder. He seemed surprised to see her.

"Didn't know you was out, Mrs C."

That makes two of us she thought as she pushed past him and into the house. Her memory had been playing her tricks lately, which she ascribed to taking too many of the magic pills that Si brought back from his clubs. She could hear Si talking to himself in the games room as he played on one of his violent killer games. She didn't want to see more of him than was absolutely necessary so walked up the stairs towards her bedroom. Once inside she sloughed off the lycra running suit and headed naked for the shower.

But the strong flow of hot water failed to calm her the way it usually did. She wasn't an imaginative women, she focused on what was in front of her and how to put it to best use. She could handle Si, in fact, she'd handled worse than him in the past in her line of business. So what was going wrong?

Why was she acting the way she was? She was trying to work out where all the missing time had gone when her mind shifted again and she got a distinct flash of memory, and it wasn't her memory.

Suddenly she was outside by the estate wall watching Skendleby mound. She'd found herself by this place quite often lately, for reasons she couldn't fathom. It wasn't a place she felt comfortable but it seemed to draw her towards it. Now she was here again opposite the mound that had put Si in such a state. There was a man on top of it with a spade. He was funnily dressed, looked like some weird kind of vicar. But it wasn't Ed. In fact, it looked to her like something out of the olden days.

She could tell that the vicar, or whatever it was, felt uneasy - he was frightened. Then something black and disarticulated, like a great bunch of rags, came bounding out of the tree line heading towards the man on the mound. It had come running out from the very place she was standing, so why hadn't she noticed it?

Suzzie-Jade was running with it and the vicar had dropped his spade and was sprinting back towards the church. She seemed to be seeing through the black thing's eyes, which couldn't be right. Then she found herself looking at something completely different. Somewhere hot, Greece or someplace like that. She'd never been there, but in a strange way it felt familiar.

She was pulled back from wherever she was by the noise of banging, and found herself back in the shower. The banging at the door was still going on, getting louder if anything. She grabbed a towel and got ready to face up to Si in whatever shitty mood he'd got himself into. She could hear his voice abusing her from the other side of the door.

"Get out here now, you slag, I've got things to say to you, things you're gonna listen to, right?"

She pulled back the bolt and opened the door, prepared for the worst.

But it wasn't what she'd expected. The door opened revealing Si's enraged and unhealthily red face, but he didn't try to hit her or shout at her. He stared in horror for a second then screamed, turned round and legged it downstairs shouting to his bodyguard:

"It's back, it's got in the 'ouse again; get up there and get it out, get it out."

She heard the man reply:

"What's up boss? What is it?"

"It's in the shower. Go and see, go and fuckin see, what do I pay you for?"

The minder grunted and Suzzie-Jade heard him rumbling up the stairs towards the bathroom. When he reached the door she saw the gun in his hand.

"Where is it, where's it gone?"

Suzzie-Jade replied.

"Nothing here, only me, innit?"

The minder looked baffled, he shouted downstairs:

"Nothing here, boss, just the missus. What am I supposed to be looking for?"

Si's voice, scared and angry, came from below.

"That thing, the shadowy one that got in before, black and rags and stuff, like bleedin Halloween. The thing the police couldn't find, the thing that killed the foreign slut and put her down that 'ole."

As he was saying this, Suzzie-Jade got the distinct image of the fantasy she'd drifted into in the shower, because the horror Si described matched exactly the way she would have depicted the disarticulated bunch of rags she'd watched chase the vicar off the mound. The thing that she'd felt herself slipping into. Instead of commenting on this she had the presence of mind to reply:

"No, nothing up here, only me and I'm not what Si's interested in."

She shut the door again, dropped the towel and returned to the shower, turning the water up to maximum power to drown out Si's shouting. Despite the relief that now he had something else to think about he'd forget about whatever he wanted from her, she couldn't relax. Strange things were happening round the place and worse, strange things were happening to her.

Later that night, after taking a couple of pills washed down with more than a couple of Tequila Slammers, fragments of her encounter with Claire in the bistro began to infiltrate her memory. Oddly enough, this didn't disturb her the way it should have done and her last thought before descending into a deep, drug-induced sleep was that perhaps it would be a good idea if she paid a visit to the little Greek detective.

****

Viv woke up late in an unfamiliar bed in a room she didn't recognise. Her memory of the night before was only partial and despite its nightmarish quality she understood that something of significance had occurred, something that chimed with her strange experiences of the previous weeks. Bright daylight was shining through the curtains. She got out of bed, crossed to the window and looked out.

It was a beautiful crisp winter's day, the sun was shining but without the power to melt the snow. She saw that the snowplough had managed to clear a channel in the road, along which traffic was moving slowly. She decided she'd talk to Theodrakis and, having resolved upon that, felt better, or at least less isolated.

Then her phone bleeped from the depths of her handbag and she fished it out to discover a long list of missed calls. What had happened while she'd been away?

Chapter 31: Hunted by the Dark

His feet were wet. Glancing down he noticed there was water bubbling up through the snow-shrouded ground. Wiping the sweat from his eyes he looked round at the dark, not much to see; flat land intersected by snow filled drainage ditches. He must be on the Moss. He hated the Moss, a poxy miasma of waterlogged peat, how had he got here? What was going on?

If he carried on he'd probably stumble into one of the deep pools that littered this damp land and drown in the black, freezing water. He stopped, stood breathing heavily trying to get his mind working. He remembered the pub and Dave saying:

"Jed, Jed you alright?"

But he also remembered the sensation of killing the old guy, the priest. One of these memories must be false but the damp stains on his coat felt and smelt remarkably like blood. However, neither of these vague recollections was anything like as bad as that other fleeting glimpse into an unreal and increasingly frightening last few hours. This one couldn't be real, made no sense.

He'd found himself outside the door of the vicar's house in Skendleby. He vaguely recalled something important driving him, something he had to tell the vicar, something he had to get off his chest. Then the door opened and there was the vicar, the stuck-up ponce he'd smacked that day on the mound before the fat lezzer had decked him. Then everything seemed to slide away, like it did in dreams, leaving just a blank.

Except it wasn't quite a blank, although Jed wished it was. He remembered the vicar, or to be more accurate, the vicars. Because as he'd stood there trying to remember what he had to say (Joyce, that was the vicar's name, he recalled), the vicar started to speak and Jed became very afraid. Not because of the words, Jed hadn't been able to understand any of them, even though he reckoned they were some kind of warning. No, it was what he was seeing that frightened him, scared him so much he began to blub until he could feel the warm tears on his freezing cheeks.

It was the way the vicar kept shifting and sliding into different forms, the way he was changing as he spoke. It looked to Jed like he was turning into something that wasn't from now, but from way back. He was turning into something older.

Everything about him was growing older, looking different, like something out of an old film. Jed hadn't remembered much from his history lessons at school, he'd skipped most of them, but he thought he saw the vicar change into the type of one they must have had back when the Romans were fighting the Spanish Armada.

Jed didn't want to look at him even though he knew that what the vicar, if he still was the vicar, was trying to tell him was important, important to him, Jed. But he just couldn't stand to look any more and the last glance he dared direct at Joyce, before he'd turned to run, revealed a gaunt figure in a mouldy black cape with a crow's beak staring out from under a cowled hood.

Jed tried to pull himself together; he looked round across the wasteland of the Moss. This felt real enough, it was certainly bloody cold enough. Perhaps what he thought he was remembering was like a series of acid flash backs that seemed real but weren't. He tried to rationalise.

Maybe he'd been smoking too much of the crazy stuff that he'd got from that whore in Stocky, the one he liked to knock about a bit. But he couldn't convince himself and his heart started pumping again. Something really bad was happening to him. He thought of his mother, hadn't thought of her in months. He heard himself begin to whimper. He had to get out, find his way back home.

Then he heard the noise.

Very faint at first, a putative pulse, but strangely threatening. Jed shook his head attempting to clear it, then he tried to reassure himself about the growing sonic intrusion: at least it sounded far off. Far off now maybe, but it was getting closer. It sounded like a duvet being shaken out, or more like a load of duvets. Then, as the cacophony drew nearer, got louder, it began to sound like duvets fashioned of old leather, creaking and scratching across the sky.

It was time to get away from here; Jed forced his feet to move into a slow jog. But this was difficult across the freezing claggy terrain where the very earth seemed to be sucking him into its greasy grasp with every step he tried to make.

While he struggled, the moon dodged out from behind the clouds and shone its silver light over the wetlands, transforming the Moss into a Christmas card scene, glittering and radiant, stretching away into the distance towards the hills. But not for Jed the comfort of a Christmas card.

For Jed the translucence brought a hideous clarity. Below the moon, picked out in night-dark relief, a dense swarm was approaching. A black mass of crows, ravens, rooks and jackdaws was hurtling across the desolate plain towards him. Then, as if at the command of some corvid emperor, the din of their leathery wings flapping was augmented by an outbreak of ferocious cawing and carking. They swept across the face of the moon and the night momentarily reverted to black in an avian lunar eclipse.

Now he was running, running for his life and screaming at the top of his lung capacity. All his life he'd never believed in anything other than gain and self-interest. Now he believed; but in all the wrong stuff, the nightmare stuff the belief of the damned. But there wasn't time to do anything about it now, as he lurched and galloped for life at full tilt across the Moss.

Then his right leg missed the grass tussock he was aiming at and plunged deep into freezing water. He was down on all fours slipping and sliding in the mud at the bottom, pulling at his leg and trying to extract it from whatever was holding it down. *Just mud*, he tried to reassure himself, *it must be clinging mud.* But it didn't feel like mud.

What it felt like, oh God, what it felt like was fingers: bony fingers, leathery fingers, several of them. Not just one hand but many tugging him down to Hell in the mud and slime of the pool. What was it down there? He squealed in terror and kicked out against the unspeakable horrors. However, the more he struggled, the deeper he sank. The sound of the birds was intense. Looking up, he saw them clearly now. Not as an undifferentiated mass but as individual beaks, claws and venomous eyes. He started to scream.

Then they were on him, all over him, ripping and tearing, cutting and gouging. Even through the agony and terror he was aware of their stench, the carcass breath, death reanimated. Within seconds his clothes were in tatters and his flesh shredded. His life force was already seeping away when he felt their frenzied weight pressing on him, forcing him down into the black water stained with his blood. His head was forced under last, tattered, torn and bloody, cutting off his screams.

Even through the terror he understood this was retribution for his attempt to demolish the Skendleby mound, and probably for more. The face of the old priest he'd killed flashed across his closed eyes. The man's face didn't seem angry, it seemed more like he understood, but there wasn't any more time. Jed's lungs were bursting and he opened his mouth to gasp for air knowing it would be filled not by air but by water.

But it wasn't. It filled with something else, something he couldn't place and for a nanosecond his spinning mind registered surprise but it didn't last. Time ran out, then blackness, then nothing.

****

Anderson had been eating a flaccid bacon roll from the canteen when the call came through. Disturbing as the message was it was almost a relief in that it shook him out of the bout of bleak introspection he'd been locked into. He'd sat slumped in his chair staring out at the Christmas market without really seeing it. His guts ached; his stomach had felt off for weeks now. He knew it was just stress but it still generated hypochondriacally induced anxiety.

He blamed Skendleby, blamed it for sucking the joy and anticipation out of Christmas. It had been the same the previous year, maybe it was ruined for good. His mood was exacerbated by the boss going AWOL. He'd been trying to reach her for the best part of twenty four hours and had just been about to try her cell phone number again when the duty sergeant called him.

"Jimmy, you'll love this, there's been another."

"Where?"

He asked but inside he knew already.

"Skendleby, of course, where all your business comes from. Body in the Moss, some poor bugger found it walking his dog this morning, there's a car waiting to take you."

He considered ringing Viv but decided to wait until he knew for sure what he was dealing with, so he just grabbed his coat off the back of his chair and headed for the stairs, too preoccupied even to wonder over the implications of the sergeant saying 'in' rather than 'on' the Moss.

There was one nice surprise though: the driver was Gemma Dixon, back on duty as a driver after arresting the attacker on the Skendleby mound the previous Christmas. She'd been honoured for that, been to the Palace for a medal. Jimmy was surprised she'd stayed in the force; she was close to making it as a singer. Jimmy had fancied her for ages but reckoned she was out of his league. She seemed pleased to see him though, and smiled before saying:

"Strange to be going back to Skendleby almost exactly a year on, Jimmy, sorry, I mean, Sarge."

He hadn't noticed the slip and decided to sit in the front next to her rather than enjoy the benefit of rank in the back. But he couldn't really think of much to say to her until they'd crawled out of the city in the snake of slow moving traffic, and even then it was only in response to her saying:

"You know, Sarge, since that night, Ges Wilson hasn't been able to come back to work, it's changed him, I don't know what to say to him any more when I go to see him."

"Was harder on you, Gemma, and you made it back."

"Messed me up though."

"You don't look messed up to me."

He wondered what had made him say that. He needn't have bothered though, she smiled. For a moment he was on the brink of asking her if she'd like to go for a drink after work; she was looking at him as if urging him on. But too late, they'd reached their destination. She turned the car off the road and onto the track into the Moss. They could see flashing blue lights ahead and he felt a tightening in his stomach and the acid bile of reflux rising in his throat.

He wasn't the only one. A white-faced constable he didn't recognise blurted out:

"Sorry, Sir, we moved him, and that's when."

He hesitated.

"That's when?"

Anderson could see he that wasn't going to get much further so he pushed past to see what the boy had seen, looking over the shoulder of an officer from the forensics team who was crouched down on his knees inspecting something lying on the cold ground. At first he couldn't identify what he was seeing, everything was blackened with peat staining and there didn't seem to be any recognisable form. The man on his knees said, without bothering to look back at Anderson:

"Hard to separate out what's what here, never seen anything like this before."

Anderson hadn't either. He stood rooted, waiting for the man to explain what he was seeing. The forensic turned his head to look up and Anderson saw that he too was pale faced and hollow eyed.

"This one here's the one you'll be interested in. Problem is he's got mixed up with these others, God knows how."

Anderson still couldn't understand.

"So, what have we got here?"

The forensic gave a mirthless chuckle.

"Right mix up is what we've got here, Jimmy. Looks like your customer's got mixed up with some old 'uns from under the bog. This other shit, the flint pot and old wood covering them, must have come up with them from the bottom. Have to get the archaeologists out when you've finished."

Anderson stammered:

"How? How? I don't understand."

"None of us understands, and none of us want to be here either. I can't risk moving any of the bits of the old 'uns, they're too fragile, but watch while I turn his head towards you, see, look there."

Anderson's cell phone bleeped and part of his mind registered it was Viv calling. A few minutes previously answering would have been his priority. Not now.

"This is his face, see the mouth's wide open."

Anderson still didn't understand.

"What's the black stuff covering the mouth?"

"Not covering it, in it."

"What are they?"

"Feathers; his mouth's stuffed full of feathers, they're the only sign of a mark on him."

Chapter 32: Haunted By Stars

In the chill gloom of twilight, Ed steered his car through the traffic choking the southerly urban fringe of the Northern Powerhouse, relieved at having discharged his duties. He'd stood in, at the last moment, to officiate at a funeral, replacing a local vicar who was unavailable following a visit from the police that the diocese was unwilling to elucidate upon.

He decided to take the minor road that cut across the fields at the back of 'The Hanged Man'. Despite the poor quality of the rapidly dwindling light, he noticed the flapping shredded fragments of black plastic rubbish bags spiked on the thorn of the hedgerows. Hedgerows badly trimmed by the council, which meant fangs of splintered, badly pollarded saplings, reached out towards the road like grasping fingers. His headlights lit up the gaunt skeleton of a stag-headed oak choking on ivy.

Since his experience beneath the Davenport Chapel, most things struck Ed as sinister. In fact, it had taken a great deal of mental strength to convince himself he wasn't mutating into a crow. This phenomenon, amongst the many problems in his life, was one he hadn't anticipated. But of all the horrors circling his mind there was one particular recent memory he found most perturbing; the visit of that creature Gifford: the criminal who had assaulted him by the Skendleby mound.

To Ed's horror, the previous evening, Gifford had called in at the rectory. The doorbell had rung and Ed had opened the door to find him standing there, arms hanging at his sides, dishevelled in stained and weather-beaten clothes. He'd looked ravaged and disturbed, but also, strangely like a frightened child. It was this last detail that had stopped Ed being afraid. In fact, he'd felt a sudden surge of pity for Gifford wash over him.

He'd been asking Gifford to come in and dry off and have a warm drink when he'd noticed the man begin to shuffle backwards, a look of absolute horror spreading across his face. Ed had reached out his hand in a gesture of reassurance at which Gifford, emitting a choked-off squeal, had turned his back and ran. It had been something he'd seen in Ed that had done it, something Gifford hadn't been expecting.

So total was this outbreak of terror that it had frozen Ed to the spot. For a moment he'd touched his own face to check he hadn't in fact metamorphosed into a giant crow. Gifford disappeared into the gloom so he'd slouched back into the rectory, closing the door in perplexity.

To slough these memories off, he switched on the car radio, but after a few dispiriting seconds listening to the news reader's summary of the increasingly violent anarchy in Athens, he switched it off and spent the rest of the journey signing *The Day Thou Gavest, Lord, Is Ended* at the top of his voice.

The relief of entering into the warmth of the rectory and Mary's welcome didn't last long.

"I've left the post in the study for you, most of it's junk but there's one handwritten envelope. Do you want a cuppa?"

He grunted assent and sloped into the study. As soon as he saw the envelope he had a presentiment and hesitated a moment before opening it. A short epistle, seconds to read, hours to digest. Some time later, looking up, he saw the mug of cooling tea in front of him. He hadn't noticed Mary bring it in. He returned his scrutiny to the crumpled page with its scrawled message.

Dear Joyce,
The exorcism on Skendleby didn't work, I think we were used. This is beyond us, beyond our dimension. We meddled in things we don't understand.
I fear something's coming for me. Be careful.
Marcus Fox.
P.S. Find Gwen, save her if you can.

But Ed already knew this: the crows had told him. He also knew that if he didn't manage to get a grip on himself he'd descend into one of his episodic bouts of depression. So for about forty minutes he struggled to turn his attention towards preparing for his numerous Christmas activities. He made no progress, couldn't put his mind to it, so the details kept slipping away. Slipping down into the chamber of terrors beneath the Davenport chapel. He needed to speak to someone; he had to share some of the hideous detail. But who to share it with?

Davenport was too unwell, Giles too weak, Steve missing. There was only one person, but he hesitated to call her. Part of his existence, his salvation, was based on Claire, based on her strength and goodness, so why did he hesitate to call her?

He knew the answer, something about her, something in her had begun to unnerve him, frighten him. He knew there was no logic in this. He pushed it from his mind and decided on Olga. He had to speak to her anyway so, suppressing his guilt over the mixture of motives that inclined him towards her, he reached for the phone.

As his hand grasped the handset there was a bleep from the cell phone on the desk. He glanced towards it and saw that Claire was calling. Perhaps the Lord was deciding for him. He answered and heard Claire's sparkling voice.

"Ed, darling, you'll never guess what I've been watching on the Moss?"

He knew, despite her tone of voice, that this wasn't going to be happy news. He was right.

"The police have cordoned it off, there's flashing blue lights blocking all the tracks."

"Why Claire, what is it?"

"A body. Ed, they've found a body. A dog walker stumbled over it early morning, bet she wishes she'd taken another route."

He felt his heart sinking; he knew this was connected to his fear.

"Do you know anything more? Like who it was?"

"That's a strange question to be asking. Ed, are you feeling guilty?"

"No, no, of course not."

"All I know is that Giles will get a call about this, he reckons that there are a lot more ancient bodies preserved in the Moss. Anyway, that's not the reason I called you, Ed. I'm worried about you, have been for some time now. I've a feeling there's something you need to get off your chest. Am I right?"

So the Lord had decided for him, he should have rung her earlier.

"Claire, I've had a strange experience, I can't understand it, can't get it out of my mind."

"I knew there was something, Ed, tell me all about it."

"You know the chamber, deep under the Davenport Chapel, that Giles found?"

"Of course, he wouldn't shut up about it for ages."

"Well, I've been down there."

"Silly of you."

"More than silly. Claire, something terrible happened to me under there, something I don't think I understand yet. Something I need to understand."

Claire's manner changed and he felt her true sensitive nature, her sympathy, reaching out across to him.

"Tell me, Ed, tell me everything, I can help you."

He needed to tell, needed to share this burden, he could feel tears stinging his eyes.

"They trapped me in there, Claire, they talked to me."

"Who Ed? Who trapped you?"

He could feel her sympathy now, it was surrounding him, protecting him. Thank God she'd rung him.

"The crows, the crows, you remember? The ones who I thought were helping me last year."

"Share it, Ed, pass your burden over to me."

He couldn't resist, it all came out, and he tripped over his words in his haste.

"They surrounded me, all of them, all their ancestors spoke to me, told me things, terrible things. Something drives them, a necklace of bone almost complete that will pave the way for a terrible birth. I didn't understand but I felt their terror. Then they piled on me, dragged me down, drowned me in their stench and rot. All the time speaking things, things no one is meant to hear."

"Ok, Ed, it's all right, you've got me with you now. Calmly now, slow and calm, Ed, there's no need to be afraid any more. Take some deep breaths then tell me what they said, exactly what they said."

"As I sank down through the layers of time they murmured to me. At one point I swear, swear I heard Homeric verse, iambic metre, dactyls and spondee. How can that be? Then deeper down below that they spoke in tongues long since dead, yet I understood them. And below that, meaning without words, before words, meaning from mouldering earth and rock, long before humanity. Then layers before the earth, from other places, and I think other universes. Claire, how can this be, am I mad?"

"No, Ed, you're not mad, trust me and tell me all of it."

"They showed me what happened at Skendleby, not just us and what we did last year; there were others before us: Heatly Smythe, one of Olga's relatives, a series of Davenports, even Dr John Dee. Corrupted and searching for missing bones amongst the shambling restless dead. Bones of evil purpose whose power extends beyond what we understand. Like us they all meddled and failed. Like us they made things worse."

He paused, gasping for air, fighting to keep control. Claire said nothing, waited for him to continue but he could feel her caring for him, feel her protecting him across the airwaves.

"All the way back to the first, long dead stars, they gave me experience, experience we should never have. I'm marked, marked for some dread purpose. But worse, I'm haunted, haunted by stars."

There was worse, much worse, but even to Claire he couldn't make himself tell it. Maybe she understood this, for she said:

"Well done, Ed, you've been very brave and you've done the right thing in telling me."

"But what must I do now? What do they expect?"

"Nothing, Ed, you've played your part, your role has ended, this message was for me. You were merely the messenger and the message has been delivered."

Even wound up as he was, something didn't feel right about this. The crow's connection had always been with him. He was about to make the point but Claire spoke across him.

"Ed, like before, you must trust me. I know what's happening, your part is over. Now listen carefully to what you have to do. Nothing."

He felt he should protest but the possibility of passing his responsibility on was too attractive so he kept silent.

"You go to the church, pray to your God then prepare for Christmas. That's your role now, leave everything to me, I know what to do. And Ed?"

"Yes."

"Above all, say nothing of this to anyone else. Absolutely nothing, or you will put those you care for in danger. Say nothing, understand?"

He thought he did, he could feel relief like warmth beginning to spread through his body. She was about to ring off but he remembered one more thing, one detail she'd need to know.

"Claire, there's something else. I just opened a letter from Marcus Fox. He was warning me, he seemed terrified, he said something was coming for us, especially for Gwen. Gwen knows something. He asked me to find her and save her. Gwen's your friend, perhaps…?"

"Of course, Ed, as you say, Gwen's my friend. You were right to pass that over too and don't worry, Ed. I'll take good care of Gwen."

Claire rang off and Ed sat back in his chair trying to breathe deeply and evenly, but relieved as he was he couldn't feel easy. He didn't have long to ponder the matter. His cell phone bleeped again. This time Olga.

He kept most of his promise and told her almost nothing of his conversation with Claire. Partly because Olga was distressed and urgently needed to see him, he agreed a time and place to meet with her, and then, almost in an attempt to reassure her (he was now glad he'd not distressed her further by unburdening his fears), he said:

"And Olga, I think you've misjudged Claire. I've just poured out my fears and feel much improved. I think she can help us."

There was a pause before Olga said in a stuttering whisper:

"Ed, I think you've made a terrible mistake."

Then the phone went dead.

Chapter 33: Past Imperfect

Leonie took him by surprise. He'd wanted something to shock him out of his mood: the black dog that always followed him into the unit, but not this.

Behind him Sophie was putting up the meagre Christmas decorations. For this year she'd bought a new tree, the old fibre optic one that had witnessed fifteen Christmases carried too many bad memories and been consigned to the bin. Its replacement was a small live one complete with roots. On top of it she placed a soft toy hedgehog with a Christmas hat.

A strange choice but it probably wouldn't have mattered what she'd done because the decorations brought back memories, and the memories haunted the unit. Since storing the Skendleby bones, the place hadn't felt right and the death of Tim Thomson, who they'd all laughed at secretly, compounded the guilt. So when Leonie tentatively approached Giles's desk it was almost a relief.

"They've sent us back the analysis on the bones."

She sounded edgy, but then she always did these days.

"What bones? Can't remember sending any."

"The Skendleby bones."

He almost jumped out of his seat.

"We put them back, we put them all back."

"Not all of them, it would appear."

"But there's no way we'd…"

She cut him off.

"We didn't but it seems Tim did. Must have been carrying out his own investigations."

"How could he? I never..."

She finished the sentence for him.

"Told him."

There was silence. Leonie pushed her hair back, tried and failed to smile then finally broke the silence.

"You never told anyone apart from Steve, did you? Maybe if you had, Tim would still be alive."

He could see her lower lip trembling, she was going to cry. There was no answer he could give; the same thoughts had been troubling his conscience. Perhaps Leonie recognised this, regaining control of herself, she said in a softer tone:

"Do you want to hear what the analysis says?"

He didn't, but knew he had to.

"Ok."

"But not here, Giles, I don't want to talk about it in here."

So they went out and found a couple of seats in one of the many identical student bars and cafes that fringed the University. In a few days most of the students would go home for Christmas and the identical bars would emptily mourn them. Over a couple of weak lattes, Leonie told him the things he didn't want to hear.

"Three bones in all, I don't know how he got hold of them but he chose well. One from the tomb, one from the sacrifice in the pit and one much, much older, from the ritual deposits beneath. It's this last one that scares me the most. According to the lab reports, it's older than is possible."

Giles was about to interrupt but she didn't let him.

"No, don't speak, let me finish. It's older than seems possible and what's even worse is that they can't find its origin from the analysis of its chemical composition. It has no source location. How can that be, Giles?"

"They probably got the samples mixed up."

"There was only one small piece, Giles, and you know how rigorous and up themselves these chemical analysts are now. There's no match for it anywhere and if they can't find where it came from then it didn't originate anywhere on Earth. Try explaining that?"

Since his trip to Samos, this apparent oxymoron didn't surprise Giles as much as it might once have done. He didn't comment. She hadn't finished.

"The fragment from the sacrificial pit seems straightforward enough. It originated somewhere in the southern Cotswolds in the mid-Neolithic. But the piece from inside the tomb, the last section of the right little finger."

She paused as one of the bar staff walked over to administer a cursory wipe to the sticky table top, before adding:

"Well, that finger joint originated somewhere between the Tigris and Euphrates, and it's pre-Neolithic. So tell me what…"

She got no further. Giles's phone bleeped and he answered.

"Giles, where the hell are you? No one in the unit could tell me."

He recognised not only the voice but also the graceless manner of his local authority boss.

"The police have got a situation on their hands in Lindow Moss. Drop what you're doing and get across there now."

****

He had plenty of time to reflect stuck in the traffic on the M60. He'd tried this route as an alternative to the long crawl down the A34, but it had been a bad choice. A series of Highways Agency posters informed him that the M60 was now a 'Smart Motorway'. He didn't know what this meant but assumed it was a motorway choked with cones restricting progress, with no sign of either construction work or workers. If this was what a 'Smart Motorway' was like, he promised himself he'd never venture onto a genuinely clever one.

The other problem with 'Smart Motorways' was that they gave you plenty of time sitting stationary in which to think. Giles didn't want to reflect but couldn't stop himself. The bones forced themselves into his mind; their provenance made no sense; how could two people who'd lived a couple of thousand years apart have met in

Skendleby? But then again, it wasn't the first time he'd confronted this. If the bones were real then the past wasn't.

Eventually he managed to inch his way off the Smart M60 onto the sluggish M56, and from there he skirted the airport to arrive at the track into the Moss. He pulled up by the flashing blue lights of the parked police vehicles. It had started to snow.

He picked his way across the part frozen bog to the huddle of people surrounding whatever horror it was they'd uncovered. He could make out the forms of Anderson and the bitch who'd tried to pin the murders on him. By the time he reached them his shoes were soaked through. And he was shivering.

Up close he could see that she, DI Campbell, wasn't in great shape; she looked queasy and unsteady on her feet. Anderson was supporting her with a hand under her left elbow, which he was pretty sure was a level of familiarity that wasn't encouraged in the force.

Anderson saw him first.

"Dr Glover, thanks for getting here so quickly, we need you to confirm a couple of things for us if you would."

Even as tightly wound as he was, Giles wondered at the strained formality of this. He nodded and moved through the huddle of police to look towards where Anderson was pointing. Everything assumed a dreamlike quality.

Maybe it was this that prevented him from seeing what he was looking at. The harder he looked, the less he saw; there was something with a blackened tongue resembling an old bonfire night Guy Fawkes, with its raggedy limbs mixed up in what looked like a thickish stew laced with bones. He realised Anderson was still speaking.

"Not like in a TV series, is it? No endearingly quirky police pathologist to give an immediate analysis of what's happened."

Giles didn't know how to respond, he just looked at him blankly. Anderson paused, then said:

"It's not like a crime scene at all, more like some ancient atrocity."

But slowly Giles's years of interpreting scant evidence on excavations began to indicate what he was looking at. This made it worse. He could make out the body of the victim now. It was strangely unmarked, with no sign of even the slightest wound, a state which made the open mouth full of black feathers all the more gruesome. But in many respects, this was the least terrifying aspect of the scene.

DI Campbell was standing by him now; he smelt the sickly odour on her breath as she spoke and felt a surge of pity for her. This was her burden, not his.

"I know this can't be easy for you, Dr Glover, but please do your best."

By now he was beginning to piece together elements of the tableau at their feet.

"All right, this is my best for now. Can't say anything about the body but the rest of this stuff couldn't occur naturally. It's an assemblage."

He could tell this didn't mean anything to them.

"An assemblage is what we call a collection of things that have been put together in a single context."

He found that slipping into academic jargon made it easier.

"Look, I'd need a team out here for days to do this properly. But my initial guess is that what we've got here is an assemblage of organic and non organic material, all of it as out of context as your victim. I can see elements of limbs, fingers from different time periods, flints, sherds of pot and a scatter of shells. Even now I'm pretty sure this stuff spans several time periods. It isn't natural it must have been put together artificially for some purpose."

Anderson said:

"But there's been people long dead dug out of here, Lindow Man and all that, you worked on those bodies yourself."

Giles was wondering how he could explain to them that this mixture all came from different times, different places, and that each element would have occupied its own discrete patch of earth at different levels, that the only way they could all be there was if some huge giant with an enormous spoon had stirred the whole of Lindow Moss up as if it were a bowl of soup. But he didn't have to.

Walking towards them, picking his way gingerly across the bog, was a smartly dressed man - Theodrakis. Both Anderson and Campbell stared towards him expectantly. Theodrakis nodded to Giles and stared at the crime scene. He stared for a long time before saying into the expectant silence:

"There is something essential about the now which is just outside the realm of science."

Viv spat back at him.

"If you think we're going to stand here listening to clever bugger remarks…"

Theodrakis put up his hand and she stopped. It was clear from his face he was as shaken as they were.

"Sorry, I was quoting Einstein, it seemed appropriate. You won't find anything here; get the body moved to the lab where you'll find he died of a heart attack. Turn this place over to the archaeologists. Then I'll talk to you."

Giles looked out over the Moss toward a distant strand of trees. A few hundred yards beyond them, hidden in the gloom, lay Claire's cottage. He stumbled off towards it, through the thickening snow.

Chapter 34: Strange Affairs

Theodrakis knew his time had come. This was what he'd been brought here for, this was his destiny. Explaining it to his colleagues wouldn't be easy. He was mulling over using Impressionist painting as an explanatory metaphor when he saw that DI Campbell was crying; the tears smudging her carelessly applied mascara. She pushed past Anderson, who was trying to console her, and blundered towards him.

"You take this over, I can't, I just can't do it anymore."

He gently placed his hands on her shoulders.

"Yes, you can, in fact, you're the only one who even has a chance, and it's why you've been brought to this place."

She didn't look convinced, just stood there head bowed with the light snow dusting her coat and hood. He felt pity but not too much, you couldn't deal with these things until you'd been broken and no one understood that better than he did. Now she seemed pretty much broken.

He looked across her to Anderson, who was fumbling in embarrassment near the body.

"Nothing else we can do here, it will be better back at HQ, this is a bad place, it feeds off misery."

Anderson didn't react but Campbell did, she was beginning to understand. Theodrakis didn't look at the body, knew it wouldn't help him in any material way; it had served its purpose - whatever was happening now was taking place elsewhere. He turned round and supporting Campbell under one arm, headed for the car. Behind him he heard Anderson mumbling some instructions to the scene of crime officers before following them.

****

Giles was fumbling for his keys when the front door opened. He recognised the heady musk of Claire's perfume, looked up and saw her. She was wearing the body hugging floor length white dress she wore on certain occasions, and he knew what would follow.

He was aroused as soon as he crossed the threshold and the gnawing pangs of anxiety slipped away without trace. She twined her left arm around his neck and pulled his face towards hers, her lips open. He slipped into the kiss, she bit hard on his lower lip.

"You took your time, lover, here, drink this."

She handed him a drink. It smelled like mulled wine but was spiced with something he couldn't place.

"What's this?"

"It'll give you strength and, believe me, you'll need strength for what I have in store for you. Now drink it before it goes cold, I was expecting you earlier."

He didn't bother to ask how she could have been expecting him. The drink was good: warming and rich, not like the sickly stuff with too much cinnamon they peddled at the Christmas market. It slid down his throat and spread through his nervous system; a lotus-eating concoction of lassitude and lust.

She took his hand and led him to the stairs, then up them. Inside the bedroom she helped him out of his clothes, pushed him down on the bed and straddled him. Giles wriggled beneath her trying to pull up the hem of her dress and open her to receive him.

But she stopped him, stopped him with surprising strength.

"Not till I'm ready, not till I've told you some things, some things you won't be able to remember afterwards."

He lay trapped beneath her, writhing in desire, hearing the words but not listening, just wanting the sharp burning need satisfied. She bent her head low over him so that her long, silky black hair covered his face, tickling his skin. She began to whisper.

"You manage to get things so wrong every time, don't you, you and your little friends? Only two bones to harvest now, the one beneath the women's house and then the one we need to grow, which will link them all into the necklace. Now poor little Ed and that butch bruiser think that Lisa is the key to this, can you imagine that?"

She stopped and laughed to herself, before adding:

"There's nothing in Lisa, she's empty; I emptied her. Their attempt to take her out of the house will lead to nothing except Olga being expelled and the others becoming my creatures. There will be a birth. There has to be to create the bone that will link all the others. That's the problem with having to work across dimensions, isn't it?"

The question was rhetorical and Giles made no attempt to answer.

"It means we have to dabble in backwater spheres like this where everything is so literal. But sadly that's the only overarching law in what you primitives call physics; you have to play by the local rules. You know gravity, religion, relativity, magic, all that childish nonsense. Believe me, it's all too too boring, but sadly that's how the game has to be played. "

She raised her head a little to see if Giles was listening, but from his writhing about beneath her it seemed his mind was on other things.

"Anyway, lover, the birth will happen where none of your poor deludedfriends will think of looking. Then it will be a relief to leave the basic metaphysics of this tediously limiting dimension."

She looked down at him almost affectionately, then shrugged her shoulders.

"But while I'm here I may as well get the pleasure that your low level life form is programmed for. Better get ready for a rough ride, Giles baby."

When it was over and they lay, post coital, Giles bruised, torn and sweating, she began to giggle.

"Sorry, honey, I don't know why but this human form makes me do childish things and I can't resist this one, so come on, wake up, I want to show you something."

He showed no sign of listening so after slapping his face a couple of times she picked up the half empty glass of water from the bedside table and dashed it onto his face. He opened his eyes and stared at her. She squealed with delight and said:

"You'll love this; want to see the image that Alekka took to her death? Watch."

He gazed up at her through the levels of sedation and saw the slim woman next to him. Then something else: something like a cross between a decomposing woodlouse and a hairy spider with large, wobbling mandibles and exterior veins, something whose boundaries were constantly shifting in a way that the physical laws governing the universe couldn't accommodate. He began to scream.

"Don't be so childish, Giles, can't you take a joke? Well, that's the last time I'm showing you my real beauty."

She sat back against the headboard, laughing as he screamed. Then she muttered to herself:

"Well, I suppose the fun's over, time to wipe your memory."

****

All she could hear was the voice, the voice and the chant, the unspeakable chant of hate and terror that had once been hers.

Lisa was dreaming, it had to be a dream. If not she was back in Hell. The voice was in her head again, the chant. The chant that had destroyed her humanity last time, the chant that had consumed her, eaten away her real self and transformed her into a hate-filled, lustful fiend. Most of it she couldn't remember except in snatches: the taste of blood, elements of fear, rage and darkness. She needed to get away from here but she couldn't move. Why was she chanting?

She'd thought the terrible thing inside her had gone; moved on to some other host from where it could expedite its inconceivable purpose. Even the thought of this and the sporadic patches of memory froze her blood.

The fear was so extreme. She emitted an involuntary squeal and as she was doing so the chanting continued. So the chanting wasn't her. Awful though this was it brought her to her senses. She must be awake, awake and in bed in her room in the women's house. So, if she wasn't performing the ululation of the chant, then who was? It sounded very near, almost near enough to be coming from inside her.

Her eyes were closed and she feared to open them. But now she could sense not only the chant building to its climax, but something else too. The presence of others, very close and edging closer. This threatening proximity was unbearable with eyes closed, so she forced them open.

They were in a circle round the bed, which had moved to the centre of the room. Seven women, hands joined, circled her bed. Claire, at the bed's foot, looked down on her. Claire, even the thought of her plunged Lisa into spasms of horror. Claire who had felt inside her and taken out the spirit of the demon which she now wore herself, even though nobody else seemed to see it. Claire, who was as far from being human as nuclear fission.

Claire, Margaret, Jenna, Ailsa, Rose, Ruth and Leonie; their eyes like owls, their noses like beaks. Through their distended mouths the ululation of the chant moved to its climax. The chant ended, they dropped their hands and their faces returned to normal as they looked to Claire for leadership.

Lisa realised she wasn't meant to see this, she should have stayed asleep. Claire looked at her and smiled, a smile like a fridge door opening, and Lisa felt her bowels turn to water. None of the others noticed, they'd eyes only for Claire who motioned for them to leave the room.

They drifted out; Rose and Jenna grinning, feeling the power, the others in a state of trance. Claire looked at Lisa from the foot of the bed, smiling as her human form shifted around her. Lisa realised she wasn't important enough for Claire to bother hiding her real nature. She spoke.

"Did you enjoy my little performance, mad girl? Do you like what I've done to your housemates? No? I thought not. But don't worry, you don't matter now, what's left of you can go and drift from mental breakdown, to care in the community, to asylum. I don't even need to warn you, do I? No, you're too frightened to say anything; not that anyone would believe you, would they?"

Lisa knew Claire was right, she started to sniffle, could feel the fat, wet tracks of tears sliding down her cheeks. Claire smiled, amiable but chilling.

"Ah bless, little mad, empty Lisa's crying. Just to cheer you up I'll let you know how this ends, shall I? Only fair really seeing as you were part of it before this body I'm currently wearing was, although I've got to tell you, Lisa, this body gives me a lot more fun than yours did."

She patted Lisa on the head with something that vaguely resembled a hand, but which was ice cold.

"Anyway, as I was saying, I've almost finished here now, everything is in place, just a couple of bits and pieces to tidy up then I'm off back to where I came from. Long before they manage to get their new Watchers into working order. I quite miss the old ones: Alekka, Vassilis, Father John and the one that used to flit around Skendleby. Still, nothing lasts forever, does it?"

She paused and then corrected herself.

"Except for us, of course."

She threw back her head and pealed with laughter.

"I will miss laughing though, everything here is so funny, isn't it? Oh come on, lighten up, Lisa, share the joke."

She waited for a reaction, Lisa just lay sniffling.

"Suit yourself then, but as I think you might be beginning to understand, Lisa, we've moved way beyond what you understand as time. Sorry, have to go now, things to do, you know how it is? Then I'll be off leaving your little dimension to whatever consequences our little joke has created. Ciao, Lisa, good luck with forgetting all this."

Claire chuckled to herself then followed the others towards the door as Lisa wept.

Chapter 35: Understanding Makes it Worse

As they were walking into the Manchester police headquarters a uniformed sergeant shouted across the vestibule to Anderson.

"Hey Jimmy, don't forget the drinks for Twiggy."

Theodrakis looked at Anderson quizzically, so he explained.

"There's a do in the City Vaults."

Theodrakis looked more confused.

"City Vaults, it's a pub."

"I know that. What is Twiggy?"

"Oh, Twiggy; he's a fat bloke from traffic who's retiring. Before the disciplinary he used to work with us."

Anderson could see from Theodrakis's expression that this exegesis of the sergeant's message hadn't helped so he cut his losses, mumbling:

"Maybe we should go, just show our faces for a few minutes."

He hadn't expected a positive response to the suggestion but to his surprise Viv spoke. They were the first words she'd uttered since Lindow.

"Yes, lets, some normality would be good for us, we can talk afterwards. I could use a drink."

She and Anderson turned back towards the door leaving Theodrakis staring after them in amazement; of all the strange things he'd seen recently this struck him as the strangest, but then this was England, a barely civilised state miles from the Mediterranean heart of European culture. He scuttled after them.

He caught up as they were entering the packed square which every Christmas housed the European market. He found being crushed and jostled against his colleagues by the dense crowd strangely comforting. A small silver band of men and women in a type of military uniform was performing one of the more sentimental of the canon of Anglo Saxon carols, and he felt his eyes begin to water.

He thought of Samos and Hippolyta then, and this took him completely off guard, an image of Mrs Carver, 'call me Suzzie-Jade', jogging round the side of the Hall towards him seeped into his consciousness. Then they were out of the market with its bright lights and Christmas odours and walking down an old street in the shadow of the gothic town hall.

The pub was packed, warm and convivial. Looking round, Theodrakis recognised several faces, it seemed the pub had temporarily become the recreational centre of the police department. Anderson pushed a large glass of beer into his hand and he realised he would be obliged to drink a pint of the liquid for which he had no relish.

It seemed that no one had any interest in talking to either Viv or himself, so he pushed a way through the crowd near the bar to a smaller, quieter room at the back where they found a table in the relative gloom of a corner. He asked Viv:

"Shall I ask DS Anderson to join us?"

"No, let Jimmy enjoy himself with his mates. You can fetch me another of these though."

She knocked back the remnants of the large glass of white wine she was drinking and Theodrakis pushed his way back to the bar, noticing Anderson whispering something into the ear of an attractive WPC who was standing close enough to lean on him. He bought two large glasses of wine, taking the opportunity to lose his pint. Back at the table he passed a glass to Viv. She took a long swallow, then said:

"Ok, I'm ready, talk to me, tell me, I need to know. What the hell is happening here? What are we meant to do?"

"Finish the wine first then I'll buy you dinner, I'll tell you as we eat."

Sometime later they sat by the plate glass window of a Greek restaurant at the side of the town hall. Outside in the cold and dark, crowds of heavily laden shoppers were shuffling through the snow towards bus and tram stops.

Theodrakis knew what he was about to say would change Viv's life; he pitied her but there was no alternative. Clearing his throat he began.

"I want to help you, DI Campbell. I pity you because you're in the same position I was on Samos; you still think there's a logic that governs our existence. But…"

He paused and refilled her glass with a deep coloured red wine.

"Drink this, it's a Nemea, a good one, I know the estate, my father nearly bought it on impulse some years back. A good wine, it will help you."

He watched her drink then began, trying to explain how to see things differently.

"I can't explain in a way that will suit the logical part of your mind. The closest I get is that the perpetrators we are chasing have a different perception to ours because they don't inhabit the same world and pursue different objectives… no, don't, please don't stop me."

They were interrupted by the waiter bringing a dish of lemon potatoes and two plates of briam. Theodrakis used the natural break.

"Eat, it's good, and while you eat, listen."

He refilled her glass then resumed.

"I experienced this on Samos. There was a place there: palatial, impossible, like something out of *The Arabian Nights*. Its owner enticed me there. I saw it, experienced it but I don't think it really existed."

He looked across at her expecting some protest, but she was listening.

"What I saw wasn't a one-off, there's a history of these places although they go by different names: Lyonesse, Mu, Atlantis, Camelot, Shangri La. They inhabit our consciousness while they achieve some purpose then fade, leaving only myth and memory. But all they really were was a glamour cast over our senses, an illusion, a confidence trick."

Theodrakis forked some of the vegetable stew and lemon potatoes on to his plate, took a sip of the wine and wiped his mouth on the napkin fastidiously.

"You will not solve the case until you understand that the murders are an insignificant consequence of what is happening, and that we play only a fleeting walk on part in the crucial events."

Now Viv lost patience.

"And you'll explain that to the Chief, will you?"

"I won't have to; it will end like it did on Samos - they won't want any more meddling from us. So the evidence from the crime scenes and a couple of convenient deaths will be given to you on a plate."

"You're mad."

"Yes, I think so; however, believe me, the evidence will suggest the murders are solved and the murderers are dead. You'll be the heroine."

Viv would have laughed at this a few weeks ago, but experience had destabilised her and she doubted her own sanity. Theodrakis continued.

"These things appear like this to enable us to play the part they need us to. On Samos, I began to wonder if the real action wasn't happening somewhere we can't even conceive of."

He picked up his wine and finished the glass. Viv knew it had taken a great deal out of him to expose himself this way to her, but she asked:

"So, if that's how it's going to happen why make the effort to tell me all this insane stuff? You didn't need to; if you're right then the case is closed."

"But it isn't really, is it? It never can be and that's not what you were brought here for."

For a second he saw a look of panic transform Viv's features. He felt he was seeing her as she must have looked as a frightened little girl. He only had one even slightly reassuring card. He decided to play it now.

"There are some slight compensations thrown in during this process, things that give us the strength to play our parts. On Samos I found love, at least I think it was love. Also, and I'm embarrassed to tell you this, I discovered I wasn't impotent."

It seemed he was more than embarrassed, either that or what he had just said dredged up powerful emotions, for he stumbled to a halt. Viv poured him more wine.

"Go on, you can't stop there. What compensation will there be for me?"

The latter part of her interjection, the question, rang with bitterness.

"I don't know, maybe it doesn't always work like this. But if it does it will be personal. Speak to Giles."

A look of incredulity crossed her eyes and he hurried on.

"I don't know where that last bit came from, forgive me, but don't rule it out."

Outside the snow was coming down hard, so hard that the dark shape of the town hall was barely visible. The waiter emerged out of the shadows with two small glasses of clear liquid. He exchanged a few staccato sentences in Greek with Theodrakis then took away the empty plates.

"It's raki, very strong and on the house, as it appears is the whole meal. The waiter said they don't want us to pay but they don't want us to come back either. Apparently they consider us unsettling and bad for business. We drink this then we leave."

She stared at him blankly before asking:

"So, you're not going to tell me what you think I was brought here for?"

"I can only tell you what I know, and it's not much. Like mine, your real role here is unclear, all I can say is that there is a part for you so I wouldn't make any plans that involve a return to London. I think you'll find that once they think you've closed the case your secondment here will be extended. The rest you will discover for yourself."

"And you, what will you do?"

Theodrakis sat back in his seat, his face as pale as the snow being driven against the window. Then he picked up the raki and swallowed it in one, before saying:

"I'm going to visit Mrs Carver."

Chapter 36: Excavations

Olga was late; she'd drunk too much last night and forgotten to set the alarm in her lonely bedroom. She had a quick shower, threw on some clothes and made a mad rush down the stairs for the front door. She had to be in Frodsham to see a client by nine thirty and it was already eight fifty-nine - no chance. Grabbing her coat from the cloakroom by the front, door she noticed the door to the cellar was open. This was strange, none of them liked to venture into the ancient bowels of the house. For a second she contemplated investigating but couldn't afford to lose a client, particularly in light of her unravelling relationship with Margaret, so she headed for her car.

Down below, Rose and Leonie heard her go.

"You must have left the door open, that was careless, she could have seen us."

Leonie shrugged her shoulders unhappily, the only answer she made. It didn't satisfy Rose.

"From the sound of the banging on the stairs it was Olga, you know what Claire told us, no one's meant to know about this, particularly Olga."

Leonie ignored this, saying:

"Let's get this finished as quick as we can, Rose, I don't like it down here."

Rose didn't like it either, it was the first excavating she'd done since the raggedy thing from Hell had bowled her off the top of the mound at Skendleby. They moved through the section of cellar where the mildewed remnants of abandoned belongings from previous tenants lay rotting, to the vault that was situated beneath the eastern wing of the house. The oldest part, which back in the late Middle Ages had been a barn. Rose found herself wondering, not for the first time, what sort of barn had a cellar.

This space hadn't been much used since, it seemed. The only light down there came from one bare electric bulb hanging from the centre of the filthy ceiling above. It was powered by a single cable that had been run from the other side. And it was cold, bitterly cold.

The two women stood shivering on an uneven floor of compacted earth whilst the gentle swing of the cord carrying the electric bulb caused their shadows to shift and flicker. A smell of age and rot filled the space and the silence was sporadically broken by creaking sounds as the old building above them shifted its weight.

"Feels like no one's been down here in centuries."

Rose agreed with her, but she didn't want to waste time talking, and anyway, in this part of the cellar sound was distorted, making it feel like Leonie had been speaking from some distance away when in fact she was standing right by her. But she couldn't stop herself replying:

"And the feeling's not helped by 'sweet little Jan' refusing to help."

The bitterness of her words was so palpable that Leonie couldn't think of any response. It didn't matter, Rose had moved on.

"You direct the arc light at the centre of the floor then move the beam slowly. If it's not in the centre we could be here ages."

Leonie did as she was told and for a few moments the archaeologists studied the uneven surface of minor undulations that comprised the beaten earth floor. For differing reasons, neither of them wanted to find anything but the evidence of their quest was unmissable. In the centre of the floor, directly below the naked light bulb, there was a patch of earth that bore all the hallmarks of having been disturbed.

Strange, since the disturbance they were looking for should have been almost as old as the barn itself, over four hundred years, while the feature they found themselves staring at was not only obvious but seemed recent, so recent that little trails of disturbed earth ran down its sides. It was as if the thing beneath the earth was straining to attract their attention. So there was no other option.

They had no intention of conducting a properly constituted excavation and recording the process, so what they were doing was the equivalent of grave robbing, and they both knew this. Fortunate then that it took so little time and effort. Within minutes they had discovered things with no natural reasons to be in such a location: feathers bizarrely preserved, fetish objects fashioned from materials unavailable in Britain. They recognised these but attempted to push them to the backs of their minds, worried that their mental imbalance would become unhinged.

Then, cradled in a small wooden container of preserved yew, they found it. Leonie, still an archaeologist at heart, suggested they explore the context but within seconds her trowel blade had scraped against the edge of an unnaturally large severed bird skull and they abandoned the pretence. Leonie lifted the strangely moist and tacky dark wooden box out of its nest and placed it on the floor. From somewhere - could have been anywhere - she heard Rose.

"Open it, better check it's what we're after."

"No, you do it, it doesn't feel right, I don't like it."

Rose didn't answer and Leonie made no move to check the box. After what could have been any length of time she felt Rose push past her and bend down. Leonie didn't want to watch so she looked away, and it was then she noticed the shadows.

Shadows of things shifting and weaving across the floor, shadows of things that didn't seem to be in the cellar. There was something about the light down there that distorted perspective, making the walls of the cellar seem impossibly distant while the roof seemed to get lower. Leonie felt like she was underground, trapped in some vast crack deep beneath the surface with all the weight of the world above pressing down on her.

Rose's shriek of disgust snapped her out of it.

"Urrghh. It's wet, it's alive. Take it away, take it away!"

Leonie looked over her shoulder at the now open box. Inside it something was flexing, moving. Something less than two inches long and narrow, flexing at some natural break in its length. Staring at this horror it gradually dawned on Leonie what she was looking at: the top two joints of a finger - a living finger. Before she could scream Rose grabbed the box, closed the lid and ran with it towards the steps leading back into the world.

Following close behind in her slipstream, and disturbed by the unhinged mewing sounds Rose had started to emit, Leonie promised herself this would be her last contact with Skendleby and its restless dead.

****

A few miles away, crouching down in the freezing black peat, Jan was thinking something similar but was too occupied by the bizarre scene in front of her to follow it up. She and Giles had been on site since the first had tentatively slipped in from the east. Not that the calibre of light had brought cheer in its wake, more an indistinct blanket of greyness. And it wasn't as if this was Jan's only worry, she recognised that in opting to be here excavating with Giles, rather than in the cellar with Leonie and Rose, she'd crossed some type of line separating her from her housemates.

This bothered her less than she'd imagined; in fact, in a strange way it was a relief. There was a distance between her and the other women, they saw things differently. At first she'd rationalised that this was because the others had bonded with each other for longer. But it wasn't that. It wasn't to do with perception; it was more like they inhabited a world of different realities. Even Leonie, her friend. How had this happened? She didn't get time to answer herself, Giles's voice pricked her thought bubble.

"Ok, let's just limit ourselves to what's right in front of us; I don't think that anything beyond these two metres will be of much interest to the police. Strange how different it looks now, almost as if it's fading away."

The end of the sentence made no sense to Jan and probably not to Giles either, as he followed up with:

"There seemed to be more stuff when they brought me out here on the morning they found the body. Certainly different stuff."

He stuttered to a stop. Jan said:

"Giles, this stuff can't be real, I can't understand it?"

"Reality doesn't function in Skendleby, does it?"

Jan ignored this, pointing instead to the layer of evidence they'd reached in the semi saturated subsoil.

"Shells, worked flint, animal bone and antler tools. Beads and nutshells, and all of it laid on what seems like a brushwood and timber platform. I didn't expect something with an age profile like this."

"So what's your archaeological diagnosis?"

"Text book Mesolithic, Star Carr comes to Skendleby but…"

"But?"

"But it shouldn't be here and even if it was it wouldn't be laid out like this as if it had been waiting for us."

"Yeah, and that's not even the strange bit."

"What do you mean?"

"I mean that when I looked at this patch of ground the day they found the body it was a different assemblage. These aren't the artefacts I saw."

"How, how different?"

"There was evidence from different material cultures for a start, a pottery culture, looked like grooved ware, the sherds I saw, much later than this. It was an artificial assemblage but an entirely different one to this; there were human bones, and bird bones. Pottery, bronze, all types of shit. I wasn't there long enough to study it closely but long enough to identify elements."

"And?"

"And, where's it all gone? This is different. How come we're finding evidence from just one context? A context that shouldn't exist."

He didn't expect an answer, didn't wait for one.

"How's this happened? It's like a revolving slide show of archaeology. It's not possible, is it?"

Jan had no answers; she was out of her depth. She threw down her trowel and stood up, fumbling for the cigarettes in the pocket of her overalls. She lit two with shaking hands and handed one to Giles. He reached up to take it and remained crouched over the small patch of disinterred human activity.

"Archaeology was the only safe part of my life; it was always there, consistent, safe, with its own rules. Never let you down like people do, it never ran off with other men; boring at times but faithful, dependable. You knew where you were with physical bits of the past. It was never frightening."

Jan stood listening, wondering where this was going.

"Jan, which bits of this are real? Was what I saw last time real, or is this? What'll turn up here tomorrow?"

He got to his feet; she saw he was close to tears.

"What's happening here, Jan? What's happened to time? If the past just shifts when it wants to then what's real? What can we believe in?

Chapter 37: Stranger Affairs

"I'm not a reliable expert anymore than I'm a reliable witness; no one would believe anything I said."

Viv smiled at him but blamed herself, if she'd handled him better he'd talk to her, and now she really needed him to talk to her.

"Please, Dr Glover, just try to explain what it was at the crime scene that changed."

At first she thought he wouldn't reply and had begun to plead.

"Giles, this is…"

He cut across her.

"What I saw when you dragged me out there to the crime scene wasn't there today. What we saw today was different in every way, which is, of course, impossible. This is why any report I make will just weaken your case. Get it? Understand?"

He was red-faced and shouting by the end of the sentence. Then something strange happened. He looked hard at Viv, as if seeing her for the first time, and his face softened, making him look younger and, to her surprise, desirable. He said gently:

"But you've been damaged by this too, haven't you? You're hurt. Like me. Like Theodrakis, you've been hurt."

"Yes, I've been hurt."

He knew there was more to come so said nothing, giving her space, and, after a few moments of silence, she said:

"Not so much hurt as damaged."

She crawled to a halt. Giles thought she was going to cry, but it seemed she was made of tougher stuff.

"Not even been damaged, I think some part of me is doing the damage. Either that or…or…"

He prompted her gently.

"Or what?"

"Or I'm haunted."

Giles laughed.

"Of course you are. Why should you be any different?"

For once with her he'd found the right thing to say, she smiled. Then everything changed as Anderson burst into the room.

"The forensics are back, you'd better come quick, they all tie up, we've cracked it. I think the nightmare's over."

****

Smiling faces, corks popping, congratulations, even a football chant, and yet Viv couldn't join in. She knew it was false.

But she hadn't time to brood; the Chief was about to speak. Despite all this, as he started she found herself thinking 'this is where he belongs, this is where he's happiest, leading a small team solving crimes'. With an open beer bottle in one hand, hefty arms bulging out of a short-sleeved shirt, he reminded her more of a bus driver at the end of a long shift than the new breed of bureaucratic chief constable.

"I'm not going to interrupt you for long, just a few words to tell you how bloody relieved I am that you've cracked it, that you lifted the web of fear from our city."

He paused for the applause, took a swig from the bottle, then said:

"When they first sent us DI Campbell I thought to meself aye, aye, here's another bloody graduate from bloody London to teach us how it's done. But the buggers got it wrong, didn't they? She's not from bloody London, she's from Oldham, she's one of us and she's cracked it for us. So raise your glasses to your guvnor, DI Campbell."

Now they were cheering her; it was like a dream. Viv could see Jimmy leading the cheering as she walked across to the Chief to say her piece. She said a few words, echoing her boss. There were things she'd learnt from him, it appeared.

When it was over and the Chief had told them that single-handed they'd more or less saved Christmas, Viv followed him to his room wondering where Theodrakis was; it was bad form for him not to be present, not that anybody missed him.

Once ensconced behind the desk in his office, the mood changed.

"Don't give me that look, Viv, I'm as iffy about all this as you, but unless the whole lab system has been contaminated then we've all the evidence we need to close the Skendleby case, which has worked out well for our political masters."

"What do you mean, worked out well?"

"Final planning meeting for Carver's Skendleby development this evening. No ongoing police activity knocks down any arguments for a delay. Bad news for your archaeologist friend, though."

A few days ago she'd have protested about the use of the adjective friend, now she wasn't so sure. Instead she asked:

"Surely it can't all be wrapped up so quickly. There's no motive for either of the perpetrators and now they're both dead they can't give their side of things. It's all too convenient."

While she was speaking, Theodrakis's words in the Greek restaurant came back to her, it had gone exactly as he'd predicted. But now the Chief was speaking.

"If the lab results hadn't got muddled up first time round we'd have got here sooner and, to be fair, it does make some sort of sense."

"Like what? What sense does it make?"

"Well, Trescothic must have paid Gifford to harass the women at the house. When it went too far and Gifford killed Kelly Ellsworth, Trescothic must have threatened him with talking to us, so he killed him too - plenty of logic there."

"And the girl at Skendleby Hall, why kill her?"

"Gifford had violent tastes, he abused his wife, knocked about the sex workers he used. He just went too far."

"She wasn't a sex worker."

"Maybe Gifford mistook her for one. He had the opportunity, he worked for Carver at the Hall."

"Ok, even if I buy that then what possible connection could he have had with Marcus Fox? And why would he go out there on the Welsh borders?."

"I don't know, I'm not bloody Stephan Fry. But whatever the reason, his DNA was all over Fox, clear as day, prima facie."

"And then he goes for a run on Lindow Common, stuffs his mouth with crow feathers and has a heart attack. Very probable."

"Look, Gifford had people after him, he owed money, he had enemies, maybe he was desperate. And you need to be careful talking about those last details, the press don't know about the feathers."

"Like they didn't know the details of the attacks last year. Are we supposed to believe that Gifford was responsible for those as well? I just don't buy it."

"Listen, we've got a dead villain with lots of previous and rock solid forensic evidence. What have you got, Viv?"

She hadn't anything other than a horrible realisation that Theodrakis was right and that she was walking through Hell.

"Are you listening?"

She hadn't been, her thoughts had taken her elsewhere.

"Sorry, Chief?"

"I was telling you about some news, good news."

Despite the positive words she felt the hairs on the back of her neck stand up.

"Seems we're going to be working together for a bit longer."

"What do you mean?"

"There's been a request from up high that you stay in Manchester, and London's agreed. Congratulations, your rank's been made substantive and if you continue like this the next step's divisional commander. Congratulations, lass."

Somewhere in the back of her mind, Viv heard a door slam shut.

****

Flakes of snow were driven into the taxi window by the wind, but peering out Theodrakis saw, to his surprise, that the gates guarding the driveway of Skendleby Hall were open. Asking the driver to wait for him he got out, shutting the door behind him. The driver obviously didn't want to wait in the dark in a place with Skendleby's reputation and the taxi roared off into the night.

Outside in the murky light, Theodrakis gingerly picked his way down the drive. He felt the landscape was watching him; it seemed alive and his nostrils filled with an odour he couldn't quite place, which was coming off the fields. It tasted, as much as smelt, like a compound of iron and blood.

Gazing across the fields it came to him that this landscape was as ancient and troubled as his Greek homeland, and that beneath its layers lay buried the same secrets and tragedies. It had a life of its own, unknowable and brooding, enduring and remembered.

The wind died and a sudden hush fell: Skendleby Hall was a desolate place. It was darker than in the fields around. Across the estate wall, Theodrakis saw the tall spire of the church and for a moment considered heading for whatever slight protection it might offer. But figuring that you can't dodge what is coming for you he trudged on towards the sepulchral silence that hung over the Hall.

Few of the windows were lit; whatever life the Hall possessed seemed long gone. He was aware of slight movement along the estate wall to his left, something was watching him. The further he walked the greater the sense of dread in his heart grew. He'd never see Samos again; whatever the future had in store for him it would find him here. Find him now.

There was a rustling from the woods, wings maybe? An owl hooted, the cold intensified. Visibility was poor but as he stared into the gathering dark he thought he saw a slice of the darkness by the wall detach itself from the beech trees and move towards him, beginning to shift violently in focus as it drew closer. He considered running; but where to and for what purpose?

Whatever it was coming for him was hastening its approach, 'Quis est iste qui venit'. A phrase from a ghost story he'd read as a student came to him. He stopped; the patch of darkness was clearer now, had stopped moving in gravity defying jerks and settled into a slow running speed. In the last few yards of its progression he felt an element of recognition.

"Been waitin' for you, took your time, innit."

He took the ice cold hand that was proffered him.

"Betta come into the Hall, freezin' out here."

Chapter 38: Northern Powerhouse

Giles saw that all the 'big guns' were present as soon as he entered the committee room and knew he was wasting his time. They'd left nothing to chance. So, tonight, Carver's Skendleby proposals would receive the go ahead with the council blessing.

There were very few protesters present; perhaps they also knew it was a lost cause, certainly not one worth turning out for on such a raw night. He shuffled into his seat at the table and a name plate was set in front of him by the clerk to the planning committee. A couple of the protesters nodded at him but from the ranks of the bureaucrats, politicians and marketing types, there was no gesture of recognition. Even his colleagues averted their eyes, not wanting careers jeopardised by association with a man bent on opposing the collective will.

The meeting had been scheduled in the town hall; it was more convenient for those with influence who wanted the venture to proceed. Giles was just in time, the independent chair, representing the 'Powerhouse Partnership', cut through the murmur of conversation and opened up with his introductory remarks.

"This shouldn't take us too long, most of the ground has been covered so I'll be grateful if all contributions can be brief and to the point. The weather is deteriorating and I'm sure that, like me, you'll want to get home tonight. I'm told that Mr Carver will be joining us in a few moments so in the meantime I invite Bruce Mont-Giraud of Dream Solutions to update us on progress since the last meeting."

There followed a flashy presentation painting the picture of a socially responsible, eco-friendly New Jerusalem that would not only enhance Skendleby but drive forward the local economy. The (in Giles's opinion) slippery and unctuous Mont-Giraud had reached the climax of his peroration and said:

"The hard working citizens of 'The Northern Powerhouse' deserve amenities that provide them with…"

He was cut off by two simultaneous arrivals: the scowling, red-faced Si Carver, and a pale and strained Sir Nigel Davenport. Neither showed any awareness of the presence of the other. Carver was greeted with a series of smiles and nods, Davenport was ignored.

The meeting was moved swiftly on to a summary of the council's backing for the project, delivered by a senior officer from planning. This proved to be a longer and duller presentation during which time Giles began to wonder where the women from the house were. Claire had told him she'd ensure they were there to support his objections.

When the meeting finally reached the stage where questioning of the project was permitted, Giles commenced his lengthy report on the potential damage to the historic landscape. The independent chair stopped him.

"Sorry, Dr Glover, we've heard all this before, have you any new and pertinent objections?"

"No, not new, I'm restating the integrity of the original objections."

"Which we've heard several times and taken due note of. That being the case we may properly move to a decision."

While the chair was making this pronouncement, Giles saw a smirk cross Carver's features and Davenport sunk his head into his hands. It was the latter that made Giles try one last time.

"Listen to this then. That land shouldn't be built on because it frightens people, just look at what the police have found there. Think about why no one ever built on it before, think why…"

The chair was about to silence him but it was Carver who delivered the 'coup de grace', shouting:

"You talk about thinking, then think about this. How much public and private money has been sunk into this project? How many people will benefit from the starter homes? How many people's health will the leisure centre improve? How many jobs will be created? All you have to put up in opposition is a silly fairy tale."

Carver didn't have to say more, everyone in a seat of office round the table was nodding and smiling. Giles slumped back into his chair and listened as the committee voted the project through. As the chair began his concluding remarks there was a hiatus among the onlookers. Davenport was on his feet, shouting:

"You'll live to regret this and no one more so than you, Carver."

He opened his mouth to say more but his hands grasped at his chest and he collapsed, clutching the area around his heart. Giles and several others rushed to him and a doctor was summoned. By the time he'd been helped onto a chair and subsequently into an ambulance, the chamber had emptied. The Skendleby project was reality.

Davenport rallied and refused the ambulance so Giles sent him home in a taxi. He tried Claire's mobile again, still no answer, he wasn't surprised - she was difficult to contact these days, almost as if she'd tired of him. He couldn't face her empty cottage or his empty house and he didn't want to get drunk, so he trudged through the cold dark streets to the archaeology unit deep in the basement of the 19th Century heart of the university.

It was empty and unwelcoming, so it suited his mood. Avoiding the strip lighting he turned on his desk lamp and sat musing in the crepuscular half light listening to the creaks and squeaks of the deserted building. After an indeterminate period of time he reached for the free copy of the evening's Journal that had been thrust into his hand by one of the numerous distributors in town.

If there was anything that could have lowered his downer any further it was the headline.

"Police crack South Manchester terror crime spree."

Half the front page was taken up with a picture of the police public briefing, while the scant text opined that the spate of attacks that had terrorised the fifteen miles stretching from the city centre to Skendleby for two years was finally over. He hadn't the stomach to read the quote from the senior investigating office, DI Campbell. Everything was stitched up.

On an impulse he rang the police, and to his surprise after a brief wait he was put through to Viv. All she said was:

"I'll ring you back on my mobile."

She did, instantly.

"I need to talk but not over the phone. Can you meet me?"

They fixed on a pub near her Didsbury flat in an hour. He was there before her and was nursing a pint when she walked in. Outside of the police context she seemed strikingly different; certainly striking. She was taller than most of the drinkers at the bar and he noticed eyes following as she walked across to him. Some probably recognised her from the paper and local TV news, but it was more than that.

"You've not solved it, have you?"

After buying her a drink these were the first words he said. He didn't get an answer, he suspected she was playing for time.

"Where's your partner, Ms Vanarvi?"

"I think Claire's lost interest in me."

There was a pause, then Giles tried again.

"You don't believe it's over, do you?"

Still no answer, he tried another tack.

"Is Theodrakis going to join us?"

"No, I need you to talk to me, tell me the things I'm missing."

"Dunno where to start, it all just like happened, and I don't know why. I'm an archaeologist, I don't believe in all this hippy woo stuff. I used to be like that pleased with himself scientist whose always on TV. But…"

She smiled at him, a warm smile, he liked it. She asked:
"But what?"

"But I've seen things and what I experience and what I believe aren't the same. The experience feels more real; whatever reality is, if it exists."

"Not particularly helpful."

"Actually it is and it's the best advice I can give you. I'll tell you something else, something that you wouldn't have believed a couple of weeks ago."

She looked close to the edge and he knew she'd believe him now.

"You know that whatever you fed to the press isn't the truth? Talk to Theodrakis; it was the same on Samos: no leads, no ideas. And then out of nowhere people confess, the DNA confirms it and they mysteriously die. Very convenient, just like here, it's all wrapped up. Yeah? Sound familiar? And believe me, the attacks will diminish in intensity and then fade altogether. Whatever local demon was engaged to perpetrate them will be stood down. It has what it wants, it's moving on."

"That makes no sense but it feels right. I feel haunted, even here in Didsbury. But I can't go back to London, I'd be scared it would follow, that it would contaminate my family. I'm trapped."

She looked so vulnerable and without thinking Giles reached out and took one of her hands in his. They sat like that for a period then she gently disengaged his hand, saying, almost beneath her breath:

"No, it's too early for that."

****

They sat in a huge, gleaming kitchen that seemed to have walked complete and unused from the pages of a brochure. Lit only by spots directed at the work surfaces, it felt distant and unreal, particularly where the light reflected off polished metal. They drank green tea and their voices, although muted, rang round the vast kitchen to peter out as echoes in the empty silence of the dark corners.

"What brought you here from Greece, must have been powerful?"

"Yes it was, very powerful"

Theodrakis was playing for time. He knew that the heavily made up woman with the tied-back hair and show pony running gear was no more real than the things that had destabilised him on Samos. And yet?

She was still talking.

"No need to worry about Si, he won't be coming back tonight. He'll stay and celebrate then sleep it off in one of the apartments he owns in town, where he keeps his little friends."

This was said without any trace of bitterness, in fact, she sounded relieved. Also, the pronounced accent and language she normally affected had diminished to just a trace. But what she said next shocked him out of his observational reticence.

"Better now you're finally here, over the months I got tired of waiting."

"What do you mean? How could you have known I was coming? I didn't know myself until a short time ago."

"That's the way they work, isn't it?"

There was no answer to that, not that he had one and even if there had been, what she said next would have rendered it inadequate.

"Better get used to it, cos like me you'll not be leaving."

Chapter 39: Assemblage

Ed picked up the scattered pieces of the crib scene, wondering who would do a thing like this, who could have done it? The church had been locked overnight and there'd been no evidence of a break in when he'd opened up that morning. Except of course from the systematic destruction of the crib.

That evening was the children's Christmas service followed by a party in the church hall, and the crib was the centrepiece. The idea he'd had the previous year of putting presents round the crib rather than a Christmas tree, linking the material and spiritual gifts, had worked well, he'd thought. Now the crib was smashed and the figures of Jesus and the Virgin were missing. Mary was away in Wales visiting her mother so wouldn't be available to cobble together a substitute.

He was wondering what to do when his mobile bleeped. Olga.

"Hi, Ed, can you talk?"

She didn't wait for an answer.

"I'm at the flat with Lisa. She seems alright but she's so quiet, like she's been drugged. I think we got her out just in time. Jan's going to stay with her till Christmas Eve when she's going back to Glasgow, then I'll take over once I've talked to Margaret. I won't be able to stay in the house after that conversation."

It all came out in a breathless gabble and she hadn't finished.

"Can you come over, Ed? I'm on my own with her until six when Jan gets back from work."

His mind switched from one anxiety to another.

"I've a bit of a crisis in church at present…"

"Ed, we have to talk. You've read all that crap about the demonic attacks being solved, and now Claire is moving into the house over Christmas. Think about that, Ed, our house which a few hundred years ago was the barn

Dee performed his procedures in, the ones in the document. The barn that my ancestor Hikman, the man who terrified Dee, owned. That's when I think all this was set running."

She was babbling now, distressed; he had no moral choice.

"Ok, I'll be there, give me a couple of hours."

He shut off the phone thinking of, among many other things, what Claire moving into the house over Christmas meant for Giles. He'd invited Giles to lunch on Christmas Day because he felt sorry for him. Giles had asked if he could bring a Greek friend. He hadn't sounded right, had babbled some stuff this Greek had told him about demons or such like. This was still on his mind when he arrived at Olga's flat.

The flat was in a suburb of Stockport described by estate agents as up-and-coming and convenient for commuting into Manchester. The second characteristic was undeniable, it was on a busy T junction opposite a rail station. Lisa didn't seem to mind; in fact, she seemed better than she had for years and made tea for them before disappearing into her new bedroom.

Ed and Olga sat on opposite sides of the small table in the cramped kitchen.

"Ed, I think you need to call everyone who has experience of what's going on in Skendleby together."

"That's hardly going to be possible this side of Christmas, and for what reason?"

"Because the focus for everything has changed. I've begun to think that we were all brought to that house for a purpose, and I think the time for that purpose is upon us."

"Oh, come on, you…"

"Just listen to me, Ed. There's something growing in that house, something that shouldn't be. I don't know what it is but I can feel it, so can Jan, that's why she's leaving. A couple of days ago Rose and Leonie dug something up in the cellar. Leonie started to tell Jan about it then clammed up. Jan says she was too frightened to say more."

Ed had a horrible idea of where all this was going, what the crows had whispered to him was happening. He took a sip of his tea, it was too hot and burnt his lips. Olga didn't notice or even pause.

"We got Lisa out just in time; she's pregnant. I know it sounds mad but all this drive for a baby in the community only started when Claire began to meddle with Margaret's mind. Whatever's going on, Lisa's pregnancy is at the heart of it. It's the only card we hold."

Ed didn't know what to say; there was a silence into which Olga dropped:

"All I know is that evil is consuming a community built on love and trust."

Ed thought for a moment she was going to cry, but she didn't; she was too strong for that. He knew in his heart she was right, except about Claire. Claire was behaving strangely and no wonder after what she'd gone through, perhaps entering the community for a while was what she needed. He knew he couldn't tell Olga this; she believed Claire had stolen her lover. He was wondering what to say when Olga cut to the chase.

"We need to pool what we know about Skendleby."

Ed made a decision.

"Ok, you and Lisa come over on Christmas day and I'll invite Gwen"

Chapter 40: Total Eclipse of the Heart

Gwen put down the fountain pen and refilled her glass from the bottle of single malt whisky. It had been intended as a Christmas gift for Marcus but she reckoned that wherever he'd got to he wouldn't be needing it. She'd sat at the kitchen table drinking since she'd finished writing, and over half the bottle was gone. Something was coming for her and she knew there wasn't much time left, so the letters needed to be dispatched with speed.

The letters had taken so long to write: one to Ed and one to Giles. She'd spared Davenport an epistle on account of his health. She was weary down to her bones and wanted the letters out and posted. What would come next she didn't know. It must be getting late, she looked up at the old grandfather clock cramped in the corner of her little kitchen; thirty seven minutes off midnight. She rubbed her eyes then picked one of the letters up to check over one last time.

St Anselm's Yard

Shrewsbury

20-12 2016
Dear Ed,

I'm sorry to have to burden you with this but I'm afraid there's no alternative. I have a premonition that my part in this business and in life's game is about to end, so it's down to you and Giles. You need to be very careful and afraid.

Afraid of Claire. You can't imagine how hard it was for me to write those words. I love and cherish her, she grew to be such a beautiful, warm-spirited young woman, but what we asked of her was too much.

Marcus was in touch with me before he was killed. He'd suspected for some time that our ceremony and exorcism last year hadn't worked. What he had only just discovered was that it worked all too well. Except it achieved precisely what we had hoped to avoid. The demon, or whatever type of evil it is that the Skendleby excavation unleashed, was far too strong for Claire. However, in her we presented it with its perfect host. We relied on her courage and goodness but we destroyed that poor girl when we pushed her into meddling with forces we could never understand.

Marcus discovered more but was killed before he could divulge it. The poor, poor man, what a tragic life. You are in great danger because Claire is searching for something and when she finds it her work here is done. After that neither you nor Giles will survive. Your only chance is to find whatever it is before she does and learn how to use it.

Sorry, but that's all I can offer. I think for me the end will come as a relief. At least in writing you this letter I've done my bit.

I hope your god will protect you,
Gwen

She stubbed out the glowing end of her cigarette in the overflowing ashtray and, moved by a premonition, decided to deposit the letters safely in a post box. She took down her old donkey jacket from a hook on the wall and was in the process of putting it on when there was a sound from the hall.

Looking out from the kitchen she saw the front door closing and a figure standing by the foot of the stairs.

"Bit late to be going out, Gwen, a few seconds later and I'd have missed you. Lucky I still had my set of keys, isn't it?"

Gwen's glance swept anxiously back towards the letters on the table and Claire's eyes followed it.

"Oh, been writing letters I see. Nice to see old traditions being maintained. Anything interesting?"

For all the heart stopping panic Gwen was able to regret the passing of the Claire she'd loved and feelings of regret and loss exceeded her terror. The Claire thing giggled.

"Oh bless, how sweet, you still want to mother me, don't you? Well, it's too late for that now old lady, now that you've started to meddle. You should have taken what I did to your friend Marcus as a warning."

Gwen couldn't speak, her legs gave way and she sank back down onto the kitchen chair.

"Well, let's take a look at what you've been writing so busily."

Claire picked up the letters from the table.

"To little Ed and Giles; how sweet."

Gwen watched in horror as Claire opened the hot metal door of the old anthracite burning stove with her bare hand, showing no sign of pain, and threw the letters into the flames.

"Sorry to have to extinguish your last gasp of hope like that Gwen, but that's life, isn't it? Not that you've got a great deal of life left."

Gwen opened her mouth to speak but couldn't. Instead, without intending to, she found herself getting to her feet.

"That's right, Gwen, now go and fetch that heavy binding twine from the drawer where you keep it."

Gwen did so.

"Remember telling me that the hook that holds the drying rack up is strong enough to take the weight of an ox? Well, let's test it with a smaller weight, shall we? Go on, tie one end tight to the hook."

Gwen did as she was told.

"Good girl, you see, it's not so hard. Now about a foot down from the hook, make a noose."

As Gwen's shaky hands were struggling with the twine, Claire picked up the half empty whisky bottle and finished it in one gulp.

"When they find you they'll see the empty bottle and the note I'm going to leave and conclude that in a fit of drunken sorrow you took your own life. A bit unfair that for someone as brave as you, I know, but this is what you get when you meddle."

The grandfather clock struck the chimes of midnight. The Claire thing giggled.

"Dawn of the winter solstice, the anniversary of your pathetic attempt to get in our way. How appropriate. Now stand on that chair, slip the noose round your neck and tighten it."

Then, for a moment, the Claire thing seemed to go out of focus, or that's how it seemed to Gwen. It gave a little whimper and reached out as if to lift her down from the chair. She could see Claire's eyes, not the demon's, looking out at her. It looked to be struggling to speak, tried once but couldn't, it was crying, the eyes stared at her, imploring, loving.

But it didn't last; the voice again, but this time harsher.

"Now kick the chair away."

Gwen took the love that the eyes had briefly offered, stored it in her heart with an unlooked for burst of hope and did as she was told. She heard the chair crash to the floor beneath her and concentrated during the brief struggle on the last glimpse of the real Claire she'd been gifted.

Envoi Christmas Day

The morning was bright with a crisp sparkle of frost. Si Carver, his head still banging from the previous night's party, noticed the letter on the mat by the front door. He hated Christmas Day, had since he was a kid, it never brought anything but disappointment. So he was pleased to see there'd been a delivery that broke Christmas down a bit for him, reduced its significance somehow. And the bloody church bells had finally stopped banging on so maybe things were looking up.

He was waiting for his driver to pick him up and take him into town to one of his clubs, where he'd have lunch and a bit of private entertainment, after which he'd sleep it off for a couple of days. In the New Year the development would start, he'd make a packet. Then he could wave goodbye to this poxy place and move on; maybe Dubai, classy there: yachts and golf.

Oddly, the thought of the development made him remember something he was beginning to dread. He looked round for that slut Suzzie-Jade to tell her he was off, and that she'd be left in the house alone. He looked forward to seeing the expression on her face. Then he remembered what her face had looked like when he'd last seen her and was relieved she wasn't here.

In fact, he couldn't quite remember when he'd last seen her; didn't recall seeing her at the party. Perhaps the thing that lurked by the estate wall and frightened him, made him feel like a scared kid, had got her. That'd be a stroke of luck. Thinking of it made him uneasy, he opened the door. Where was the driver?

To kill time he looked down at the letter; no stamp, no postmark. Someone had delivered it by hand. Maybe it was from Suzzie-Jade. Maybe he'd done a better job of frightening her than he'd thought. The letter could be her goodbye note, that'd be convenient, save him from having to pay her off.

But it wasn't from Suzzie-Jade. It took him some time to remember the writer at all. A short letter, just a few lines, in red ink.

Dec 25th
Dear Mr Carver,
I know how much the 'Devil's Mound' and the things that come out of it frighten you.
I can help you be rid of it. Perhaps we should meet; don't worry, I'll make the arrangements.
Yours sincerely,
Claire Vanarvi

****

Midday, and Ed walked into the rectory from church having preached the family Christmas service. It was well attended and his remarks well received. The only slightly unsettling note was that the crib had reconfigured itself with a full cast. The Virgin Mary and the baby were back; perhaps it had just been a practical joke.

He hadn't time to dwell on it, he was returning to participate in a strange Christmas lunch. Giles had accepted the invitation but had asked that if along with Theodrakis he could bring someone else otherwise condemned to spending Christmas Day in solitude. In the event the day grew stranger than he'd anticipated as the guest list grew in a most unexpected manner.

To his surprise, the extra guest Giles brought turned out to be the chief investigating officer of the Skendleby murders, who he recognised from TV and newspapers. The woman who had given Giles such a hard time but who now seemed on very good terms with him. But this seemed quite appropriate, part of a new alliance against the forces of darkness.

Lucky that Mary was so easy going. In fact, he was the last to arrive for the feast and there was a cheerful buzz emanating from the large drawing room where a log fire was blazing.

He was surrounded by people who were on his side and feared the things he did. For a moment he let the feeling of relief wash over him and he noticed that even Lisa was smiling. Mary was the perfect hostess for gatherings of this nature.

"Here, Ed, have a glass of this, it's Moet, Colonel Theodrakis brought three bottles with him."

She nodded towards the immaculately turned-out, diminutive Greek, who raised his own glass in a toast to Ed.

"Thank you for bringing me into your home on Christmas Day, Reverend Joyce."

Everyone crowded round him shaking hands or kissing his cheek; Mary took this as a signal to head for the kitchen but was stopped by Theodrakis.

"I'm sorry to impose on your hospitality, Mrs Joyce, but I fear it might be necessary to set one last place."

His timing was perfect; at the end of the sentence there came a chime of the doorbell. Mary opened the door.

"Mrs Carver! How nice to see you. Merry Christmas!"

Mary returned to the room followed by Suzzie-Jade who was wearing a neat and almost demure black dress, her hair tied in a plait. She handed a carrier bag to Mary.

"My contribution to the feast, a couple of bottles of Si's best cognac, he won't miss them."

She turned her smile through 180 degrees to include everyone in the room, then walked over to Theodrakis, who she kissed with surprising intimacy.

After a long traditional Christmas lunch the company gathered round the fire intending to talk and drink Carver's cognac while Mary and her mother slipped away. Mary to make up beds in the numerous unused bedrooms for the unexpected guests, and her mother to watch the TV.

Remembering what the crows had told him, Ed made them stand in a circle and hold hands. Looking round at each face in turn, he began a short prayer, wondering what power such a strange assortment could possibly muster. Then, as the dark began to gather, they toasted the absent Davenport and settled to an attempt to unravel the current state of the Skendleby haunting, each wondering where they would be the following Christmas. Outside in the night, snow settled thickly on the churchyard.

****

As the old sun sank blood red behind the woods and fingers of shadow crept towards the house, the women, minus Jan and Olga, were settled in the Gathering Room prior to the evening's celebration of midwinter. They'd exchanged gifts and blessings and the champagne was open. It had been a far harder year than they'd anticipated, but an air of optimism filled the room. Margaret, the leader and heart of the house, was responsible for this. She had foretold an encouraging portent. This in itself was encouraging as Margaret had experienced the most difficult year of all of them. A rustle of expectancy filled the room as they saw the door begin to open.

Claire, in a long white dress hinting of an earlier age swept in. She was radiant, almost glowing, and her eyes sparkled with intense light. But it was her right hand that attracted their attention. It held an object that was like a cross between a thermometer and a toothbrush. She held it aloft, calling out to them.

"Rejoice sisters, there will be a birth; the birth foretold. This is our midwinter nativity, now we can begin the great changes that will sweep the old orders away, wherever we find them. You are blessed, you are chosen to serve. Come rejoice."

The women shuffled towards her to congratulate, share and touch. Across the fields towards Skendleby, anyone abroad on that cold night would a have seen the night sky above Devil's Mound begin to glow.

20-05-15

To be concluded in "Green Man Resurrection"

Marcus Brown

Lightning Source UK Ltd.
Milton Keynes UK
UKHW04f0028190918
329130UK00001B/157/P

9 781785 075421